THIS VIOLENT RECKONING

THE CURSE OF THE BLESSED
BOOK TWO

R. DUGAN

THIS VOLENT RECKONING
Copyright © 2025 by R. Dugan

All rights reserved. Printed in the United States of America. No part of this book may be used or reproduced in any manner whatsoever without written permission except in the case of brief quotations embodied in critical articles or reviews.

This book is a work of fiction. Names, characters, businesses, organizations, places, events and incidents either are the product of the author's imagination or are used fictitiously. Any resemblance to actual persons, living or dead, events, or locales is entirely coincidental.

For information contact:

R. Dugan
PO Box 1265
Martinsville, IN 46151
reneeduganwriting.com

Cover design by Saint Jupiter
ISBN: 978-1-958927-27-4

Second Edition: July 2025

10 9 8 7 6 5 4 3 2 1

978-1-958927-27-4

Dedication

To happy endings
and the happiness we find along the way.

Orleth

- Peaks of Kharanklad
- Bayar
- Erdineen's Mines
- Amasandji
- Tariaga Falls
- The Aldsen Wood
- Kaishan
- Danje
- The Orlethian Channel
- Jungsai
- Chanar
- Dabantai

The Ocean

Part One

The Hunter and The Prey

Chapter One

Together to the End

Elynor Azorius woke in the dark, chilled and with the hair-raising sensation of being in motion.

Not on her beloved waters that had called to her since girlhood. Not on the Ocean Caeruel, fording a path of hope through uncharted waves. The movement that rocked her was not gentle and familiar as a lullaby; it was crooked and cruel as a nightmare.

She lay quiet and still for a time, anchoring herself within the familiar and the not—a swaying and clacking all around her that made her think of Bernian and Gregor, her driver and footman, lifelong servants and companions to the household Azorius. And from that she deduced, before she'd even opened her eyes, that she was in a carriage of some sort.

When she did finally peel open her lids like heavy sails slow to unfurl, she saw that it was not a carriage at all, but a cage.

The wood-and-iron prison was a small box, only the slatted window on its door allowing in a faint breeze and the smell of clean air. Everything else stank of sweat and dirty bodies and fear, and Elynor lunged away from those lethal fumes, gripping the iron bars with shackled hands and gulping for a breath that didn't pour nausea into her gut. She cast her gaze wildly about the undergrowth that trundled by, but nothing looked familiar. The hardy, rich foliage at the heart of the Amasandji *Khulig,* one of six in the Kingdom of Orleth, had given way to sterner stuff: thick pines and stout brush that signified a harsher terrain.

They were moving away from Danje, the coastal port where she was meant to find *Khul* Ergene, ruler of the land of Orleth, and plead for aid to halt a war. North, she guessed—toward the Bayar *Khulig,* stomping grounds of the raider Kirsagan al Bayar and his people. The ones who had captured them...how long ago had it been? Unconsciousness in bursts of earthy fume left her head addled; but the stiffness in her joints suggested it had been days, at least, since the Orlethian raiders had ambushed them in the thick of their grief and tossed them into this cage.

Now they traveled; now she was lost, without compass or stars to guide her way. And once they reached the dangerous crags and deep mines of the northernmost territory in Orleth, Elynor doubted they would ever step foot outside them again.

She twisted around on her knees, facing away from her panic presented in unattainable freedom, and cast her gaze about the box. It was too small to stand straight in, but long and wide enough to stretch out. The gloom was not absolute with the shafts of stunted light peeling past the frame of her body, and when she shifted aside, she saw that she was not alone.

There were five other people in this box. One of them was Sylvester Munrow, the golden-haired bard stripped of all his fine trappings.

But here. Alive.

With a gasp of relief and anguish mingled, Elynor scrambled across the cage and hovered over his body, unsure of where to touch. There was a deep, ugly gash along his temple, and his eyes were tightly shut. Pain etched the lines of his face even in sleep.

Elynor shook his shoulder and called his name, but to no avail.

Terror and loneliness were an open gulf in her chest, the waves crashing into her ribs, and she wanted desperately to sob. But what good would tears do? Kirsagan's raiders would not care for her tears. And she had cried enough.

Elynor gripped the talisman that hung around her neck, breathing in her courage and breathing out her panic. Breathing out her grief at the familiar stamp of it on her palm, the yawning ache of missing the man who had given it to her. The man who was...

She choked on the memory. On the notion. On the latest of many griefs that tied her throat tighter than a bosun's knot.

Death hung a dark veil over Elynor's shoulders, thicker and weightier than sailcloth. It threatened to smother her entirely, wrapping her head in the murky shroud of farewells spoken before they had fallen prey to these raiders.

Hold it tightly, mal ga'el...let it give you strength.

Strength—the strength of the killing Blessed who has brought them this far. Who had died on the journey to bring them to Danje, to thwart the plans of warmongers in their home kingdom, Erala.

She could not give up. She could not let that strength lie fallow, when he had entrusted their quest for salvation to her hands.

She would lean into his strength. Even if Sharek Ransalor was dead—even if he was no longer here to give it from his own hands.

Trembling, but breathing more deeply now, Elynor drew Sylvester's head onto her knees. She would be here when he woke, if that was all she had to offer. And then, together, they would plan.

From the corners of her eyes, she took stock of their companions. Four unwashed bodies jutted into the sunlight, bent with hopelessness. Two men and two women: the women fit and muscular, the men broad-chested and corded with veins. One slept with the smaller of the women tucked into the curve of his body. The other two sat at opposite walls, clear strangers. The woman stared vacantly ahead. The man's chin was to his chest, deeply asleep.

Elynor battled wave after wave of isolation like a child caught in a rip current. She couldn't see the shore. She could only desperately cling to hope that she would not tire before it came into view.

To give her restless fingers something to do, she smoothed Sylvester's hair. She murmured to him, "I need you to wake, Sly. We have things to discuss."

He did not stir.

She shook him gently by the shoulder. "You must think of our future children! Kolden, Marideg, and what was the last one...Brec'hed Morvannou?"

Nothing. Not even at the jest of the first night they'd met—a night when there had still been hope. For them, for Erala, for...

"Think of Sharek." Elynor's voice snagged, and it was an effort to keep speaking: "Think of how you loved one another. We have a promise to keep. We can't let things end as they are."

"I'm afraid you've little choice in the matter, lass."

Elynor nearly jumped. That voice belonged to the man sitting against the wall across from them. His chin still touched his chest, but now Elynor could see that through his enviously-long lashes, his eyes were open, taking bleary stock of the floor between his sprawled legs. His shackled hands hung limp in his lap, his brown skin dull in the light.

Elynor set her teeth to keep from snapping so loudly she'd alert their captors. "I don't know you, and I'll thank you not to tell me my business. But there is always a choice, and my friend..." For Sylvester was her friend, wasn't he? And she was finished with telling people they were less important than they were to her, before it was too late to tell them at all. "My friend and I have important things to do."

"Didn't we all, before Kirsagan al Bayar found us," he snorted lightly. "There was a fresh bottle of *arkye* waiting for me back at home, and now here I am, sober as a bone and about to be sent where I can't even beg a cup of *argai* from a poor man's bowl."

Elynor glared at him. "Is that all you think about? Fermented mare's milk?"

"In all its consumable forms. One of the few good things this kings-damned spit of land has to offer."

Elynor's heart clenched at his choice of words. "Are you Eralanite?"

"Does it matter? Now they'll call me a slave. Whatever we were before matters nothing. We'll all be the same to them in the mines."

Elynor draped her arm over Sylvester's, gripping his hand. "You may be resigned to that fate, but I'm not. Nor will I ever be."

The man chuffed lightly, and his eyes slid shut. "We'll see."

They carried on for hours, the patterns of light changing through the iron door, and when their progress finally ground to a halt there was more stone around them than before. The pain of entrapment stabbed Elynor's limbs as the raiders bantered outside the box, Kirsagan's voice the loudest and harshest of them all. When he swaggered into view, his long, dark braid swaying between his powerful shoulders, her heart voided its usual recess, and slick, hot hatred filled in.

If the raiders had not attacked them on the beach the morning after they'd shipwrecked here, if Sharek hadn't been forced to push his body yet again to escape them, then perhaps...*perhaps*...

It was easier to direct the blame outward than toward herself, so Elynor let it loose.

Kirsagan strutted to the door, accompanied by a lithe, willowy man who held a ring of keys. The man opened the door, and Kirsagan shouted inside, "If any of you *busars* would like to relieve yourselves somewhere you won't have to sit in after, now's the time."

They were making camp, stone rings and kindling cropping up wherever the raiders set to work, and Elynor's heart clenched with memories of river rocks and willow bark and tired eyes watching her across the flames.

"My friend is injured." Her grief added a roughness to her voice that she loved, for it made her seem stronger than she felt. "I'm not leaving this cart until he's seen to."

"Then sit in your filth for all I care." Kirsagan beckoned the other prisoners out.

"Please!" Elynor shouted. "Do you really wish to arrive at the mines with one man less than this pitiful offering you've already brought?"

Kirsagan hooked his thumbs in his belt and rocked back on his heels, eyeing her shrewdly. Elynor understood his doubt—after all, the last time he'd given her an inch of leeway, she'd jammed a knife into him and gotten away. But she wouldn't run now, not with Sylvester lying senseless and nothing but miles of rocky terrain around them.

Finally, tersely, Kirsagan spoke to his man. "Tolon, search him for life."

The man clambered into the cart, and all the prisoners withdrew—all but the one with whom Elynor had conversed. He showed no signs of caring at all as the raider crouched beside his ankle and bent over Sylvester, feeling the pulse at the side of his neck.

Suddenly there was a wild cut of limbs, and Sylvester was sitting up and jamming one of Sharek's hidden knives into the bottom of Tolon's jaw. Elynor shrieked as blood showered her pants, and Sylvester yelled at her to run.

So she did, diving out the cage door, tackling Kirsagan to the ground. She picked herself up and ran, with Sylvester staggering behind her, down the steep hill the carts had just climbed.

A thick, black-shafted arrow whizzed past Elynor's ear so close it nicked the skin, and she gasped, tacking sharply left, almost colliding with Sylvester. He righted her with a hard shove, and they kept moving, careening downhill as the camp broke open in shouts and Orlethian curses behind them.

There was a body of water nearby—a foothill lake. Elynor could smell its rich minerals on the wind. If they reached it, if they swam across, they would be free.

She pulled Sylvester's sleeve. "This way!"

They crashed recklessly through the sparse undergrowth, vaulting fallen trees and skirting carriage-sized boulders, and Elynor's heart jammed into her throat as roughly as her toes jammed into the front of her boots. Her veins sang at the thought of seeking refuge in the water, a territory she could conquer without question—nevermind that it would be icy and deep, and kings knew what horrors would lurk in its foreign depths. Better than the horrors chasing them, still firing their bows, still calling down curses.

And then an arrow stabbed through the back of Elynor's calf.

She didn't feel it at first, was not aware of why she'd fallen until Sylvester hauled at her arm, shouting her name, and when she staggered up she felt the chafe of the barbed arrowhead in her muscle. She made it two steps, then crumbled down again with a scream that pierced her own ears.

"Go without me!" she sobbed, shoving at Sylvester's arms. "Go to Danje—bring help!"

"Never," Sylvester snarled. "I won't leave you to face these barbarians alone."

"Sylvester Munrow!"

He crouched beside her, taking her shoulders in his hands. "We do this together, Elynor. We're all either of us has left. You'll need me to take care of this...of *you*."

She looked into his eyes, serious and shocked but without a hint of fear for what was coming toward them through the undergrowth. And she swallowed her own panic, and another scream, so that she could choke out instead: "*Together*."

Then Kirsagan's men descended on them.

Chapter Two

Allies and Enemies

That night was among the worst in Elynor's life, not far behind the one where her mother had disappeared or the one where her father had died.

The raiders had their way with Sylvester first, pummeling his face into mince while Elynor thrashed and fought and screamed at them to stop.

Only when the bard was limp to their blows did they turn their attention to Elynor. They hit her, too—a series of hard kicks and punches to the ribs and stomach that hurt worse than anything she'd ever felt—worse, even, than the arrow in her leg—leaving her gasping and sobbing for breath. Then they half-dragged her back to the camp, the arrow still in her leg, and flung her and Sylvester back into the cart. They slammed the gate shut and locked it, and there was no food or water offered through the bars.

For uncountable hours, Elynor lay on her side, quietly weeping—from the sensational agony for once rather than the constant company of grief. Her leg was a bloodied mess, her stomach bruised, and her ribs throbbed with every breath. She had never wanted to die before tonight, but the escape seemed absurdly welcome. To slip into some dark abyss and never awaken to Kirsagan's enraged face again; to not wrestle with the pain of losing her father and Sharek. To not carry this terrible burden of Erala's fate on her shoulders.

Her body gave way at last to void dreams, nonsensical visions of Bracerath's Landing back in Bast, and her father's joyous smile before death had stolen it, and the Caeruel. She dreamed of sailing, every sensation so pure and true it tingled in her fingertips and massaged the muscles of her arms. In her dream, she wept at the glory of freedom. She vowed to never again take it for granted.

And then she came awake screaming, because the arrow was yanked out of her leg.

A sweaty palm covered her mouth to muffle her cries, and she realized the drunkard was holding her down, and Sylvester with his mangled face had pulled the arrow out. He looked at its sharp definition, shaking his head.

"This is going to become infected," he mumbled through swollen lips.

Panting and shaking, Elynor looked at the man who restrained her. His eyes were full of thought as he watched her.

"Brazen, what you did," he remarked. "I told you we had no choice."

Elynor pushed his hand down so she could hiss, "I didn't see you trying to run."

"Already did. Difficult to manage when you're sobering up. And they've watched me too closely since."

Elynor had no retort, so she turned her head to look at Sylvester. "Are you all right?"

"Not in the least. That was the only knife I managed to stash, and now you're risking infection." He sniffed thickly, ripping off a bit of his cloak and binding it around her leg. Elynor bit the tip of her tongue so hard it bled, squeezing her eyes shut and freeing more of those endless tears. She only dared look again when Sylvester's careful ministrations ended, and his hand descended on her shoulder instead. "But we'll think of something, Elynor."

"Elynor," the man echoed. "That's an Eralanite name."

Elynor sat herself up painfully and clutched her throbbing middle. "I thought such things didn't matter to you."

"They don't, usually. But I know Eralanites…hard to break and desperately clever. So perhaps we stand a chance, after all."

Elynor and Sylvester exchanged a glance, and the bard said, "Does that mean you'd like to help us dream up an escape?"

"Means I have an entire cupboard of *arkye* waiting for me back in Danje, and it'd be a shame to waste it." He offered his hand. "I'm Sam."

"Elynor." She gripped his hand and let go at once. "This is Sylvester."

"Can't say I'm pleased to meet you," Sam said, "but I'll be pleased to part ways as unlikely allies once we're free, and never see your faces again."

Elynor couldn't help but agree.

Chapter Three

Impossible Choices

The Peaks of Kharanklad sprouted in jagged umber fangs from the Orlethian terrain, and for some days Sharek Ransalor and Iracabeth Azorius moved in their shadow, climbing the steep flanks through the lower crags—chasing after the raiders.

With every dawn, Sharek's senses unfurled wider, like a flower blooming again after a harsh winter. He heard the melody of the world so clearly—the songbirds and animals, the wind whispering through the pines and underbrush—and he sensed Iracabeth's restlessness, a tightly-strung fiddle stroked to the same tune as his own desperation.

Until now, he hadn't realized just how much of his clarity had been stolen by the poison dealt from an old friend's wicked blade. Though his weakened body still ached like the remnants of a bad chest sickness, and at times breathing hurt so badly he had to sit down and rest, at least he did not feel death's cold grip around his throat anymore. Those days of dying in increments as they'd crossed the Caeruel and the lands of Orleth were nothing but a nightmare that stalked his waking memories now.

And that he owed to Iracabeth's powers as a healing Blessed.

At a steady clip, they passed wild meadows of stunted amber grass that danced in Sharek's vision and deep jade pools of mineral water where the scent of damp stone invaded his nostrils until long after they'd passed by. A piece of Sharek's spirit ached to stay and gaze on these things a while longer; Orleth was wilder somehow than Erala, a land of unconquered pockets and untamed wilderness, and it was easy to go days without seeing a single curl of smoke from the *gers* stashed along the clefts.

Because of the raiders, Iracabeth explained one night as they made camp near a small pond; only ascetics lived this high in the Peaks of Kharanklad, men and women who'd retreated to the refuge of the mountains when the indulgences of Orleth's populace became too much for them.

"It is for their faith that they go," she said, building up the kindling for their fire. "The world has changed for Orleth. Once they were a reclusive people, steeped in their own ways and traditions. Now Missians bring their beliefs of the omnipotence of man across the borders, and Eralanite sailors bring talk of the Holy Throne and the Infallible Sovereign. But Orleth once held fast to the belief in the *Burkhan*, figures the same as the Empyreans you pray to, Sharek. Some say the Hunters originated on these shores, even. So men return to the mountains to live the lives of their deities in self-denial and piety."

"My father told me such stories of Orleth's beliefs. And that Hunters might come from here." Sharek set the flames and fed them tinder, handful by grudging handful. He hated to stop, but his lungs felt cold and rigid in this thin air, and his body begged for rest.

"Your father was a Hunter?"

Sharek nodded. "He taught me all of this...the tracking."

Iracabeth nodded slowly. "He would be proud of you, I have no doubt. You've far exceeded this healer's expectations. A man without your talents might have given up in the foothills and gone back to recover, yet you convalesce as you climb. It's...fascinating."

Sharek shrugged. "I am how I am."

And how he was was a killing Blessed, as gifted to take life as Iracabeth was to save it; he was an assassin whose next mark would not be Rowan Varodan, who had poisoned him and Elynor's father both, or Gavannon Al-Morral, whom Elynor had first hired Sharek to slay for ordering Alden Azorius's death.

No. It would be Kirsagan al Bayar who next tasted Sharek's merciless steel.

"How you are is extraordinary. I'm sure your father would have agreed." A beat, and then Iracabeth laughed. "But listen to me! That is a parent's prerogative, after all. We believe our children capable of any feat, no matter how extraordinary or impossible."

"Did you believe that of Elynor?"

Iracabeth's smile faded. "Yes. And I still do."

Pain burned in Sharek's chest—pain which was not his to feel. The agony of abandonment which he had watched Elynor hold in hand with her worry for him, and her grief for her murdered father, while she had sailed and struggled with all her might to find her estranged mother. To save *him*. "Then why did you leave her?"

Iracabeth stared into the flames. "It was the hardest choice I've ever made. But I knew that my gifts would bring ruin on Alden and Elynor, and she deserved better than that. He knew the risks when we married, and still he chose that life. She did not."

"I think she would've preferred to have you and the danger both. She's a stronger woman that you know."

"But would she have had to become strong, if not for the pain of our parting?" Iracabeth's lips tipped, but there was no amusement there. "I believe she *is* strong...particularly to have come this far in search of me. But I am a healer, Sharek. There has not been a Blessed like me, born and named, in some time. If I had been found, I would have been enslaved to the King at best. And what that would have done to Alden and Elynor, I shudder to think. People do not belong in collars."

"Then did you truly flee to Orleth for her sake, or for your own?"

Iracabeth's eyes shuttered. "Some days, I wonder that myself."

A wolf howled in the distance, bidding farewell to the sun as it slipped between the peaks. The air grew sharply colder, but Sharek didn't mind. The chill sharpened his senses, and the world seemed to move through the patterns of frost lace around them, intricate and delicate in these frigid hours.

"She is fortunate to have someone who cares so much for her honor and her wellbeing as you do," Iracabeth said after a time. "Even as a child, Elynor was precocious. She loved ships and the seas more than people. I feared she would be friendless as she grew, and that someday she would wake up and find herself lonely. I'm glad she has you."

"I am her servant." Though the words were ash, Sharek let them sift between his teeth. With the threat of his death passing away each day, he would soon assume his former role: the assassin hired to kill Gavannon Al-Morral.

But Iracabeth shook her head. "I know my Elynor. She would not sail across the Ocean Caeruel and brave these wilds for a mere servant." Her gaze danced over Sharek, touched with intrigue. "Though I wonder what in the Emperium possessed her to hire an assassin."

She didn't know, then. She hadn't heard about Alden's death.

It wasn't his place to say. But an ache yawned in Sharek's core as he held his silence to her veiled question, rubbing the empty side of his neck where his talisman had always hung and squinting up at the moon-limned mountain peaks.

Not far to go to the place Iracabeth believed they were traveling: Erdineen's Mines.

He prayed to Sabrathan, Lord of Light, Greatest of the Empyreans, that Elynor and Sylvester would still be alive when they found them…and that the Empyreans would give Elynor the strength for the confrontations that were yet to be had with her mother.

Chapter Four

A Brutal Land

Elynor came to fear when the caravan stopped almost as much as when it traveled. While they climbed the mountain passes, the raiders left them alone; they were too busy keeping the horses from stumbling into treacherous holes unmasked by recent torrential rains, turning the road to a mudslick.

During the daylight hours, Elynor, Sylvester, and Sam plotted; the unhappily-sober Sam told them everything he knew about Kirsagan and his people, and what their destination was. And from that, Elynor and Sylvester attempted to weave a plan.

At night, when the caravan stopped, the raiders had their fun with the prisoners. Sometimes they drugged them and drank with them and made them play the part of fools; sometimes they used them for target practice. Sometimes they dragged them off out of sight of the fires they built at the trail's edge, and Elynor tried not to think of what was being done to them out there.

There were six wagons in the caravan, each one full of prisoners. Elynor hoped, perhaps cruelly, that the raiders would be so occupied with the other five that they'd never bother with the last one.

And the same day she started to foster that reprehensible wish, they did.

They pulled the unhurt women out first, and the man who was intimate with one of them followed her as if they were bound by an invisible tether. No one looked twice at Elynor and Sylvester, and that was a relief; but Sam tested the door, swung it open, and slid out of the wagon with casual grace.

"What are you doing?" Elynor hissed, slithering up to the door. "You know we need a horse if we're going to flee!"

"And they'll catch you if you try," Sylvester added with a chin nod toward the raiders. They were feathered around a broad fire, passing bottles of spirits back and forth and plying the prisoners relentlessly with them.

So. It was one of those nights.

"That they will," Sam drawled. "I'm not trying to escape. Hoping they'll spare me a drop."

Elynor glared at him. "You're despicable."

"Been called plenty worse, and for better reasons." Sam whistled, and one of the raiders fetched him and dragged him to the fire.

"How can they do this?" Elynor spat. "Any of it?"

"I don't see Kirsagan," Sylvester observed. "Something tells me his people are more arrogant and less cunning than he is." He propped his shoulder against the wall, then his head. "We'll have to remember that when we do make our escape."

"If we do." Elynor tallied the raiders for the tenth time; they numbered over two dozen, and many were proficient archers. If she'd known that, she would never have attempted the first escape. And then they would not be in such dire straits for the second.

Sylvester clapped her on the shoulder. "It's going to be all right, you know. I've survived worse than this. Not *much* worse, but..."

"Name one thing."

Sylvester's mouth twisted to the side. "Well, there was this terrible occasion where a woman shoved me out onto the beach in front of a mob of guards, and left me to run for my life while she stole a ship."

Elynor snorted. "She sounds like a remarkable friend."

"I've had worse." He winked with a trickle of mirth in his eyes. Her heart thudded painfully in turn.

"So have I."

"Yes, Sharek mentioned your girlhood friend tried to poison you. Really, I don't know how you've survived this long, with your judge of character—"

Out by the fire, something smashed apart. Raiders leaped up and back from the flames, shouting as they circled up around someone thrashing in the mud. Elynor and Sylvester swapped wide-eyed looks; then the bard shoved open the door, dropped from the cart, and started running. And Elynor, who would not leave him to face the raiders alone, limped after him, leg burning and throbbing with every step.

By the time she thrust herself through the ring of bodies and knelt at Sylvester's side, no one was paying attention to her. They were all staring at one of the women from Elynor's cart, the one who never acknowledged any of them. She was crumbled up on her side, jerking and foaming at the mouth. A smashed clay jug of spirits lay just out of reach of her hand. Sylvester crouched over her, peeling up her lids, listening to her breathing, feeling her pulse.

"What's wrong with her?" Elynor demanded. "Sly?"

"I don't know." His frown was sharper than the clefts of the mountains around them. "She won't survive if she doesn't empty the contents of her stomach. I need herbs, a thick oil, *something*!"

None of the raiders moved. Elynor gripped Sylvester's shoulder and pushed herself unsteadily to her feet. "Help her! She's important to Kirsagan—important to you!"

"She's as good as dead." The raider who'd fed wine to the woman stepped toward Elynor now. His gaze was oddly fixed, not sober in the least, and hungry for something no feast could fulfill. Elynor tensed sharply, shifting back from him.

"No." Sam threw out an arm in front of Elynor, his gaze narrowed on the man. "There's a lot I'll stand by for, friend, but not that. You just back your ugly arse away, before I feed your head up into it."

A few of the raiders chuckled, but the man hefted his belt and leered, stalking closer to them.

Elynor had dealt with her share of handsy sailors, and her father had taught her how to put them in their place with a few well-aimed blows, and threats on top of that; but she'd never been this heavily disadvantage in such an encounter, bearing on only one good leg.

"What are you doing to do, eh?" The raider crowded up into Sam's face. "Think I don't know who you are? What they say about you in the cities? You can't protect anyone or anything. Not your title, not your reputation—not even a child."

Elynor jerked back at the insult, but Sam *lunged*.

He and the raider went down in a scuffling heap, and the others closed in—not to break up the brawl, but to keep either man from fleeing. Coin traded hands in a dazzling stream, and they hooted and jeered, their sickening prisoner already forgotten.

Sylvester gripped Elynor's wrist, yanking her against his side. Her senses danced, dizzy with disbelief that Sam was fighting, that he'd attacked one of the raiders, and that Sylvester was concerned for *her* in this moment at all.

She tried to tug free. "Sly, the woman—"

"It's done." Sylvester's tone was low and brittle. "She's dead."

Elynor froze, staring at him.

Dead. They'd killed her with that drink. And Sam...

She twisted around, stumbling on her injured leg, and as Sam rocked back and pounded his fists together, readying to dive back in, Elynor grabbed his arm. "Enough!" she roared, and even the raider froze. "Enough."

Sam's eyes cut to her, sharp and vicious, and Elynor shook her head. She hoped he was still in his sane mind enough to see that she didn't want him to defend her honor at the cost of his life.

Cursing, Sam whipped his arm free, swiveled back toward the raider, and caught another punch, this one to the nose, knocking him to his seat with blood pouring into his mouth.

Elynor stepped over him and spread her arms, facing the furious raider. "I said, *enough*!"

"What is this?"

Kirsagan al Bayar's voice boomed across the rocky encampment, and it seemed that even the fire banked with terror at his voice, just as his men and women shied away. Off to her left, Sylvester whispered Elynor's name, a panicked thread of sound.

Kirsagan returned from kings-only-knew-what, belting up his trousers, his steely eyes flashing to Sam, bloodied, and Elynor standing over him; to the raider with the mangled face who'd tussled with Sam; and then to the woman lying dead on the edge of the circle.

He grew very still.

"Boal," he breathed, "you ruined the wares?"

The man who'd dueled Sam shrank back. "I...it was...how was I to know she couldn't hold her spirits?"

Kirsagan stalked toward him, and Elynor hobbled backward—not quickly enough. Kirsagan smothered her face with his hand and shoved her away, and she reeled, her wounded leg buckling, pain screaming along the nerves and aching muscles.

Damp hands caught her upper arms, and Sam held her firmly back against his chest. A strange feeling shot through her as his fingers closed over her shoulders—a safety she hadn't known since the last time she'd stood on a ship's prow with her father, and he'd held onto her just like this, steadying her as the waves bucked beneath them.

But she was not safe, not even with Sam holding onto her or with Sylvester at her side. Not when the raiders surrounded them in a silent, shivering circle, and Kirsagan and Boal stood at their midst, a storm of tension heating between them.

Boal had seemed so tall a moment ago when he loomed against Sam. But next to Kirsagan's scarred fury, he crumbled up like tinder, consumed.

"That woman was Blessed with strength," Kirsagan seethed. "You knew it. You knew the drugs we used to keep her subdued."

"I—I forgot."

"What you did was thought about your appetite instead of my coffers!"

He lashed out without warning, and the smash of his fist against Boal's face brought the splintering of bone. Elynor sucked in her breath, nausea rolling up her throat as Kirsagan slung the raider to the ground and straddled him.

"That one would've fetched us a *Khul's* ransom of *tolvors*, and now what've we got? A corpse to feed to the overseer's *dogs*?" He dropped blow after blow against Boal's face, breaking up the pitiful chorus of his cries. None of the raiders moved to their friend's defense; they were silent as gravemarkers, watching Kirsagan smash Boal's face apart.

Jagged white slices of bone jutted through the torn skin. Kirsagan kept hitting, even when Boal's voice was gone, nothing but a gargling mess of spitting blood.

Another blow. This time it caved in his temple, and Elynor saw something within, thick and glistening—

She retched, and Sam spun her into Sylvester's hands. The bard wrapped his arms around her and murmured, "Don't look."

Elynor had not hidden her face from anything in years. Perhaps in her whole life. But in her mind, all she could see was that slick thing peeking out of Boal's temple, and if she dared look again, she would vomit. And who could imagine what rage that would provoke in Kirsagan tonight.

Finally, the dull slap of meaty fists on shattered bones ground to a halt. Silence stretched across the rock, taking Elynor's face in its soft fingers and turning it so that she could squint at Kirsagan. The raider unfolded from his crouch, dropping Boal's body onto the rock...what was left of it. The face hardly resembled a man.

Kirsagan wiped his own bloody jaw on his wrist and turned, surveying each of the stunned, silent onlookers, one after the other. "This is what happens to anyone who costs me another *tolvor* of my hard-earned profit on this journey." His eyes fixed on Elynor as he said it, and she shuddered. "Put them back in their cage."

Elynor had never been more glad to be locked behind iron bars. At least something separated her from Kirsagan now.

The other man and woman huddled at the back of the cart, arms wrapped around one another. Elynor sat next to Sylvester, and Sam slumped across from them. Sylvester quietly removed the handkerchief Elynor had given him, the one that bound his brow, and offered it to Sam for his bloody nose.

It was deep into the night before any of them fell asleep; the man and woman first, and then Sylvester. Elynor supposed he could manage it because he'd seen so much as a healer. She, on the other hand, could not shut her eyes without seeing Boal's brainmatter, a gritty vision that jerked her awake with bile flooding her mouth again and again.

The fifth time it happened, she gave up trying to sleep, and searched out Sam's face in the dark.

He was awake, watching her.

"What?" Elynor muttered.

"Didn't expect that," Sam said. "What you did tonight. Wealthy women aren't usually the first to throw themselves on blades for others."

"Who says I'm wealthy?"

Sam waved a hand. "Everything about you—your bearing, your speech. All of it."

Elynor raised her chin, shifting as his words prodded a part of her that had curled up and gone to sleep after her father's death. She hadn't behaved much like an heiress since then; she'd had no room for that woman full of lofty ideals and happiness. Something dark and ugly had slithered into her place. And also something strong and strange, that was willing to fight for what was hers. Whether it was the Fleet, or a Blessed she called a friend, or the people who deserved her help.

"Well, drunkards in the backs of slave wagons aren't usually the first to defend a woman's honor, either," Elynor said. "But you stood for me, so I stood for you. I'm...I used to be a woman of my word."

Except when she'd promised Sharek she would save him.

She laid her cheek on the wooden siding, peering out the moon, her throat too tight for words. After some time, Sam grunted, "There may be some hope for you yet, lass."

"Why?" she croaked. "Because I try to keep my word?"

"No. Because you've got an arrow wound in your leg and you had Kirsagan's eyes on you, and you still have enough salt left after that to stick out your chin at me." Sam flashed a razor smile in the dark. "That will keep you alive in the mines, if the infection doesn't kill you first."

Fear skittered down the notches of her spine. "You say that like you've been there before."

"Haven't. But I've heard stories from someone who has."

Elynor slowly dragged her gaze back to him. "Who?"

Sam dropped his back hard against the side of the wagon, and this time it was him who peered out into the dark. "Someone who doesn't give a damn if I live or die in these mountains."

Elynor snorted quietly. "Forsaken love?"

Sam rubbed a hand over his arm, rucking up the sleeve a bit. "You could say that."

For the first time, Elynor noticed he had scars—not wounds from being captured by Kirsagan, but old, knotted brown threads that traveled up from his wrist to the inside of his elbow. Her fingers followed a similar streak along her own arm—a fresher wheal, only a few weeks old.

Sam caught her imitating his movement, and he dropped his hand, scowling. "Doesn't matter. No one's coming for us. But at least we don't have to share the rations around as many mouths after all."

"That's all you care about?"

"It's all I can afford to. And it's all you can, too, if you and your friend want to survive in the mines."

Minutes later, he was snoring, as if their conversation had released him from whatever kept him awake.

Elynor was not so fortunate. In fact, she didn't sleep at all that night. She watched him instead, looking down at the sleeve he'd left rolled up, and at the scar twisting through the hair on his brawny arm.

It really was just like hers.

It was a rigging scar.

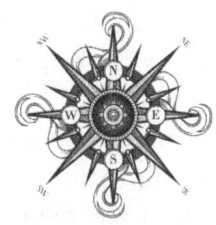

Chapter Five

Bayar

The raiders' caravan slowed as they ascended the steeper paths of the mountains. According to Sam, their destination was not the expensive salt mines of the lower peaks, but the upper mines, where gems were harvested for trade. Elynor knew of these gems, often used to supplement *tolvors* at the markets; she even had a necklace of them, a gift from her father. But she had never wanted to see them in their rawest form and had no desire to pluck them from the rock with her fingernails.

She woke from dreams of this—of dark shafts and purloined workers with dull eyes, all refusing her pleas for help—and heard singing.

Sylvester was singing.

It was almost peaceful, lying with her back to his leg, feeling the vibration of the music in his body. The wagon rocked, a vicious cradle, and around them the other destitutes dozed. Even Sam, usually muttering and swearing long into the night, snored away. For the first time since their failed escape, Elynor and Sylvester were the only ones awake.

"How can you sing at a time like this?" she murmured.

He stopped. She felt the shrug that lifted his whole body, even his folded legs. "We cage birds to decorate our homes in Erala, and it never silences them. If they can sing in captivity..."

"A bird sings because it still has hope. It doesn't know any better."

Sylvester's fingers fitted to her shoulder. "*I still have hope.*"

Elynor had little. In the days they'd spent winding up into the mountains, her throbbing leg and Kirsagan's close watch had stolen her vivacity. Grief had seeped back into the holes it left behind, and now she ached—for her father, for the lost dream of her mother, for home.

For Sharek.

She knew Sylvester missed him, too; she'd seen him gazing out the barred door back the way they'd come with tears in his eyes. But she couldn't offer her own sadness to comfort his; it was still too private, too precious, too mysterious, all the ways she missed Sharek. All the guilt she felt for sending him to his death.

She twisted her head to look up at Sylvester now, and found him staring out the door again. Sadness stamped his roguish face, and she nudged his leg. "Why did you propose to me, the night we met in Northumbra?"

"Because you're desperately lovely," he said without missing a beat.

"Fair. But we've been together for weeks now, Sly, and the man who named our three children in the middle of a tavern is not the same man who boarded a vessel and drugged its sailors to win our escape."

Sylvester chuckled quietly and went back to humming for a bit. Then he said, "After all these years a bard, I've developed a reputation, you know. Carefree, unmoored, loving and leaving always. So when you came in, knowing my name and searching for me...well, you terrified the rocks off of me, Elynor. So I tried to do the same."

"You succeeded," she admitted. "I could have kicked you in the face, I was so embarrassed."

"Truth be told, we were never in any danger of being married. Love doesn't interest me, and romance is for idealists, not for men forever running from place to place, terrified of being found."

"Who would dare chase a bard?" Elynor asked. "Or is it because you move into other people's homes when they're away, and make them so angry they want to hunt you?"

Sylvester's laughter was without mirth this time, and Elynor heard his head thump against the wall. "No, I move into their homes *because* I'm running. It might not look it, but I live a very dangerous life. I could never conceive bringing anyone else into danger with me. Any woman who shared my bed would also share my fate, and no one deserves that."

Elynor rolled over, propping up on her elbow to peer at his face. There was no jesting there, no humor at all. He truly believed *his* was a dangerous life. "It isn't illegal to be a bard, you know."

"You would think." He looked down at her, his eyes dancing with sadness. "Did Sharek ever tell you of Ardeth Lamruil?"

"Not that I can recall."

"He was also a bard," Sylvester said, "and also a Blessed. A legend they told of in Ollanthyr, from years ago. They say he had powerful music inside him, and that he hid it in his performances. He became a man of renown, sought after for his songs. It was rumored he could cure depressions, lift the lowest spirits, soothe babes and even pull men back from the brink of death with just a touch of his music. But the Kings of Yore learned of a Blessed serenading them in their own halls, and they began to hunt him. He lost his lavish life, his accolades, everything. And in his memory, the title of bard is tarnished. We do not play in fine halls anymore, and there are some who believe we all descend from Lamruil. So we all deserve to be hunted."

There was a strange allure to his words, the practiced tones of a professional storyteller; and when he was quiet again, it was as if the moonlight had dipped lower to listen between the iron bars. Sympathy tugged at Elynor's heart, and she squeezed his knee. "You are no Blessed, Sylvester. You're a good man, and a good bard. You deserve to practice your craft without fear."

"Ah, but if I *were* Blessed, it would be different for you, wouldn't it?"

Elynor scowled, taking back her hand. "I didn't say that."

"You hardly need to. I hear it in your tone." He stretched out his legs and tested his bonds with a groan. "Rowan may be a disgusting pit stain, but he has a good cause, trying to free the Blessed. Why should a talented bard and a man Blessed with music be treated differently? Who gave the sacrosanct the right to decide what is permissible and what is forbidden?"

Elynor wanted to say it was at the discretion of the King; but the Kings had also decided that men like Sharek and women like Elynor's mother had no value but what they offered to their kingdom in the bonds of slavery—and Elynor no longer believed that. She'd cared for Sharek's fate as much when he'd gone to Rimbourg, fit and healthy and ready to kill Al-Morral, as in his last days when all he'd managed to do was take one step after another. His value had not been diminished, not in her eyes.

"I don't know who gives us the right," she admitted. "I don't know who truly decides which men are equal and which are slaves." Yet even as she said it, her hand crawled up to graze Sharek's talisman.

"Perhaps we're all equal, and it is men who justify making slaves of whomever they do not understand. Or of those they fear."

The wagon jolted suddenly, and their progress ground to a halt. The other prisoners stirred around them, and Sam picked up his head so smoothly Elynor doubted he'd been asleep at all. The raiders swarmed outside, calling in the Orlethian tongue, cheering and backslapping. Elynor's skin crawled. "What are they saying?"

"That we've reached Bayar." Sam's tone was low, inflectionless. "Tomorrow, we enter the mines."

Then tomorrow, they would disappear.

Elynor's heart stuttered, and dizziness spun her head. They could not allow themselves to be written out of the narrative here, footnoted only in tales of the mines, forced to till the rock until death found them in those dark warrens. Not when Rowan was in Danje and war still loomed. They had to do *something*.

But as usual, Kirsagan let out the other prisoners and latched the gate with Elynor and Sylvester still inside.

"Sam!" Elynor hissed between the bars, and he hesitated. "Would you bring us healing herbs, a bit more food...*anything* you can find?"

His eyes swung back to her, sharp and calculating. Then he lifted his chin and moved off with the others.

Sylvester slumped against the wall. "I hate to rely on that one to fetch our supplies."

"What else can we do? We're useless," Elynor scowled, driving her heel into the floor.

"We will find a way out of this, Elynor."

The only response her body gave was a dull throb from the hot, swollen flesh of her leg.

Chapter Six

The Killing Blow

The world throbbed around Elynor when she woke the next morning, so that she couldn't even discern if they moved toward the mines. The erratic pulsing of her senses filled her with nausea. She squeezed her eyes shut and clawed desperately for sleep, but Sylvester's hand on her head brought her back to the discomfort of waking.

"I need you to stay here with me, Elynor." The bard's voice sounded strange, all traces of music gone. "Give me that water, will you, Sam?"

"It's all we have left." Sam's tone grated with irritation, as if Elynor and Sylvester had personally climbed into Kirsagan's cart to steal his water and his peace.

"Better we go thirsty than this wound goes unflushed."

A rush of prickling heat swarmed Elynor's leg, but after a moment it simply married into the rest of the pain there. She managed no more than a feeble whimper.

"This is infected," Sylvester cursed. "I fear blood poisoning if she doesn't receive treatment soon."

How ironic. Poison, yet again. Elynor didn't know if she should sob or cackle.

Sam scoffed. "I thought you were a healer."

"Yes, I am, and I'll just harvest some herbs from my arse-cleft! They hardly feed us, I certainly don't have the remedies I need to treat an infected wound." Sylvester's hand left her head and the cage began to sway. "Keep her awake. I'll try to convince our captors not to be *complete* barbarians."

An open palm struck Elynor's face, not hard, but enough to jolt her eyes open. She groaned at the sight of Sam's filthy, bearded face hovering above her, framed in moonlight. "Your friend said not to sleep. Something tells me you ought to listen."

Elynor swallowed a moan. She was hot and cold at once, and her whole body ached. Sleep seemed to be the only relief. Was this how her father had felt in his last hours? Had Sharek?

By the Holy Throne. She didn't want to think of either of them.

Sylvester was shouting now, and the cage rocked dangerously, but it all seemed muted, like floating on her back, ears submerged beneath choppy waters.

Sam shook her roughly. "Stay awake. Talk."

"About *what*?" Elynor groaned. "I don't have a prize shelf of *arkye* or a love affair with an Orlethian mare to entertain you."

The man's chest rumbled—almost a laugh. Or perhaps a congested cough. "You must have something you love as much as I love the milk. A family? A man? Profession?"

The Fleet. She could picture it as clear as anything: the shipyard, the harbor house, the great vessels framed by the dying sun. What had Al-Morral done with it in her absence? Had his magistrate found a way to twist the two wills by now? Was he ripping the Fleet out of her hands while she raced to stop his wicked schemes?

But she wasn't racing anywhere. She was trapped in this kings-damned cart, and Rowan was free to hatch his nefarious plot however he wished.

Sam tapped her hard on the temple. "*Talk.*"

"I love to sail." The words dragged a pang of longing across her chest, one she'd stuffed away as they'd ridden deep into Orleth to save Sharek. "It's my passion, my family's lifeblood."

"So you sailed to Orleth, did you? You and the lad?"

"And our companion."

"What did you sail?"

"A cog."

He snorted. "What a heap of horsedung. Cogs can't cross the Caeruel."

"My father's could." A touch of pride edged Elynor's voice.

Sam's face shimmered in the firelight bleeding through the cage bars. "The damned fool changed the rigging."

Elynor frowned. "What do you know of rigging ships?"

"Plenty. I've done my fair share. So tell me how he did it."

"Well...with the lines, he...he bound them together in a pattern, sail-to-sail." She was forgetting the proper words to express the art of what her father had accomplished, but the pride that filled her at the thought of him was beyond the infection and fever's reach. "He saw everything in patterns and new designs. He was a brilliant man."

"So I've heard."

"You've heard of my father?"

In the shifting angles of firelight, Sam's face was inscrutable. And then Elynor realized the angles had changed because someone was answering Sylvester's summons.

A sense of imminent danger spiked through her, peeling back the tarnished folds of feverish confusion. She struggled to push herself up, and Sam helped her with a rough pull to the elbow as the cage door swung open, knocking Sylvester off-balance.

They dragged him out first. Barely had his body smacked the stone ground than one of the raiders loaded inside and snatched Elynor by the hair. Dizzy lances of pain stabbed into her skull as the woman hauled her out and cast her down beside Sylvester, and as the bard leaped up, someone else knelt on top of Elynor, yanking open the rip of her pants where the stained fabric clung to the edges of the arrow hole.

There was laughter, and coarse talk, and then something harsh and thick poured over the open wound. Pain slashed through Elynor's leg and dug its claws into her hip so hard she screamed, shooting upright, dislodging the raider on top of her. Sylvester cursed and clobbered Kirsagan, laughing nearby, and the man took him down without so much as swiveling, his elbow jabbing Sylvester in the throat and dropping him in a retching heap.

Elynor glared up at Kirsagan, clutching her wounded leg, every muscle seizing as if she'd stepped into icy water.

"Ungrateful lot, aren't you?" Kirsagan turned to Sylvester and drove a kick into his groin. "I give you food, you try to run." Another kick, this time to the stomach. "I give you healing, you attack me."

Sylvester curled into himself, clutching his middle, but it was a useless defense against the raider's iron-clad boot.

"Spend all that defiance tonight!" Kirsagan roared, balancing his intoxicated frame with upraised hands as he slammed his foot again into Sylvester's abdomen. "Once you reach the mines tomorrow, there's going to be nothing left to spend but sweat—" another kick, "and blood—" and another, "until you're used up and thrown into the heart of the mountain like the rest of the rot!"

The next blow flipped Sylvester over his back and sent blood misting from his lips. Elynor screamed, fumbled upright, and broke down again. Kirsagan swung his leg back for another strike, and Sam piled out of the wagon, slamming into the raider and knocking him off-balance. He spun himself to stand over Sylvester, fists raised. In that moment, he looked less like a captured drunkard and more like a seasoned tavern brawler. "I've never cared much for brutes who'd kick a man while he's down."

Kirsagan lunged at him, wielding an amber bottle of spirits like a club. The two men tussled briefly, locked at the arms and wrists, winging and swiveling through the shifts in firelight while the raiders hooted and laughed. They could afford to laugh, to enjoy this, because no matter how hard Sam or Elynor or Sylvester fought, there was no escaping their fate.

Then the bottle shattered against Sam's skull, and he went down, weaving and bleeding.

"Cost me a perfectly-good bottle of Eralanite spirits!" Kirsagan roared. "And that's coming out of *your* hide!"

They had both crumbled now, Sylvester and Sam, fighting to catch their breath and their wits, and Kirsagan advanced on them. And for a moment, in the shimmer of firelight against stone, Elynor saw Boal go down under Kirsagan's fists, she saw his brainmatter spilling out and she remembered what Kirsagan had promised to do to the next person who crossed him.

And so, though she could hardly bear it, she dragged herself up on her good leg and threw herself in front of them.

For a moment, she and Kirsagan glared at one another in the cuts of fire and moonlight, and no words were said.

Then Kirsagan gripped her chin, towing her face so close to his that she could smell the spirits on his breath and see them dancing with the shadows of murder in his eyes. "I am very much going to enjoy seeing you disappear into that dark hole for your first and last time. I've never met a woman who more deserved to be broken."

He thrust her backward, her injured leg buckling, and she broke down next to Sylvester. Faint pressure circled her hand as he gripped it and squeezed, but over the tide of pain flushing along the length of her body like a battered stretch of shore, she couldn't muster the strength to squeeze back.

She was already broken. The mines would simply land the killing blow.

Chapter Seven

Hunter's Brew

THIS SOLSTICE SPEECH WAS going to be the death of him.

It wasn't that there weren't plenty of accolades to give, or achievements to laud. Crown Prince Jamyson Venator could've filled twice as many scrolls as he'd been given to work with. The trouble was that his heart wasn't in it anymore.

Erala's accomplishments this past year seemed a jest next to the events that had taken place in recent weeks. And every time he put quill to parchment, he pictured Gavannon Al-Morral's smug face when he was named Friend of the King; or his ears rang with the dull *crack* of his supposedly infallible father's hand against the tiny cheek of Jamyson's five-year-old sister as she wailed for her falsely-imprisoned mother; or he imagined his stepmother, Queen Cecile, caged in the dungeons, eating cold bread rinds and hard cheese; or he thought of Elynor Azorius, his lifelong friend and reluctantly-betrothed, and the letter she had sent in a forbidden script, warning him in brief about all of these harms.

And, in light of it all, his will to write failed him entirely.

He ought to just have his bodyguard and closest friend, Vestan, write the kings-damned speech. What did it matter?

A knock sounded at the door, and Jamyson snapped, "Enter."

THIS VIOLENT RECKONING

"If you dare," Vestan added from his seat at the dining table, where he flipped through his copied notes from the former physician's logbook. Jamyson shot him a glare, but the guard only shrugged.

A page entered, her angular face sickly pale against her green livery. "Your presence is requested immediately in the King's chamber, Sire."

"Well, that never bodes happily," Jamyson muttered, tossing down his quill and shoving his chair back.

He and Vestan crossed halls that teemed with whispers—something about a messenger arriving in the dead of night, a distressed, exhausted man with a note for Gavannon Al-Morral. Some claimed he'd ridden his horse to the barbican, where it had promptly dropped down and died; others said the man had run down the bridge himself, bloody and sweat-soaked, his mount already long dead. The current of sameness to all the rumors was a sense of urgency and importance, and Jamyson quickened his stride until he was practically running to the King's private chamber.

His father waited for him there, seated at the round dining table with Gavannon Al-Morral at his left—the position that had once belonged to the Queen. The righthand seat, always Jamyson's, seemed large enough to engulf him today. He was too agitated to sit.

"Your Eminence." He flicked a glance to the side. "Al-Morral."

"Jamyson." The King's tone was oddly gentle. "Thank you for joining us."

"What is this about?" Jamyson asked. "Why summon me here and not to the audience chamber?"

"We thought this was a conversation better had in private." The King's gaze slid to Al-Morral, and Jamyson fought not to bristle. The King shouldn't be conferring with an outsider about how to deal with the Crown Prince.

He folded his arms to hide the furious fists his hands had formed. "I'm listening."

Al-Morral leaned forward and slid a waterstained letter across the table toward Jamyson. "I received this correspondence from one of my captains this morning. I'm afraid it contains terrible news."

Jamyson's heart began to pound. "What is it?"

The King's gaze brimmed with damp compassion—too much of it. A cloying, sickening sympathy that reminded Jamyson of the day he'd been told his mother had freed heretical Hunters from the dungeons. When his father had consigned her to execution for treason.

"Elynor is dead, Jamyson. She fled detainment by Gavannon's men, and a rogue wave broke her ship in pieces. She has drowned."

His words—they were nonsense. They were *impossible*. Jamyson's thundering heart and swimming head could not make sense of them—he could not feel them any more than he could feel the edge of the table his hand had fallen to.

His knees were buckling. His chest hurt. Why did everything *hurt*, when he was being dealt such a lie?

Elynor was the strongest and cleverest woman he knew. She was more than a good sailor...she was an uncanny one. A mere wave would not conquer her. The ocean she loved more than any man, more than life itself, would not be the death of her.

"What proof do you have?" he bit out through gritted teeth.

"Eyewitness accounts by the men aboard *The Iracabeth* and *The Incharan*," Al-Morral said. "*The Farcomb*, Kings rest her, was destroyed by the same wave. Elynor's resistance led to the deaths of many sailors, good ones...loyal men to the kingdom."

"I am sure it comes as a surprise to learn Elynor was capable of such callused disregard for the lives of others," the King mused.

"She isn't," Jamyson growled. "If she fled, it was for good reason."

"You know her better than most, Sire." Al-Morral spread his hands in a feint of helplessness. "If you can fathom her mind in these matters, please, I welcome it. Anything to dull the pain of what she's done to me, and to the Fleet, and our kingdom."

Hatred pumped hotter and faster than the blood in his body. Jamyson wanted to strangle this self-sure Fleetmaster. Every moment he was in Al-Morral's presence, Elynor's warning letter about him, about her father's murder, about a threat of war...it all made better sense.

Gavannon Al-Morral was a master of deception; and if Jamyson called him on his lies now, without proof, the King would dismiss him. He would dismiss the evidence of a letter from a deranged, ambitious girl.

A dead girl.

"As you said," he muttered. "I know her."

"You *knew* her," the King said. "But she is dead now, and there is nothing left to know. This was justice for her crimes—the justice she fled our kingdom to avoid."

"I pray it was only for that reason she fled, Your Eminence," Al-Morral said.

A hush stole through the room, muting even the wind against the windows. Muting Jamyson's ears with a roar of fury.

"What do you mean, Gavannon?" the King asked.

Al-Morral slowly sat forward, banding his fingers together. "I have wondered often in these last weeks why Elynor fled to Orleth, of all places, when her attempt on my life failed. Why not go to the Farrow Mountains, or disappear into the desert beyond Oss Namore? Why flee from Erala entirely and risk the waves?"

The King frowned. "An excellent question."

"Unfortunately, I fear the answer to it is not quite so excellent," Al-Morral said. "I believe Elynor fled to be with her allies. *Orlethian* allies."

"Orlethian allies," King Marcus echoed sharply. "And to what end?"

Al-Morral held the King's gaze with an almost irreverent steadiness. "What if her father's death and her attempt on my life were not merely about gaining control of the Fleet? What if Orleth had its hand in this alongside hers, to provoke some sort of reaction? Perhaps even conflict?"

"That's ridiculous!" Jamyson snarled. "Orleth is a peaceful ally of Erala. They would never meddle in our affairs."

"Alliances shift every day among men, Sire," Al-Morral said. "It is foolish naivety to believe they do not also shift between lands. Orleth may grow weary of our trade agreements. They may seek a greater profit. They may even begin to dream of retribution for the Blessed...you know how they feel about such matters."

"Their greatest flaw," King Marcus growled. "Peace is profit. We all know this. But I will not have Orleth flex its might by influencing My people, and I will not tolerate meddling in Eralanite affairs. If I discover they had any hand in Alden's death, they will find the profit and trade arrangements become *very* disagreeable indeed."

Horror speared through Jamyson, vivid and sharp, leaving an ache under his ribs and choking his voice.

"I have a man in Orleth already, a spy sunk deep into their ranks," Al-Morral said. "Even now, he searches for evidence of treachery in the *Khul's* household. I pray he will find none, but one cannot be too careful."

"True. We must remain strong," the King said. "Aqqor's shores are our strong hull facing Orleth's shores, and if that crafty woman turned against Me before her timely demise, we must be sure to present a strong western face to our so-called allies. Gavannon?"

"I am at your mercy, Your Eminence."

"I fear we are at yours," the King said. "With Elynor gone, and with her family's name forever tarnished by these misdeeds and the attempt on your life, the Fleet must be remanded to another. We cannot afford to lose a step."

"I wholeheartedly agree, Majesty."

"I can think of no one more qualified, more capable, or more trustworthy than you," the King said. "Gavannon, henceforth I relinquish deed and title over the Azorian Fleet to you. I trust you will build her up even greater than Alden ever did."

It was like watching a nightmare come to pass. Jamyson almost expected to be ripped awake by Vestan shouting at him to get up before he missed breakfast. But his guard was standing behind him, breathing shallowly, stiff and silent—as horrified as Jamyson himself.

"This is such a great honor, I cannot even comprehend it." Al-Morral pushed back his seat, bowing deeply. "I will return to Bast at once to oversee the Fleet."

"No!" the King barked, and Al-Morral froze halfway through rising. "No, you will remain here. Until these matters are solved, we do not know if...if Orleth might send another assassin, as they might have sent against Alden. You are safest in Kaer Dorwenon, surrounded by the Kingsgard."

After a thoughtful moment, Al-Morral lowered himself back to the seat. "Your wisdom ever exceeds my own, Your Eminence. I will remain."

"*I* would like to be excused," Jamyson said.

The King hardly spared him a glance. "Yes, you may go. Take all the time you need to grieve."

Jamyson was not going to grieve. He was going to tear something apart on the training pitch, because he couldn't tear apart Gavannon Al-Morral.

Jamyson and Vestan were on the pitch for hours, dulling blades and wrecking shields, and it did little to calm the wild, wicked edge of Jamyson's rage. He worked his way from throwing knives through polearms and battle axes, ending on the sword, which became such a fierce fight between him and his guard that half the Kingsgard in training paused to watch and cheer and place bets.

It wasn't until he'd pinned Vestan and put the blade to his armored chest that Jamyson realized it was not his guard's face he saw. It was still Al-Morral's.

"How did he position himself *this* perfectly?" Jamyson raged when they returned to his chambers. He paced while Vestan sat on the table, wrapping a bandage around a shallow slice on his palm from one of the throwing knives, and a servant drew Jamyson's bath. "He's been here less than a month, and already he's the King's *trusted adviser*."

"Some men are born manipulators, Sire," Vestan said.

Jamyson whipped around and stalked back across the chamber, scowling as the servant rushed out. "Did you hear the way my father sounded when He ordered him to stay? It was pathetic. *Desperate*. This isn't about Al-Morral's safety, not unless my father is secretly in love with him! There's something else, something I don't understand."

Vestan shrugged, and Jamyson skinned from his clothes and climbed into the tub. The water's heat did nothing to soothe his rage, or the wounds he'd accumulated during the reckless training session. He was back out and toweling off before the bath had even begun to cool.

"That's it. I must go to my father," he said. "Tell Him what I suspect about Al-Morral. I have to stop this before it gets any further out of hand."

"Do you truly believe He'll listen to you?"

Jamyson lashed the towel around his hips and sat down hard on the bed's edge, gripping the sheets on either side of his body as he bent forward. "A month ago, I would have. Now...now I'm not so sure."

Vestan sank down beside him, looking off into the dining chamber. "So, what else can we do?"

Jamyson propped his elbows on his thighs and rested his folded hands against his mouth. "I don't know. Get a step ahead of Al-Morral somehow. Thwart this ridiculous notion that Orleth wants war. And clear Elynor's name." Heat pricked his eyes. "I owe her that."

Vestan stared down into his hands. "She was a good woman. I'll miss her."

The blow of that grief had not begun to strike Jamyson yet. He couldn't believe Elynor was truly gone—or that her inheritance had passed to the man she'd insinuated was responsible for her father's death.

There was a knock at the door, and this time it was Esmae who entered—the love of Jamyson's life, and the enslaved daughter of a magistrate who had hung for the same crimes as Jamyson's mother.

For once, not even the sight of her freckled face or the soft scent of rose soap from her deep red hair raised his spirits, though he mustered what imitation of a smile he could on her behalf. "Esmae. To what do we owe the pleasure of this visit?"

"I've just been informed I'm to be a caretaker for the royal siblings from now on?" Disbelief lilted the words into a question.

"That took long enough," Vestan muttered. "It's been *weeks*."

Jamyson scoffed. "Well, the King has other things on His mind, apparently. Like kissing Al-Morral's pompous arse."

Esmae tilted her head. "Something tells me this has less to do with the King, and much more to do with His noble son."

"I might have suggested something along the lines of it."

Vestan rumbled with deep laughter. "You know when Jamyson plays at being humble…"

"That he's waiting for someone *else* to praise him." Esmae joined them at the bed, sitting on Jamyson's other side. "Jamyson, truly, thank you. It seems no one in this kaer knows what to do with a slave when her mistress is disgraced. Ever since the Queen was imprisoned, I feel as if I've been disappearing into the cracks. And not in a good way."

"If it were up to me, her imprisonment would mean your freedom."

"But we both know the King would never hear of it. My status is not just a punishment against me. I carry the burden of my whole family's guilt. It will be a lifetime sentence."

Jamyson took her hand and squeezed it. "Not when I'm King."

Esmae's eyes sparkled with dark mischief. "I didn't say it would last *my* whole lifetime." When he didn't scold her for the treasonous suggestion—the next step in their familiar dance—Esmae turned her body toward him, still gripping his hand. "Jamyson, what's the matter?"

"Elynor is dead." Even when he spoke the words himself, they didn't seem real.

Esmae clapped a hand to her mouth, paling so starkly her freckles sprang out like mudspatter on her face. "*No.* How? *When?*"

Jamyson told her the story as it had been told to him, and by the end of it Esmae was shaking her head, her face firm with anger.

"I don't believe it. Not without a body, not without some proof beyond Al-Morral's witnesses," she said. "We've seen what he's done, and we have Elynor's letter. The man is corrupt. He would lie about her death if it profited him."

"And it has," Jamyson grunted. "Now the Fleet is his."

"So, we know that," Vestan said. "But why can't the King see it?"

Neither Jamyson nor Esmae offered an answer.

They all sat in silence for a time, pressed close together, and Jamyson was grateful for the comforting warmth of the most trusted people in his life. Even if Elynor was somehow a traitor, even if this kaer felt less and less familiar with every passing day, at least his faith in Vestan and Esmae was not misplaced.

Dusk swallowed the sun before Esmae smoothed down her skirts and stood. "I should go. Apparently I have bath duties with Isaac and Isla from now on."

"Good luck," Jamyson monotoned. "They turn into vicious imps at the first splash of water on their skin."

"I think I'll manage." Esmae hesitated, looking between them. "If there's anything I can do, you'll both let me know?"

Jamyson forced a smile. "You'll be the first we come to."

Esmae smiled, dipped at the waist, and hurried through the dining room toward the door. Jamyson rubbed his face with both hands and tried to conceive of sleep, so that he could think clearly and tackle this problem fresh in the morning—

"What is this?"

Esmae's tense, lilting question brought Jamyson's hands down from his face and sat him up tall. She was standing by the dining table, where she'd paused to push in the chair Vestan had vacated at the page's summons that morning. Lying open on the table were the copied notes from the logbook.

Vestan and Jamyson leaped up together, and Jamyson said, "Old Anna's scribblings. Apparently *Vestan* forgot to stow it away before we left the room."

As the guard spread his hands in an apologetic shrug, Esmae bent over the book. A distracting thread of hair tumbled loose from the knot on her crown and grazed her jaw, and Jamyson imagined sweeping it back into place, burying his hands in her hair, and—

"Whose treatment prescription is this?" Esmae demanded.

Jamyson and Vestan swapped a sharp glance, and Jamyson stepped behind the changing screen to don his trousers while Vestan went to the table. "We don't know. She annotated each patient but this one. Why do you ask?"

"I know this formula."

Jamyson forewent the tunic as he rushed to join them. "Do you?"

"It's a very unique blend, very rare, but, yes." Esmae tucked the strand of hair behind her ear as she glanced up at him. "It's called Hunter's Brew. An ancient recipe from the days of Yore. The refugees in Oss Belliard made several batches for my grandmother."

"For what ailment?"

"Mind sickness, Jamyson."

Jamyson stopped breathing. Stopped thinking anything.

His own mind turned to a dim hum without thought, without reason. He knew they were both looking at him. Knew they were drawing the same conclusion that he was—about the patient without a name. About the Brew. About the goings-on in the kaer of late, with the Queen, and the royal siblings, and Al-Morral.

About Anna's sudden execution.

"It's the King," Vestan said when no one else dared. "The King has mind sickness."

"He must have hung Anna because she knew," Esmae croaked. "Because He feared word would spread."

Jamyson dragged out a chair and collapsed into it, running a shaking hand over his mouth as he stared at the book.

An infallible King with a degenerative illness that warped judgement, planted paranoia, and destroyed memory. A ruler relying on a feckless Fleetmaster to be His compass, His conscience, His moral guide and His protector from the things He feared. And this secret, which Old Anna had died for revealing.

It would tear Erala apart.

He could not let it happen.

"Burn the notes," Jamyson sat forward, bracing his hands on the tabletop. "And don't breathe a word of this to anyone. For the kingdom's sake, it stays between us." Vestan and Esmae swapped heavy glances, and Jamyson's chest throbbed. "Do you both understand me? If the people learn the King's mind is unraveling, it will crack the very foundation of their beliefs. It could lead to a revolt, and with Al-Morral at His ear, I can't allow it to come to that."

After a long moment, Vestan nodded, took up the book, and brought it to the roaring hearth. He tossed it into the flames.

"And what will you do, Jamyson?" Esmae asked, sinking into the seat beside Jamyson's as the smell of burning paper filled the room.

He reached for her hand, and she gave it, winding their fingers together—her grip a bastion against the shadows that crawled away from the consuming flames as they devoured the only evidence he had of his father's deteriorating mind.

Besides the things he had witnessed for himself. All of the small tells that betrayed the King's cursed hand.

"Hold Him together as long as I can," Jamyson rasped. "And try to keep Erala from unraveling with Him."

Chapter Eight

A Kinder Death

Erdineen's Mines were a dungeon unto themselves. They were agony unimaginable, pain incarnate.

They were to be Elynor Azorius's tomb.

She did not recall their arrival here but in fits and bursts. She might have wept at the jagged maw of a mountain hall with fangs of stone riving toward her chest when someone—Kirsagan or one of his men—had carried her inside.

The next she knew was shadow, warm and dank; then pain cracking open the muffled dark, thundering up her leg like a tide gathered out from the sea and dumped against the coast with unforgiving might.

Heat, inside and out. The rattle of coin trading hands. Argument. Laughter. A quiet lullaby sung above her head...a song of the sea.

Her father's fingers in her hair. No—Sylvester's. Sam's.

Sharek's.

Sharek.

Sharek.

She dreamed of him, strong and sturdy as a ship's mast; she dreamed of him sick and ailing, his very life a fraying sail rope slipping through her wind-ripped fingers. She dreamed of their farewell at Tariaga Falls, his hand wrapped around hers, the talisman clutched between them.

Hold it tightly, mal ga'el. Let it give you strength.

She had no strength left to spare.

She dreamed of poison and infection, of parting with her father forever. Parting with Sharek.

She parted from herself.

She roused in darkness to the *thump* of something heavy dropping and rolling on stone. Warmth shifted beneath her body, and she was aware she'd been moved only when pain erupted along one side of her body, clawing itself out from her leg to dig frigid talons into every inch of her. Heat, then a chill so brazen it ached, dripped from the top of her head to the soles of her feet; it was an effort beyond reason to pry her tacky eyes open and find the face of a stranger looming above her.

A stranger...but she did not care. She could hardly blink his features into focus with the dimness of the world behind him, freckled with glimmers of lanterns hung on cords.

This was Erdineen's Mines.

This was her deathbed.

"Get her up." The man's voice was chilly darkness, like the world around them—black and seething and dank. "I want that bucket full of gems by sundown, or it's coming out of both your hides."

"You're welcome to try, you won't find gems coming out of *these* orifices." Sylvester's voice looped the last word out into staggered syllables.

A jest—one she might've laughed at if she'd had the voice for it.

Filthy hair, once amber like sheaves of wheat, ruffled along the corner of her vision. Sylvester's fingers, bloodied and torn by the stone they'd picked at for hours—days...perhaps even weeks—framed her face with a gentle pressure.

It mattered little how gentle he was. Her whole body ached at his touch, and she hardly held back a whimper.

"Elynor, listen to me," the bard urged, "you must get on your feet, do you hear me? We're meant to be mining, this is no place for sleep."

Sleep. Mining. Her gaze crawled past him to a bucket overturned on its side.

Her bucket. She'd dropped it. *She* had dropped, fallen like a chunk of ore sliding from a worthless hand, straight in the midst of her labor.

Labor she'd been doing for hours. Days. Weeks. It all ran together like blood from her leg. Blood from a wound.

Blood running from Sharek's side when he'd stumbled into Bracerath's Landing, calling her name—

A tear slid from her eye, and Sylvester caught it hastily with his thumb.

"I can't, Sly," she mumbled. "I can't."

"You must!" Though still low, the bard's voice seethed with desperation, his fingers tightening on her face as her head lolled. "Elynor, look here—if not for me, do it for the children!"

A weak laugh built up in her throat, but what escaped was a sob. "I'm so tired. Sylvester, I can't do this."

She did not *want* to do this. This work, this place...she did not want to pick at the rock or stumble back to the chamber she and Sylvester and Sam shared with all the rest of the miners.

Days. It had been days since Kirsagan had shuffled them off the cart, since she'd been bound and shackled, the pickax thrust into her hands. Lifting it was already a chore.

Ever since she'd held her father's hand and watched the life slip from him on a final breath, she'd feared death so much. Had fled from it in her dreams. Had trembled at its mere notion in her waking hours.

But death could be better than this.

"Elynor, do not give up," Sylvester begged. "Don't make me face Rowan alone."

Another tear joined the first, falling from her other eye. "We aren't going to face him, Sly. We're going to die here."

His eyes widened. Horror, shock, anger—she did not know. Nor did she care.

She let her eyes fall shut and her head slump in his hands; and she did not answer him when he righted her, when he shouted her name.

She did not open her eyes when the guard cursed. When Sylvester's fingers peeled away and rougher hands snatched her under the arm. When the chain slithered through her manacles and the guard wrenched her against him, she did not fight.

Sylvester howled her name. Someone else—Sam, she thought—swore and spat threats. She did not care.

She couldn't care. Because caring would necessitate she fight for her life. And Elynor Azorius was so spent from fighting.

Heat burned through her whole body as the guard hauled her up against him, his voice reaching her as if from a distance. "If you won't heed me, perhaps you'll heed the Overseer, then."

And he dragged her away, Sylvester still crying out after them in anguish. In rage. In farewell.

Chapter Nine

The Mercy of Sharek Ransalor

The hole that fed down into the mines reeked of waste, illness, despair—and far worse. Death lived and breathed in these winding, watchful hall of stones, lived in by raiders and guards and Empyreans-knew what else. The worst of all that Orleth had to offer.

Sharek's nostrils stung with the stench as he and Iracabeth slipped into the mouth of the Mines, passing the bodies Iracabeth had dropped by arrows shot from the treeline beyond. The verge of greenery might have betrayed lesser invaders, but not a killing Blessed and a mother whose daughter lay captured in these shadows.

These men had never had any hope of surviving.

Darting past their corpses, Sharek and Iracabeth entered into the antechamber of the mines; halls branched off from the room of high stone, each as dim and rank-scented as the last.

Iracabeth slowed and glanced toward Sharek, her face grim with determination. "Which way?"

He strained to hear the distant chime of picks biting into stone. Strained to catch every whisper of sound that would lead him to those he'd come to kill—and those he'd come to save.

"These shafts," he pointed to two adjacent, one before them and one spreading off to the right, "their echoes are the same, carrying the same voices. They likely lead to the same place."

Iracabeth's fingers tautened audibly over her bow's grip. "Very well. I'll travel down one, you the other. I'll cover your flanks."

Sharek nodded, spun his blade once, and took off down the shaft ahead.

There was no time to worry for his aching lungs, for the exhaustion of so much trekking on foot that grazed at the contours of his consciousness. There was only this place, which had swallowed Sylvester and Elynor whole.

Nothing mattered but that he reach them.

Guards dotted the tunnel along his way, their outlines fracturing the dim glow of the ore that snaked through the walls; Sharek gave no heed to their faces, gave them no moment to cry out after they caught sight of him. With twice the ferocity with which he'd conquered Al-Morral's home in Rimbourg, Sharek cleaved through Erdineen's Mines. Everyone patrolling these halls was of little consequence to him; every one was a captor, a thief of bodies, a privateer who profited off the suffering of others.

There was no place here for shame or regret. Only for the very talents that might have made him a coveted asset to them, had they been the ones holding the blade and he at their mercy.

But there was no mercy here except what Sharek might choose to give. And he had none to spare for these people at all.

He only slowed his wild, ruthless dash down the ore-limned tunnel when the swell of voices turned from an echo to a force, hammering against his ears…one louder than all the rest. Strident. Accustomed to being heard and heeded.

Sharek knew that deep rumble of a voice, laced with cunning and cruelty—though he knew it as if from a feverdream. A dream of sand and ocean, of panic and pain…and of pride. Pride in Elynor as she'd outwitted this foe, with none of Sharek's prowess for killing or Sylvester's wily ways of running from trouble.

Sharek knew that voice, and bristled with loathing at the roar of laughter it rose on, high enough to brush the cavernous vaults of Erdineen's Mines.

Kirsagan al Bayar.

Sharek slowed at the mouth of the tunnel, squinting at the harsh light that fell through a gap between the Peaks of Kharanklad into this central chamber. Its walls were high and jagged, speckled with lichen and other creeping growth, the sun beating down on the room from directly above. The tunnel he stalked through was one of many breaking off from the broad span of dark rock in the heart of the Mines, a channel of sorts through which miners seemed to be herded.

By whip. By chain. By bow.

Kirsagan and his raiders perched atop a crop of rock in the chamber's heart, its broad width encircled by stone steps, the slosh of spilling wine and the gritty rip of teeth through tender meat spilling down from where they sat.

They gorged themselves, enjoying the spoils of their conquests, while down below the chamber pulsed with the movement of slaves driven by the whip, turned this way and that through the tunnels.

Sharek pressed his tingling spine to the stone, shut his eyes a moment, and breathed deep, hunting for familiar smells among the cold waft of the stone, the sweat of the prisoners here, the brilliance of exposed ore seething in the veins of these Mines.

When a smell of faded herbs and wood oil reached his nose, his eyes shot back open. A breath of relief staggered through his abused lungs.

Sylvester. He was here, in this room.

But there was no sound, no scent, no sight of Elynor.

Heart thundering, Sharek lifted his gaze along the span of rock to where the raiders sat, feasting and drinking, glorying in their catch.

His fingers curled sharply around his sword.

Then he was running, lunging clean over a line of chain slithering around the room and feeding down one of the tunnels, to which prisoners were bound by the ankles; he was past them already by the time they gathered their voices to shout in shock. Before the guards could fumble for their weapons and cry a warning, he was halfway up the rock face; and when he flipped over top of it, landing in a crouch, Kirsagan and his men had not yet risen, their hands scarcely on their blades.

Sharek held himself in abeyance for one moment. Just long enough for morbid recognition to alight in Kirsagan's drink-reddened gaze.

"You," the raider choked.

And then Sharek was upon him.

Never before had he truly gloried in death; it had always been a cruel necessity from the moment he'd felled Fausto Hagan—his father's murderer—until now. But this death...it would not plague his conscience. It would not haunt his dreams.

For the first time that he could ever remember, Sharek Ransalor knew what Rowan must feel when he killed—satisfied, triumphant, delighted, even, as his blade slammed straight through Kirsagan's chest, then whipped free and slashed his head from his shoulders.

Then plucked the blade from Kirsagan's cruel hands as the raider toppled dead before him. And he kept killing.

Killing these raiders who had made his friends suffer. Killing these raiders who had stolen Elynor and Sylvester from their purpose, from freedom, from *him*. He brought them down one after the other, his ears roaring with their swift shouts silenced by the efficient edges of his blades. It was some moments before any voice broke through the thrum of battle in his ears—and then, it was not one of theirs.

"*Sharek*!" Sylvester cried out from below—exultation, disbelief, warning. Then he bellowed again, wordless, wild with rage, the sound nearly lost in the clatter of singing steel.

Sharek hurled the last raider's corpse aside and whirled to spot Sylvester just below the rock crop. He was one of the prisoners bound by a chain, being led along the far side of the chamber—and he had turned on a nearby guard wielding a crossbow, looping the binding links of his shackles around the man's throat; the weapon was discarded beside them while they wrestled, but it was a brief skirmish. For even unarmed, this Orlethian was stronger and fitter than Sylvester, who reeked of hunger and pain despite the distance.

In a moment, the guard was free, throwing Sylvester down and raining blows on his midsection. Another prisoner snarled profanely at the abuse, writhing in his own shackles, fording back toward them until the lines of his chains caught him at the ankles and sent him tumbling down to the floor.

All of this Sharek breathed in between one moment and the next.

Then he leaped.

It was a short, silent, deadly descent—and yet still Sharek was not faster than the arrow that came whipping from off to the side, slamming into the guard's ribs, jolting him sideways. He stumbled straight into the cut of Sharek's blade, removing his head from his shoulders in a single clean slice.

The chamber erupted with panicked shouts—prisoners and guards alike—as more arrows rained from the tunnel entrance adjacent to where Sharek had arrived. The strongest among the chained miners whirled on their captors, dealing out blows no doubt months or years in the waiting. The sound of shattering bone and blood spattering rock filled Sharek's ears, not only from his own movements; he carved a crescent of slaughter around Sylvester, warding off any guards who turned their way. Then he whirled back, tossing his blade aside and sliding to his knees beside the bard.

"Sly, look at me," he growled, and Sylvester's eyes squinted open painfully, his breathing labored as he clutched his ribs. "Do you see me? How badly are you hurt?"

"Sharek Ransalor," Sylvester breathed, and with every blink, the sheen across his eyes brightened, until at last it spilled over in twin trails carving down his bearded cheeks. "*Sharek*, truly? I'm not dead...you're here?"

"Here for *you*, my friend." Sharek swept an arm around Sylvester's far-thinner frame—thinner, even, than when Sylvester had bowed under his weight on the slow trudge to the side of Tariaga Falls—and embraced the bard, hauling him up from the floor.

A gasp of sound, nearly a sob, wrenched from Sylvester; then he clapped hold of Sharek in an embrace just as strong, and did not let him go for some seconds; when he at last pulled away, he was weeping in earnest, though still he smiled. "I don't believe it—*how*? Your Empyreans?"

"Iracabeth," Sharek said, and Sylvester's eyes blew wide, his hands dropping away. "She returned not long after you left."

"You mean that if we had just *stayed* with you, Elynor and I wouldn't be in this—?"

Her name was a violent wind blown from an ocean storm, barreling through Sharek, sharpening his purpose along the brutal edge of its passing. "Sly, where is she?" he demanded, shaking his friend by the shoulders. "Where is Elynor?"

The dampness in Sylvester's eyes dried in a blink. His mouth tightened with a dangerous sort of focus...one more people would fear, Sharek was certain, if they knew Sylvester Munrow as well as he. "The Overseer sent for her. She's badly off, Sharek, her leg—"

Sharek hauled Sylvester up with him, steadying them both on their feet. "Which way?"

Sylvester gestured vaguely past him, then took a wobbling step in his wake when Sharek turned that way. "It's a maze in here, you'll never find your way alone—"

"We both know that isn't true."

For Sharek Ransalor was not here to spare lives; and his senses, as if knowing that to be a certainty, already found paler twists in the path—places where the rock was impressed by more sets of bootprints traveling toward than away, leading down one tunnel where prisoners in this place went and did not return.

A chamber of death. A chamber of ended lives.

If not yet, then it soon would be.

Sharek jerked his head at Sylvester, motioning the bard alongside him; then he crouched, freed a band of keys from one headless guard's waist, and tossed them to Sylvester. "Free as many as you can and lead them out. Iracabeth will cover your flanks."

Sylvester's mouth opened and shut, a protest living and dying on his lips at the look Sharek leveled his way. Then, cursing, he limped to the nearest prisoner—a man with a brawny build, bloodshot eyes, and a bearded face, the one who'd wrenched at his chains when the guard had kicked Sylvester—and freed him. "Help me, will you, Sam!"

Entrusting the stricken prisoners to Sylvester's capable hands, and his friend's life to Iracabeth's level aim, Sharek whirled back to that tunnel where the luckless went to die.

He did not know how long it was—how much stone and stale air lay between him and its end. Him and Elynor.

But when a distant, anguished scream grazed his ears, it did not matter. It did not matter how his lungs burned or how his body begged for rest.

Sharek was running harder than if his own life had hung at stake.

Chapter Ten

Falling Star

The Overseer of Erdineen's Mines was elegantly cruel everywhere Kirsagan al Bayar had been ruthlessly so. Elegant in the look of him, his clothing tailored to a lean and powerful frame, hair slicked to his scalp with tallow, posture and poise immaculate. Elegant in his chamber, a warm and heated thing in the belly of the Mines which might well have been anywhere, with its sophisticated furnishings and well-rendered hearth.

Even the weapon he carried was as polished as it was brutal: a sleek leather whip, the sort that horsemasters in Kaer Dorwenon wielded to break mounts to their will.

She could not peel her eyes from that whip as the Overseer paced before her, and she hung slumped over her knees where the furious guard had cast her down before he'd retreated to take post with a handful of other men at the walls. One leg throbbed far harsher than the other, a familiar ebb and flow of pain wailing in her wound just as it had for many days...and seemed it would until her last.

To and fro, the Overseer paced, hands perched on his waist, fingers an inch from the immaculate black whip coiled serpent-like in his belt. Elynor watched it slither in the firelight and wondered how many had tasted its cruel bite in this hopeless place...and whether she would be the next.

"My guards tell me you do not work," the Overseer spoke the trade language in clipped tones, which suggested he had learned it for necessity rather than interest.

How many captured Orlethians and Eralanites both had vanished into these mines? How many sailors and common folk put picks and chisels to stone in the interest of these captors, and whittled away their own hope as they mined ore and jewels, day by day? How many were missed, and loved, and often thought of—but given up for lost?

Emotion hitched Elynor's throat.

She had so few awaiting her return; Jamyson, perhaps, but he had the Throne to think of, and her note about Al-Morral, assuming it had reached him; and Bernian and Gregor and Millicent, and the servants at Kaer Lleywel. But all of her family was missing, or dead; there were so few who would mourn her, and none who would know where to search even if they wondered after her disappearance.

There was no one who could come to her aid.

Dull resignation seeped into her throat like a tide pool filling, and she blinked dampness from her eyes.

"Well?" the Overseer halted before her, and it occurred to Elynor then that she had not answered his remark about her performance. Or lack of it.

What was there to tell him? That until just recently, she had been an heiress who rarely toiled, except at the rigging to her heart's desire? That she was not strong in the way this cruel world demanded...that she had wept for a hired Blessed whose death was on her hands, that she still yearned for a mother who'd twice forsaken her, that she clung to the frail edge of life by the tips of her fingers when some aching part of her dreamed of letting go?

When she opened her mouth to retort, all that escaped was, "My leg."

The Overseer's head canted. "I beg your pardon."

Not a question so much as an invitation to reframe her retort. To spare herself whatever that cruel fate was that lurked behind his knotted mouth, his pulsing jaw.

"My *leg*," Elynor croaked, forcing her gaze up from the severe cut of his lower face to his cold eyes and creased brow, "if you haven't noticed...Kirsagan al Bayar made a...a mess of it. If you intend us to work, perhaps you should...*invest* in our wellbeing."

The Overseer's tongue grazed his lips, just the tip of it. "Is that what you think?"

Fiery, screaming agony erupted through her body as the man dropped before her and gripped the arrow-wound in her leg, digging his thumb into the hole torn through flesh and muscle. Sylvester's paltry dressings gave way, and Elynor's entire world blackened in the eclipse of a pain that overshadowed all else.

She floated for a moment in a void that somehow knew pain, its edges humming, thrumming with the ripples of agony rising up from her leg.

Then he pushed in again. This time it jolted her back, a scream tearing from her so viciously it cracked her body into a violent arch, feet digging into the stone, spine vaulting into a bow as she struggled to tear free of his grip.

The Overseer held her fast, dragging her back to him by her wounded leg when she writhed to escape. His voice sliced through the havoc of anguish in her head, cutting the piercing windstorm scream in her ears. "Do you think your *wellbeing* matters to me? Kirsagan brings a dozen like you a month! I took a risk on you, he said you had a fire that would set this place ablaze...all I've seen is a worthless, sad, *sniveling* waste!"

His thumb slid from the hole in her flesh, and Elynor's vision blurred and blossomed with violent, dark spangles. She rolled onto her side, gasping, retching, fighting to cling to consciousness.

No retort rose to her tongue. Every erratic thud of her heart hurled an inescapable truth into her spinning head.

The fire Kirsagan had witnessed on the shores of the Caeruel, the never-ending burn to escape, to press on, to dodge his advances and see her task completed...

Some piece of that had collapsed at the falls. Had laid down and died beneath a tree, beside an abandoned *ger*.

What was she, against the might of men like Kirsagan, against Rowan and Al-Morral? They had outwitted her. Beaten her from afar. Perhaps this was her punishment after all for defying the Holy Throne, for doubting the King, for placing her heart and hope in the hands of a heretic.

She was going to die in these mines. Likely in this very room. And she would be forgotten, and replaced, and the world would go on living.

Or the world would burn beneath Al-Morral's schemes. Sylvester would wait for her to return, and she never would.

Gasping in a staggered breath at that notion, Elynor planted her hands on the rock, digging her nails against their unbreaking might until the edges chipped, and slowly she levered up the top half of her body; she rolled painfully over her uninjured leg to glare up at the Overseer, who crouched above her, his thumb slick with her blood.

"I am not what you think of me," she hissed. "I am *dauntless*."

And though the word did not feel true, it felt brave. It felt like every sweet scrap of courage she lacked, soaking into her very bones. And when the Overseer blinked, eyes flicking to the guards who held the walls, a faint thrill of triumph rushed through her.

She had pretended for so long—to be the compliant heiress awaiting justice, the undoubting sacrosanct following her King, the woman of faith, of hope, of unbreakable will. She could pretend again, if it took her back to Sylvester.

If only to say goodbye.

She caught hardly a glimpse of the Overseer's eyes in the torchlight, the glow in them shifting from startled to seething.

Then his hand was around her jaw, yanking her up at an awkward angle, his knee crushing her injured leg. He shouted louder than her sobbing scream: "You will be *nothing* when these mines have finished with you! If you won't work, you won't *live*!"

Elynor fought to muster a retort past the fizzing nausea in her throat, past the pain of his fingers digging into her jaw—

And then she heard it. Heard it before she even saw it. The sound of a falling star rushing across the sky, of a blade cleaving through the dark. And then a figure, robed in shadows, emerged from the tunnel mouth with a wordless snarl, and at the sight of him Elynor lost her breath. She lost her sanity and her sense.

All that was left in her was his name, gliding over her lips like a prayer to the Empyreans who must have sent him.

Sharek Ransalor stepped into the cavern's light, arms spread, a blade strapped to the inside of his left wrist. That was all he had.

It would be enough.

The Overseer let go of Elynor's face, eyes narrowed. "Who are you?"

Sharek's gaze was riveted on her, deadly and brilliant and so heartachingly *beautiful*.

"I am hers."

And then he attacked.

Elynor had seen him fight Dru Farwell spiders and struggle free on the Orlethian beach from Kirsagan's raiders, but this was nothing like that. This was Sharek the killing Blessed, utterly unleashed.

He leaped onto the shoulders of the nearest guard, snapped his neck with both hands, and pushed off to meet the next one, blade in hand. And then the next. And the next. Furious shouts as the guards converged soon turned to panicked screams. In a matter of seconds, the stone was paved with blood. Elynor swayed in place, her nose scathed with the old-meat scent of spilled entrails, and the Overseer fell back from Sharek's onslaught. His eyes hunted wildly for a weapon that would do him any good, and then he spun and snatched Elynor by the arm. He yanked her in front of him, hurling Orlethian abuses in her ear, scrabbling a blade loose from a sheath on his thigh and putting it against the side of her neck as Sharek brought down two more guards.

"I'll kill her!" The Overseer's voice, stripped of the smug might of a moment before, broke with terror.

Three guards still standing, Sharek froze. Then, slowly, he revolved toward the Overseer and Elynor. His chest heaved, his skin faintly gray. His eyes were glassy, but they were riveted on her.

And all at once, he moved; he racked between the two guards, thrusting them against the walls, then stabbed the third in the chest, whirled, and flung the knife. Elynor felt the brush of its passing, heard the slice of it driving straight into the Overseer's open mouth.

She shoved his arm away as he tumbled so that his knife would not rake her neck; the motion set her swaying like a ship on storm-rocked waves, and all at once Sharek was there, his hands catching her arms when she tumbled down. They struck the stone together, and his fingers dropped to the side of her neck, feeling for a wound, a mark of the blade.

"Look at me, Milady...look at me!" His tone was rougher than she'd heard it yet, urgent, fervid with terror. "Are you hurt? *Elynor!*"

"No," she panted, the words half-strangled by nausea, by terror, by agony—by the impossibility that he was *here*.

"Thank the Empyreans." His fingers knotted in the matted, miserable mess of hair at the back of her head, and he drew her in, his lips grazing her brow with a fervency that surged tears to her eyes.

This could not be true. Sharek was never so brash, so forward. And the way his hand cradled her head, as if he held all the world in his grasp, as if he would never let go...

But, by the *Throne*, she ached for it be true. For this to be something more than a delirious death-dream.

"When Sly told me they'd taken you, I feared I was too late." Sharek's ragged voice chafed against her will, her valiant efforts not to be drawn in by this illusion of fever and desire. She trembled in his grasp, and he drew back, framing her face with his broad, scarred palms. Terror of a different sort bolted through his gaze. "Milady, what—why are you weeping?"

"Am I dreaming?" Elynor croaked. "Is this a fever dream?"

Sharek stiffened; his brow furrowed, and he looked all around them—the blood, the bodies, the havoc he'd wreaked. "You must have very violent dreams, Milady."

The sound of his voice this time—no longer rough and vicious as when he'd spoken to the Overseer, no longer warped with fear for her—severed the rope that moored her to disbelief and doubt. Elynor cast out to a sea of relief that did not care for the impossible, did not care if she was dreaming this, and she wrapped her arms around Sharek's neck, breathing in the smell of mahogany and vetiver layered with the sweat under his skin.

"You're here," she rasped. "I don't care how, I don't care about any of it. Thank your Empyreans. Sharek...*Sharek*."

After a tense moment of surprise, his arms came under hers, his hands clutching her shoulders, and she felt him take a long breath, heard it rattle slightly in his chest and felt the wind of its passing on her skin as he buried his face in the crook of her neck.

"Elynor."

At the brush of his breath on her skin, she broke. She relinquished to the sleep she'd fought for so long, and let herself slide down that dark slope again, knowing that somehow Sharek, killing Blessed, cheater of death, would be waiting to greet her at the bottom.

Chapter Eleven

The Rules of Mediocrity

"**W**HAT ARE YOU GOING to do about Al-Morral?"

Vestan's voice, quiet as ever, disappeared into the fog that girdled the east-facing belvedere. He and Jamyson had both been awake since before dawn, the prince needing to pace and his faithful guard ever at his side. Now that Jamyson had burned off his wild energy, they stood on this balcony, where they'd been for hours, losing the sunrise in the thick mist that curled up from the valley floor far below.

Jamyson perched his arms on the railing and stretched his back out, resting his chin on his elbow. "I don't know."

Vestan propped his own elbows backward, watching the walkway behind Jamyson, regarding its doors and stained-glass windows with a vigilant eye. "You believe Elynor's letter? That Al-Morral was somehow involved in her father's death?"

"I do. Why else would he arrive at our door and insinuate himself into royal affairs with accusations against Elynor herself? And why presume her death—or sink her vessel, if he was telling the truth?" The mere thought stuck like a dagger in his throat; it was some effort to speak around it. "There's something he hopes to gain...and now we know why my father can't see it." Jamyson dragged a weary hand down his face. "All this strange behavior, all His poor decisions of late..."

Vestan grunted. "How's Isla?"

"Healing, thanks to Orson's brews. She's already forgiven Father, I think, with all the gifts." Jamyson rocked back and braced the heels of his hands on the railing, sinking his head beneath his shoulders. "It's Elliott I'm worried about. He's questioned me every day about Father's choices. He asks for his mother ten times a day, and the governess and Esme both say he's acting out."

"He's coming face-to-face with the lie the whole kingdom believes about the King's wisdom," Vestan said. "Even grown men and women question it. How can we expect children to fathom an infallible King who imprisons His wife and strikes His daughter? They know deep in their hearts it isn't justice."

"Well, I've known for a long time He isn't without His faults," Jamyson said. "And now we know we were never wrong. He's just as prone to failures as the rest of us."

"And Al-Morral may be His greatest." Footsteps scuffed stone, and Vestan's elbow jabbed into Jamyson's ribs. "Company."

He swiveled away from the railing as Gavannon Al-Morral himself appeared through the haze of fog. A cloak billowed from his shoulders, pinned at the throat, its clasp bearing the emblem of Erala's royal family: the dagger and the crown, enshrouded with roses. The mark of the Kings of Yore defeating the Hunters. Jamyson bristled to see the Fleetmaster wearing it.

Al-Morral halted, his eyes flicking between Jamyson and Vestan. "Up early for a morning stroll, Sire?"

Jamyson folded his arms. "Bold of you to assume I slept at all."

"That's a pity. In these troubled times, we all need to be well-rested and keen of mind."

"Troubled times?" Vestan echoed.

Al-Morral's gaze rested on him a moment longer, and Jamyson tensed at the disdain in his lifted brow and sideways smirk. "The King has not forgotten, nor is He pleased, that the Crown Prince's life was threatened while his personal guard was off collecting wares in Dorwenon. Where were you when your prince needed you most?"

Jamyson's chest hitched at the reminder of the mad scheme of his—a gamble with a belladonna tincture to draw attention from the healer's rooms—that had helped set all of this in emotion...that Al-Morral had twisted to his advantage, driving a wedge between the King and Queen with false accusations that she'd poisoned Jamyson himself.

He'd be damned if he let a wedge be driven between him and Vestan next.

So Jamyson stepped forward, angling his shoulder between the two men. "*If* my father has a grievance with my guard, He knows I will gladly hear it from *Him*."

Al-Morral did not fall back at Jamyson's advance. Another mistake. "Mediocrity among the servants and *slaves* of this kaer has been the standard in the past, but the King grows weary of it. We have traitors and would-be murderers in our midst now, even among the royalty themselves. Inadequacy in those who tend them will not be tolerated."

"By whose enforcement? Yours?"

"The King's," Al-Morral said smoothly.

"Well, you'd know all about mediocrity, wouldn't you, Al-Morral?" Jamyson stepped toward him, arms still folded so he would not lash out the way he ached to. But he barred the way from the Fleetmaster to Vestan, and did not recoil at the raised brow it earned him. "A man made nameless until his business partner's untimely demise. The King wouldn't know your name if not for that boon."

Al-Morral scoffed low in his barreled chest. "How would Elynor feel, I wonder, to hear you call her father's death a boon?"

"Feel? Or *felt*?" Jamyson bit the words out. "I think you're mixing your stories."

The Friend of the King studied him for a long, long moment.

"No need to repay a friendly warning with accusations," he said at last. "Your father has seen my strengths in rooting out deceivers and traitors among us. It is my honor to use my talents in service to the Holy Throne."

"Is that why you're out patrolling so early? Looking for evidence to put someone else in the dungeon?"

"Bold of *you* to assume I was not patrolling all along, Sire." Al-Morral's lips tipped into a sleek grin. "You should be grateful I stumbled upon the Queen's illicit activities. I may very well have saved your life."

They were chest-to-chest now, the blood roaring in Jamyson's ears, his racing pulse begging him to swing at Al-Morral's head. "Something tells me my wellbeing was not your greatest concern."

"You ought to be wary of your tone, Prince Jamyson." Al-Morral's stinking breath fanned his face. "Your Father has not forbidden me from keeping watch over *your* affairs, as I do all the other nobles."

"Threatening a prince is treason." Vestan stepped shoulder-to-shoulder with Jamyson.

"So is questioning the King's judgement, *Blessed*."

Stalemated, Jamyson and Al-Morral glared at one another. Then the Fleetmaster shrugged his shoulders deeper into his new cloak and stepped back.

"We'll be seeing plenty of one another in the weeks to come, I'm sure. I hope in time we'll reach an understanding, Your Highness. After all, we both desire the very best future for Erala. There's no reason we ought to be at odds."

He flashed one last smile, then brushed past them. Jamyson kept his back to the man, hiding his fists in his armpits and drowning his rage in long, deep breaths until Vestan's hand descended on his shoulder. "Sire?"

"Watch him," Jamyson growled. "Sooner or later, I'll expose him to my father. I want him gone from this kaer before he harms anyone else."

Quiet as a spirit, Vestan slipped away.

Chapter Twelve

Comforts and Conflict

Elynor did not know how long she slept, but her dreams were odd.

It was the Ocean Caeruel she visited there, its waters chopped by vicious winds, and yet it was no challenge at all to sail it. She was traveling toward something frightening, something larger than she was prepared to face, but her father's voice was with her in the wind that filled the sails.

When the time comes, you will know the way.

The prow crested another thick, spirited wave, and at its peak, Elynor saw what she had been sailing toward: the Fleet, flying murderous Gavannon Al-Morral's standard, spread out across the horizon.

The horrific *boom* of a hundred cannons filled her head, and Elynor snapped awake with a sharp breath.

She was indoors, somewhere softly-lit and smoky, and there were people murmuring nearby about fallen trees and waterfalls. As if they had heard the sound from her dreams.

This was not Erdineen's Mines, the last slice of the world she had known. The shadowed pits of rock and ore where skin-traders had held her and her friends captive were gone. This place hummed with safety and hominess instead.

The mines were not her tomb. They were only a memory.

A door opened and shut, and a figure moved into her tearstained sight. Her chest snagged to a halt at the vision of his face, living and well.

It was still so strange to see him again. It still felt like a dream. But she knew it was not, now that she was awake and the fever pulsing in her skin and muddling her head had abated.

Elynor licked her lips. "Sharek."

He lowered himself cross-legged before her face. "Milady."

"Please don't start that nonsense again."

His lips twitched, and he reached over to tug the blanket up around Elynor's shoulders. "How do you feel?"

"My leg doesn't hurt." It was a surprise when she realized it.

"It's been treated for infection, and there was some numbing solution in the bindings...don't ask me to remember its name."

Elynor peered up at him. He seemed so relaxed, so at ease here. It was almost unnerving. "Where are we?"

Sharek's eyes flicked to the side. "Your mother's *ger*. I...carried you here."

By the Holy Throne...after all they had endured together, *that* was what brought a rush of heat to her cheeks?

Sharek, mercifully, ignored it—though some of his prowess as a killing Blessed must have signaled her body's betrayal. Instead he told her what had happened after she and Sylvester had left him, believing him at the precipice of a death he had not wished them to witness; and what they hadn't known about Kirsagan and his raiders who had caught Elynor and Sylvester up in the absence of Sharek's talents; or the state of this secluded sliver of Orleth called Tariaga Falls—that its abandonment had all been a ruse.

Elynor's heart leaped between relief and resentment at every turn of the tale: relief that her mother, Iracabeth, had been there, that she'd healed Sharek. And resentment at the lie of the *ger* that had chased Elynor and Sylvester away from Sharek's side and straight into Kirsagan's hands.

"She treated everyone's injuries once we escaped from within the mines, and then we returned here. You've been asleep for many days." He paused a moment. "I was...concerned, when you didn't wake. But your mother assured me all would be well."

"Where is she?" Elynor demanded.

"Checking the fish traps. She'll return soon."

Elynor wondered if her mother was avoiding her. She resolved not to dwell too heavily on that, and focused on Sharek instead—taking in his long, dark hair hanging tangled but clean to his shoulders, and the healthiness of his complexion, and the softnesss of his eyes that set her heart stuttering. "And how are *you*?"

"Uncomfortable," he admitted, which was entirely at odds with how he leaned his weight on his hands and unbent his spine. "The poison left a scar on my lungs that will only heal with time, if it heals at all. The trek up and down the mountains was difficult, to say the least." And then he coughed into his elbow, so thickly Elynor winced and her stomach tightened.

Perhaps she would always carry this fear that when he coughed, she would see blood.

"I'm sorry you had to endure that," she said when he was quiet again.

Sharek's eyes settled on her, bright in the dimness of the *ger*. "I would walk it again a thousand times for you, Elynor."

Warmth spread through her chest, and with it a famished curiosity. She put out her hand, and Sharek helped her sit up so she could take stock of the *ger*. It was a fine place, cozy, she supposed, though she preferred the pristine halls of Bracerath's Landing. Sylvester sat against the opposite wall, shirtless with his middle thickly wrapped in bandages; disheveled flaxen hair tumbling around his bare shoulders, he played idly with an instrument like a lute, but with a neck half as tall as the bard himself. His fingers didn't seem to have any trouble with the strings regardless.

To her shock, Sam dozed beside the fire, flat on his back, snoring deeply. Or pretending to snore. It was difficult to tell with him.

"Where are the other prisoners?" Elynor asked.

Sylvester shrugged. "They left us after two days of walking. Apparently our company was not agreeable to them once we weren't all subjected to each other's filth. Sam was the only other one too beaten to have a choice about following a healing Blessed to her place of refuge." His words were light, humorous, but the way he looked at Elynor was fathomless.

They had seen much together, endured much in Kirsagan's caravan and in their handful of days in the mines—days Elynor could scarcely recall. They had each faced the choice to leave the other behind, and chosen not to.

She would not soon forget it, and she doubted the bard would, either.

Then the door of the *ger* opened, with a cool wind that swept aside all thought of raider caravans or the mines, or any life beyond these walls.

For there was her mother.

Chapter Thirteen
The Curse of the Blessed

IRACABETH AZORIUS LOOKED PRECISELY how Elynor had envisioned her: as an older mirror of herself. The source of her dark hair, her stern mouth, her smoky eyes.

And now, the source of her rage.

"Elynor," Iracabeth breathed, the fish basket tumbling from her arms. "Look at you. Oh, your father's letters did you no justice. That fire in your eyes—"

"You should have been here." Elynor's words trembled out, brittle with anger. Beside her, Sharek stiffened.

Iracabeth stepped toward her. "I know, Elynor. Listen to me, Seabird, leaving you was the hardest thing I—"

"No." Elynor couldn't let her continue, couldn't think of all the years between when her mother had abandoned them and this moment. All that mattered was *now*. "You should have been *here*, Iracabeth. Where you said you would be in your letters. All of this happened because of you."

Her mother drew up short, brow slanted with confusion. "Elynor. I had no idea you would come searching for me after all this time."

"You have no idea about many things," Elynor snapped. "The things we had to endure..."

Sylvester stopped plucking the strings. Sam snorted and turned his head away.

She had thought Sharek was dead. *Dead.* And she'd had to grapple with that, and with imprisonment, because Iracabeth had fled. Just as she'd fled from Bracerath's Landing when Elynor was a child.

Perhaps that was not a sensible argument, but she didn't feel like being sensible for once. Her mother was here, and what did she expect? That Elynor would crumble, weeping and forgiving, into her arms? How could she?

Iracabeth had saved Sharek. Had tended Elynor's leg. Had healed Sam and Sylvester, it seemed. But she had also left her family for the freedom to learn these things—freedom Erala did not offer to those with talents that evaded the sacrosanct.

Her own mother was a Blessed, and Elynor had never known.

All these things were too horribly tangled together to separate, and Elynor was not strong enough or keen enough to sort them out. She wanted to be furious rather than sensible.

So she leaned back into the heat of that fury and let it consume her.

Behind Iracabeth's frozen form, the door slid softly shut. An unfamiliar girl around Elynor's age tiptoed over to Sylvester and quietly began to tend his bandages.

The sight of her was a spark on the tinder of Elynor's temper. "Who is *that*?"

Iracabeth cleared her throat. "My assistant, Rue—"

"And how long has she been with you?"

If Iracabeth knew the question was a trap, then she did not fear it. Or else she did not care. "Since she was a child."

Elynor scoffed under her breath. "How simply you replaced me. And did you replace Father as well?"

"Elynor."

"Did he approve? Did Father approve of your new life in this place?"

Iracabeth's eyes hardened. "Your father knew that I came here to escape oppression. And not only me. I did not come here for myself."

"You cannot possibly expect me to believe you came here for *us*!" Elynor snapped. "I needed a mother, but you...you simply found yourself a different daughter."

"Rue is not my daughter! She is my *assistant*. She helps me find Blessed who need our help."

Sharek sat a bit taller, kneading his chest, his brows drawn together. "She is a dragnet."

The girl's hands stilled, and she shot a frightened glance toward Iracabeth. They stared at one another for a long moment. Then Rue nodded.

"Yes, Sharek, she is," Iracabeth said. "When her Blessed parents discovered her talent for finding their kind, they cut out her tongue. So she fled from them. She stole aboard a ship to come here, and I found her. I raised her, taught her Orleth's language of handsigns so we could communicate. Now we find our own kind, and we heal them. As we healed you."

Elynor's resolve to hate this girl, this other girl Iracabeth had raised, cracked like thin ice. Sympathy wormed through her defenses.

"That was how we found Sharek," Iracabeth added. "Rue sensed power in our meadow, and so we came, even fearing the raiders. But what we found...*who* we found..."

Sylvester touched Rue's wrist, stilling her hands. His face was full of deep thought. Rue sat back on her heels, watching him; then she turned to Iracabeth, her fingers flying in complicated twists.

"It was not Sharek she sensed," Iracabeth said heavily. "She didn't know who she sensed. Until I brought you all back here."

"But why not?" Elynor demanded. "Why couldn't she sense Sharek?"

"Because," Iracabeth said, "Sharek is not Blessed."

Her head swiveled, and she locked eyes with Elynor.

"*You* are."

Chapter Fourteen

The Hunter's Heart

IT WAS NOT FOR the scarring in his lungs that Sharek struggled to breathe.

Beside him, Elynor was as still as a woman carved of stone, her fingers splayed on her knees, her wide eyes riveted on Rue. On this powerful Blessed, a dragnet—the only one Sharek had ever met. The only one who could truly know these incomprehensible things Iracabeth was speaking.

"That's impossible," Sharek croaked. "I am...I am a killing Blessed."

Rue shook her head, dark ringlets storming against her brown skin. Then she spread her hands in a broad, helpless shrug.

"I know what you are, Sharek." Iracabeth's tone was grave. "I knew it when I saw how you healed. How your body worked with my craft to mend itself. And these senses you have, your way with the world, the things you heard and scented in the mountains, things that no sacrosanct human *or* Blessed ever could..."

With every word that dripped from her mouth, he knew.

"You are a Hunter."

Sharek shoved to his feet and started to pace, wild energy shrieking over his nerves. His footsteps slapped the *ger's* wooden floor like a death march. He dragged his shaking fingers through his knotted hair. "No. No, that is not possible."

His *father* had been a Hunter—a noble man, a fierce warrior, a protector of Erala. Sharek was a murderer, a hunter only at the behest of the Sanctum.

"It isn't as impossible as you might think," Iracabeth said. "When two Hunters join..."

"My mother was human."

"Are you certain of that?"

Was he? His memories of her were vague, blurred by years of work for the Sanctum. She had seemed human to him. But perhaps she had hidden what she was, hidden her strength and power, her way with animals and with nature, to keep him safe. To keep men like Fausto Hagan from learning that the Hunter bloodline lived on through her son.

Through Sharek Ransalor.

He'd been thrown into the Sanctum without question, assumed a killing Blessed for what he'd done to the man who'd beheaded his father. And after Rowan had trained him, there'd been little doubt of what he could do—for Rowan was truly Blessed with the power to kill, and Sharek had imitated him flawlessly. But what if Sharek's strengths were not in killing only, but steeped in the might of the Empyrean-empowered Hunters? His speed, his keen senses, these things that made the kill possible, but never preferable like it was for Rowan...

He fell against the wall, bracing his hands on his face. "Empyreans help me."

"That girl is a liar." Elynor's voice was low and calm, but vicious. "He is not a Hunter. I am *not* Blessed."

Rue scowled and signed furiously at her. Sharek did not know the words, but he suspected she did not take kindly to being called names.

"Rue is right, Seabird, you are," Iracabeth murmured. "Alden and I have known ever since you were young. That was why I truly left, in the end. I could not risk my power bringing attention to yours."

"These are lies! Cruel lies to cover your own selfish decisions!" Elynor shot to her feet, stumbling on her injured leg, and Sharek lurched away from the wall to help her. But she cast up a hand to halt him, her glare fixed on her mother. "I know what I am, and I know Father...he would never have kept this from me."

"He feared to lose you to the Sanctum," Iracabeth said. "We both did. We thought it better if he raised you, kept your talent hidden by training you on the waves, and I left so that no one could ever trace your lineage to a Blessed mother who'd passed the blood down to you."

"Enough! Enough of your lies!" Elynor screamed. "I am not Blessed!"

"If you won't believe what I say, ask Alden. He will confirm it."

"He'll confirm nothing!" Elynor shouted, and it was a mark of the potency of her dry rage that there was no break in her voice at the mention of her father. "He can't, because he's *dead*."

A hush gripped the *ger,* so abrupt Sharek was keenly aware of the breath leaving Iracabeth's body.

Then she fell back a step, her hand flying to her throat. "That—no. Elynor, that cannot be. I would know. I would *feel* it."

"It is true—a Blessed killed him, because they're a curse, and I am *not one of them*!" Now Elynor's voice did crack from the force of her screaming. "I'm not one of *you*!"

And then she knocked her mother aside and limped from the *ger*, leaving the door open behind her.

Sylvester, silent in his shock, looked at Sharek with a stricken gaze. Sharek shook his head. "She didn't mean it."

Iracabeth buried her face in her hands. "Oh, Empyreans...what have I done?"

Rue stood and wrapped her arms around Iracabeth. The healer clung to her tightly, her body racked with sobs. And Sharek, whose own head was a hive of humming disbelief, left the *ger* for the solace of the wilds.

For some time, Sharek walked, watching the world around him fade toward dusk. He measured his pace, letting his injured lungs rest, and the openness of the world soothed his frantic disbelief. His cringing mind relaxed, and then his thoughts flexed, reaching out to mull over possibilities. To consider the chance that Iracabeth might be right about him.

It would explain so many things. How he had never developed a thirst for killing like Rowan had. How the craft still sickened him after all these years, when other killing Blessed began to relish it. And how he had endured so much. Survived so much—and not only since Rimbourg. There were those Blessed with survival whose bodies adapted in whatever way was necessary to keep them alive, but he knew he was not one of them. He was an efficient killer, but it was possible his senses and strength made him that way.

The strength of a Hunter.

And if it was true, then he had never been in so much danger in all his life.

The King allowed the Blessed to serve the sacrosanct, to use their talents for the good of the kingdom. But there was no place for Hunters in Erala. They were killed on sight, as Castian Ransalor had been, and their sympathizers were cut down as well, or enslaved to teach lessons to anyone who dared shelter the few Hunters who remained. If a dragnet ever came to the Sanctum and learned the truth of what Sharek was, then it would be over. Aeson Thalanor would personally behead him.

Could he ever go back? Did he dare stay away and give Aeson reason to hunt him? And could he truly defeat Rowan, who was killing Blessed, when Sharek himself lacked those advantages?

He walked on, tormented by possibilities and by the crushing weight of the truth, until the path climbed around the side of the falls and ended in a rocky outcropping above a raging river. Beyond it, over the distant treetops, the Peaks of Kharanklad jutted in the distance. And on that shelf of stone, Elynor sat, arms wrapped around her knees, watching the sunset as it painted the treetops in pink and gold and turned the western faces of the mountains to pure amber.

Sharek could see so far, and in such great detail. He could smell the salt of Elynor's tears with her back to him. How had he never realized it before?

He cleared his throat, and Elynor sniffed sharply, thumbing her nose. "I should have known you would track me."

He hadn't meant to. But perhaps he had been following the imparting of her passage through the undergrowth around Tariaga Falls without even realizing. His body suddenly felt foreign, his senses undependable, this shell of skin caging a spirit that was familiar within sinews he no longer understood.

Sharek made his way slowly onto the outcropping and lowered himself beside Elynor. They were silent for some time, gazing over the valleys of the Amasandji *Khulig* below them. Then Elynor said, "Do you think it's true?"

Sharek wished he could give her the answer she wanted. But he murmured instead, "I think it is."

Elynor's hand rose to his jaw, a startling touch—but not an unwelcomed one. She turned his head toward her, moved it left and then right. He tried to keep his gaze fixed on hers and not look at her mouth, her half-parted lips so near to his.

"That ring of gold around your eyes, whenever it grows dark," Elynor said. "I first saw it in the Dru Farwell, when you fought those spiders. Is that a Hunter's trait?"

Sharek shrugged. "It must be. All my senses are."

She let go of his face. Leather snapped with a dull pluck, and Elynor held out his talisman to him. "Here. They're truly your powers now."

Sharek stared at the token, his mother's necklace, and agitated laughter rose in his throat. *Her* token of Sabrathan—not his father's gift to her, but hers in truth.

How had he never thought to wonder why a human woman carried a talisman of the Empyreans? It was Nymeria who had insisted he learn the Hunter's Prayer from his father, after all. Nymeria who had urged him to follow in his father's footsteps in so many ways.

Not only Castian's footsteps. *Hers*. She had hidden her heritage to keep him safe, but she'd guided him on the paths of their people nonetheless. She had known all along what he was.

A Hunter. The son of Hunters.

He took the talisman from Elynor and tied it behind his neck. The weight was wonderful, the cord swollen with his own sweat and blood. It felt like it was his more than it had ever been before. More than anything else in all the world.

Elynor dug her fingers into her temples, rumpling her hair with feverish scratching. "He knew. Father *knew* about my craft. All this time...that was why he didn't hire any Blessed. Because it was like hiring *me*."

Sharek watched her from the corners of his eyes—her sharp, frenetic movements, her profile touched in the dying light. "He loved you."

"No. Love would have offered honesty. Perhaps he was afraid that having a Blessed daughter would lose him the Fleet."

Sharek didn't believe that, and he knew that sensibly, she didn't either. But sense had no place in these stunned moments when the world was unraveling, so he didn't try to speak rationality to her. He simply sat beside her and offered his silence for her to lean into.

Darkness unfurled its blanket across the sky before Elynor spoke again: "It's sailing. I'm a Blessed sailor."

Sharek had already surmised that. Her talents to bring them to Orleth's shores were incontestable, given what her parents knew.

"That was why Father kept me on the waves," Elynor added. "Why he made the Fleet my inheritance. Because he knew how I would crave it, as you told me once, the way Blessed always crave their craft. And he hoped that if I was taught the talent, no one would ever question where it came from. Whether it was learned, or...inherent."

Sharek nodded.

"I'll never sail again." Elynor's voice was brittle, calm, full of conviction, and she reached into the seam of her pants and withdrew her compass. She cocked her arm to throw.

Sharek caught her wrist; when she looked at him, he shook his head.

He saw her now as clearly as he had the night in Kaer Lleywel when they'd spoken of their dead fathers—she was still his mirrored echo in their grief, and now in their disbelief and uncertainty. Their lives upended, their pasts in tatters, their futures unclear.

He was a Hunter and she was Blessed. Nothing would ever be the same again. But still he saw her, and he knew her heart. The compass was her talisman, her bond to her past. Her last gift from Alden. And like Sharek and the necklace from his mother, when the shock and hatred dulled, when the world and their own lives made sense again, she would want it back.

After a moment, Elynor tugged her arm free. She shoved the compass into her pocket. "I won't return to the *ger*. Not tonight."

"I'll stay with you, then," Sharek said. "If you like."

Elynor looked away across the valley, shoulders shaking with a tremulous intake of breath. Then her hand crawled across the gap between their bodies and slid into his. "Stay. Please."

Her hands were callused, roped with small scars from the sailing lines. They were cold and wet, clammy with sweat and tears.

Sharek had never held anything so perfect or precious in all his days. He did not know how to let go.

So he squeezed her fingers. And she squeezed back, and after a moment, laid her head on his shoulder. Sharek held very still, even when her tears marked his sleeve, and decided that if all he had faced led no farther than this moment, in this place, with her...then he was content to have faced it all.

After a length of silence, Elynor whispered, "I'm glad you're here."

She said it the way he said his prayers; as if it made today, and all the uncertain tomorrows after it, easier to bear.

It was the same for him; everything was easier to face with Elynor Azorius beside him. Even death. Even this new life, knowing what he truly was.

He leaned his cheek carefully atop her head. "I will never be anywhere else when you need me. Not even if death should come between us again. I will crawl back from the grave for you, as many times as you call me. I know nothing else feels certain to you now...but trust in that."

A wet breath rattled her parted lips, and her grip strangled his, desperate as drowning. It was all the plea and promise either of them needed, on this night where the world as they knew it shattered before them, and an uncertain dawn awaited beyond the shadowy hours ahead.

Hand-in-hand, they watched night overtake the world.

Chapter Fifteen

Battle for the King

DAY BY DAY, JAMYSON watched his younger brother turn to stone.

It was only them on the training pitch today, and Vestan somehow managed to disappear into the fog despite being six-and-a-half feet of solid muscle, sharp wit, and imposing glares. And it was Jamyson who'd insisted on coming out here so early, far earlier than he and the Second Prince were usually even awake; because he'd heard Elliott sassing his governess and tutors like a seasoned Kingsgard soldier and that, in light of everything transpiring with their father, could not be allowed.

Elliott needed to spend his rage before it got him killed.

In the unstable climes of Kaer Dorwenon these days, Jamyson felt like the thread holding everything together—looking after his younger siblings, keeping the nobles in check, and keeping one eye on Al-Morral.

And with every other spare moment of his time, he watched over his father.

King Marcus's bouts of forgetfulness were worrisome enough; He'd asked Jamyson six times in the past week if he had begun to work on the speech for the Winter Solstice, and each time Jamyson had reassured him it was nearly done. Which was troubling, but not unnavigable; what concerned Jamyson more than his father's forgetfulness were the fits of temper...and the cruelty that came where the two met.

First He had struck Isla, which was unforgivable enough; but now He seemed to have forgotten He'd landed the blow at all. When He'd seen the yellow splotching around her eye two days ago, he'd had the royal siblings' sword mentor thrown in the stocks for doing the deed himself.

So now Jamyson was training his brothers and sisters with the blade, besides all his other princely duties.

Not that he minded, except that ever since he'd taken over the task, rumors about Elliott were starting to grow worrisome in their own way.

All these thoughts cut through his mind, one after another like quick blade strokes, and then Elliott broke his guard and jabbed him in the ribs so hard he lost his breath. Stabbing his own wooden practice sword into the frosty grass, Jamyson held up a hand. "Break."

Elliott frowned. "Why don't you ever wear armor when you train?"

Jamyson shrugged; the truth of it was, he didn't like to feel encumbered by armor. He relished the thrill of knowing every blow that might land, practice sword or not, would do him real damage. But he didn't want to put those kinds of thoughts in Elliott's head.

Vestan joined them then, thrusting a canteen into Elliott's hand. "He has a knack for making trouble that no prince should."

"I don't recall asking you," Jamyson drawled.

"Well, I thought the Second Prince deserved an answer. And you were busy staring at him with the vacancy of a newly-neutered billy goat."

"Much as I appreciate your loyalty to my siblings, Vez, you're making me sound ridiculous."

"Apologies, Sire. I know you need no help with *that*."

Elliott smiled reluctantly as he passed the canteen to Jamyson. It was better than his scowls all these past weeks, but it still wasn't anything like the roaring laughter Jamyson had come to expect from his oldest half-brother.

Like Jamyson had learned painfully and long ago, Elliott was in the painful process of learning that the Infallible Sovereign of Erala was not really so infallible—that the illusion of the King's all-consuming wisdom was really just that, an illusion. But he also had to learn—and Jamyson was determined to teach him—that they must uphold that generational lie.

If they did not, Erala would crumble for certain. And they would fall with it.

Jamyson thrust the canteen back into Vestan's hands, then swung an arm around Elliott's shoulders and walked him along the edge of the pitch to cool down. "Your governess tells me you're acting out. Throwing fits."

Elliott pocketed his hands with the scowl that was rapidly becoming his new trademark. "I'm thirteen. Too old for her to tell me what to do anymore, like she does Isaac and Isla."

"That's right, you're nearly thirteen. So I'd expect you to behave like it, not throw tantrums when you're given a chore or a task to do." Jamyson gave him a sharp shake. "Listen to me, Elliott. With things being as they are in the kaer, you can't afford to go around kicking your heels or spreading talk about Father. Do you understand me?"

"Why not? He hurt Isla!"

"I know." Rage cracked Jamyson's voice—he couldn't help it. He'd been the one to put the pieces back together after that night. He'd been the one his siblings turned to, with their mother imprisoned and their father turned to a stranger before their eyes. "But this is about more than us. It's about the kingdom. And for the kingdom's sake, everyone must continue to believe in Father's wisdom."

"But *why*?"

Jamyson halted, taking his brother's slim shoulders and holding fast until Elliott grudgingly met his gaze. "Because when I become King, and you become First Prince, we can't have the people doubting *us*."

Elliott's eyes widened, and the fierce frown melted away. Slowly, he nodded. "When I'm First Prince, and then Crown Prince, I'm going to write a law that makes it *illegal* to hit little girls."

"I think that's a good law, Elliott." The words, bright but fierce, rolled through the fog, and Jamyson turned to see the rest of his siblings crossing the training pitch, led by Esmae.

He couldn't resist flashing her a smile despite the serious conversation topic, particularly when Elliott puffed up with pride at her praise.

Then he was mobbed by Isla and Isaac, and Sylvie, next youngest after Elliott, who trotted after them, offering Jamyson a shy smile that cracked his heart in two. She had been so quiet ever since the King struck Isla, timid and refrained, as if she expected to be hit next. He missed her fountain of chatter about all things politics and baking, her greatest passions.

He missed how things had been when the King could still be trusted with *some* things.

"It's almost time for lessons," Esmae said. "Governess Mariana asked me to walk the energy out of these three before they started. I see you've already taken care of that with Elliott, Sire."

Isaac hauled at Jamyson's hand. "When can *I* train with you?"

"Once you weigh more than a soaked sack of grain." Jamyson hauled his brother up easily under one arm.

Isla swatted Jamyson on the backside. "You put him down!"

"I don't think so." Jamyson bundled her up under the other arm and jogged down the pitch, and Elliott grabbed Sylvie's hand and dragged her into a chase, their playful shouts swirling the fog.

If Jamyson never managed to do anything else right by his kingdom as the prince who knew too much, at least he could still make his siblings laugh while their mother rotted in the dungeon for supposed treason and their father became a figure untrustworthy, seated high on a Holy Throne they could never approach again.

Ahead of them, where the pitch cornered, the thick autumn fog pulled apart and a figure stepped into Jamyson's path.

"Good morning, Your Highnesses." Gavannon Al-Morral's smooth voice was unmistakable even before his countenance came into view: dark mustache and beard freshly shaved, hair slicked back, eyes darting from face to face.

Jamyson slowly lowered Isla and Isaac onto the trimmed grass, his nerves tingling with the need for a blade in his hand. "Come for a training session, Al-Morral?"

The Fleetmaster's smile was bitter like ice framing the edge of a pond. "Hardly. I'm no match for you in the sword, Prince Jamyson."

"Good. I'm glad you're aware of that."

Tension burned the mist around them. Elliott stepped up to Jamyson's side, scowling. "Did Father send you?"

Al-Morral's brows rose. "I see no reason why He should. He only has me watching the nobles He cannot trust. *You* are trustworthy, aren't you, Prince Elliott?"

Elliott jutted his chin. "More than *you*."

Jamyson laid a quieting hand on his brother's shoulder, his pulse kicking. He hadn't dared breathe a word of his suspicions to his siblings—that Al-Morral was directly responsible for their mother's imprisonment on false claims—but perhaps Elliott had drawn that conclusion himself.

The Friend of the King flashed that smug grin Jamyson despised. "The King Himself named me trustworthy. Surely His own son is not questioning His judgement?"

Jamyson took Elliott's other shoulder now, drawing his brother back a step from Al-Morral and into the breadth of his own chest. Sylvie shrank behind him, and Isla and Isaac gripped his legs. "The only thing anyone is questioning," Jamyson said coolly, "is why you're out walking the pitch this early if not to train."

Al-Morral's gaze traveled between all of them, his smile fixed. "The King sent me to inquire if you've finished the solstice speech."

Jamyson let out a long breath in increments. "Tell Him it's nearly complete. I'll have it to Him by week's end."

"See that you do."

Footsteps brushed the grass, and behind him, Esmae said, "Is everything all right?"

Al-Morral stilled, his eyes skipping to her like an arrowhead changing targets. Jamyson didn't realize he'd tensed until Elliott squirmed, forcing him to loosen his fingers.

"I don't believe the Friend of the King owes His children's slave any explanation." Al-Morral bowed toward the royal siblings. "Good morning to you." He vanished, the fog swallowing him like a vengeful spirit.

"I don't like him," Isla whispered.

Esmae lifted the princess onto her hip. "No one does."

"The King does," Vestan said, arriving at Esmae's side. "And I'm afraid that's all that matters in this kaer."

Jamyson turned Elliott and thrust him into Vestan's hands. "Take them to their lessons. I have to pay someone a visit."

Chapter Sixteen
Vicious Fingerprints

Jamyson rarely visited the dungeons of Kaer Dorwenon. Not since his own mother's imprisonment in his boyhood had anyone he loved been left to rot in this dank place—he'd made certain of it; and before that, he'd never believed anyone in the dungeons deserved his attention. They were all traitors and criminals as proven by his father's infallible wisdom.

Walking the stone halls paved with slick shadows in the belly of the mountain, his torch's guttering flame hardly slicing the dark, he wondered now just how many of them truly belonged here, and how many had been sentenced unjustly, without a proper trial, because the King's word was always law.

Urgency bit at his heels until he jogged past the cells carpeted in straw and lit by thin rays of sun tumbling through from skylights high above. If he did not hurry, someone would notice his absence; and if Al-Morral or the King found out he'd come here, it could spell death for Queen Cecile.

Jamyson arrived at her cell, the brightest lit of them all. Someone had brought her blunted knitting needles and a small mound of books. There was also a distinct smell of chocolate cake mixed with the musty straw and the scent of the relief bucket.

Apparently, he needed to have a private conversation with Sylvie, too.

The Queen raised her eyes at the torch's light, and her expression registered no surprise as she beheld him. She was gaunter already than when her husband had thrown her into this cell, dressed in tattered rags rather than the royal gowns Esmae had prepared for her every morning since she had become slave to the Queen.

Guilt tore at Jamyson's chest like vicious claws, and he planted the torch in the sconce on the wall so he could grip the bars. "I'm told they've been treating you fairly."

"As fairly as any woman can be treated who's been falsely accused." Cecile's voice was still queenlike, sharp and unshaking. "I know I came into your life at a difficult time, and that things have never been particularly warm between us. But you must believe I did not try to kill you, Jamyson."

"I know you didn't," Jamyson said. "I never believed it for an instant."

Because his near-death had been at his own hands...something he could never confess, or risk his life and far many more. But the accusation that had been leveled against her, excising her so precisely from the confidences of the King...

Cecile's breath rushed from her, and she rose swiftly, stepping up to the bars to wrap her fingers around his. "I think it was Al-Morral. I think that man is plotting something...something to do with your father."

Jamyson studied his stepmother's face carefully. If he said too much, he might find himself in this cell with her—or in her stead. "You know why He hung the physician instead of allowing her to retire."

Cecile shifted her feet and averted her gaze.

"It's all right," Jamyson added. "I'm not here to condemn you to that fate. But I need to know that you know."

"The mind sickness, yes," Cecile whispered, her fingers fetching away from his. "He told me of it. Wept about it openly, in fact. And then He hung Old Anna to silence her, and He did *this*." She spread her hands along her soiled skirts. "I can only imagine I've kept my head despite what I know because underneath it all, He still loves me."

Jamyson rested his brow against the bars. "How long do you think He has?"

Cecile's shoulders bobbed. "My own grandfather had the mind sickness for many years. It does not take life quickly. But it does take meaning from it much swifter. He's already grown so forgetful and so angry, in so short a time. He is not the King the people loved. The man *I* fell in love with."

They stood there, wrapped in firelight with the shadows tracing their bodies, and Jamyson knew the words must be spoken. He had to hear for certain what had plagued him for years—had to hear it from the one the King trusted most. It was the only way he could move forward. "He was never infallible, was He?"

Cecile pressed her lips together and stepped back, studying him carefully. "Jamyson, one day you will take the Holy Throne, and you will have a queen of your own. And she must learn to keep secrets, as I learned to keep them. As I suspect your mother did. It is not the King who truly has power...it is the tale of His infallibility which lends strength to His hand. And now that He sickens, Marcus will surround Himself with people who believe that lie at all costs. If you do not wish to join me here, I suggest you play along."

Jamyson dragged a smile onto his face, but it did not hang well. "I should have made the effort to know you better when we still had time. We could have been friends, I think."

"You are a friend to my children, and that means more to me than anything else." Cecile cleared her throat. "How are they? Sylvie's crept in to see me, but I've forbidden it now."

"Good, she shouldn't risk it with things as they are," Jamyson said. "They're adjusting. Elliott is angry. Isla still has nightmares from time to time of Father hitting her. You've seen how Sylvie is. But at least Isaac seems all right." He hesitated, then added quietly, "Esmae has taken part of their care. Not their education, but seeing to their needs."

Cecile wiped a hand down her face. "Well. I wouldn't have allowed it, but she's a good slave. She'll serve them well, as she served me."

It was the only praise Esmae would ever receive from her old mistress, so he didn't press for more. "One last question."

"Anything."

"I can't very well ask the court physician for this, but I want to know what will happen to Father next."

Cecile backed up to her stone bed and sat on it, her vacant gaze fixed on the shadows of the corridor. "The paranoia will steepen. His decisions will become more reckless and His memory dimmer. I fear for Him at the Winter Solstice, Jamyson. When all those lords and magistrates are gathered together, if they see Him that way..."

"I'll do something," Jamyson said, though he wasn't at all certain of what. "I'll protect Him."

"I'm not certain He deserves your protection."

"I'm not doing it just for His sake. I do this for the people."

Cecil's lips curved. "That speaks less to the King He is, and more to the man *you* are. Be careful, Jamyson. This is a battle for His mind, and for the kingdom's very heart. You will have enemies everywhere you go."

Jamyson pondered hard on that as he emerged from the guardhouse above the dungeon's spiraling stone well and slipped into the heart of Dorwenon. The mist from the Valley of Embra had burned off and the city had begun to bustle. People hurried among the markets, homes, and merchant booths. Wells pumped and children laughed.

Here, at least, life continued as normal, unaware of the King's perilous position.

And, it seemed, unaware of Gavannon Al-Morral—a shadow who cut across the edges of Jamyson's sight, hurrying down the central road with a plain hood cast up over his features. He was well-concealed in that drab attire, but his bearing, and the quick glimpse of his face as he surveilled the market, was unmistakable.

Jamyson halted, frowning.

What business did the Friend of the King have in the heart of Dorwenon? The life he'd built on vicious lies and treachery was in the kaer alone.

Jamyson turned up his own hood, pivoted smoothly, and gave chase.

Al-Morral moved with the intensity of purpose, passing taverns and hawkers without so much as a sideways glance. For nearly a quarter mile, Jamyson pursued him through Dorwenon's streets; then he ducked behind a vendor's stall as Al-Morral slowed outside the Inn of Tryst, a hostel of middling reputation among the townspeople. He flashed a fleeting look up and down the street, his attention lingering on a pair of Kingsgard at the market nearby, haggling for venison jerky with a vendor. Then he slipped inside.

Jamyson didn't dare follow him any further. Al-Morral's presence might not raise eyebrows the Inn of Tryst, but the Crown Prince's certainly would.

Still, the encounter haunted him; Al-Morral had among the most lavish suites in Kaer Dorwenon. He wanted for nothing better found in a squalid inn than the King's own halls.

He'd have to have Vestan keep a closer watch on Al-Morral after today. Expand his authority to follow the Friend of the King beyond the kaer walls…and find out why he was lurking in this place specifically.

Chapter Seventeen

Abigale's Schemes

No matter how many moments he stole away from Kaer Dorwenon, tangled up in the sheets with Abigale Cainwell at the Inn of Tryst, it was never enough.

    Gavannon craved her when they were apart. He longed to walk the city's dusty streets and the kaer's splendid halls with her. And as much as the position of Friend of the King suited his needs and advanced his purposes, none of it could compare to her words of love spinning his head into a tangle of nonsense or the way she smiled when he told her how clever and lovely she was.

    He might have traded it all for a quiet and successful life in Bast as master of the Azorian Fleet with her by his side—if they did not deserve better.

    Today, he was too distracted to lie with her, his mind on the encounter with the Prince at the training pitch that morning. No matter what he did, Jamyson did not seem to trust him. And that mistrust was fanning out to touch those who trusted his word above the King's: his guard, and that precocious slave who'd nearly caught Gavannon framing the Queen for Jamyson's brush with death. And now the royal siblings were joining his resistance.

    Abigale's arms slid around Gavannon's waist from behind as he fell back onto the bed's edge with a groan. "What's the matter, my love?" He moaned again into his hands, and she poked his ribs. "Gav, I thought things were progressing well at the kaer! Why are you moping?"

"It's the royal siblings," he grumbled. "The King and Queen might be a fractured front, but Jamyson and his brothers and sisters hold fast. The King delights in them. He's *proud* of them."

He could not keep the tinge of scorn from his voice. How many years had he hoped his own father would see his accomplishments, would be proud of *him*? And he had been a child built of steel and bloody fists who'd brought home bread and ale for his drunkard father, who'd earned them a few *duais* here and there in hopes they'd add up to a fortune and a future.

He'd done everything for the man, and then his father had gambled off those *duais* and belted Gavannon afterward like the loss was his fault. Yet these pampered royal siblings did nothing but knock wooden swords together and chase each other through the halls, and their father already thought they were brilliant.

"Well, aren't you fortunate," Abigale said slyly, "that the royal siblings are the next piece of my plan?"

Gavannon straightened. "Are they?"

Abigale slid from the bed and pulled her thin chemise over her head, then retrieved her journal from the small writing desk at the corner of the room. She sat beside Gavannon, hip-to-hip, and laid open her notes. "I've given an awful lot of thought to the younger princes and princesses. Now that their mother is dealt with, they're vulnerable, tended by an elderly governess and an Incandaeic slave girl."

That slave was a thorn in Gavannon's side. He did not like how keenly she watched him or how she was frequently wherever the Crown Prince went. He wondered if Jamyson held something over her—if he had made her his spy somehow.

But a slave could not implicate him. Abigale was right that it was the royal siblings he must be concerned with.

"What are you plotting?" He tucked a strand of her hair behind her ear, the better to see her face when she turned that fierce smile to him.

"You have the King's ear, my love. You must convince Him to send the children into exile. It will cut down the support around Jamyson and shrink the number of successors between you and the Holy Throne. And then, once the Crown Prince is dealt with, only the King Himself will stand between you and that power."

The appetite for security and position dampened Gavannon's mouth. "And how do you suggest I do that?"

Abigale sat back, her mouth puckered in thought. "We will need at least a shred of real evidence against them to make the King doubt their loyalty. Rumors alone won't do."

"I ought to be able to churn something up regarding Prince Elliott. The nobles whisper about him frequently. Shouldn't be too difficult to turn the King against him."

"Suggest to Him a school in Bast—Mahony's School for the Nobility will be fine, I should think," Abigale said. "It's where Elynor's father and mine sent us for a few years. Tell the King you can send for a teacher from there. I'll pose as a tutor of the fine arts and ramble on about the quality of an education at Mahony's and so forth. You'll have all the leverage you need to convince Him it's a good place to send his children."

Gavannon took her chin and pressed his mouth to hers. "Have I mentioned of late how I cannot wait to marry you?"

"Soon, Gav." Abigale's laughter against his lips sent tines of heat dancing along his nerves. "I'm not certain the King will believe I'm a simple tutor if the magistrate of Dorwenon weds us here."

"There's nothing simple about you at all, Abigale Cainwell. And nothing in the kingdom can conceal that."

But as much as he meant the words, he still trusted her plan to work, just as it had with the Queen. Abigale's schemes rarely failed.

Chapter Eighteen

Women of War

The night she learned she was Blessed was among the worst of Elynor's life. And the days after it were little better.

She did not return to the *ger* for some time. She sheltered in a lee of rock Sharek found near Tariaga Falls where she could curl up in her cloak and be alone with her thoughts. And then he left her, at her own request, while every memory of every sailing expedition she'd ever taken with her father and with the Fleet spiraled through her mind.

She had never looked closely at these memories, never taken hold of them and dusted them off to notice how clear they were. The most vivid she had. But of course they were; every recollection of the water was. Because she was Blessed with sailing, one of the variegated talents that blooded these people. *Her* people.

She was Blessed. And Sharek was not.

Every day when he returned with rations Elynor could barely stand to eat, his tension was visible as he grappled with the dangerous truth that he was a Hunter, hated in their home. Like hers, his life had been a lie.

She felt closer to him than she had to anyone since her father's death. And it was for his sake that she finally picked her way down from the mountain and returned to the *ger*. She felt oddly calm when she arrived, as numb as that first night after her father had died.

She found the *ger* lighter by one body. Sam was gone; he hadn't even left her a note of farewell.

Her heart panged with the now-familiar throb of abandonment even from a man who'd been a reluctant ally in perilous circumstance and little more...though Elynor could hardly blame him. The tension in the *ger* was almost unbearable from the moment she returned, laid eyes on her mother, and then promptly ignored her in favor of lying down next to the fire and thawing out her frozen limbs.

Elynor did not know who to be furious with at any moment: her mother, Rue, or even Sylvester, who never stopped plucking his newest instrument—a *shudraga*, Iracabeth called it. Sharek, wisely, kept out of her way, except to offer more food or ask her how her wounded leg was faring.

He was eager to travel to Danje—eager to be finished with Rowan Varodan. And perhaps to be finished with her, and this complicated thing they'd become: a Blessed in secret, hiring another Blessed, who was truly a Hunter.

Sylvester was likely writing a song about it in his mind.

Finally, huddled around the fire one night while Iracabeth and Rue slept, Sharek, Elynor, and Sylvester made their plan to escape.

"We must travel on foot, and that will take time, with Elynor's leg and my lungs being as they are," Sharek said. "But it's better than no progress at all."

"I'll miss this place," Sylvester sighed. "Rue cooks an excellent fish."

Elynor rolled her eyes. "Erala's fate hangs in the balance, but certainly, let's stay behind for well-made trout."

"It's salmon, actually, and you know, you might be less cranky if you ate more than three mouthfuls at every meal."

"I don't recall hiring you as my personal cook, so I'll thank you not to tell my eating habits to me, Sly."

"Habits? What *habits*? You *don't eat*!"

"Enough," Sharek interrupted. "The days are growing colder. We may see snow by week's end. Best if we leave tomorrow."

Elynor silenced a shiver. "Tomorrow, then." And she snuffed the flames.

There was a kings-damned conspiracy afoot, and Elynor knew it for certain the next day, when Sharek and Sylvester offered to empty the fish traps while Rue was out gathering herbs, leaving Elynor alone with her mother.

"It's good Rowan's poison didn't kill you, because I'm going to murder you myself," Elynor hissed as Sharek readied the quiver and slung it over his shoulder.

He blinked, innocent amber eyes not fooling her in the least. "You need to rest your leg as much as possible. A journey to the water's edge and back again is a waste of your strength."

"There is death in my heart this day, Sharek Ransalor, and it's all for you."

"I'm honored." He smiled crookedly and led the way out of the *ger* with Sylvester quick on his heels.

Pair of traitors.

Iracabeth sat against the wall, restringing her bow, and Elynor stubbornly ignored her as she gathered her things. The gentle whisper of her father's voice reminded her that she and her mother had not seen one another in more than a decade, and after today, they might not ever be reunited again. And Elynor did not know how she felt about that, or about how the memory of her father was becoming more warped with each of these revelations. Posthumously, Alden Azorius was shaping into a man she no longer knew.

After some time, Iracabeth rose and went to the pile of furs and musty blankets near the door, where Elynor surmised she hid her medicine satchel when she pretended the *ger* was abandoned. She watched her mother from the corners of her eyes while stoking the fire, preparing for the fish they would eat tonight.

Iracabeth joined her at last, just as Elynor had feared and hoped she would. Her arms were laden down with a small wooden box.

"Take this with you." Iracabeth set the box before her. It had a strange, cloying smell of herbs, too potent, like an incense dish. "It will gain you favor with the *Khul*, enough to meet her face-to-face."

Elynor eyed the box suspiciously. "What is it?"

"Nothing you want to see now."

This offering was surely meant as a kindness. Now that they knew Sharek was not a Blessed—and because Elynor would not allow herself to be forced to live as anything other than sacrosanct, no matter what power she'd inherited from her Blessed mother—they would need another status by which to gain audience with *Khul* Ergene, the ruler of Orleth.

"Thank you," she said curtly, and slid the box together with their sparse belongings: Sylvester's medicine satchel, the weapons he and Sharek had stolen from fallen raiders, and the *shudraga* and a bag of herbs, which Rue had shyly handed off to Sylvester that morning when they'd announced their imminent departure.

Iracabeth sat across the fire, watching Elynor through the flames. "Sharek told me why you seek an audience with the *Khul*."

Elynor scowled. "To stop a war, yes."

Iracabeth was quiet for a long time, gazing at the flames. "I'm not certain it should be stopped."

Elynor froze, her eyes snapping to her mother's face.

"You are Blessed, Elynor," Iracabeth murmured. "If you return to Erala, with things as they are now, at best, you will live in hiding for the rest of your days, fearing to be found. At worst, you will be hunted relentlessly, and if captured, turned over to the Sanctum until your talents are bought by the sacrosanct. You will be enslaved on the very ships you were born to command as a Blessed sailor and as the heiress to the Azorian Fleet. You deserve better."

"And what is better?" Elynor snapped. "A Blessed on the throne who will repay years of prejudice with more in kind? Because that is what Rowan wants!"

"I didn't say that. I only wonder if it's your concern at all."

"Erala is my home! Of course it's my concern!"

"You could stay here, in Orleth. Blessed are all but worshipped in this land. You could use your craft in freedom—revered, accepted. Loved. You could learn of the Empyreans--"

Elynor cursed. "So now you're a heretic as well as a liar and a Blessed? I suppose I shouldn't be surprised. It was *you* who told me the stories of them...were you an Emperium-lover even before you left us?"

Iracabeth's gaze remained steady even at Elynor's scathing tone. "You wore a token of Sabrathan when we found you in the mines. I saw it when Sharek brought you to me, to tend your leg. What is that if not heresy?"

Elynor's cheeks heated, and she looked away. "That was Sharek's."

"I see. So you would call him a heretic as well?"

Elynor had no answer for that. It was all so tangled up within her—the King she'd been raised to worship, the Empyreans, the Blessed and the Hunters. "This is not about Sharek. It's about you and your ridiculous ideals. I can't sit in a *ger* or track Blessed in the wilds while my home is torn apart by a war waged on false pretenses!"

Iracabeth dropped her gaze back to the flames. "I'll grant that Rowan and Gavannon's methods are barbaric. But the *Khul* is reluctant to make any movements that will jeopardize trade for her people, and in instances like these, sometimes barbarism is necessary. Erala is steeped in the old ways. It will not lightly release its slaves. It's possible that only war would set our people free."

Disbelief shook Elynor's hands. Her own mother, a supporter of this war—or at least unwilling to prevent it. Allowing lies and murder to march forward for the gain of their people. "Fine. Believe in Rowan's misguided ideals if you wish. Let him start this war, and let other people fight the battle for a free Erala on your behalf. But you're forgetting that the price to start all this was Father's life. And if you consider that a worthwhile sacrifice, I have nothing more to say to you."

She snatched a cloak from the wall and stepped out, slamming the door behind her.

Elynor found Sharek and Sylvester sitting near the base of the falls; if they were fishing, it was not in any way Elynor had seen before.

A conspiracy, indeed.

The sound of the water, which had so often drawn her to places like this in Erala, was a snare to her feet now; even moreso were Sharek and Sylvester's voices, raised above the roar of the waterfall, their backs toward her. Elynor slowed beneath the weeping fronds of a willow tree, tucking herself behind its thick white body to listen.

"A Hunter, Sharek," Sylvester said, tossing up his hands.

Almost inaudible under the distant thunder of the falls, Sharek sighed. "I know."

"I mean...*rocks*. How did we never know—how did we not *realize*—?"

The same question Elynor had asked herself during those long days holed up in the mountain cleft, wondering how she could ever face the world again.

"We were trained to see a Blessed craft in the things I did," Sharek said. "Not the instincts of a Hunter."

Sylvester was quiet for a time. Then he said, "Does it frighten you, old friend?"

Sharek huffed with curt laughter. "It scares the breath out of me, and not just because of these scarred lungs. But stopping Rowan comes before this. Before everything."

A splash drew Elynor's attention around the tree just as Sharek lunged from the shore, catching a salmon in his bare hands and tossing it on the ground beside Sylvester. The bard watched it flop about, then looked at Sharek. "We've been friends since Ollanthyr—since before you went into the Sanctum. How did we *never* notice?"

Sharek waded back to shore and mussed Sylvester's hair on his way to retrieve the brace of fish from the traps. "Because you're dull as a stone, and I've killed too many people to question if it was Hunter instinct or Blessed power that made it possible."

"True." Sylvester stood and stretched. "That Rue...it's good she made her way here. Could you imagine Aeson Thalanor with his hands on her? How different our lives would be?"

Sharek held Sylvester's gaze for several long seconds. Then his eyes snapped straight to Elynor.

Embarrassment flushed her cheeks. She pushed off from the tree and limped out to join them, cleaning her palms on her pants as she went. "I decided to come anyway."

Sharek's brow climbed. "I can see that. Why are you so angry?"

How could he tell? Did he hear her heart racing? Feel the tingle of blood singing against her cheeks? Or was her expression simply that transparent? "My mother believes we should let Rowan have his war. To set the Blessed free."

Sharek swapped a glance with Sylvester. The bard nudged Elynor with his shoulder when she sat. "And what do *you* think?"

"That nothing justifies what Rowan and Al-Morral have done. And that it's our duty now more than ever to stop them."

"That much, at least, has not changed." Sharek offered her one of his rare smiles.

The undergrowth parted further down the streambed, and Rue emerged from a nettle bush, kicking free with a scowl. She hesitated as she saw them all clustered on the slope, and her eyes traced back to the *ger*. Then she slung her bag securely over her shoulder, marched up to them, and motioned in sharp, deft cuts—one of the Orlethian languages Elynor knew absolutely nothing about. But judging by how fiercely Rue's hands flew, cutting between them and the *ger*, they were being shouted at, and some of it had to do with Iracabeth and Elynor.

Sylvester sat forward, hands folded to his mouth, fascination oozing from his wide-eyed features. "May I take a guess?" When Rue's eyebrows arched, the bard grinned. "You're not too pleased with how we've made Lady Iracabeth upset since we came here. And...possibly she deserves better than us."

Rue nodded, rolling her hand to motion him on.

"And we should apologize?"

She nodded more vigorously this time.

"I'm not sorry my mother is upset," Elynor snapped. "She should be. She abandoned me, and she helped my father keep the truth of what I was hidden from me. You don't understand, Rue—she's never abandoned *you*. And pray to whatever powers you believe in that she never does. You don't want to fight with that pain."

Rue took another step forward and signed sharply in Elynor's face. Then she stabbed a finger into Elynor's breastbone so hard it hurt.

"I don't know what you want from me!" Elynor burst out, shoving her hands away.

Rue rolled her eyes, jabbed both thumbs to her temples, and wagged her fingers as she blew out her cheeks and puckered her lips.

"I think she just called us fools," Sylvester chuckled. Rue fixed him with a withering stare, then flipped him a rude gesture well-known in all the kingdoms. The bard blinked. "All right, well, I understood *that* one."

Rue stuck out her tongue, gathered up her herbs, and marched to the *ger*. Elynor dragged herself upright, more unnerved by her furious signing than she cared to say—and bitten with a kernel of regret she'd rather not feel. "We should go, we've already wasted too much time. Will you two retrieve the things from the *ger*?"

"You've already said your goodbyes?" Sharek asked.

Elynor raised her chin. "I have nothing to say."

Sylvester cleared his throat. "Elynor. She's your mother."

Elynor pinned him with a frosty look. "She might be, but you're not. Don't tell me my business again, Sly."

And that was the end of that.

Chapter Nineteen

Treaty and Testing

JAMYSON HAD TO REMIND himself that he'd chosen to relegate himself to these kitchens with the stone hearths belching heat against his back, with the kaer cooks and servants rushing around the tables. This was not a punishment, whatever his fever-hot skin might otherwise suggest.

Knives winked in the sunlight and pots blistered with steam all around him. Normally Jamyson wouldn't care to know how his meals were cooked or by whom—just that someone brought them on time. But he'd asked Sylvie if there was anything she wanted to do with him, and she'd brought him a recipe for boysenberry and *Aljalam* cake—some Orlethian recipe.

She hadn't warned him it would be so kings-damned *hot*. Now he was cooking without his shirt and enduring sidelong looks from the servants that made him fully aware how his warrior's physique protruded like a broken bone from the skin of this place.

But his sister did not. Sylvie looked and acted like she belonged here, as much as she ever did on the training pitch or in the library or at court. Arms akimbo, sugar dusting her dress and cream spotting the tip of her freckled brown nose, she watched him measure out a portion for the recipe. "I said one cup of caster sugar, Jamyson."

"Yes, and—?"

"That's salt."

He cursed, and for the first time in weeks, his sister smiled. She relieved him of the measuring utensil, checking him with her hip as she took his place at the preparation block. "You know, you didn't have to do this. I'm all right. Really, I am."

Jamyson spread his hands on the edge of the block, watching her measure out the caster sugar. "If that was true, I don't think you'd be making so many trips into Dorwenon."

Sylvie stilled, frightened face swinging toward him. "Are you going to tell Father?"

He flicked the cream from the tip of her nose. "Do you think He already knows?" It was a trick question, and he despised himself for asking it. But he had to know how much she suspected.

Sylvie shrugged. "Governess Mariana says He knows all. So He must know about my trips to Dorwenon. He's as good as sanctioned them."

Jamyson watched her add the sugar. "And what does Elliott say about all this?"

Sylvie set aside the measurer and carried the pot of sugar, butter, and zested and juiced *Aljalam* citrus to the fire, where she began to heat it. Jamyson followed her, hands in his pockets, and leaned against the thick siding of the oven as he watched his sister work. It was only when a good deal of the servants had scattered to bring the King's afternoon meal to the dining hall that she whispered, "Elliott says He isn't all-wise. And that I'll get into trouble if He finds out."

Jamyson folded his arms and dipped his body to catch her eye. "You know I would never let anything happen to you. Or to your brothers and sister."

Sylvie's smile wobbled. "I know. But Isla."

With a sigh, Jamyson lowered his head into the curve of the stone and smoothed his hand over its knobby edge. "I shouldn't have hesitated that day."

Sylvie stopped stirring long enough to squeeze his arm. "You aren't King yet, Jamyson. There's only so much a prince can do—even the Crown Prince. And your title doesn't protect you from our laws any more than a common man when it comes to defying the King."

Jamyson raised a brow. "Your books told you that?"

"They tell me plenty. Like that a woman can never rule."

"And that's a pity, because I can think of a princess who would make an excellent ruler. Probably a better one than her reckless older brother. She's wise and kind, and clever—very clever. And not bad with a sword, either. And did I mention she has a truly frightening love of sweets?"

Sylvie flashed him a smile. "Thank you, Jamyson."

"What are you thanking me for? I was referring to Isla."

Sylvie chuffed in mock offense, slapping him with the flat of the wooden spoon. Jamyson reached past her to grab the saucepan and carry it back to the block, grinning when she shrieked that he needed to be more careful about sticking his hands into hot ovens.

They were quiet for some time, mixing and pouring batter, the Head Cook peeking over their shoulders and offering the occasional grunt of approval. Sylvie grinned at these morsels of praise, and Jamyson wondered if she'd begun to spend her time here so much because her talents were recognized regardless of her womanhood, and she saw a brighter future in the kitchens than with a throneless marriage to a lord or magistrate who craved higher standing with the King.

Heart panging, Jamyson wondered if things had always been this bad, and he'd just been too preoccupied to really notice.

"Done!" Sylvie announced as they slid the cakepan into the oven. Jamyson slapped palms with her, then wrapped his hand around her shoulder and pulled her against him. She leaned into his side, twining her arm around his waist. "We should do this more often."

"I agree." Despite how Jamyson was sweating, and how famished he was after smelling the food cooking all day, the smile on his sister's face and the ease in her tension was worth every rumble of his stomach.

Sylvie was solemn for a bit, her head tucked against his side. Then she looked up at him. "No more visits to Dorwenon."

Jamyson kissed her hair.

"Did I come at the right time, or do you two still need a moment to finish that cake?" The laughing voice rolled from the doorway, sending a new flush of heat through Jamyson's body.

Sylvie disentangled herself with a grin. "Esmae! You're going to *love* what we just made."

"Of course I will." Esmae winked as she joined them. "I just wish you'd invited me. You know how much I love baking."

"Next time," Sylvie vowed. "And after lessons, we'll each have a slice—you and me, and the boys and Isla..."

"Just as long as we can all eat with our shirts *on*."

Jamyson curled his lip and snatched his shirt off an abandoned chopping block, yanking it over his head. "Time for lessons, Sylvie."

She heaved a heavy sigh. "I feared as much." She removed her apron, then rose on her toes to kiss his cheek. "Thank you for this morning."

"My pleasure."

Sylvie scampered out, shrieking as the Head Cook swatted her on the haunch. Jamyson and Esmae laughed, and then Jamyson motioned with a tilt of his head, and they left together.

It was difficult to keep a respectable distance until they could find a secluded corner of the kaer to disappear into. Jamyson's heart thundered by the time Esmae gripped his hand and hauled him around a corner into a deserted hallway. She took his cheeks in her hands as he braced his above her head, and for a time they simply kissed.

Jamyson, reluctantly, was the first to break it. He rested his brow against hers with a sigh. "I've missed you."

"And I you." Esmae's fingers settled lightly over his hips. "Ever since I took over duties with the royal siblings, and with Al-Morral skulking about these halls..."

"Don't remind me." This clandestine romance would be the perfect gossip for that Fleetmaster to take to the King, and Jamyson didn't want to consider what would become of them if his father ever learned.

"Actually, I'm afraid we do need to discuss him." Esmae pushed Jamyson back lightly. "Al-Morral, that is."

"What's wrong?" Jamyson rested his hand on the household sword, thin and short, bound at his hip. "Did he accost you?"

"No, although I've heard him speaking with Mariana and the children occasionally while I'm cleaning their chambers." Esmae frowned at the mouth of the corridor, then pitched her voice low as she faced him again. "He's proven himself very skilled at listening in on things, Jamyson. And I think...I think that until we've found a way to oust him from the kaer, perhaps we shouldn't have any more meetings like this."

Jamyson's pulse stuttered. "You want to end things?"

"Burning sands, no! Not *end* them. But we can't afford to give Al-Morral a weapon to use against us. And I fear that's what he'll try to do if you continue to defy him. And because I saw him plant the belladonna in the Queen's chambers, I'm a threat. We invite more danger if we steal moments like this while he lives in the kaer."

Jamyson struggled against the selfish, bitter part of him that resented being held hostage by a commoner in his own kaer. He had always loved the thrill of sneaking about with Esmae, the risk and reward of moments like these in darkened corridors and narrow recesses between their duties. He didn't want to give any of it up. Did not want to give *her* up, even for a short time.

He tucked the red threads of her hair behind her ear and cradled the column of her neck. The clash of their skin was starkest there—ivory-white and rich brown. "Are you certain?"

"As certain as that I despise it with every fiber of my being. It's what we have to do, to keep ourselves and those we love safe."

Jamyson bent his head a bit, his pause a plea for permission. Esmae met it with her hands in his hair and her lips pressed to his for the last time in kings-only-knew how long. Jamyson tried to memorize the taste of her mouth, the feel of her lips, the way her tongue slid against his. It was over far too soon, a need for breath triumphing over a need for touch, and when they drew apart his desire and regret were mirrored in her eyes.

"We will stop him, Esmae," he said. "And then this will all just have been a horrible dream."

Esmae brought his hand down from her neck and kissed his knuckles. "I will count every second between now and that day."

With a last graze of her fingers to his jaw, she straightened her rumpled dress, drew her shoulders back, and slipped from the hallway, the shackles on her ankles singing a farewell dirge. Jamyson rested the bar of his forearm against the wall and bent his brow to his wrist, chafing his fingertips as he stared blankly at the wall. A thin, throbbing strand of his heart unraveled and trailed after Esmae.

The Crown Prince wasn't a murderer, but today he wouldn't mind being finished with Al-Morral for good and all.

Dismissing that violent notion, Jamyson returned to his rooms. He had patrol duties with the Kingsgard today, and he'd need to be back promptly to receive Vestan's report from a very particular mission this morning.

"Jamyson!"

The call echoed down the hallway just as he reached his chamber. Jamyson paused with his hand on the door as doubt and unease trembled through his guts. Then he plastered on a smile and turned back with a smile. "Your Eminence."

King Marcus didn't move like a confused, paranoid man, except that His flicking eyes took in every Kingsgard and servant who passed with a kind of suspicious intensity no all-wise ruler should ever foster. Jamyson wondered if anyone else noticed it...and prayed they didn't.

"I was wondering if you had my speech prepared." The King halted beside Jamyson. "The one for the Winter Solstice."

At least He wasn't asking him if he was going to write it. Again. "Just finished it this morning. I'll bring it out to You."

But the King followed him into his rooms as if Jamyson had invited Him in. He lingered at the dining table while Jamyson sorted the speech out from the stack on the desk and brought it to Him. There was a vacancy about the King's features as He stared through the painted-glass windows toward the overcast sky.

Then, abruptly, He asked, "Jamyson, have you seen Cecile this morning?"

Jamyson halted, heart thudding with dread. "What do you mean?"

"I mean that I can't find the woman anywhere. No one's seen her, apparently. Or her slave girl."

Jamyson mustered a half-smile as he surrendered the speech. "I suspect that's because none of them have visited the dungeons of late."

The King regarded Jamyson for a long moment before He took the scroll from him. "Of course that's why. And I'm glad to know you haven't gone to see her either. It's treason to consort with the Queen. And I cannot trust My nobles not to ply her for information about Me."

Jamyson was absurdly glad he'd had this conversation with Sylvie just this morning. It hadn't been named treason to visit the Queen before, not when Jamyson had gone to see her at least. But now...

Any flicker of gladness in his heart went out like a snuffed candle.

The King was feeding His paranoia to hide His forgetfulness—making the lapses in His memory the fault of everyone else. And now Cecile would rot in the dark, friendless and uncared for, because her husband would make it illegal for her to be seen. And if Jamyson didn't want to join her, he would have to play along with the King's sham.

He summoned the faces of his siblings to mind, and Vestan and Esmae, and plastered on another unconvincing smile. "My hope is that Your nobles will remember their love for You. All the good You've done for them, and for this kingdom." That, at least, was not a lie.

The King tapped the scroll in His open palm. "We'll learn the truth of that at the Solstice. I intend to have every lord and magistrate sign a scroll swearing their absolute fealty to the Holy Throne. Any man who defies Me thereafter will have his lands taken, and then his life. And anyone who declines to sign it will lose his head there and then."

Shards of ice pierced Jamyson's bones, freezing his feet to the stone as his father thanked him for the speech and strode from the room.

The lords and magistrates had already made such vows. Their fealty to the Infallible Sovereign was absolute, tracing all the way back to the Kings of Yore. But if they signed away their loyalty as being to the Holy Throne, and not to the bloodline of Venator, then anyone who took the Throne would own the lives of the people and all the lands of Erala, to do with as he wished.

Jamyson could think of only one person who would profit from such a change.

Chapter Twenty

Salt and Spitfire

It was as a solemn trio that they traveled toward Danje on the coast.

Sharek was indeed slower than before, his lungs scarred by the poisonous blow Rowan had dealt him, and Elynor still limped from the wound in her leg despite her mother's—and now Sylvester's—ministrations. Sylvester carried the Orlethian medicine satchel from Rue, and that *shudraga* strapped to his back. Elynor tried not to feel that her mother's spirit haunted them as they crossed the Amasandji *Khulig* and entered Kaishan. She tried not to regret that she'd never said goodbye.

But she could not escape other thoughts, and the knowledge of what she was. It gnawed at her like hunger pangs.

Though her heart had longed for the Caeruel's dark shores and the broad fathoms of the waves from the moment they'd moved inland, now her stomach writhed with raw nerves at the mere thought of seeing the ocean. And of *sailing* it.

She had made a vow the night she'd learned what she was: she would fight the Blessed's inherent addiction to their craft by leaving the lines to trained sailors who'd earned the right to be so called. And that meant they would have to charter safe passage home to Erala when the matter of Rowan was done with, rather than sailing themselves.

It was a problem she would solve once they reached Danje.

"Elynor."

An earthenware bowl thrust under her nose, and she looked up from her slouch at the fireside. Sylvester was tending a small cookpot, and Sharek stood before her, offering a bowl that smelled vaguely of stew.

Elynor shook her head. "I have no appetite, thank you."

Sharek's brow drew low. "Elynor. You must eat."

The look they shared—her in bitter defiance, him with steady eyes—reminded her of picnics in Bracerath's Landing and all the ways he'd looked after her when she'd been no more than his hirer.

How things had changed. In times of Yore, her people had descended from his.

Elynor took the spoon and stirred the broth listlessly while Sharek returned to his own seat, and she watched things bob in the bowl before she took her first sip.

The exquisite taste stung like salt on her tongue. She had expected a thin broth, a bit like drinking filthy bathwater. But the flavor was surprisingly robust, and the textures, while odd in combination, were not unpleasant. She shoveled in her second spoonful, then her third, realizing the pains in her stomach truly were from hunger.

"This is superb!" She hid a mouthful behind her hand. "What *is* this?"

"Old Hunterish recipe," Sylvester said. "*Multem.*"

"*Multem.* And what goes into it?"

"Whatever you can find. You see, *multem's* never made the same way twice. It's just a stew thrown together from whatever Hunters happen to have on hand at the time."

Elynor peered at their sparse rations. "And what do *we* have on hand at this time?"

The bard shrugged. "A bit of this and that. Some Orlethian herbs that taste suspiciously like rosemary and garlic, a few riverbank vegetables, rat, hare, snail—"

Elynor almost spat out her mouthful. "That's disgusting!"

"No, it isn't, and you know it isn't. I've just upset your sensitivities is all. You were singing its praises a moment ago."

Elynor swore, and Sharek smiled. "Many things sound terrible when given too much thought. But if you present them just as they are, you find the wonder in them."

Elynor shot him a waspish look, and when he met her gaze with that fearless half-grin, a strange feeling churned in Elynor's guts. She shoveled another grudging bite of multem into her mouth, but she would not let these men cheer her up. And she would not be convinced that removing the name from anything somehow made it more beautiful.

She found herself thinking of Sam that night, when she lay down and could not sleep; thinking of his gruff commendations that she would survive the dangers ahead because of her salt and spitfire. Her father had told her similar things of the stuff from which she was built.

Strong and sturdy as a ship, he'd always said. Steady as she goes.

If Elynor was a ship, she'd had a hole blown into her hull and she was taking on water swiftly. After the flooding came the sinking, and she was no longer certain she had enough salt or spitfire to pull herself out of the depths.

What was she, after all? A ship or a seabird? An heiress or a Blessed? What was she when everything she'd ever known about life was the stuff of secrets hidden beneath treacherous waves?

What *was* she?

She feared she might never know.

Chapter Twenty-One

Doubts and Dissenters

It had taken weeks of preparation and careful strategy, listening in at the proper doors, impressing himself gently but firmly on the right nobles, and gathering information while artfully dodging the harried governess and the Queen's clever slave; but it was finally time to remove another hinderance on his path to a secure future and a war that would outfit him and Abigale with everything they needed to prosper.

The King was in His private solar when Gavannon found Him, where He took His meals in privacy and the Kingsgard had orders to allow no one entrance but the Crown Prince and the Friend of the King. That privilege alone was enough to puff out Gavannon's chest as he strolled into the ornate stone chamber, tipping his head to the guards. They nodded back stiffly; it was clear they didn't like him—or perhaps didn't like how swiftly he'd insinuated himself into their King's graces—but they would learn to love him when *he* sat on the Holy Throne.

Gavannon halted with a flourish and a bow. "Your Eminence!"

"Gavannon." The King's tone was always the same when Gavannon arrived: striving to be boisterous but underswept with a current of relief.

That kind of current could skate the belly of a ship and turn it on its axis. Today, he intended to make it do just that.

"I hope all is well, Majesty." Gavannon joined the King at the circular table where He pored over a pile of lists and books, quill in hand.

"Yes, all is well," King Marcus said. "I've just been reviewing the speech for the Solstice. It...it seems..." He trailed off, a worried crease between His thick brows. "Why don't you have a look?"

Gavannon happily obliged, searching over the artfully inked words for a hint of untested mettle he could use to introduce doubt about the Crown Prince's schemes and intentions. But it was quite good, Gavannon had to admit. The Prince had clearly written speeches of this caliber before. Perhaps the King had noticed His own wit failing some time ago and delegated such important orations to deter suspicion.

"I find no fault in it, Your Eminence." Gavannon lowered the scroll, saw the King brushing at another paper, and frowned. "May I ask what it is you're doing now?"

"Preparing the treaty the lords and magistrates will sign at the Solstice," the King said absently.

Gavannon gently took hold of the quill, slid it from the King's hand, and flipped it over so the nib, rather than the feathered shaft, touched the paper.

The King looked up at him, eyes flashing with some guarded emotion at which Gavannon's guts clenched. He hadn't forgotten Old Anna, the court physician who'd hung for what she knew. If the King suspected *he* knew...

"Perhaps you could write this treaty," King Marcus murmured. "It is delicate in nature, and I have many tasks to complete before the Solstice."

"It would be my honor, Your Holiness." Gavannon bowed low to hide the glee streaking his lips.

This was an unexpected boon. He had convinced the King days ago to craft the treaty; being bidden to choose the words of it himself would ensure their success.

After all, the wording would have to be precise if he was to have control of Erala when he took the Throne. Otherwise, they would pass to Jamyson and his siblings by the Blood of Yore, which would provoke a coup. Another delicate detail Abigale had spotted and sorted out, like she'd sorted out dozens of swindlers in the Guild's bookkeeping over the years.

The musty air, frosted in stone dust and the autumn chill seeping through the open shutters, filled with the sound of scratching nibs for a time. Gavannon wrote the treaty to his liking, and the King referred to guest lists in silence. Then, all at once, the King said, "I am considering pardoning Queen Cecile at the Solstice."

THIS VIOLENT RECKONING

Gavannon's hand froze. He bit back the kind of scathing retort that would have sent even the most seasoned sailors scampering belowdecks during his captaincy, and kept his gaze fixed on the parchment as he said, "To what does the kingdom owe its infallible King's benevolence?"

The King's hands rasped over His face. He wasn't shaving anymore; perhaps His hands were no longer steady enough to hold the razor. "I've considered that Jamyson's poisoning and what you saw of her purchasing herbs in the market...the two might not be related. Cecile has been a good and loyal wife, and while she and Jamyson have had their differences over the years, it was always to be expected. But *murder*...I have never seen that in her."

Gavannon recognized the snag and uncertainty in His tone, for it caught against his own; the long weeks he and Abigale had been apart after he'd departed his home in Rimbourg had shorn his strength to thin fibers. But his future depended on an isolated King.

He cleared his throat. "Whatever Your Majesty deems best. I am certain nothing has been kept from You in deciding this matter. Not even the rumors."

There was a tense pause. "Rumors?"

Gavannon did not think he imagined the shard of fear piercing the King's tone.

He nodded. "I hear them among the nobles. They wonder if perhaps the infallible wisdom You possess is from the Throne itself, not from the Blood of Yore. They seek to place puppets in Your stead...young puppets, easily groomed." He raised his eyes to the King. "The royal siblings are quite shaken by their mother's imprisonment. Talk about the kaer is that they've become rebellious—particularly young Elliott. He's grown to question Your word and wisdom. And Princess Sylvie has been about the market in Dorwenon, trying to creep into the guardhouse above the dungeons."

The King's hand settled over His stubbled mouth. "This cannot be."

"They are young and full of difficult feelings. I understand that. When my own mother was taken from me..."

He did not have to lie his way through the quaver in his voice at the horrific memory: his father's drunken fists around his mother's throat, squeezing until she went limp, and how the bastard had ordered Gavannon to bury her in the yard and never speak of her again.

Gavannon shrugged off the spirits of that night like a damp coat. "The nobles may use so much grief to their advantage in time, Your Eminence. They may turn the children against You."

The King's eyes were clearer, sharper than they had been in some time. "And what do you suggest we do about this, Gavannon?"

We. The word solidified his resolve like new steel. "I suggest sending the children to Mahony's School for the Nobility in Bast. A few years away ought to sever their ties to their mother and teach them the value of Your wisdom."

King Marcus was strangely quiet, His gaze fixed on the solar window. Gavannon's scalp bristled with a sudden chill.

"You know I've made my home there for some time, Your Eminence. It is a good city," he added. "I know a tutor at the school who could meet with You personally, to assuage any concerns—"

"No."

Gavannon grimaced. "My Lord..."

"No, exile is not enough for them."

He stared at the King, thin blades of dread pricking his chest, telling his heart to beat faster. "Your Eminence, I am not certain I understand."

"Send them away to a school where they can gather other children of the aristocracy to their despicable cause, and return to steal My Holy Throne?" King Marcus all but spat the words. "*No!* They've taken after their mother with this defiance, trying to twist the noble lines to their own ends. I will not have it. Not in My lifetime."

"Your Majesty, surely it isn't like that. Children are young, they can be—"

"*Silence!*" The King roared, and Gavannon's traitorous pulse stumbled like he was facing his father in a darkened room again, the powerful fists of drunkenness raised above his body, ready to pummel him. "I will not stand for this treason. I showed mercy to Cecile, and she repays Me by turning My own children against Me? No, there is no place in Kaer Dorwenon for doubters and dissenters."

Gavannon shoved back from the table, his pulse thundering in his ears. "Your Eminence, I beg You to consider carefully what You're saying."

"The King does not need to consider! The King's word is infallible law!" King Marcus heaved brutally through flared nostrils. "This is My law, and you will take it to the Kingsgard yourself: I want those treacherous whoresons and daughters taken to the dungeon. In the morning, they will be made example of, so that anyone who thinks to use My own blood and body against Me will rue the very day they first held those schemes!"

Those blades of shock and horror pierced into Gavannon's heart so swiftly and sharply, he felt it stop. Then he felt nothing at all, staring at the raging King.

At last he jumped to his feet, swept out a shaky arm in a low bow, and hurried from the chamber. The moment he left sight of the wide-eyed Kingsgard, Gavannon started to run.

Sense returned to him when he all but fell through the door of Abigale's room at the Inn of Tryst, startling her so badly she jumped up from her writing desk with a yelp, going for the knife in the drawer. She froze when their gazes locked, and Gavannon fell back against the door, still struggling to breathe. The whole run from the kaer, he'd felt the spirits of soon-to-be-hung children lunging at his heels, the sunset bleeding like death along his face.

Horror sprinted down the paths of his body. Gavannon started to shake, yanking his hands back through his hair.

"Gav, what's wrong, you're pale as a corpse—look at me!" Abigale stepped into his path and gripped his wrists. "What's the matter?"

"I've done something," he rasped, "I did not mean—I did not *think*—"

Abigale's eyes sharpened. "Is it the King? Has He found you out?"

"Worse." Gavannon shook her off. "It's worse, Abigale!"

"I don't understand—"

"He's going to execute the children."

Abigale froze, her hand clapping other mouth. "He—He wouldn't *dare*. Would He? Because of what you said?"

Gavannon jerked his chin and started to pace again, raking his fingers down the sides of his neck. "He believes they've betrayed Him, that they're plotting to kill Him and take the Holy Throne. I tried to convince Him it was all conjecture, speculation, but He'd hear none of it."

Abigale's breath strangled. "By the Throne. He's truly gone *mad*."

Gavannon halted, a terrible weight crashing over his head like the most suffocating wave. "What do we do, Abi? We cannot let Him murder children, but I can't intercede if we're to keep this strategy afoot."

Abigale crossed the room and took his hood, drawing it up over his disheveled hair. "You must go to Prince Jamyson. Tell him you overheard the nobles plotting, and that they convinced the King to remove the contention for the Throne. Keep your hand out of this, Gavannon. Let him make the risk and take the consequences of saving them."

As usual, her solution cleared his mind. Gavannon took her cheeks in his trembling hands and kissed her; then he tore back out of the Inn.

Chapter Twenty-Two

A Game of Exile

Now that the speech was done and the nights grading steeply colder, Jamyson filled up the late hours training with Vestan in his own chambers. With the dining table shoved off to the side and the hearths roaring, it was wide enough and warm enough to practice their footwork in close quarters. Jamyson relished the release of tension—something besides worrying about his father and thinking about Esme, and counting how many days had passed since he'd been able to do much more than catch her eye as he turned his siblings over for their morning lessons.

The knock of steel to steel cracked through the room, shocking him back to focus as Vestan parried his downward thrust. They pivoted in lockstep and whipped around one another, each aiming for the other's exposed back. Their swords snagged in an overhand cross, guard to guard, back-to-back, and Jamyson smirked over his shoulder. "Finally learned how to block that one, did you?"

"I believe that's *my* line, Sire."

They pushed free and spun back, drilling through a flurry of blows, and Jamyson's concerns peeled away. He loved this kind of training—unarmored, in close quarters, with Vestan's Blessed strength guiding the other sword. It walked the perilous line between powerful lessons and complete insanity. If Vestan didn't control himself, or if one of them lost their footing, or if the King caught His son training without armor and with real swords, it would be disastrous; which was why Jamyson so enjoyed it. He couldn't afford to lose control, and that sharpened his senses and aligned his focus like a sighted arrow in a bowstring.

He and Vestan clashed, chest-to-chest this time, planting their boots and bracing against each other's guards.

"Ready to give up, Vez?" Jamyson taunted. "You're looking a bit sweaty. Smelling it, too."

Vestan grinned. "All I smell from *you* is fear, Jamyson."

Laughing, Jamyson kicked his guard in the stomach, shoved backward, and raised his blade high.

The door burst open. Cursing, Jamyson yanked the sword behind his back. Vestan froze with his still in hand, eyes fixed wildly on Jamyson.

But it wasn't the King who came crashing inside. It was Gavannon Al-Morral, unkempt and panic-stricken.

It was *glorious*.

Jamyson balanced his sword point in the mortar of the stone floor. "You know, it's considered polite to knock before entering the Crown Prince's chambers."

"There's not time for formalities," Al-Morral said. "Your Highness, I come bearing troubling news."

Jamyson heaved a sigh and rolled his eyes. "Your *presence* is troubling news to me, Al-Morral."

"It's about your brothers and sisters."

A chill danced over Jamyson's sweat-soaked skin, commanding his absolute attention. "What about them?"

Al-Morral struggled through a few more gulps of air, shaking his head. "The King has entrusted me with a secret. He believes the nobility are priming to turn the royal siblings against Him."

"I wonder where he might have gotten *that* notion," Vestan growled.

"I intend to seek the truth of that in the coming days. But the threat is more imminent."

Jamyson grimaced. "The dungeons."

"Worse. He intends to have them hung at sunrise."

Jamyson stared at Al-Morral as time turned sluggish, his thoughts bubbling slow and dark, congealing thickly like one of Sylvie's caramels. Then a low *bang* erupted through the room, so loudly all three men flinched, and Jamyson realized his sword had fallen from his fingers. As it jumped and clattered on the floor, he whirled. "Vestan."

The guard sheathed his blade with a swift nod and retrieved their cloaks from the coat tree in the corner.

"You must get them out of the kaer," Al-Morral urged. "The King expects me to deliver orders for their arrest. I'll have the Kingsgard called to the opposite end of the kaer. That should buy you some time."

Jamyson nodded, his mind already racing through possible places his siblings could hide. But he still struggled to grasp that this was happening—that his father could've become deranged with paranoia so quickly.

"Wherever you're taking them, do not tell me," Al-Morral said as Jamyson and Vestan joined him at the door. "Best if the King can't find out the truth from more than a few of us."

Jamyson fixed the Fleetmaster with a glare. Though the panic in Al-Morral's face seemed sincere enough, this could always be a trap.

But even if it was, Jamyson had to go. He couldn't gamble with his brothers' and sisters' lives that way. "If I ever learn you had any hand in this..."

"I would never willfully bring harm to a child."

Jamyson couldn't say if he believed him, but that didn't matter right now.

He and Vestan darted out into the corridor and sprinted away.

Darkness spidered its cruel fingers across the thin neck of dying daylight seeping into the kaer as Jamyson and Vestan reached the deserted corridor outside the royal siblings' chamber. Though Isaac and Isla would be asleep already, Jamyson pounded on the door. Esmae answered swiftly, wide-eyed, her braid partially undone. "Jamyson?" Behind her, Elliott and Sylvie perked up at the table where books lay open around them.

The sight of their faces spurred his resolve, and he took Esmae's shoulders and walked her swiftly into the room while Vestan shut the door behind them. "We need to get them out of the kaer. Elliott, Sylvie, get into your riding clothes."

They leaped to obey, but Esmae snatched Jamyson's arm as he went to the beds where Isaac and Isla were stirring and grumbling at the commotion. "Jamyson, what is it? What's happened?"

"My father is going to have them put to death at dawn."

Esmae ripped her hand back. "Burning *sands*..."

"Vez and I will get them out tonight." Jamyson sat on the edge of the bed and brushed the hair from Isla's eyes as she glared up at him. "I know you've just gotten comfortable, but we're going on an adventure."

"What kind of adventure?" Isaac mumbled as Esmae took him under the arms and sat him up on the edge of his bed.

Jamyson met Vestan's eyes as the guard helped Sylvie into her warmest cloak. "A game of exile."

Sylvie's eyes widened. Elliott scowled as he strapped his small dagger around his waist. "Is this about Father?"

Jamyson plucked a kicking, moaning Isla from the warm covers and set her next to Isaac so Esmae could stuff her feet into her boots. Then he went to Elliot, pulling him behind the changing screen and squeezing his shoulders. "Father is ill, Elliott," he kept his tone to a hushed whisper. "His illness makes Him think He can trust no one. That includes all of us. The best we can do is move you and your sisters and brother out of the kaer until He recovers. You understand?"

Elliot swiped his sleeve against his nose. "He's never going to recover. Is He?"

Jamyson gripped the back of his brother's neck, pressed a kiss to his furrowed brow, and marched him back out into the room. Esmae had buttoned Isaac and Isla into their coats and silenced their whining with a piece of Sylvie's boysenberry and *Aljalam* bread shoved into their mouths.

"Take the servants' stairwell behind the statue of King Yorick on the second level," she said. "It leads straight to the laundering balconies, and those have steps to the side of the bridge."

"But what then?" Sylvie demanded.

Esmae flashed her a smile. "I'll meet you there with bags of food. Jamyson and Vestan will tell you what to do next."

Jamyson flashed her a quick, grateful glance. Then he passed Isaac to Vestan, picked up Isla, and herded the older two from the room.

Al-Morral had made good on his word so far; no Kingsgard spotted the corridors along the way. The siblings and Vestan thundered down two flights of stairs at the opposite ends of corridors, reached the statue of King Yorick, and slipped behind it. The way beyond was dark, but Jamyson knew it well. He and Elynor had crept down it on several occasions when they were hardly order than Isaac and Isla, dodging their mothers' exasperated shouts after another bout of mischief making.

Life had felt so full then, nothing but summer days and swords and song; but this night was dark enough to eclipse everything, fashioning Kaer Dorwenon into a foreign prison or a glittering stone tomb. And the King was its undertaker.

When they emerged onto the laundering balconies, Isla moaned at the frigid bite of the wind. Jamyson ripped off his cloak and draped it over her, and to his surprise he didn't feel the cold at all. His skin was flushed with a balmy warmth as he led the others down a series of steep stairwells along the flank of the kaer, then up its sheer side to the barbican. A strange smell wafted on the air as they approached, and Jamyson motioned his siblings and Vestan to a halt, set Isla down, and crept up onto level ground alone.

The smell came from a brazier. The guards around it were slumped unconscious, and Esmae stood beside them, a scarf wrapped around her nose and mouth, a satchel of food slung over her back.

Jamyson pulled his shirt over his nose as well. "Sleeping powder?"

Esmae shrugged. "You know how enamored Incandaeics are with the arts of subtlety."

"I love you," Jamyson said.

Esmae handed him the satchel, her cheeks rounding above the scarf in a smile. "How could you not?"

Vestan, seeming to sense no danger, led the children up the steps. Jamyson steered them away from the brazier and deeper into the shadow of the barbican. "You'll go down into the valley and out to Ventia. You can catch a barge from there to Bast and then make your way south, to a village called Lleywel. Its kaer belongs to a friend, and I trust her people to look after you. Few know of it, and those who do won't think to search for you there."

Sylvie frowned. "But what about you?"

Jamyson met Vestan's eyes over their heads. "Vestan is going to take you. Esmae and I will stay behind and free your horses. Yes, even your new pony, Isla. We'll make the Kingsgard think you've fled by horseback."

Quietly, Isaac started to cry.

"Come with us, Jamy," Sylvie begged, gripping his hand. "It's not safe in the kaer anymore."

Jamyson shook his head. "I wish I could. But don't worry, Vez will look after you until you're somewhere safe."

"It's not about us, idiot!" Elliott snarled. "You said Father doesn't trust any of us! That includes you!"

That was true. After tonight, Kaer Dorwenon would become a more lethal place than ever, especially for those close to the King. But Jamyson couldn't leave; not when the people stood beneath the unseen guillotine of the King's mind sickness, helpless to defend themselves. And not when Al-Morral was burrowing deeper and deeper into the kingdom's affairs. "This is what being Crown Prince means. Someday you'll learn that for yourself."

"I won't have the chance if Father hangs you instead of us!" Elliott hit him hard on the chest. "I want to stay with you, help keep you safe!"

"I'll be all right. Listen to me, Elliott! There's no more time to argue." Jamyson caught his brother's fist as Elliott swung at him again. "You can help me by keeping your brother and sisters safe. Do you understand me? You lead now."

Elliott jerked back, tears shining in his eyes. "I hate you. I'll never stop hating you for sending us away."

"Good. Let that hatred keep you warm until I see you again."

With a half-sobbed curse, Elliott plowed into him, flinging his arms around Jamyson's waist, and Jamyson clutched his tangled, thick curls and kissed the top of his head. Then he shoved his brother toward Vestan, threw the food into his arms, and nodded to the guard. "Take them and *go*."

Vestan scooped up both Isla and Isaac and took off at a run down the bridge. Sylvie sprinted after him, and Elliott lingered a moment, gazing at Jamyson with teary eyes. Then he slung the sack over his shoulder and darted after Vestan.

"Do you think they'll be all right?" Esmae whispered.

"I hope so." Jamyson glanced down at her, the chain winking between her ankles, and a wild notion possessed him. "Now is your chance, too. While the Kingsgard is distracted. No one would notice if you went with them."

"And leave you to face the King alone?" Briefly, she cradled his jaw. "I fear that more than I hate these chains. Now let's loose those horses."

The stables were located off to the side of the kaer's first courtyard, and Jamyson and Esmae sprinted toward them through a silence hanging heavy with dread. Jamyson's heart was in his throat, his hands shaking so badly it seemed to take an eternity to saddle and loose Isaac's horse. By the time he'd done it, Esmae had already sent off Sylvie and Elliott's. Her poise was remarkable, her calm like a balm.

"You've done this before, I take it," Jamyson tried to joke as they tacked up Isla's new pony together.

Esmae's nod was grim. "When the Kingsgard came to Oss Belliard, I was in the stables, helping the Hunters escape. That was the only reason the guards believed I wasn't privy to my father's crimes...I claimed I was at market." She slapped the pony's haunch, chasing it from the stable.

Before it took a dozen strides, the warning bell began to toll.

Jamyson swore, jerking his gaze up to the inner balconies. They were swarming with archers.

Jamyson lunged toward the kaer door, but Esmae seized his arm. "No, Jamyson! The Kingsgard will follow you straight to them. Come with me!"

They bolted through the dappled shadows as quickly as Esmae's shackles would allow, the moon peeking and hiding its face behind thick clouds. Jamyson still didn't feel the cold breeze, but the chill was inside him, a thick, icy chain coiled in his chest. He could barely breathe as he and Esmae skidded out onto the north-facing belvedere and caught themselves on the railing, looking toward the mountainside that homed Dorwenon.

Those bright flashes of moonlight between the cloudbank showed the dim tracing of Vestan's body against the sheer rock face. He climbed with all four children strung across his body like pieces of armor—front, back, and sides—his Blessed strength equipping him for the desperate climb. But Jamyson could hardly fathom the strain on Vestan's body. He felt every strand of his own will reaching out, trying to bolster and support the guard as he made the perilous trek across the mountainside.

Esmae's fingers covered his on the railing. "They'll make it, Jamyson."

And then, as if the will of the world itself was destined to prove her wrong, the first arrows unleashed.

They hurtled through the dark like tines of lightning, smashing into the rock all around Vestan. Isla's thin, high scream carried through the valley, and Jamyson wrenched forward against the railing, straining to see every detail.

Vestan hurled himself faster, scraping for handholds in the rock. The archers lined the bridge now, firing wildly as if they didn't dare take true aim. As if their very fingers at the bowstrings questioned the wisdom of this. The sanity of it.

But they believed in the King's sovereign will too much to defy His orders, and these orders *had* come from Him. Al-Morral could have said nothing and let the siblings be butchered in their beds; if this was his doing, they would already be dead. But this had the reek of a queen at the gallows or in the dungeons; of a physician falsely accused, sent to her death to hide the secret that could bring Erala to its knees.

This was the King's hand on every bow, loosing every arrow.

Esmae's fingers gripped Jamyson's so tightly he lost all feeling in them. "He's going to make it. He *must*."

"Climb, Vez, climb," Jamyson chanted under his breath.

They were nearly out of range. Nearly to safety along the rock wall.

And then one lonely archer chose to trust the King's word over his own sense. One archer planted himself at the end of the bridge, drew slowly, and aimed true. Jamyson watched him fire, the long thread of the arrow's passage dragging the breath out of him as it whistled into the night.

It slammed into Vestan's side, between Isaac's legs, and his cry rang through the world like a death knell.

Esmae's fingers separated from Jamyson's. Her breath caught.

And then Vestan let go.

He toppled from the rock wall, the screams of the royal siblings whipping the air, and then they struck the treetops growing up along the foothills, and there was only silence.

Silence.

And then bellowing rent the night, grief-stricken roars of agony, and Jamyson realized it was him, that he was clawing at the railing, trying to climb over it, and Esmae was holding onto his arm to keep him from leaping. She put her shoulder into his chest and hurled him against the side of the kaer, pressing her hands into his shoulders as he twisted and fought, his gaze fixed on the place where his siblings and his friend had fallen, where the trees had engulfed them and taken them to the depths.

He could not reach them.

He could not save them.

Jamyson broke down to his knees, and Esmae fell with him, pulling him against her. He clung to her arm as sobs hacked from his throat, as he felt his heart crack in pieces, five fragments of his very essence winking out like snuffed candles.

The King had done this.

The King had sent His own children to their deaths.

Chapter Twenty-Three

The Price of the Throne

Gavannon hovered at the window of Abigale's room, watching torches bob down the bridge at the kaer, moving toward the sharp grade from Dorwenon to the valley below. The Kingsgard moved in rotation at the King's command, searching for the bodies of the children and the man who'd taken them—the Prince's bodyguard, or so the rumors flew. No one but a Blessed would dare defy the King and help the traitorous siblings out of the kaer.

They had been at this for two days, two sleepless days, and Gavannon had forced himself to watch, to face what his actions had wrought. He'd tried to hold the Kingsgard at bay as long as possible, but someone had noticed the children creeping down a corridor and reported to the King. He'd ordered that they be shot on sight.

It had been out of Gavannon's hands. It all felt out of his hands now.

"Gav, come to bed." Abigale sat up among the sheets. "Staring won't bring them back."

"But we did this, Abigale. *We* did this." He slid his hand from the windowframe as he glanced back at her. "Maybe we should put an end to this now, before worse things happen."

Abigale pushed her hair from her eyes. "The King is an absolute madman, Gavannon. This only proves it. If He's left on the Throne, don't you think *that* will be worse? We need to depose Him as soon as possible. It's the only way to keep this kind of thing from happening again."

"It wouldn't have happened *now* if not for us! Perhaps we should've been content with the Guild and the Fleet, and left it at that."

"And do you think the King's mind sickness wouldn't have reached us there, in time? We underestimated His cruelty, yes, and His depths of paranoia. But now we know. And because we know, it's *our* responsibility to stop Him."

Gavannon rubbed a hand down his face. "I just don't know anymore. Four children are dead because of us."

"No. They're dead because of *Him*." Indignation laced Abigale's words. "The plan was perfect, Gavannon, they would've been safe and looked after in Bast. But what sort of man would rather murder His young children than send them into exile?"

There was wisdom in those words, and his fear was not only for more innocent people to be harmed; it was fear of what the King would do to *him*, and to Abigale, if He learned what they plotted against Him.

If a man could be so cruel to His own children, what would He do to his tenuous friends?

But Abigale was right. If there was no King, there was no concern. Gavannon had known this would be a messy ordeal, and that the road to the Throne would be paved with blood. He did not condone it to be the blood of children, but what was done was done. They could either be cowed, as if by the wild blows of a drunken man…or they could stand up to Him and take vengeance for those children.

Gavannon's hands formed slow, determined fists at his sides. "After the Solstice, we move against Jamyson. The Prince already suspects I had something to do with the King's verdict. We'll deal with him soon." And carefully, so that no more blood was shed unjustly.

Abigale joined him, wrapped in the sheet, and slid her arm around his waist. With her chin on his shoulder, she too stared through the window. "Those poor things," she murmured as the Kingsgard marched down the slope. "I hope it was quick."

Gavannon hoped for that, too.

They lingered at the window well into the night, watching the procession descend into the valley to search, letting the sight of the torches sear into their minds so that they would never forget the cost of this path to the Throne.

Part Two

The Cursed and The Blessed

Chapter Twenty-Four

City of Jade and Gold

Danje was set inside a great wall that ran its roots deep and far, out into the Caeruel itself; its uppermost edge huddled in the low clouds that eddied in from the Caeruel. They came upon it after weeks of trudging, where the jungle abruptly ended at the westernmost face of the jade wall. Elynor struggled not to feel the tug of briny winds and ocean currents against her very spirit as she stood with Sharek and Sylvester, waiting for the guards to draw open the opulent doors.

They risked much coming here after jaunting about on Orlethian soil undocumented. They would have to lie about why they'd foregone formalities when they'd shipwrecked so close to the city. But Elynor did not regret that choice. Not when Sharek stood beside her, carrying Iracabeth's box, eyes fixed steadily ahead.

No. She did not regret it for even an instant.

The doors finally broke apart with a groan, and they entered.

The first stretch of Danje's limits was exactly like the jungle they'd just left behind, except that pale *gers* dotted the underbrush and torches were staked along the path, winding through another few miles of jungle. Children skipped and laughed, warming their blood beneath the chilly midday sun, and their mothers chatted in gatherings along the trail. A few curious eyes wandered toward the trio, but it was clear they were not unused to travelers.

Their quiet, safe lives made Elynor's heart ache. Not so long ago, she'd been like one of those children. And now she could not bear to think of all the ways she was different.

They traveled under mottled shadows as the dense foliage gave way to rusty inclines, and then they crested a small knoll and looked down at the heart of Danje. It was breathtakingly large, budding like a flower in every direction, distinct avenues and clusters of homes and shops flourishing away from the *Khul's* palace at the center. The rooftops were paved with stones and clustered into uniform knots, each district its own color. The distant harborside sported seafoam and blue tiles that married with the vivid reflection of the cloudless sky on the water's face. The great gates of the wall hung open, allowing ships to enter through the Orlethian Channel.

Elynor's heart throbbed worse than her leg. She longed for the water—*ached* for it. And she hated that desire, despised the way her gaze sought out all the ships at port, their sails trimmed, their magnificent bodies at rest.

She wondered how many were Eralanite vessels. How many were her father's design—how many ought to be hers.

She sucked in a harsh breath and shook her head. This was not the time to think of the Azorian Fleet. It was the time for action; so she set the pace down the embankment toward a district capped in yellow domes and the palace beyond.

Danje was as bright with activity as with color. There did not seem to be an untended shop or a street corner empty of hawkers, and the constant echo of sound reminded her of Bast, sleepless and drunk on produce. Everyone in the yellow-roofed district sold housewares, from handcrafted furniture to expensive silk drapes to mattresses stuffed with every material imaginable, straw and water and downy feathers.

As they went, Elynor recalled things the captains had told her around bowls of soup at the harbor house when she and her father often entertained them after long voyages.

"Each district has its own specialty," she said as they left the buttery stone buildings behind and stepped under a canopy of rich currant tones. An exotic smell of sizzling meat and curry rubbed her nose. "This is the spice district, I think. And we just left the commodity district. Next will be the weapon district. And then the palace."

"I wonder if they have a music district?" Sylvester mused.

Sharek didn't speak. A familiar tension set the lines of his body and his eyes swept the markets with cagey refrain. Elynor wondered if he expected Rowan to leap out from some shadow and finish what he'd begun with Sharek in Rimbourg.

But they passed unaccosted through the spice district, then through the weapon district—though Sharek slowed, wide-eyed, taking in the booths full of blades and flails and tools of disembowelment with which Elynor was mercifully unfamiliar. Sylvester had to grip his arm and steer him through.

At last, they left the districts behind and faced a broad pavilion that ended at the moat encircling the *Khul's* palace. Gilded and jaded, it gleamed like a jewel in the late-afternoon sun. The water in the moat winked the same shade of green that veined the palace's outer wall and capped its tiered domes, casting sickly ripples on their skin as Elynor, Sharek, and Sylvester walked along its edge.

There was only one entrance to the palace itself—a narrow bridge joining a great outer plaza to the palace's gate—and between them and the *Khul's* home stood a contingent of guards, helmed and armored, watching over the doors at the bridge on the plaza's side.

Elynor's scalp prickled. Though she had committed no offense warranting imprisonment or death, suddenly she feared for her neck.

Sharek bowed to the guards and spoke in the trade language toward their feet: "We seek an audience with the *Khul*."

"On what grounds?" The man who answered in the same tongue spoke it without inflection, but his eyes glittered.

"We have a gift," Elynor said, and prayed it was true. Her mother had never told her what was in the box, and out of sheer spite, she'd avoided looking.

The guards leveled their spears, but they nodded Sharek to set down the box. He obeyed slowly, a practiced effort; she knew by now that he spent much of his life learning how to seem disarming to everyone he was not hired to kill. Then he opened the box, and the guards swore at the stench previously masked by salt, herbs, and leather.

Elynor covered her nose and mouth. Sylvester recoiled, sleeve to his face, coughing in disgust. Sharek, at least, kept his calm visage as he reached casually into the box and withdrew the head of Kirsagan al Bayar, blood crusted on his severed neck. "Is this tribute enough?"

Wide-eyed, the guards stepped aside.

Sharek boxed the head again, swung the parcel into his arms, and strolled over the bridge. Elynor and Sylvester swapped disbelieving glances, then hurried after him.

"Did you know that was in there?" Sylvester hissed.

"I suspected. I could smell it. Clearly, Kirsagan was not a man beloved by this land. I believe we did the *Khul* a great service in dispatching him."

Elynor was inclined to agree; for the very doors to the palace opened before them now, and though the guards flanked them in wary watch, they entered the *Khul's* home unhindered.

The world within the golden walls was oddly peaceful. Hardly even a sound from the bustling districts made it through to the quiet outer courtyard, a long stretch of tiles paved with gemstones and lined with baths. There were doors set into the walls, perhaps for rooms to house the esteemed guests who milled about the courtyard, wrapped in the *dahl* cloaks that sold so well in Bast—their furred cuffs and brass clasps whispering of wealth and station. A collection of imported trees grew in stone soil beds dotting the courtyard, and at the very center was a fountain in the shape of a tree. Six figures knelt among its roots, pouring out cisterns that filled the basin below. Whatever it was, it didn't smell like water.

The guards led them across the outer courtyard to a broad turret that bisected the palace. Its staggered cap flashed almost blindingly bright as their escort of two guards conferred with two more at the doors, and then those opened up to them as well.

Elynor, Sharek, and Sylvester stepped as one into the audience chamber of *Khul* Ergene.

It was surprisingly well-lit for having no windows, only a broad circular skylight in the tiered cap, which was indented higher than the rest of the roof. By that light, Elynor spotted an ensemble of attendants and guards flocking the walls, ready with food and weapons should a need of any sort arise. A fire burned in a stone-lined pit sunk into the middle of the chamber, surrounded by four golden pillars, and beyond that were the steps up to the royal seating.

Khul Ergene was a tall woman even when she knelt on her broad, thick cushion, her angles soft but her upswept eyes sharp as daggers. They glinted the same jade green as her palace accents and the long, lacquered nails of her hands, folded on the lap of her artful, gold-accented ebony *dhal*.

On the cushion to her right was the *Khuless*, her heir—the fiercest-looking woman Elynor had ever seen, and one she knew of only from stories told by sailors whose knees still knocked at the mention of her.

A woman near Elynor's age, the *Khuless* had forsaken the *dhal* for black trappings instead, a fitted breastplate of armor and long sleeves that linked over the middle fingers on each hand and a pair of swords strapped to her back in a cross. Though she perched on her knees like her mother, in her the posture was reminiscent of a panther braced to leap.

And to the *Khul's* left, kneeling with his arms akimbo and hands braced on his thighs, was a man Elynor had never seen except in her nightmares.

But she knew him by Sharek's descriptions of the woad and iron markings that tangled down from his stubbled hair.

Perched in a place of power at the left hand of *Khul* Ergene—the seat usually reserved for her warlord—was Rowan Varodan.

Chapter Twenty-Five

Reconciliation

With a soft, humming whine, Sharek's ears began to ring.

Across the rotund *ger*, he and Rowan stared at one another, while *Khul* Ergene's guards approached her dais and one bent to whisper in her ear. Shock broke across his old friend's face—his would-be murderer, the man who had poisoned him and left him to die or drown and then crossed an ocean to start a war—as Rowan bent forward on his knees, halfway to rising.

Sharek's whole body snapped tight for battle, and his side panged—not with the usual latent ache in the new scar there, but with the memory of Rowan's blade going into him. It was a recollection so sharp and true he sucked in a hard breath.

To his left, Elynor shifted, and her eyes shot to him, glittering with vengeance on his behalf. On his right, Sylvester visibly stiffened, and Sharek smelled sweat gathering in the bard's pits.

These were the only things that seemed real in a world of fractured madness. For here was Rowan, the man they'd come for, the one they'd crossed an ocean of their own and battled death and despair and vicious raiders to kill; and he was sitting in a place of authority beside the most powerful woman in the land of Orleth, which they must stop from going to war with their own kingdom, Erala.

A war Rowan was very much in favor of.

Sharek had expected things to be complicated, but *this*...

Khul Ergene's gaze was as cool as steel, edging on boredom. "I understand you come bearing a gift."

No one moved. Or spoke. Sharek had assumed Elynor would handle this encounter; the heiress of the Azorian Fleet had interacted with the people of Orleth on behalf of her father for many years. She knew their customs and cultures more keenly than Sharek or Sylvester could ever hope to. But instead she held still, quivering as she stared up at the dais. She seemed entranced by the sight of Rowan.

Her father's murderer.

All at once, Sharek's purpose returned to focus. His plans. The things he could and could not do.

He stepped in front of Elynor and Sylvester, shielding them from Rowan's gaze as he approached the steps of the *Khul's* dais—letting himself be exposed and leaving off any glimmer of self-preservation.

If he and Rowan were to brawl, let it be here, now. And let Rowan debase himself before this woman who clearly thought well of him. Sharek was one of the last sons of Ollanthyr, and he would conduct himself with honor because of that. He would make his parents and the Empyreans proud.

Though it betrayed his sensibilities when Rowan was within range of a killing stroke, Sharek went to one knee and set the box he carried at the base of the steps. "We have this prize for you, *Kuhl*."

"And what is it?" The *Khul's* flippant tone suggested she was used to receiving gifts.

Sharek opened the box, and every weapon in the room primed toward him, leveled to strike at the ill twitch of a finger. He refused to let their hostility unbalance him as he drew out the head of Kirsagan al Bayar. The *Khuless* sat up taller at her mother's side, sharp as a knife; Rowan's eyes fell to half-mast. But it was the *Khul* who Sharek cared for now, her gaze narrowed on him.

"I am a killing Blessed." The lie he'd lived for most of his life felt smooth and sensible as it skimmed from his tongue, particularly in Rowan's presence. "And I've come with proof and tribute of my talents. I seek sanctuary in your city."

He prayed to the Empyreans she did not have a dragnet who could ferret out his lie. He did not know how the Orlethian people beheld the Hunters, and he wasn't eager to learn if they shared Erala's hatred of Sharek's true kind.

If so, he was about to lose his head.

And then Rowan said, "He speaks the truth."

Elynor's breath caught—in rage, or in shock to match Sharek's, a swell of disbelief that strangled his breath. The *Khul* turned her glittering gaze on Rowan. "You know this man?"

"I do." Rowan's eyes had not left Sharek's face. "We were like brothers. He is the only one left like me—a killing Blessed. If he says he needs sanctuary, then it's true."

"And his companions?"

"They are not Blessed," Sharek lied quickly. "But they sailed the Caeruel at my side and for my sake. I was dying, and they gave all they had to see me cured."

Rowan's eyes flickered. The *Khul's* did not. Her daughter said, "We received no vessels carrying three Eralanite travelers into the harbor."

Sharek bowed his head. "We were shipwrecked along the coast, too far south to make the journey until now. I had to recover first."

Rowan's gaze was searing, but he did not address the poison that had nearly been the death of Sharek; too frightened to implicate himself of attacking a fellow Blessed and thus destroy whatever ruse he'd concocted with the Orlethian royalty.

"Then you are welcomed here, Blessed." The *Khul's* voice warmed like sunlight spreading across stone. "The troubles you faced in Erala are at an end. Rise. Your people bow to no one here." The absurdity snagged in Sharek's throat, but he straightened, dropping Kirsagan's head back into the box. The *Khul* watched it go, her high-boned features tightening into a frown. "We have hunted that raider for many, many seasons. You will tell us the tale of how you ended him at a banquet we will hold in your honor."

A *banquet*. In his honor? Sharek had been fortunate to have a mocking toast made in his name once or twice, but banquets were hosted for royals who knew what to do with thirteen different forks and six courses. He'd killed more people at banquets than he'd actually sat at them.

Empyreans help him.

But he could not afford to protest. Not with Rowan bunched at the *Khul's* side, prepared to leap on his first show of weakness.

The *Khul* gestured to her guards. "We have been troubled by lapses in our security of late. You will be escorted to a chamber where you may take board until you find accommodations to your liking in the districts."

Sharek dipped his head. "You are most kind, *Khul* Ergene."

A door opened off to the side behind the dais, tucked into the *ger's* rounded edge where Sharek had not noticed it before. Too much of his attention was on Rowan, waiting for the moment he would attempt to finish what he'd begun with

Sharek's side in the small port town of Rimbourg. But Rowan remained poised on that dais, sitting like a prince, until the door shut behind Sharek, Elynor, and Sylvester and they found themselves in the palace's inner courtyard.

It was much more expansive than the outer yard, diamond-tiled and framed in columns and colonnades, with swaths of grass and low hedges trimmed around pools and circular fountains. A towering citrus tree hung its branches over the heart of the courtyard, ripe with a glossy sunset-colored fruit Sharek had never seen before. Its fragrance fletched the air with notes of pure water and honey.

"*Aljalam*," Elynor murmured. "It's their kingdom's symbol, the Tree of Life. It blooms all year...the crop is unique to Orleth. They sell for twenty-five *duais* apiece in the Port of Bast."

Sylvester whistled lowly. "And you can just walk up and pluck one here? I think I'm going to enjoy myself."

Elynor's jaw hardened. "I won't."

Sharek suspected that was very true.

The guards led them along the courtyard's tiled edge to a walled walkway that divided the open-aired plaza in half. They entered a stairwell and walked the interior mezzanines to one of the curved doors, seemingly at random, hewn with an image of the *Aljalam* tree. The quarters within were spacious; no beds, but a respectable number of cushions that could be assembled into sleeping spaces. Sharek had certainly slept on worse. There was a small privy screen in one corner, a washbasin beside a modest armoire, and the back wall was taken up by windows that looked down over Danje's multifarious rooftops.

Those windows were troubling. Rowan could break inside with ease.

Sharek fought to keep his countenance blank as he nodded to their escort. "Please express our gratitude once again to the *Khul* for her hospitality. And tell her I will...dine with her whenever it pleases her."

The guards nodded, bade them ask any attendant in the palace to meet their needs, and then they were gone, shutting the door softly behind them.

"This is a trap," Elynor said at once.

"I don't think that it is." Sylvester cocked his head, his sandy forelock swinging across his brow, genuine puzzlement alight in his eyes. "Rowan could have let the *Khul*'s suspicions arouse, let her deal with us herself...but he vouched for Sharek instead."

"That's why I'm certain it's a trap." Elynor hurled her small satchel onto the nearest cushion and sat, raking her fingernails along her scalp from temples to nape, over and over. "And what was he doing at *Khul* Ergene's left hand? That position would normally be taken by her *Daishi*, her warlord. Or by the *Khulen*, her son."

"I saw no sign of either." Sharek placed his back to the door and folded his arms, training his gaze on the windows. He could almost feel the glass bowing under his weight, buckling, the air whistling past him as he fell—

"Rowan killed them." There was no uncertainty in Elynor's voice.

Sylvester grimaced. "We don't know that."

She tossed her fingers through her hair more quickly, deft with agitation. "*Why* in the King's name do you keep *defending* him?"

"Because we can't strut around this palace accusing him outright! You saw him just now. While we were shambling about in the woods, getting kidnapped by raiders and bleeding to death and whatnot, Rowan's established himself here. At the *Khul's* left hand, no less!"

"Whatever his plan to incite war, it's already advanced." Sharek skimmed his thumb along his lower lip. "Far advanced."

Guilt found a perch on his heart and sank its talons deep. If he had only healed sooner...if he had not sent Elynor and Sylvester away to be captured by Kirsagan...if they had not stayed so many days with Elynor's mother while he and Elynor fought to understand the new truths about themselves....

But here they were.

"We can't stay here." Elynor's voice was brittle. "He will kill us."

"I have no doubt of that." Sharek thumped his head back against the door. "We'll take measures to protect ourselves."

Her hands fell into her lap. She stared at him, lips parting in shallow breaths. "You want to stay anyway. Close to the man who poisoned you? Who killed my father?"

"It's a different dance now, Elynor. Different from what it would have been if we'd come to Danje sooner. We can't warn the *Khul* of his intentions when he's insinuated himself into her graces. For whatever reason, she has cause to trust him. And not us."

Elynor's gaze tracked slowly around the room. Sylvester pulled the *shudraga* from his back and plucked its neck—something to calm himself when his hands were already shaking. Their unease bore down against Sharek, dark as the sunset dragging the veil of night across the windows.

When Elynor's stomach grumbled loudly, Sharek sprang at the opportunity. "I'll find us something to eat."

Sylvester glanced up hopefully. "The fruit from the *Aljalam* tree, perhaps?"

Sharek snorted. "I'm not convinced a bard's tongue is sophisticated enough for such delicacies."

"More sophisticated than yours, you—"

Sharek shut the door on what promised to be a clever and wholly-deserved epitaph, and turned back the way the guards had led them.

He'd made it only a few steps when an arm latched around his throat from behind and a leg swept both of his, throwing him off-balance. Before he could recover his wits, he was dragged backward into a deserted room, the door kicked shut before his face.

"Sharek, listen to me—"

That familiar voice, that breath close to his ear, a spirit of countless training sessions in the undercroft pitches of the Sanctum, unleashed him.

Sharek speared an elbow backward, and Rowan curved to the side, dodging effortlessly. His sturdy fingers whipped Sharek around, and Sharek's eyes searched wildly for a knife.

There was none. Rowan's empty hands took his shoulders and drew him in, and then he was hugging him like a brother.

Sharek froze, from thought to nerve and muscle. He hung limp in Rowan's embrace, uncertain of what to do.

"Thank the Empyreans you're alive," Rowan rasped. "You don't know how glad I am to see you."

The words pierced the fog of Sharek's disbelief. He swept up his elbows, broke Rowan's hold, and shoved back from his reach. "Glad to see me? You broke off a knife in my side and threw me out a window!"

Rowan arched a brow. "We are killing Blessed, Sharek. If I had wanted you dead, your body would've been discovered in Rimbourg at dawn."

Sharek's breath caught against the backs of his teeth. That was truer of Rowan than of him, but Rowan could not know that. "What game is this you're playing?"

"It isn't a game." Rowan streaked a hand back along the stubbled hair that furred his scalp. "The moment I did it...in Rimbourg, when I attacked you, I knew it was a mistake. No killing has ever felt wrong to me before, but this...*you*. I couldn't stop *thinking* about the entire kings-damned thing. Gavannon told me to pull my head out of my arse, but I couldn't. It's all I thought about on the crossing here. I'm not used to regretting a task, but I regretted what I did to you from the moment I put that knife in your side. I thought, with the window...with you out of my reach, whether you lived or died was your own choice. I wouldn't have to feel guilty about what came next." His shoulder fell against the wall, his smile sharp and deprecating. "It didn't help. I felt guilty anyway."

Sharek kept his body rigid, hands in fists, while he searched Rowan's posture for the imminence of attack. "You forget that I know how skilled you are at deception. You wield lies as easily as blades."

"But tonight, I'm unarmed."

It was true that Sharek did not see a knife in his hand. But that did not make him harmless, and Sharek would prove it. He had no time for these lies.

He lunged, and Rowan did not resist. He barely even coughed as Sharek hurled him up against the wall, and with a small trill of panic, Sharek realized it was because *he* was not as strong as he had once been. The poison—Rowan's poison—had left him weakened.

Hatred and rage brought his hands around Rowan's throat. Still, Rowan did not fight. Not even when his chest began to heave for breath.

"If you can do it, you're a stronger man than me," he choked, "but I beg you, Sharek...remember me. Remember the plight of our people. Set them free."

Freedom.

Sharek had tasted freedom these past weeks—with Elynor, with Sylvester. Even dying of poison in his blood, he'd been free. But there was still the Sanctum, and in the Sanctum, countless Blessed. They were not his people, but he'd lived among them as if they were. He'd shared in their suffering, and never felt free. Except when Rowan was there with him.

And what was he *doing*? If he killed the *Khul's* left hand, he would bring death upon himself, and on Elynor and Sylvester. They still had no means of escape back to Erala.

Sharek wrenched backward, throwing up his hands in surrender. Rowan shrugged up from the wall, gasping for breath and rubbing his throat, a twitch of a smile on his face. "Ironic, isn't it? The last two killing Blessed can't seem kill each other. We're two halves of one coin, Sharek."

"I am nothing like you." There was a private triumph in knowing it was absolutely true, and he was not destined to become like the man before him—insatiable for murder.

Rowan straightened his *dhal*, flicking a glance toward the door. "I'm expected with the *Khul* soon, but before I go, I wanted to ask you how you did it. How you survived."

Unease sizzled in Sharek's nerves. He had no reason to believe Rowan had truly taken sympathy on him, that he was even capable of feeling remorse. Except that Sharek was standing here, alive, still drawing breath, when Rowan could've jabbed a knife into his kidneys and left him to bleed out on the mezzanine rather than dragging him into this room for a clandestine conversation.

Perhaps he was afraid to break the *Khul's* good will, too. But, that being so, he could have sat back and done nothing, and let the woman's suspicions lead to imprisonment or death for Sharek and his friends.

"It was with the aid of an Orlethian healer," he said at last.

Rowan nodded slowly. "I hear tales of one. She travels between the *Khuligs* of Amasandji, Jungsai, and Dabantai, they say. A woman who is healing Blessed."

Rage tightened Sharek's jaw. "If you lay a hand on her—"

Rowan was in his face in an instant, close enough for Sharek to smell fermentation on his breath. "I will *not* kill my own kind."

They gazed into one another's eyes, the heat of anger boiling the air between them. Then Rowan stepped back, shaking his head.

"I know you have a low opinion of me," he said. "Of everything I've done, and what I still must do. But someday, I hope you find it in yourself to believe my word as you once did: I'm sorry for what I did in Rimbourg, Sharek. And if this venture in Orleth profits me nothing else, I'm glad it showed me I won't pay the cost of your blood on my hands with all the rest when I face death."

He brushed past Sharek and went to the door. Bristling at the notion of his back exposed to Rowan, Sharek snapped around to watch him go. "When a man breaks a poisoned blade in your side, you can never trust him again."

Rowan paused, his scarred fingers clenched the doorframe. "Perhaps not. But when he could have put one there again, and didn't...I hope that counts for something."

And like a spirit, he was gone.

Chapter Twenty-Six

Dangerous Games

When Sharek returned to their room, empty-handed and grim, Elynor and Sylvester both shot to their feet.

"What happened?" Sylvester demanded.

"Rowan."

Elynor was at his side quicker than he had ever seen. Her fingers hovered just over his scarred ribs, shy to touch him, but her eyes pierced like daggers. "*Did he attack you?*"

Sharek rubbed his throat. "No."

Elynor let out a heavy breath that cut short as her eyes narrowed. "Then what did he want?"

"To...apologize."

She barked with harsh laughter. "*Really?*"

Sharek held Sylvester's gaze, and the bard said slowly, "I can't say that surprises me."

Elynor rounded on him. "Have you both become jesters now?"

Sylvester flashed his palms. "Rowan and Sharek have a unique history from the Sanctum. Those thorny bonds are difficult to untwine. Though I confess I'd love to know the details myself, old friend."

Sharek went to the window, peering out over the multicolored tiles on the rooftops beyond the moat. Some of the districts had fallen to slumber as night washed over the city. Others were just beginning to truly awaken. The music district throbbed with light and color. "He says he regrets what happened in Rimbourg. That he seeks reconciliation, and...that if he wanted me dead, I would be dead."

"You nearly were," Elynor hissed.

"But by the poison. Not with his knife in my neck. I know that counts for little to those who are not killing Blessed...death is all the same to you. But when you know how they are, how they behave..."

The silence was prolonged, and Sharek could hear by the struggle in their breathing that Sylvester and Elynor were fighting to still consider him as killing Blessed because that was the role he was forced to play here in the palace.

"You really believe he feels remorse?" Sylvester asked.

"I can't be certain what measure of remorse a man like Rowan is *capable* of feeling. But I do know this: he could have killed me tonight, and he didn't. And that may be to our advantage."

"How do you mean?" Elynor asked.

Sharek smoothed his hand over the windowframe and imagined what it would be like not to spend every moment looking over his shoulder, bracing himself for Rowan to aim a blade for his back. It did not matter so much whether Rowan truly felt guilty. It mattered if Sharek made him think he believed it was true.

He turned to them. "I'm going to accept his reconciliation."

Elynor's burning slap turned his head before he'd even registered that she was before him, or that she was going to hit him at all. Sylvester bit his knuckles, but still a quite "*ooh*" of sympathy escaped him.

It hurt surprisingly more than Sharek had expected. The sting in his chest was worse than in his cheek.

That was twice tonight his Hunterish senses had failed to alert him of an imminent attack. Somehow, Elynor's set his hands rattling worse than Rowan's.

"That is my father's *murderer* you're thinking of forgiving," she seethed. "How could you do this? How could you *forgive* him?"

"I didn't say I would. But I am going to do whatever I must to ensure Alden's daughter does not share that fate." Sharek met her eyes, his own watering from the bark of her hand on his face. "And if that means making peace with Rowan so that I can get close enough to expose his lies, then so be it."

Elynor's lips parted. Her eyes widened slightly, and she took a step back with such sharp haste, Sharek tensed. Most people who moved so quickly around him were feinting before a strike. "I'm so sorry. I shouldn't have hit you."

Sharek ached to tell her it was all right, but it wasn't. As conflicted and furious as she was, as much pain as she was struggling through, he did not deserve to be hit. She had no right to hit him like an overseer in the Sanctum.

"It's forgiven," he said instead. "I'll give this until the banquet the *Khul* intends to throw in our honor. That will be long enough to seem as if I've truly considered Rowan's remorse."

Sylvester joined him at the window, clapping a hand over his shoulder. "I hope you know what you're doing, Sharek. Rowan's a dangerous man to play these kinds of games with."

Sharek knew it. But he had also learned the danger of being the one at the end of Rowan's knife. Between the two games, he'd rather play this one.

Chapter Twenty-Seven

Rumors of Royalty

"Thisis barbaric."

Gavannon heard the cut in his own words, how vicious they sounded as they bounced off the walls in the small room at the Inn of Tryst. He stood at the window, buttoning his fine shirt—hand-crafted by the Blessed haberdasher who served the men of the royal family—and he tried not to see the face of his own leering, feckless, drunkard father glaring back at him in that sleek, mustached countenance.

"I agree." Floating from the bed behind him, Abigaile's voice was full of false cheer. "Speeches. Utterly vicious. How dare we attend?"

"It's not the speech itself that disturbs me," Gavannon grunted. "It's that all of us are going to stand in that courtyard and lie and smile and act as if it's somehow conscionable that the supposedly-infallible King of Erala had His own children shot off a stone wall to their deaths. We'll all have to make believe, somehow, that we *support* that." He fumbled the fine teak buttons and slammed his palms into the windowsill instead. "And I'll have to stand at His left hand and smile and make them all think the royal siblings were little traitors, when He's the one who's dangerous to the kingdom. When He reminds me of my own father."

"I know. And you're right, I shouldn't joke." Abigale rose to join him, her reflection annealing into focus on the glass: honeyed hair braided back, kohl lining her gleaming eyes.

She wasn't dressed in court finest; in fact, her muslin dress was fairly plain. She wouldn't be attending the King's speech within Kaer Dorwenon today; her presence in the mountain city of Dorwenon itself was Gavannon's uttermost-kept secret...though he ached to have her at his side for this despicable thing today.

He slid his hands from the windowframe and turned. "We must take the Holy Throne swiftly, Abigale. Before any more lives are lost."

She nodded, fastening the last three buttons of his shirt. Then she raised her eyes to his, full of steady determination. "We won't let those children's deaths be in vain, Gav. I'm laying out the strategy for how we unseat the Crown Prince." She planted a kiss on Gavannon's tense, flickering jawline. "Soon the King will either die of this ravaging mind sickness or He'll cede the Throne to someone more capable than Him. And we'll ensure you're regent when that time comes."

Hope was a small, fragile thing fluttering in Gavannon's chest. "No hint of rumors against Jamyson so far?"

"None. He's a busy but fair man, they say. He doesn't often have time to be with the people, but when he does, he's always making them laugh with his antics. He's chased off countless rogue Blessed who tried to sack Kaer Dorwenon, and wearing nothing but his nightclothes if you believe the tales. He's proper and charming and he loved his siblings—everything the heir to the Throne should be."

"Of course he is," Gavannon muttered, shrugging into his coat. "Well, keep digging. No one descended from the Kings of Yore is without his secrets. We already know the King's infallibility is a lie. There must be secrets Prince Jamyson is keeping in his royal armoire, too."

"Whatever it is, we'll find it. It's like my father used to say: the best business deal you can make is to hold another man's secrets against him."

Gavannon chuckled and kissed her hair. "Let's hope our enemies don't turn that tactic against us, hm?"

"What secrets do we have?" Abigale laughed, pushing him gently away. "The daughter of Guild Cainwell's leader and the Fleetmaster of the Azorian charter...we only do what's best for the Kingdom of Erala. Which happens to also be what's best for both of us."

That was true. For too long, the balance of trade had tipped in favor of Orleth across the Ocean Caeruel. It was time for Erala to stop bending the knee for precious imports, and show the *Khul* and her people that this kingdom was not to be taken lightly.

And if the war that was coming lined Gavannon and Abigale's pockets with more *duais* and *tolvors* than they knew what to do with—well. Very soon, they'd have royal coffers to pour their earnings into.

Chapter Twenty-Eight

The Tightening Noose

The day after King Marcus gave a formal speech to the people of Dorwenon—to be carried out to the four provinces of the kingdom of Erala by messengers—about His children's betrayal and the desperate flight that had tragically ended in their untimely deaths, everything went quiet within Jamyson. Dull and dark.

He'd been forced to stand on one side of the King, with Al-Morral on the other, to bear witness; to nod grimly and act as if he believed a word of it. To hear Elliott, Sylvie, Isaac, and Isla's names be smeared and decried by the King, and to watch the people reluctantly accept it as truth.

After that torturous session, Jamyson fell into his bed and did not get up for three days.

He might've thought he was ill, except the court physician declared him fit as anything. There was no treatable cause for his aching bones or throbbing chest or for the headaches that came and went. Or for the terrible nightmares, the screams and the moonlight, that woke him most nights in a frigid sweat; or from the way he found himself looking at the door every day, waiting for Vestan to come strolling inside, eager to get to training.

Jamyson diagnosed himself with a broken heart.

A Crown Prince still had duties, and him more than most. But he could hardly bear to walk through a kaer robbed of his siblings' laughter, or to train with the Kingsgard—some of whom had been on that bridge, firing the arrows that fateful night, and none of whom understood his patterns and his mind or worked through drills with him as well as Vestan had. And he couldn't bring himself to hold Al-Morral's gaze for more than an instant whenever their paths crossed in the halls.

The Fleetmaster had left off antagonizing him for now, and that was good. For his sake. Jamyson was still convinced his father hadn't reached the conclusion of His children's betrayal on His own. Someone had goaded Him, intentionally or not. And that someone, Jamyson suspected, was Al-Morral.

Jamyson wanted nothing to do with either of them, or with his princely duties while he mourned. But he had to do them anyway.

And when that thought finally settled, clarity returned to him. The pall of desperate grief peeled back, and he saw the sunlight again. His appetite returned and his sleep eased. The crooked edges of his heart crawled back together and stitched themselves into the semblance of something that could beat again, forging a new man who could carry on despite everything.

He went back to overseeing the preparations throughout the kaer for the Winter Solstice. He trained harder and better with the Kingsgard, half the time drilling them as much as they drilled him. And when he passed Esmae in the corridors, her radiant red hair and mudspatter freckles the brightest color that lingered in his word, he flashed her quick smiles and ran his fingers over her arm so that she would always know how grateful he was for everything she'd done for him. For his siblings. For a family that didn't deserve her goodness.

Despite everything he'd done to carry on, it was still with a heaviness in the pit of his stomach that he answered summons from his father one day to the solar where the King spent the majority of His time these days...preparing for the Solstice, or so was the muttering among all the servants according to Esmae's reports.

Jamyson knew better.

"You asked to see me, Father?" he said the moment he slipped inside. His voice managed to remain steady and sincere despite the disgust churning in his gut.

"Ah." The King looked up from the stack of parchments before Him. "Jamyson?"

With a pang of new and unwelcomed grief, Jamyson wondered if His father didn't remember summoning him—or if He wasn't certain He'd guessed Jamyson's name right. Nonetheless, he forced a smile and bowed his head. "At your service, Your Eminence." He outright ignored Al-Morral, hovering at his usual position at the King's side. The kings-damned bastard wasn't worth his attention.

"Yes, I would like you to deliver a message to the people," the King said. "Inform them that Queen Cecile was executed last night."

Shock rooted Jamyson to the flagstones and wrapped his tongue in knots. His eyes flicked to Al-Morral, and there was no hint of emotion in his face. If he cared that an innocent woman, the King's own wife and mother to His murdered children, had been put to death, he made no show of it.

Jamyson sucked in a deep, steadying breath. "Your Majesty. With all due respect...*why*?"

"Because she stirred up insurrection in her own children," Al-Morral said. "What more would she do with the people, if given the chance?"

"Unless your title is *Your Majesty*, I wasn't speaking to you."

"Enough," King Marcus said. "I will not have the only two men I trust at one another's throats. But Gavannon is right. The Queen was dangerous, even locked in her cell. She did not have the people's best interest at heart. It was the only right course of action."

Heat blistered the back of Jamyson's throat and stung his nose. He'd promised safety for his siblings and for Cecile...and he'd failed them all.

"The people won't like it," he croaked. "First the royal siblings, and now this...and an execution done in secret, in the dead of night? They'll question all of it."

"The people should be grateful the Throne is rooting out such weakness and deception at the kingdom's very heart," Al-Morral said.

"And they must trust the infallible word of their Sovereign, as is proper," the King growled. "I want you to make it clear to them, Jamyson: anyone who stirs up doubt about the Queen and her children will share their fate. Gavannon, you will instruct the Kingsgard to keep an ear to the nobles for such murmurings. Their status will not protect them from the noose."

He was speaking of executing His people at the first sign of dissent.

That growing fear scrabbled across the floor to Jamyson, clawing his boots, stabbing into his chest. Would there even be a kingdom left for him to piece back together at the end of this? "Father..."

"Need I remind you, Jamyson," the King said, "that when I say noble status will not protect them, that includes you."

The words struck him like a blow to his crumbling heart, stopping the breath in his lungs.

The King had not even looked up from His parchments. His tone was matter-of-fact.

Jamyson swallowed his shock. His rage. His *hurt*. None of it would do him any good. "Understood, Majesty. I'll deliver the news to the people forthwith."

"You should know," the King added as Jamyson turned toward the door, "there will be other hangings soon."

Jamyson's heels snagged on the flagstones.

"Gavannon has sought out the nobles who worked to turn your siblings against Me. They will be hanged publicly at the Solstice as a warning to the lords and magistrates of what is to come if they defy the Holy Throne and the Infallible Sovereign." When Jamyson mustered no retort that superseded the shocked tangle of his tongue, the quill began to scratch parchment again. "You may go."

Feeling as if a noose had been loosed from around his own throat, Jamyson all but jogged from the room. He descended from his father's turret on shaking legs and staggered at once into the nearest alcove, where he bent against the wall and covered his mouth with his hand.

His kingdom and his father were falling apart. And all his attempts to keep it from happening seemed to be utterly in vain.

After a moment, he couldn't stand the solitude. He went to the only person who could speak sense into his own madness.

Esmae, and the siblings' governess, Mariana, had both been without real work to do ever since that horrific night. But the King hadn't seemed to notice, and Jamyson wasn't eager to draw attention to them. He'd quietly found other work for both women: the governess in Dorwenon, with a pension for her years of service, first with Jamyson and then with his half-siblings; and Esmae in the kitchens, where she'd loved to bake with Sylvie.

It seemed the least he could do for both of them. The kitchen staff also kept very much to themselves, something he knew Esmae appreciated; they would never scorn her there for her family's ill repute.

The heat of the ovens blanketed Jamyson's skin but did nothing to thaw his frozen center as he scanned the flocks of servants. Esmae wasn't difficult to spot, red hair peeping from a handkerchief as she scrubbed inside one of the ovens. Jamyson sidled over to her, and when he was certain no one else was looking, he tapped her back. "I need to speak with you."

He caught no more than a glimpse of Esmae's surprised look from inside the dark flue before he hurried to the pantry. Five minutes later, Esmae slipped in after him and shut the door at her back. She came to him at once, peering up at his face in the gloom. "Jamyson, what's the matter?"

"Cecile is dead." Esmae caught her breath at his blunt delivery of her mistress's fate. "More are going to follow."

"Oh, Jamyson..."

"Father wants me to deliver the news to the people, to threaten them on His behalf with more of the same if they dissent at all, and I can't—Esmae, I *can't*." He wrapped his arms around her, and her fingers danced along his spine and spun into his thick, tight curls. He squeezed his eyes shut until his brow ached, and hid his face in her neck. "I can't tell the people. I can't put that burden on their shoulders."

Yet even as the words left him, a warm rush of rationality soaked through his skin. He *could* do it. With the right words, the right tone and charisma, he could spin the warning into no more than a cautioning tale. He could keep Erala from crumbling. He just had to think hard enough.

As if the thoughts came from Esmae herself, she whispered in his ear, "You'll manage, Jamyson. Somehow, you always do. No matter how awful things are, you'll protect your people. I know you will."

"Your faith gives me strength," Jamyson murmured against her freckled skin. "It makes me believe even when I have no belief in myself."

"Well, I will always believe in you, Jamyson Venator." Esmae unwound herself from his grip and framed his face with her callused hands. "Even to death, even to the Emperium and beyond. But I know that isn't enough. You *must* find a way to believe in yourself. It's how you'll hold this kingdom together."

Jamyson tilted his head into her touch. "I know."

"Then go and call the people. Tell them what your father sent you to say. But show them that you will lead them out of this darkness and back to the light. They will learn to believe in you as strongly as I do."

Jamyson shut his eyes, drinking in her words—letting them saturate every inch where his own courage failed. He kissed the palm of her hand, then brought it to rest over his heart. "You keep this beating."

Esmae's smile flashed in the dark, and she turned their hands swiftly so that his rested against the left side of her sternum, his fingers wrapping her shoulder, her heart pulsing rapidly under his palm. "It beats for you."

Jamyson swooped forward and kissed her. Then he let her go, to spare them both.

Chapter Twenty-Nine

To Death's Door

Perhaps Sharek was being dramatic, but he thought he might die tonight.

In the days preceding their honorary banquet, he had crept out of the room often to inspect the palace. It was an excuse to gently flex his senses, to introduce himself to them as he now knew they truly were: not weapons to heighten his killing prowess, but innate power to craft a stronger, better Hunter. And he did feel that, even on the nights when scaling the colonnades left him breathless and forced him to crouch on the upper mezzanines and rest, his lungs throbbing like he'd scaled a mountain in the coldest winter.

He was strong, despite his scarred lungs. He was neither Blessed nor sacrosanct. He truly was a Hunter, like his father. Like his mother, who he hadn't seen since his first killing had landed him in the Sanctum, in the hands of Aeson Thalanor.

Sharek was what Erala feared.

During those long nights inspecting the palace, he found it full of guests. He numbered them at well over a hundred, and he begged Elynor and Sylvester to make conversation with them in the courtyards.

Through those conversations, he learned that most of these guests were Blessed; far more had chartered passage to Orleth than Sharek had ever known. He wondered if Alden Azorius had been aware of them—if the Fleet had smuggled these Blessed away to freedom as it had Iracabeth, before they ever faced interment in the Sanctum; if this had been Alden's gift to the wife he might never see again, and to the daughter who hadn't known then that she was Blessed at all.

Sharek wondered how different his life might have been if he'd been raised by his mother in his later years, rather than by the brutal Sanctum guards. He wondered if killing Rowan would've come easily to him then.

It was difficult to see him tonight, the first time they'd laid eyes on one another since Rowan had apologized for Rimbourg. Now the killing Blessed sat at his place of honor on *Khul* Ergene's left, but down the length of the banquet room, his eyes met Sharek's.

Sharek's stomach cringed and his side throbbed.

They'd come late, mostly because Elynor had all but outright refused to go. Resistance still dragged in every inch of her stiff body, and she scowled at the hall while Sharek mapped its many entrances and possible escapes. He numbered three doors and five times as many windows offering a view of the inner courtyard on one side and the moat and city on the other. Ergene kept a watchful eye on her domain from both sides, at the head of the long, low rectangle of a table with its middle hollowed out. In that hollow were platters of lamb, vegetables, and potatoes, dumplings, rice, noodles, and cakes. There were no chairs; everyone perched on cushions. It was unlike anywhere or anything Sharek had eaten before, but the aroma of smoky meat and sugar told him he was going to enjoy it very much, if he could force the first bite past his clenched jaw.

He plastered on a grin and strutted toward the head of the table, where three cushions had been laid out: two to the side of *Khuless* Mide, one beside Rowan. Rowan's eyes tracked his every moment until they halted and bowed their heads to the *Khul*.

"You are welcome here tonight," Ergene said warmly. "Eat and drink your fill."

"We are *most* honored, esteemed *Khul*!" Sylvester adopted his bard's tone again, breezy and boisterous, filling the whole room. "We do not deserve such honor...but we will happily stuff ourselves with it."

He sat on the cushion closest to Mide, who cast him a look that suggested she would've preferred the company of a pig freshly returned from the sty. Elynor remained on her feet, hands in fists, trembling as she stared over Ergene's head at Rowan, who busied himself spooning onions and potatoes onto his plate from the slit-open belly of a whole roast.

Sharek rested a hand on Elynor's shoulder and spoke into her ear. "You need to sit, and eat. Keeping up appearances will keep us alive."

"I can't," she said. "My father's killer—I can't break bread with him."

"Elynor. This is about stopping him, not killing him." He squeezed her shoulder, troubled at the way the bones jutted against his hand. "Steady as she goes, Lady Azorius."

Then he took the seat beside Rowan, to spare them all.

"Welcome, brother." There wasn't a trace of animosity in Rowan's voice, and he heaped a portion of two different kinds of food on Sharek's plate. "Don't ask me to pronounce any of these things, but a man could gorge himself every day on them. Much better than the slop they fed us in the Sanctum, eh?"

Sharek watched him through hooded eyes. Then he took up his two-pronged utensil, stabbed a piece of lamb, and offered it to Rowan. "You first."

Rowan arched a brow, but he took the offering and ate. Only then did Sharek submit to his helping.

The hall hummed with conversation, and this was the portion that made Sharek want to perish. There were nine people at the nearest seats who seemed the most conversational and keen, and each one goaded him for different aspects of Kirsagan's death-story: how he died, where he died, when and by what weapon and whether he'd suffered or not.

Sharek wished the ornate rug would swallow him whole. He just wanted to eat, and the aristocracy would rather be spoon-fed tales of slaughter.

Rowan chuckled under his breath now and again, flashing smirks at his discomfort like the wink of a dagger being drawn, then sheathed again. Sharek hated those looks.

"You must forgive my ministers," Ergene said during a brief lull in the conversation. "Six of them deal directly within the *Khuligs*. They have been unsuccessful in hunting Kirsagan for some time. No doubt your straightforward success intrigues them."

Sharek shrugged and swallowed, the bite scraping down his throat. "Kirsagan captured the two people I cherish most. Failing to find him was not a possibility for me."

Sylvester grinned, but around the row of bodies between them, Elynor gazed at Sharek with peaked brows and wide eyes.

"But enough about Kirsagan," Sharek added when one of the ministers opened her mouth. "I am curious for a tale, as well. How did my *brother* gain such a position of high esteem in the palace of the *Khul*?" His question, carefully formed, held a twofold purpose: he needed to know how deep Rowan's roots were laid here, so that he could better plan how to sever them. And he needed the Empyreans-cursed attention of nine people at once to stop being on *him*.

Rowan poured himself more fermented milk and propped his elbow on Sharek's shoulder. "You always did like to use me as a shield against conversations."

Sharek forced a smile for the *Khul's* sake, but in his heart, betrayal danced with regret. It was true, after all. He'd looked to Rowan to have his back in every possible way.

Rowan swirled his cup and said, "I uncovered a plot."

Elynor snorted, then waved off the *Khul's* quick glance. "Bit too much spice in the meat."

Ergene turned back to Sharek. "The *Daishi*—what Erala would call a *warlord*—was plotting against me. His intentions were to cut down the ministers and replace them with those he trusted. The *Urvach*, they called themselves. A band of fearsome warriors."

"With a hatred for Blessed," Rowan added. "It's difficult to comprehend what they plotted to do once they ascended to power."

"But thank the Empyreans you uncovered their deception," Ergene said.

Rowan's smile was chilling. "It was my pleasure, *Khul* Ergene."

Sharek heard a whisper of chafing cloth and popping knuckles, so soft he doubted anyone else would notice. But he cast a glance down the table and saw *Khuless* Mide had fisted her hands on her thighs and was staring at her own hardly-touched portion with steady ferocity. There was a smell of dampness and salt he did not think came from the dishes.

A swift look at Elynor showed him that she was watching the *Khuless* as well. A thoughtful frown lined her brow.

"Well, thank the Empyreans indeed," Sylvester said, either oblivious or covering for their distraction. "We would have come to a hostile city if that *Daishi* had been in power. I propose a toast!" He raised his glass. "To Rowan!"

"To Rowan!" the whole table took up the call.

Khuless Mide shot to her feet, bowing at the waist. "*Madra*, I must assemble patrols. The *Urvach* could reappear at any time."

Khul Ergene nodded. "Go."

Mide strode from the chamber, tracked by her mother—and Elynor.

The meal could not pass quickly enough for Sharek's liking. The *Khul* seemed much less conversational after her daughter's abrupt departure, and that left Sharek with only the choice of speaking with Rowan or the ministers. He would have preferred holding a conversation with Kirsagan's severed head to either.

At last, Ergene rose, lifting her cup high again. The chatter among the Blessed, aristocrats, and ministers died away. "We owe this gathering tonight to the Blessed at our table. This man has freed the *Khuligs* of the threat of Kirsagan al Bayar and his raiders. Because of him, our people sleep more peacefully at night. Fewer Blessed are vanishing into the northern mines."

Sharek stiffened. He hadn't been aware that Kirsagan targeted Blessed in particular, but he supposed it made sense. The way the man had looked at him on the beach. The scathing comments he'd made. The way Rowan was gazing at him now, his eyes full of pride.

"To Sharek and his friends," Ergene toasted, "and to all the Blessed. Long may they live."

Heat seared Sharek's cheekbones and traveled into his eyes as he dipped his gaze, then his head, to the cheers around the table. He would have thanked Rowan to attack him right then, or the Empyreans themselves for bringing down the roof. He rubbed the back of his neck as the applause swelled. With the other hand, he chafed the token of Sabrathan against his neck.

And then he glanced at Elynor.

The tightness of her jaw had eased. She was smiling for the first time since they'd left Tariaga Falls.

His whole chest lit like a torch suddenly struck to life. A different sort of warmth altogether filled him. And for the sake of her smile, Sharek raised his head high.

⁓⁓

They finally escaped the hall at nearly midnight, and Sharek was glad of his warm, full stomach when the nip of the cold wind passed straight through his clothing. He would have to submit to the ceremonial *dhal* the attendants had brought to their room. Or worse, he would have to go marketing.

Best to leave such nightmares for another time.

"You've been awfully quiet." Sylvester nudged Elynor as they crossed the courtyard. "What's on your mind?"

"*Khuless* Mide," Elynor said. "Did you see how she reacted to your toast?"

Sylvester grinned. "Why do you think I made it?"

Sharek shook his head. "You two are dangerous."

Sylvester mock-bowed, but Elynor seemed too keen on her own thoughts to notice. "The *Khul* may trust Rowan, but I doubt Mide does. Perhaps she would be an ally against him if we pressed her."

"By *we*, I take it you're volunteering," Sharek said.

Elynor grimaced. "I'm afraid I don't have much interest in making friends here."

Sharek swapped a look with Sylvester, who shrugged. "I'll do it."

Elynor snorted. "You?"

Sylvester swung around to face them, walking backward with his arms folded behind his head. "I'll have you know that I can be quite charming when I—oh. *Ah*."

"Sharek!"

He froze in midstep, his muscles cording with strain as he turned to follow Sylvester's cautious gaze. Rowan jogged to a halt behind them, his gaze flicking from face to face. He dipped his head to Sylvester—and Sharek heard the graze of Sylvester's stubble on his upturned collar as he nodded back—but at Elynor, he simply stared. Their gazes could have melted the flesh from one another's bones.

Sharek sidestepped between them. "You wished to see me, Rowan?"

"To speak with you. Privately."

Sharek blew out a long breath. He'd been preparing for this moment ever since he'd decided to plunge forward full-headed into stopping Rowan the only way he knew how. And now that they were aware of how he'd become so trusted by the *Khul*, it was more imperative than ever that Sharek sidle into Rowan's graces the same way.

"Go on without me," he said to Elynor and Sylvester. "I'll be all right."

Sylvester watched him for a moment. Then he said, with uncharacteristic softness, "I'll never forget the last time you sent me away like that, old friend."

It was a low and well-aimed blow, and Sharek could've embraced him for it. Rowan shifted his weight subtly, his gaze tracking around the mostly-deserted courtyard. Elynor said nothing, and she didn't stop scowling even when Sylvester took her arm and tugged her away. Sharek could feel her eyes burning straight through him, trying to reach Rowan with a last hate-filled stare before they mounted the steps up to the mezzanines, and the shadows swallowed them.

Rowan jerked his head. "Walk with me?"

Sharek obliged, his hand grazing the knife in the seam of his trouser pocket. He had resolved not to go anywhere unarmed in this palace when Rowan was free to stalk its paths.

They walked beneath the waving arms of the *Aljalam* tree, its fragrant citrus scent buttering the air. A few Orlethians gathered at its wide trunk, pinning notes to paper garlands that crisscrossed its face.

"What are they doing?" Sharek asked.

Rowan waited for the people to disperse before he answered. "Sending prayers to the Empyreans. Most don't speak to them like you. It's too informal. But they believe the Empyreans planted the Tree of Life, so they must return every now and then to look in on it. The notes that vanish are the prayers that will be answered in time."

Sharek watched him walk to the tree and finger the garlands. "You believe that?"

Rowan snorted and let his hand fall. "I believe *someone* is stealing the notes. Doubtful it's the Empyreans." He turned back, his gaze glittering. "Then again, here you are, alive. So perhaps the Empyreans do listen, after all."

Sharek refused to believe that Rowan, of all people, had prayed to the Empyreans for him; but the remark opened the door for his next maneuver as he stepped under the boughs with Rowan. "I've been considering what you said the night I arrived. About your...remorse."

"Oh?" They circled the tree together and emerged back into the moonlight.

"I'm not certain I believe it. But as for reconciliation...I want that. Being at odds with the only other killing Blessed would make my assimilation into Orleth difficult at best."

Rowan's brow wrinkled. "Assimilation."

"I've had much time to think since Rimbourg...about what you said. How we were enslaved to the Sanctum," Sharek said. "I was Aeson Thalanor's weapon even when our paths crossed in Al-Morral's house. I couldn't see the sense of what you said. I couldn't begin to covet freedom."

"And now?"

Sharek pocketed his hands and shrugged. "Now I've tasted it. Seen it. My intention was to be healed here, and then return to Erala. But now...I don't think I can go back to how things were."

Rowan halted, turning to face him. Suspicion sketched the slant of his brows. "Then you see the wisdom of war?"

"No." Sharek held his stare unflinchingly. "I've had enough of war, Rowan. Bandit wars. Wars between lords. I'm through with it. All I want is a quiet life in Orleth, and Elynor and Sylvester want the same. If you'll leave us to it, you and I will be reconciled."

"You expect me to believe that the Azorian woman wants peace?"

"Better peace than being married off to Jamyson Venator."

Rowan grimaced. "So, the King hopes to sink His talons into the Fleet as well." He rolled his neck and shrugged his shoulders loose. "No matter, that. It's out of our hands. And Sly?"

"You know damned well Sylvester is better off here."

Rowan's lips twitched. "All right, Sharek, peace. Peace between us."

When Rowan offered his hand, Sharek shook it firmly. He had entered the arena now, taking the first step onto the battle floor. He could not afford to show a hint of refrain from here forward.

Rowan held his gaze steadily, and added, "But this war will happen, whether you are part of it or not. If you want your peace, you'll have it. I'll ensure no one drags you into this. But keep out of my way."

Sharek let go of his hand. "Beginning reconciliation with threats?"

"I didn't threaten you, did I? I asked you, brother to brother, not to interfere. You felt you had to run from Erala. I feel I have to fight for it. I have that right."

And he did. But not at the expense of Erala itself, the kingdom Sharck's people had been tasked by the Empyreans to defend. Not at the expense of the sacrosanct, misguided but mostly innocent. And Sharek knew it would break Elynor's heart, arranged marriage or not, if harm came to Prince Jamyson. She cared for him too deeply to stand aside while Rowan and Al-Morral marched this war to his doorstep. And if she was in this, then so was he.

"You have my word," Sharek said. "Erala is nothing to me now that I've left its shores. My focus is on my new life here."

"Good." Rowan slung an arm around his neck and guided him toward the great *ger*, and the walls on either side of it that divided the inner and outer courtyards. "Come have a drink with me, then. *Arkye* for me, goat's milk for you. I'm assuming you still don't drink much, you pious fool."

Sharek made himself laugh at that. And as Rowan led him away, a budding sense of responsibility flourished in his chest, hotter and brighter than any flame of pride.

He was a Hunter. Defending Erala was not only his calling, it was his very reason to exist. And defend it he would, even if he had to walk shoulder-to-shoulder with Rowan from here to the grave and escort him personally to death's door.

Chapter Thirty

The Call of the Sea

Danje's jade-and-gold palace was suffocating. Beneath the waves of its political climate, Elynor was drowning.

It had once come so easily to be diplomatic and poised; to carry out tactful conversations with visiting Orlethian dignitaries, and to haggle with their best merchants and their ship captains, had been a pleasure and a thrill. She had always been rooted deep in the fathoms of her name and title, of her inheritance, knowing who she was.

But Elynor did not feel like an Azorius anymore—whatever that even meant. Azorius the liar, like her father, who'd kept so many secrets from her; Azorius the runaway, like her mother, who'd fled to Orleth when Elynor was just a girl and sent letters to Alden but not to her.

Azorius the Blessed. What Elynor was and had always been. And had never known she was.

She ought to be helping Sharek and Sylvester insinuate into the Orlethian matriarchy so they could somehow unravel Rowan's vicious grip around this land and save Erala from the enemy's schemes. But, by the Throne, she just couldn't *do* it. It was some days before she could muster the energy even for a jaunt outside the palace. Otherwise, she slept a good deal—even more than she had after her father's death. The exhaustion hung like shackles from her body, anchoring her to her cushions in the small chamber, and whenever she began to rise the anger toward Rowan struck her in the chest so hard she curled back up in a heap and let the rage burn through her like a fever again.

Finally, she couldn't stand it anymore...the confines of the room, or Sylvester often in the corner, plucking that *shudraga*, or the thought of Sharek playing friendly with her father's killer. She needed to be out of the palace, where it was safe and she could think of something other than Rowan or Alden or what *she* was. And she needed to be useful in a way that only she could be.

The notion jammed into her like a sliver from a ship's railing, burrowing deep, and that was when Elynor began to plan.

That plan finally goaded her out into Danje's multicolored streets beneath a cool midday sun, her companions in tow. She still limped a bit from the arrow wound in her leg, and every joint ached, but she set her face determinedly to the east and pushed through the marketing crowds like a prow through calm waters. She knew where she needed to go, and what she had to do there.

Sylvester hung back a bit, examining a handful of Orlethian wares. Sharek kept close to Elynor's side, his suspicious and uncomfortable gaze swimming over the faces around them as if the danger was here, and not in the palace...in the man he spent many of his evenings with, trying to pry information from him.

Elynor wished she knew a word for how she felt about this entire affair. Jealousy. Fury. Despair. Those were all angles of it, but none of them properly named what whirled in her belly, sucking the water from her shores and out to sea, leaving her bare and dry at her core.

"Where are we going?" Sharek asked when the rooftops around them changed from the saffron-red of the spice quarter to a mellow blue. "I take it not to search for a proper home, as you told the *Khul* this morning."

"And as you told Rowan?" Elynor quipped. "No. I'm going to secure us safe passage home. Our *true* home."

Sharek's brows rose. "An Azorian vessel?"

Elynor slid a hand over the bulge in her trouser pocket: the compass her father had intended to give her for her birthday, the one she'd found with the letter that had shaped an impossible future—and carried a name that was important to her schemes now. "Someone my father knew."

They wound through a maze of white buildings, grinning avenues of pearly teeth capped in blue tiles, and as the scent of the harbor grew stronger, Elynor's heart began to pound. The assertive aroma of fish and brine, the subtler notes of wood varnish and the special soaps the Orlethians used to treat their sails, spun her head like sweet wine. If she closed her eyes, she might have been walking through Bast, those familiar avenues where she grew up. That port city she knew like her own name.

But she would never belong in Bast again, if she had ever truly belonged at all. She had no right to be so adept at things she hadn't earned, and her father's intentions to train her—after he'd given her a vessel of her own, no less—were a ruse. He'd known she wouldn't need lessons to sail, and she'd proved that with their cog when they'd crossed the Caeruel. Her father's plot to hire a seaman tutor had been a clever lie to cover her Blessed expertise, but that didn't mean Elynor couldn't twist his lie to her advantage.

They reached the end of the living quarter in the mariner's district, and Elynor's feet caught on the cobblestone road, her heart drumming to a halt. A falcate of white stone hung before them, then dropped away into a half-honeycomb of switchback streets dished out in a broad crescent around the harbor's edge. At the bottom was a fisherman's market full of chatter and the echoes of daily life. And then there were the wharfs, and the ships, and the water.

Her heart lunged back into motion, scraping her ribs so hard she gasped, and Sharek's gaze jumped to her as she stepped forward. The longing for the sea was so powerful, every fiber of her being ached for it. She could already feel the lines chafing her fingers and forearms; her ears churned with the snap of sails and the breaking of waves beneath the bow, and her legs trembled to imagine the powerful surge of the deck beneath them, a taunt, a dance—

"Elynor." Sharek's hand grazed her shoulder, and then it was gone, but it was enough to suck her back from that perilous edge. To return her to herself and remind her of her promise: though she had no choice but to sail home, she would not man the vessel that took them there...no matter what her traitorous Blessed blood craved.

She drew in several deep breaths to steady herself. Then, with the greatest effort anything had cost her since she'd abandoned Sharek at Tariaga Falls, she turned back to him and Sylvester. "We're going down to the market."

The familiar fragrance of Eralanite foods misted the air as they descended into it the blue-tiled mariner's district, but by that time Elynor was too sore and sour to feel more than a rub of homesickness against her breastbone. Her leg panged with every step from the long descent down, and her head practically ached from the effort not to look at the harbor and get lost in the glint of its waves. Better than any sunrise. Better than staring into any man's eyes.

She shook away the thought and steeled her focus. The sea was as far beyond her reach as her father's spirit or the memory of who she'd been before her disastrous reunion with her mother. She would do what she'd come to do.

She stopped at vendors here and there to ask for a man whose name she'd read only once, who was said to be a master of all things seacraft and sailing in Orleth. A man she had no doubt could bring them safely back to Erala if she could find where he did his business.

A man named Samwel Morlai.

But the reactions to his name were not what she had expected. There was none of the reverence the people of Bast held for the mention of men like Alden Azorius or even Gavannon Al-Morral. The steady eyes of hawkers darted when Elynor asked. The broad, warm grins of the boothkeepers shrank and chilled, and they shook their heads and silently pointed her on her way. As the dimness of the early sunset began to unfurl across the market, Elynor stalked back to Sharek and Sylvester, hands tossed up in fury. "I fail to see why this is so difficult!"

Sharek leaned against the side of a building, arms crossed, a sympathetic smile bracketing his mouth. "Well, if you weren't snarling at everyone you asked..."

"I am not snarling!"

He held up both hands, but now that smile became a full grin.

Sylvester released a longsuffering sigh and straightened from his slouch next to Sharek, throwing the *shudraga* into its sheath on his back. "Allow me."

He sauntered up to the nearest booth, and Elynor slumped next to Sharek, staring at her feet. It was the only way to keep her wandering gaze from the waves and all the things she couldn't have.

After a moment, Sharek nudged her. "I haven't seen you smile but once since we came here."

Elynor fixed her fiercest scowl toward the path. "I haven't felt like smiling."

"We're all alive, and together. I would think that's reason enough."

"Until Rowan butchers us in our beds."

Sharek was silent. Elynor groaned, rubbing her sunkissed cheeks, and just then Sylvester returned, jerking his thumb over his shoulder. "Samwel Morlai's up this road a ways. The white building etched with sea flowers on the right."

Elynor straightened sharply. "How is it that *you* managed to ferret that out in just a few moments? I've been at this for more than an hour!"

Sylvester gave the *shudraga* a loving flick. "I asked nicely. And it helps I don't have a face that looks like a slapped arse."

"No, but you have the arm of one," Elynor snapped, and hit him on the shoulder for good measure.

They walked into the shadows of the honeycomb, and Elynor's heart skipped. She was going to meet a man who'd had personal dealings with her father. What if he knew things about Alden that she didn't? What if her father's last wishes for her were deeply embedded in this man's opinion of her? If he expected to meet an heiress poised to receive her own ship and inherit a whole Fleet in time, he would be sorely disappointed...but she hoped she could still navigate that.

She was hanging an awful lot on hope these days. And what had her father told her?

Hope anchors no ships.

Elynor was adrift, desperately running up her sails and praying to catch the wind. She didn't know what else to do.

Morlai's place was indeed distinguishable, set apart by the flowering tiles around the keyhole-shaped doorway which looked as if they'd been painted by a talented child. A lonely sign creaked above the door, announcing *Morlai's Mariner Shoppe*. It clearly hadn't been treated in some time, and the damp breeze had swelled the wood, mildewing its edges. Suspicion rolled through Elynor, dark as a storm-churned wave.

"This looks promising," Sylvester's remark echoed her thoughts. "You're certain this is someone you want to meet with, Elynor?"

"My father trusted him," Elynor said—and faltered.

Her father had seen fit to lie to her about her mother and about what she herself truly was. He'd also trusted Al-Morral. Could she truly depend on his estimation of people?

But then, what did she have to lose for trying?

Squaring her shoulders with the pantomime of the aristocrat she'd once been, Elynor marched through the door.

Everything in the foreground of Morlai's shop wore a fine patina of dust except for the shelves full of bottles behind the counter, and the table on this side of it. A hooded man sat at that table, a graveyard of empty jugs and tipped glasses around him. He didn't look up or turn back his hood as Elynor, Sharek, and Sylvester entered the shop.

"We're closed," he slurred.

"I can see that," Elynor said. "Samwel Morlai?"

"S'what they call me."

Elynor reached into her pocket as she approached the table. "I have something of yours that I'm willing to trade back to you in exchange for safe passage to Erala."

Her father's compass landed on the table with a dull *clunk*. Sharek let out his breath on the whisper of her name, but she ignored him. He'd kept her from tossing the compass the night she'd learned what she was, but that hadn't made her want to keep it. At least it could buy them a way home.

"Now, that's interesting," Morlai said, and at the tilt of his tone, Elynor's heart clenched.

She knew that voice.

A low hiss of shock slid through her teeth as the woolen hood fell back, dark eyes lifted to hers, and she found herself face-to-face with Sam.

Chapter Thirty-One

Daring for a Challenge

"*You*," Elynor hissed, and boots creaked on stone behind her as Sharek and Sylvester tensed.

"*You*," Sam echoed in that same gruff voice that had brought Elynor both frustration and comfort in Kirsagan's cage. "Grief looks ugly on your face, girl."

"This isn't grief. It's *rage*." Elynor planted her hands on the table and bent toward him, shoulders curling, body trembling. "I should have known. That kings-damned scar on your arm—it *is* from rigging."

"Clever. Thought you might've sorted it out sooner or later. Hoped you wouldn't."

"Back in the raider caravan—you knew who I was, didn't you?"

He lifted one shoulder in a shrug. "Eralanite name."

"Then why did you never once think to *mention* any of this? Your connection with my father? With *me*? Didn't that mean anything to you?"

"Helped you escape, didn't I?"

"Yes, and then you abandoned us in my mother's *ger*!"

"Because you had nothing I wanted." Sam poured a generous helping of *arkye* from one of the bottles, the pungent notes of sour yogurt almost bringing her to gag. "Heard the story you told the woman. I left as soon as you stormed out."

She lurched back from the table, scowling. "Well, you have something *I* want. Is it true you're the master of sailing in Orleth?"

Sam banged down the bottle. "Was."

"Good. Because, as I said, we're going to need someone to ferry us back to Erala."

Sam pushed the compass back to her. "Find someone else. Don't want this. Or you."

She ignored the sting of his words. Why should she care if he wanted anything to do with her at all? "There is no one else. You came personally recommended by my father."

"Ah, you mean the slippery codfish good for nothing to either of us now he's dead?"

Elynor nearly lunged at him across the table, but Sharek hooked her elbow with his hand, putting his back to Sam so he could speak into Elynor's ear. "That won't help."

Even through the scarlet haze of rage that coated her vision, she saw he was right. Sam's half-lidded, bloodshot eyes were fixed on her, daring for a challenge—for another reason to toss her out of his shop.

She yanked her arm from Sharek's grasp. "So you'll only speak to me if I have something you want?"

"That's how it is, girl."

Elynor straightened her rumpled clothing. "Very well."

Then she marched from his shop before she could more deeply consider snatching up the *arkye* jug and smashing it over his head.

Dusk netted the harbor in a dull shroud as they stepped out onto the street and Sylvester shut the door. Then he whistled lowly. "Sam, *our* Sam, is the man your father wanted to teach you to sail. Imagine that!"

Elynor hardly could. Whenever she'd given fleeting notion to Samwel Morlai since finding the compass and the note, she'd pictured a man like her father: noble and carefree, booming with wisdom and eager to be on the waves. Never had her visions involved a drunkard so inept he'd walked straight into the hands of raiders; a man without a hope or desire to escape until they'd all but handed his freedom to him. A man who couldn't be trusted to captain his own two feet, much less any vessel.

Had her father's judgement truly been so misguided? Or was something else at play here?

"What now?" Sharek murmured.

Elynor raised her chin. "Back to the palace, I suppose."

But not for long. Thanks to her voyage in Kirsagan's wagon, she knew the way to Samwel Morlai's heart. All she needed now was the *tolvors* to acquire it.

Chapter Thirty-Two

The Bard's Victory

It was well past dark when they returned to the palace gates, held open by guards who bowed them deeply on their way. Elynor's feet dragged, and Sylvester's spirit scraped the glittering tiles right along with her.

He couldn't say he was surprised by any means that Sam had crossed into their path again, but he hated to see how dejected Elynor was about it. And how dejected Sharek was on her behalf.

He really needed to make less miserable friends, but he couldn't help himself.

They slipped into the courtyard, where Sharek brushed out an arm to halt them. Sylvester flicked his gaze around the baths and walkways, expecting to see Rowan lunging from one of the palace shadows. But he only saw *Khuless* Mide.

Her presence, and her solitude, were shocking after days of trying to find her without a brace of guards at her side. She didn't seem to notice them, either; she was prostrate before the casting of the Tree of Life, as still as the six stone men that girdled its trunk.

Sylvester glanced at Sharek. He was watching him already with raised brows, asking a silent question.

A question that Sylvester, quite unfortunately, already knew the answer to; after all, he might not find the *Khuless* alone again.

Sylvester waved a hand, motioning him and Elynor to depart. They went, Elynor with a few curious backward glances, and when they were gone Sylvester approached the fountain. He made certain every step was deliberately loud so he wouldn't startle the lethal *Khuless*. But Mide didn't raise her forehead from the glossy tiles even when Sylvester stood directly beside her.

He cleared his throat. "May I sit here?"

Slowly, Mide pushed herself up until she rested on her haunches, in the same rigid posture as she'd taken on the cushion in the *Khul's ger*. Her gaze was fixed on the statue of the tree. "You are a guest of this palace. You may sit wherever you wish."

Sylvester lowered himself onto the rim of the fountain and pretended to study it while he stole glances at the *Khuless*. He'd spent days mulling over how to pry her for information about her distrust of Rowan, but seeing her tonight sent all those plans askew. She looked strangely sad.

"Were you praying?" Sylvester asked. Mide shot him a cool look, and he added, "I have a friend...the Blessed I came here with. He also prays."

Sylvester himself had little time for prayers. He wasn't certain anyone would listen if he tried, so he let Sharek do the praying for them both.

"I pray to the *Burkhan*," Mide said after a moment. "They who created both man and Blessed. Your people call them Empyreans."

Sylvester forced a choked smile to his lips. The thought of having his own people was foreign. He'd been wandering on his own for so long, bereft of home and family. There were the sacrosanct, the Blessed, and the Hunters. And there was Sylvester Munrow, who belonged to no one.

"Are these the Burkhan?" he gestured to the figures kneeling about the tree.

"No. They are the Blessed for whom the *Khuligs* are named." Mide pointed to each in turn. "Amasandji, Bayar, and Kaishan. Jungsai, Chanar, and Dabantai. It is said they appealed to the *Burkhan* during a great famine and war when men preferred to fight rather than pray."

"I can hardly imagine such a time," Sylvester said dryly.

Mide went on as if she hadn't heard him. "The *Burkhan* heard their prayers and saw their hearts were pure...they alone among the people of Orleth sought not struggle, but peace. So they grew for them the *Aljalam* tree, and when they brought its offerings to the warlords and told the story of the *Burkhan's* mercy, all fighting ceased." The *Khuless* spoke softly, with the cadence of a storyteller. "This is why the Blessed are so loved in our kingdom. It is why they deserve our trust and respect."

Sylvester bent his chin to his fist. "My friend tells me the Burkhan planted the *Aljalam* tree in the inner courtyard. Is it the one from your story?"

Mide's countenance hardened. "That is what they say."

"It seems strange, to have a stone casting of the same tree only another courtyard away," Sylvester smirked. "But it's a good story nonetheless. I'm a bit of a storyteller myself, you know, being a bard. I take it you're used to telling that one?"

Mide rocked to her feet, the remoteness of her face turning to pure stone. "What do you want from me?"

"To speak about Rowan, as a matter of fact," Sylvester admitted. "I knew him before, and his presence here...surprises me."

The *Khuless* watched him for a long moment, her upswept eyes narrowed in harsh assessment that made Sylvester feel laid bare, as if Mide could see for herself what he was. As if everything he did began in lies and was doomed to end in pain.

"I have patrols to assemble," she said. "But at week's end, if you haven't found a home yet, I will dine with you in my chamber, and I'll tell you what I know."

It seemed too easy a victory. Sylvester didn't know how to trust it. But he also *needed* desperately to win something here. Elynor had her purposes with Sam now, and Sharek had Rowan to think about, but Sylvester...what good was he? A charming bard, an average healer, and a liar on the run from his own truths.

He truly did need this. So he sent up a prayer to the empty black nothingness for one small favor, and bowed his head. "The honor would be mine, *Khuless* Mide."

She offered a last glittering stare before she turned, swords chinking in their cross at her shoulders, and strode from the courtyard.

Chapter Thirty-Three

An Illusion of Necessity

In death, Vestan Cragon went home.

He returned to the perilous climes and mountain meadows of the City of Delv deep in the heart of the Farrow Mountains; to dark caves of endless depth and towers and ramparts of such stature they rivaled the peaks from which they were hewn. He felt the heat of the Delvin forges on his face, heard the beating of hammers on steel that chiseled life into the weapons they forged. He felt the nip of the icy wind against his limbs and knew that for the first time since he'd been captured and ransomed off at a Blessed auction in the foothills—bought by a Kingsgard for sport and finally sold to the Crown Prince to do with as he pleased—he had at last come home.

He saw his sister Glavia dancing, wildflowers woven into her hair; he saw his sister Seia fighting, daggers flashing as she sparred with their uncles and aunts. He saw his father, a magistrate of his own making, white robes clashing with the dark farrowrock borders of their world as he brought traders in to see the weapons they made in secret, better even than the legendary blacksmiths of Fallhelm. And he saw his mother, fierce and steady as the rock where they homed, her golden eyes tracking the traders with the intensity of a wolf scenting rivalry on the wind.

Here the dream became a nightmare.

Herbs spun his head into tatters, dulling his Blessed strength. Ropes hacked around his wrists and ankles, a collar choked him if he struggled. A soiled gag in his mouth made him retch when he tried to scream. The peaks and strongholds disappeared, lost to his blurry eyes.

But this time, he did not open them to the back of the trafficker's wagon. He opened them to firelight, and to a cave.

Vestan sucked in a harsh breath that set his body aflame, particularly his left side. A groan bubbled up his throat, and that also hurt. He squeezed his eyes shut, then peeled them open again.

Still in a cave. Lying on his back, looking up at the curve of the rock high above. The sound of rumbling water filled his ears.

So did the echo of screams. So did the smash of branches buckling beneath his body.

A hand touched his shoulder. "Lie still."

Vestan jerked, thinking to reach for his blade, but his limbs were too heavy. When he craned his head to peer down at himself, he found one arm was splinted and in a sling, his middle was thick and bulgy with bandages. And at his left, a woman crouched on one knee. Watching him.

Vestan flinched again, teeth gritting. "Where are the children?"

The woman raised a hand for peace. "They live."

The breath rushed out of Vestan so quickly his head spun. He laid it back on the stone. "Good. That's..." The memory of their hazardous climb and the searing agony of the arrow burrowing into his flesh tore through him again, and he groaned. "Rocks. I let *go*."

"You are not to blame for any of this. The Kingsgard is...they are brutal men following the commands of a savage King. You did what you could."

Vestan strained to lift his head again. Wariness pivoted sharply in his gut, forming slick, nauseating coils. "Who are you? How did you find me, and how do you know what happened to us?"

The woman hooked down the cloth that covered her nose and mouth. She had a fine face, softly wrinkled and golden-brown. Her eyes were also tawny, though not quite as bright as his mother's had been. "They call me Ria. My people have watched over Kaer Dorwenon for some time. When you and the children fell into the water, we found you and carried you away before the Kingsgard could finish what they began with the arrow in your side. We have been treating your wounds for many, many days."

Vestan moved his unhurt arm gingerly, prodding his side. It ached, but not terribly. He didn't feel hot or feverish. "How is it that you and your people know how to drag a man back from the brink of death? And how did you find us without being followed, with the Kingsgard swarming the foothills?"

Her lips twitched, but she said nothing.

Vestan sank back, piecing together what people had such knowledge of healing and could move about unseen. "You're Hunters."

"We are." There was neither shame nor fear in Ria's voice. "And you must be Blessed with strength. It's the only way you could have survived that fall while shielding the children."

Vestan groaned, planting a hand into the cave floor and pushing himself up. "I must see them."

"Carefully," Ria warned. "Hunters know many remedies, but we are not miracle makers. If you tear something that's already bruised inside, you'll be at the mercy of the Empyreans to heal it."

"I'll take my chances." Vestan broke down as he rose, and Ria slid a hand under his arm, muttering about the stubbornness of men.

The cave went back some ways, sloped and dim. They must be somewhere in the Valley of Embra, at the feet of the King—who had sanctioned the deaths of His own children.

Hatred bubbled hot and violent in Vestan's chest, but he silenced it. For the love of the Prince he'd come to call friend, even brother, he had gotten used to doing that.

Finally, they emerged in a stone oasis where a portion of the rock high above had cracked inward long ago. It formed a thin skylight through which the sun's rays poured down, limning the edges of a rainwater pool that spanned half the width of the cavern. There were many unfamiliar faces here, at least two dozen by Vestan's first tally. And four that he knew.

Isla and Isaac splashed in the shallows of the pool, flicking water at one another and laughing. Elliott lay on the shore, hands folded behind his head, staring up at the skylight. Sylvie perched beside him, her leg splinted like Vestan's arm.

The sight of them consumed Vestan with relief more potent than his rage, and he sagged. Ria helped him to the edge where the cavern broadened, and he braced his shoulder to the rock and slid down until he sat. Lightheaded, he simply watched them.

He'd been so certain they were dead as they fell; that he'd failed not only them, but also Jamyson—his king, even if he only carried the title of Crown Prince. But someone had seen fit to grant them mercy.

He dragged his gaze to Ria as she sat beside him. "Why are Hunters watching Kaer Dorwenon?"

"We have a vested interest in this kingdom and those who profess to lead it," she said. "It has taken us much time to gather enough Hunters and Blessed to even consider making the journey here...to learn the intricacies of the kaer's inner workings."

Vestan's skin prickled. "*Everyone* here is a Hunter or Blessed?"

Ria nodded. "Warriors, seamstresses, readers, storytellers, plotters, smoothtalkers...for months now, we have watched, and we have learned. We have seen the King's cruelty soar to new heights. It's difficult to convince so many to move as one, but when we saw what happened on the bridge, and saw you fall...it truly united us, for the first time."

"Your people weren't reluctant to save the children of the King?"

Ria's eyes flicked to him. "Some of us were mothers and fathers once. We would not punish children for their birthright."

"Does that include Jamyson?"

"Should it?" Her tone was mild but her gaze piercing.

"He's a good man who cares for the wellbeing of his kingdom. He isn't like his father."

"I know that." Ria waved a hand. "Merely testing where your loyalties lie. Though I fear what will become of him when he takes the Throne. A great many wicked things have been done in the name of the kingdom's wellbeing. Cruel men are not made from cruelty alone. They're made from the illusion of necessity."

"That's sadly true. But Jamyson is an ally."

"Time will tell just how much of one, hm?" Ria cocked a brow. "We mean him no harm. And it's all right to be suspicious. We are strangers to you, after all."

He shrugged his unhurt shoulder. "It is difficult to trust anyone, having been a Blessed in service to a King who detests us."

"The King detests many things." Ria watched the children play for a time. "It's strange, you know. Hunters and Blessed had little ambition for the Throne in the times of Yore. We were content to watch over Erala and work our craft from afar. But the Kings of Yore turned against us out of fear, and now it seems the only way to live a peaceful life is if one of our kind seizes the Throne." She rubbed her fingertips gently in the hollow of her throat as if to ease some long-ago ache. "Sometimes our greatest enemies are the ones we make by our own deeds."

Vestan thought of Jamyson—what he must be feeling toward his father now, believing his siblings were dead by the King's command. And what the reckless Prince would do with that belief, and without Vestan there to speak some measure of sense to him...

Urgency panged in his limbs, and he pushed himself up against the wall. "I must return to Kaer Dorwenon."

"Your leg is badly sprained," Ria said. "Your arm is broken. You're held together by the very talented needlework of a Blessed seamstress. But we are more than a week's hard walking from Dorwenon, and the wagons we used to carry you here are away on other business. I do not think you will survive the journey, but I won't stop you if your determination remains. You are a free man."

Vestan hesitated, watching the royal siblings. They hadn't noticed him yet, enamored in their play and in their own thoughts. But they seemed at ease, and not in the least bit mistreated. It was strange to see them here, surrounded by Blessed and Hunters, unafraid. He wondered how long he had slept, how many days it had taken to convince them that these people did not deserve to be sent to the gallows simply for being what they were.

Or perhaps their father's betrayal had caused them to question everything. Perhaps that was why Elliott looked as if he was chewing over a difficult problem and Sylvie's face was sketched in such lines of sadness.

Vestan didn't sit back down, but he said, "I'll give it some time. The royal siblings were entrusted to me. I won't leave until I'm convinced they're safe and healed."

"A wise choice." Ria smiled. "I believe they'll approve."

Just then Isla caught sight of him. With a shriek, she bounded from the water. Isaac raced after her, crying out, *"Attack the bodyguard!"*

And then Vestan was consumed with trying to keep the rest of his limbs from being broken by two enthusiastic five-year-olds.

Chapter Thirty-Four

Truth and Lies

*K*HULESS MIDE SPARED NO expense in the feast for herself and Sylvester at week's end, an affair held in her private chamber—which was every bit as opulent as the palace's dining hall. Winged jade lizards wrapped around pillars that framed the sleek black glass floor, and the sunken aisle, set with cushions and a low table, ended at a broad set of steps leading up to her bed, vanity, and armoire. A wide window took up nearly the entire back wall, overlooking the city.

Sylvester couldn't ascertain if Mide was the sort to gaze over Danje with power-famished eyes. She was unsettlingly quiet for most of the evening, a duel of greater silences between them until Sylvester finally decided to pepper it with tales and humming and laughter.

Mide stared at him as the attendants brought a pot of lamb stew to the table a half-hour later. "Do you ever stop talking?"

He shrugged. "I've never tried."

Though he did find his thoughts wandering a moment to a Blessed permanently silenced—yet one he'd had little trouble understanding.

Rocks, he should have said farewell to Rue before they'd left Tariaga Falls. He'd taken the time to learn the handsign for it, but he'd been too full-body blushed to show her before he'd scuttled out on Sharek's heels from Iracabeth's *ger*.

Mide's pert voice strung him back to the present. "Perhaps you should make the attempt, before someone at this table removes your head."

"Well, if you promise to mount it fashionably, I just might allow it."

The spirit of a smile flicked the corners of her lips up, then settled them again. "You remind me a good deal of someone I once knew."

"Do I? And was he also rakishly handsome, quick-witted, and blessed with a singing voice that could make the Empyreans weak in the knees?"

"No. He was agitating and energetic and a pain in my backside every step." Mide skewered a cube of meat and studied it. "And I miss him."

Sylvester grimaced. "I'm sorry for your loss. I too know such pain."

Mide's eyes flicked to him, chillingly focused. "It has been a year, and still it does not lessen."

Sylvester nodded. "It's been quite some time for me. Yet still it's nearly constant, the ache. You find yourself looking everywhere for them."

"Finding things to share with them," Mide murmured, "and looking around for them only to remember they're gone."

"And realizing that every new thing you learn is something about you they will never know." He swallowed. "It was my little sister and both of my parents."

Mide dropped her gaze to her stew. "I am sorry for your loss as well." She waved the attendants away; when the doors had shut, she said, "What does Rowan have to do with it?"

"With my loss, nothing at all. But my friend Elynor..." Sylvester folded his legs at the ankles and leaned forward, clasping his hands. "Did Rowan tell you why he came here?"

"Seeking sanctuary from Erala. Blessed are imprisoned there. They are less than dirt beneath the feet of the sacrosanct."

Sylvester's heart twisted. "Did he tell you what he was seeking sanctuary from?"

"No. His explanation was brief. Vague." Mide paused. "He was lying." It was not a question.

"We have cause to believe that Rowan's intentions with the *Khul* are not pure," Sylvester said, "and that it's more than sanctuary he seeks."

Mide folded her arms. "Go on."

"Rowan killed Elynor's father. And he came here to start a war between Orleth and Erala, to set his fellow Blessed free."

The silence stretched on, and Sylvester's heart pounded for fear he'd said too much. Perhaps Elynor had misjudged Mide's anger at Rowan; and now Sylvester might have given away everything, consigned himself and his companions to the gallows, or whatever equivalent Orleth used.

"Now, that *is* refreshing," Mide said at last. "Perfect honesty from Eralanites."

Sylvester cocked his head. "You seem quite certain of that, *Khuless*."

"I am...for I too am Blessed. I have the power to sense lies."

Sylvester jerked back in shock. "Well! You might have said so sooner! And here I was sweating about how the *rocks* we were going to convince you of any of this, when Rowan sits at your mother's left hand!"

"That's precisely why I didn't tell you. I wished to see if you'd be honest with me." She drummed her cushion, making a soft *swish* in the beaded fabric. "Rowan seeks to start a war."

"Have you learned as much from him?"

"No. He's been careful to avoid me thus far...he knows what I am, so he's wise to keep out of my way. Wiser than others." Her eyes narrowed. "Your friend Sharek. He isn't Blessed."

Sylvester's muscles coiled tightly. "You've known that since he presented Kirsagan's head, I take it."

Mide nodded. "But I also knew Rowan spoke the truth when he said they'd once been like brothers. That Sharek *is* killing Blessed. He believes the lie of what Sharek is, and I find that *fascinating*."

"It's all very fascinating, yes, and very complicated. What I personally find the most fascinating of all is why you didn't expose Sharek outright."

Mide's eyes flicked to her swords, lying at her right and left sides. "Ever since Rowan arrived, things have been strange in this palace. My mother has been absolutely taken with his every word. She seems to trust it over mine."

"And what reason would she have for that?" Sylvester asked.

Mide's mouth twisted in a scowl. "She believes my judgement to be clouded by loss, and...by betrayal."

Sylvester frowned, thinking of the feast, and Rowan's tale, and how furious Mide had become. "The *Daishi*?"

Her piercing gaze rose to him. "You are very perceptive."

"Rowan staged the entire thing, of course," Sylvester murmured. "The so-called *Urvach*?"

"They gave witness against the *Daishi*. And that was the odd thing—I sensed no lie in them."

Sylvester bit the side of his thumb, gazing into his stew bowl. "There are Hunterish herbs that make one agreeable to almost anything. I wonder if Rowan didn't drug those people and feed them a lie about their own part in this...a lie so powerful it could even deceive a Blessed."

"Whatever he did, it was enough to convince my mother," Mide said. "She hung the *Urvach* we found and banished the *Daishi*. But he told me as he left that we'd been misled. And there was no lie in his words."

"I assume you told the *Khul* this."

Mide sat back, a mirthless smile bracketing her mouth. "And that was where her faith in me met its end. She believed *I* was lying to her on the *Daishi's* behalf. That I was too grief-stricken to fathom yet another loss. She has placed me on assignment with the patrols ever since, and Rowan, the seething snake, grows closer to her by the hour."

Sylvester rubbed his chin. "What was your relation to the *Daishi*?"

Pain flashed like lightning in the shadowed depths of her upturned eyes. "He helped raise me...his were the first arms to hold me after my birth. He taught me the way of the sword, and of honor. He was the closest to a father I have ever known...and I suspect that's why he didn't hang with the *Urvach*. Even in the depths of her betrayed heart, my mother was grateful to him."

"Well, hung or not, Rowan has what he wants. He's all but taken the *Daishi's* place. And what better way to prompt a war than from a warlord's position?"

Mide inclined toward him, intensity written in every line of her body like a taut *shudraga* string. "But how will he do it?"

"That, we aren't certain of," Sylvester admitted. "Not to the last note. But we know he'll somehow lay blame for the death of Alden Azorius at Orleth's feet, and then his accomplice in Erala will bring word of it to the King. We suspect they positioned themselves perfectly at the ears of the King and *Khul* to provoke them with ill whispers to war."

Mide's countenance darkened, her jaw tightening. "My mother is already frustrated with the trade agreements of late...she believes they hang too heavily in Erala's favor. If the King hurls accusations of meddling, and with Rowan whispering in her ear, she may indeed seek retribution."

"And if our lands go to war, countless lives will be lost." Sylvester rubbed his brow. "The Fleet Elynor's father worked so hard to build will become a vessel for slaughter. And the only ones who truly stand to profit are the ones who have taken enough from us already."

Slowly, Mide nodded. "We will need help. Rowan is Blessed, and supposedly he uncovered this great conspiracy. We must find clear proof of his true plan if we're to remove him from my mother's side."

"Sharek is already searching for that. He's intimated himself back into Rowan's trust already. Now he's seeking a way to thwart him."

Mide took up her swords and sheathed them. "I will send word to the *Daishi*. He may be disgraced, but his counsel would be valuable."

Sylvester rose as well, bowing with an arm across his chest. "We are most honored for your trust in us, *Khuless* Mide."

"Anything," Mide stuck out her hand, "*anything* to remove that serpent from my mother's side. I will call on you when I have information."

Sylvester shook her hand. "Until then."

"One last thing," Mide called after him as he went to the door. "About Sharek. What is he really?"

Sylvester froze, gripping the ornate doorknob. A hundred answers tumbled through his mind, each one more useless than the last.

Slowly, he looked back. "For Sharek's sake, I can't tell you that. It's his choice who learns it. I would sooner die than give him up."

Mide studied him for a long moment, head tipped, the knot of her hair on the crown of her head not tilting an inch. "And that, I absolutely believe."

Chapter Thirty-Five

Convince or Be Killed

It was uncomfortable, but not unusual, for Sylvester and Elynor to be bound up in their own affairs while Sharek was left with little to do but desperately avoid having conversations with strangers in the palace. Sylvester was often in the musicians' district, which helped keep up the ruse that they really were searching for a home here; and Elynor kept to herself, preferring not to speak of things like her mother and father, or of her status as Blessed.

Tonight, Sylvester was with *Khuless* Mide at a dinner Sharek had not been invited to, and Elynor was doing small jobs, of all things, around the palace.

So Sharek sought out Rowan.

"Well, this is a surprise," Rowan drawled, folding his arms and propping his shoulder to the doorframe of his room across the courtyard. He'd answered the summons in only his trousers, his killing might slumbering in his casual appearance and posture. "I've felt like I've had to chase you for a moment of your time these past few days."

Sharek shrugged. "I'm bored tonight."

"Because you need to kill something."

It was a sly test. Rowan knew Sharek was the only killing Blessed who'd never really felt compelled to kill—and now Sharek understood the truth of why that was.

But he couldn't tell Rowan that; so he turned the question instead. "How do you manage it? I'd think if you were killing your way through the city, the *Khul* would have words."

"There it is, that tone of accusation." Rowan ducked back into his room, snatched a long coat from the foot of his bare bed, and tossed it on as he stepped outside. "I settle it with rats in the sewers, mostly. You know a kill is a kill."

"True." Sharek stepped out of his reach. "Then let's go hunting rats."

"*You're* suggesting a hunt?" Arms akimbo, Rowan ran a mocking gaze over him. "What have you done with the real Sharek Ransalor?"

Sharek offered him an empty smile while chills cantered down his spine. "I'm not the same man you left in the Sanctum to go off on your campaign with Al-Morral."

Rowan's smile slid from his lips as his hands slid from his waist. He wandered forward to Sharek's side. "I should have made you my price. Told Gavannon I'd have nothing to do with him unless he found a way to bring you as well. But I saw my opportunity to make the difference we always talked about, Sharek. I had to take it."

Again, Sharek shrugged. "We're both free now, aren't we?"

"Maybe so. Maybe not." Rowan led the way down into the courtyard. "I've thrown off my shackles, but you still follow around the heiress who hired you."

"Elynor is a friend, not a hirer."

"Is she? A friend who decides your fate?" Rowan's smile was pitiless. "A friend who could turn you over to Aeson Thalanor if you ever returned to Erala, and you would have no say in the matter? Sharek, you can't have any sort of relationship with someone who holds that power over you. You can never be friends or more with a woman who owns your agency."

Sharek bristled. "What would you know of it? You, who throw your friends through windows."

"I only have two friends…you, and Gavannon. And with you, I would take that back." The moonlight painted stern lines of Rowan's brow and pierced his eyes. "Gavannon set me free to do the work I'm called to do. Can you say the same?"

Could he? He and Elynor had rarely discussed what his fate would be once they returned to Erala; when he'd been dying of poisoning, it had seemed a false hope. And now they were entangled in this, so tightly Sharek felt the thorns of Rowan's way of thinking pricking his skin, letting doubt infect the wounds left behind.

He checked Rowan's shoulder in passing. "We have rats to hunt."

Rowan had blocked out a small portion of the spice district where the alleys crawled with rats. He and Sharek posted themselves on a ledge jutting from the side of a building and watched for small movement in the dark, and Sharek hated to admit he relished it. He didn't enjoy the kill itself as Rowan did, but he basked in the unfurling of his senses. His sharp gaze and sensitive ears picked up the movements of the rats far quicker than Rowan's did; he could spot a rodent slinking through the stone seams at the alley mouth while Rowan was still looking the opposite way.

But he let him have a few kills, to keep suspicions from mounting.

They made a game of it all night, tallying their kills, leaping down from the ledges and shoving each other out of the way to reach the rats. Rowan cheerfully bagged them afterward.

"I haven't lost my taste for that *multem* you used to make," he remarked when Sharek shook his head, watching the fifteenth rat disappear into the sack. "Though it was better sometimes than others."

"It isn't my fault we had hirers who sent us to the most barren crags of Ventia." Sharek sprawled out on the wooden awning that formed the ledge. "Difficult to find anything to season *multem* with there."

"True. But have you ever tasted such waters?" Rowan's eyes gleamed nearly as bright as his tattoos. "I could have lived on those for the rest of my days."

Sharek studied him sideways. There'd been a change in Rowan's demeanor here; his smile came quicker, less cruelly. And his voice had lost some of the Sanctum-fed roughness, as if he sought to intimidate less and beguile more. "Tell me something. You truly believe this war of yours is the only way to set our brothers and sisters free?"

Rowan squinted one eye shut, peering up at the moon. "I do."

"And that's worth any price to you? Any life? Even a child's?"

"What do you mean?"

"That boy in Rimbourg, the one who told you about me. Cillin. Did you kill him?"

Rowan shook his head. "I killed his dog. But not the boy. Gavannon wouldn't permit it. He has his lines he will not cross." His eyes flicked to Sharek. "As do we all, it seems."

"And you heeded him because he's your friend?"

Rowan scoffed. "Because if I didn't, he'd return me to the Sanctum."

Sharek cleared his throat. "Yes, that sounds like freedom."

Rowan stiffened. Then he lunged suddenly, so suddenly Sharek had no time to brace himself for an attack; but Rowan vaulted over him with a light handspring, chasing down a rat in the alley below. He returned to the awning empty-handed and scowling. "I thought you swore not to interfere with my plans."

Sharek bobbed his shoulders, hoping Rowan couldn't sense his racing heart. "And I'm not. I'm only curious if you truly know the sort of man you're allied with. He sacrificed his partner to begin this war. Are you certain he won't turn on you?"

"Gavannon and I want the same thing. So, yes. I'm certain."

Sharek stared across the rooftops toward the winking gem of the palace, visible on its slight incline at the heart of the city. "Elynor and I do not always want the same things. But even then, I know she won't betray me."

"Leave it alone, Sharek."

So Sharek did. He'd done what he intended: he'd introduced doubt into the alliance between Rowan and Al-Morral.

A small part of him whispered that he was not here to introduce doubt—he was here to prevent this war at all costs. He had not come to turn Rowan away from this path, but to stop him from walking down it by any means necessary.

And yet the thought had lodged now, and would not let go.

What if he could convince Rowan, rather than killing him?

Chapter Thirty-Six

A Fleet for Passage

Aftera fortnight of labor about the palace, Elynor finally earned enough coin to purchase an armload of *arkye*. And at long last, she returned to the mariner's district to barter with Samwel Morlai.

She went alone this time, not knowing for certain what the evening would require. Visions of herself threatening Sam at knifepoint danced through her head as she descended among the array of brightly-colored rooftops to the mariner's district and hurried down the shadow-stamped street to his shop. She entered without knocking and found Sam precisely where she'd left him last, spinning a cup on its edge and staring unblinking at the wall. His gaze drifted to her, slower than a buoy on calm waters, but something lit in those ravaged depths when he saw the offering she carried.

"Well, well. You know the way to a man's heart, that's for certain, girl."

"I'm not interested in your heart," Elynor said. "I want your story. And I want to know what it will cost to hire your services."

Sam eyed the bottles, fierce with longing. "I don't sell them anymore."

Elynor set the basket of bottles on the table and unloaded one. "Just your story, then." She had to learn if her father's judgement had truly been so clouded that he'd been swindled by an Orlethian drunkard, or if the fine make of the compass in her pocket told the truth of a far more intricate tale unfolding here.

"Suppose a bit of seaman's storytelling couldn't hurt, after you've been so generous and all." Sam took the bottle and gestured to the chair across from him. "Pull up a seat, if you dare."

Elynor dared.

Sam produced a second cup from the floor and polished it out with his sleeve, set it before her, then poured for them both. He drained the entire glass in one pull; Elynor sipped hers and found the taste as palatable as sour cheese. But she hadn't expected this story to come for only the cost of a basket of *arkye*.

"So," Sam drawled, "what did you want to know?"

"How you came to be like...this." Elynor waved a hand at his entire person, caring little if that was offensive. "You're not the sort of man my father led me to believe you are."

"Your father..." Sam helped himself to another glassful but didn't drink this time. He swirled the milky contents, staring into their depths. "Your father was my last hope. My charter back to Erala."

Elynor blinked. "*Back* there?"

"Aye. I was born on the coast—Port of Bessidia. Crossed the channel when I was a lad, parents perished in the crossing. I made landfall in Orleth with naught but the skin on my back and the grog that filled my empty belly aboard the ship. But the hunger was awake in me after that voyage. Hunger for the sea."

Hunger, deep and festering, terrifying in its might...

Elynor could hardly breathe the words. "You're a sailing Blessed."

Sam toasted unsteadily. "That I am."

Elynor ripped her gaze to the door, every muscle bunched for flight. Yet even as her body prepared to hurl itself from the presence of another Blessed—a man who was just like her—a strange longing churned in her gut. The same moment she'd realized she was Blessed, she'd also lost her bearings of the first person who'd given her hope they could be more than half-human abominations—because Sharek was not Blessed. He was not like her. She was alone, and this gruff drunkard from Kirsagan's cage was exactly the same kind of cursed.

Slowly, Elynor peeled her fingers from the table's edge and picked up her glass again, welcoming the sour sting of the alcohol this time. It helped steady her nerves. "I see," she said weakly.

Sam burst into deep laughter. "You have an opinion on the Blessed."

Elynor forced a smile to her lips. "An ever-changing one." They both drank this time, and Elynor slowly unthreaded her thoughts from one another. "You said you don't sail."

"Aye," Sam groaned as he finished the cup and immediately poured another. Elynor's liver panged in sympathy for his—or perhaps that was her stomach, protesting at how little she'd eaten all day, and now she was bailing sour milk into it.

"That compulsion all Blessed face," she said. "How do you resist it? And why?"

"The why is how," he said. "You pour. I'll talk." Elynor happily obliged. "Used to be I was the greatest seaman in Danje. I had my fill of sailing whenever I pleased. When I had my feet on land, I was making all sorts of things...lines and models, carvings and threads, your little compass there." He gave her a pointed look, and Elynor produced the compass and slid it across the table. Sam eyed it, but he didn't touch. "*Khul* Ergene took notice. So did her offspring, *Khuless* Mide and the boy...*Khulen* Tamachi."

Elynor nearly choked on her next sip. "Mide has a brother?"

"Had." Sam's haunted gaze anchored to the tabletop. "Stuck to me like a barnacle, that one. Always wanted to sail. Harbor first, under his mother's orders, but he wanted to go further...and that's like being ordered by the Crown Prince. So his sister covered our trail one night, and I took him out on the Caeruel."

Discordant notes of longing pinged through Elynor's head as if Sylvester sat next to her, plucking his *shudraga* out of tune. She could almost feel the *Khulen's* eagerness to be out on the waves, and more strongly than that, she felt *Sam's* eagerness. He must have taken very little convincing at all.

"Rogue wave came up from nowhere," Sam went on. "Drove us straight toward the wall. I was the best there was, but the sea was better. Broke apart my flagship and drowned half my crew. And the lad..." His hand rattled, and he banged the glass down so hard Elynor jumped. "Tamachi had half the mast speared through his chest. I'm no Blessed healer. Nothing I could do for him out on the sea, on that wreckage. Nothing but hold him." He topped off his cup, raised it to his lips, then lowered it. "I can still hear the lad's sobs."

Elynor let him drink in peace—what little peace a man with his past could find—while she digested the horrific story. No wonder the *Khuless* and her mother were so frosty with each other; Mide had let Tamachi go, putting her faith in this Blessed sailor, and it had ended in disaster.

"Lost everything after that," Sam grunted. "*Khul* took my ship, my *tolvors*, my good name. Left me this shop, but told me if I set sail one more time, it was the guillotine for me."

Rage shook in Elynor's chest. "That's not hers to decide."

"It is if all the ships in the harbor are hers."

Elynor finished off her glass, a slight hum working its way into her fingertips. She drummed them on the tabletop and poured herself another. "What about my father?"

"Ah, that codfish. Thought he was the chance to redeem my sorry hide." Sam peered at her with half-hooded, bloodshot eyes. "Alden commissioned that compass of yours and offered me a job teaching his heiress daughter how to sail. I may not have the faith in my skills I once did, but sailing's in my blood. I was willing to take the risk, to leave this land and start over where I was born. Cleaned myself up, sent him the compass, told him I'd smuggle aboard an Azorian vessel as soon as he sent word. But word never came."

Of course it hadn't. Because Rowan and Al-Morral had thwarted all their glorious endeavors.

This time, Elynor drank to silence the sting of that loss.

"Took word not long ago he'd died, untimely-like," Sam went on. "Can't say I took it well. Got so soused, I wandered out onto the coast just to be close to the waves. And that's where Kirsagan landed me, like a fish hooked out of the sea. And that's where you and I met."

Elynor finished her drink and refilled them both. The pleasant tingle in her hands was crawling toward her face now. "What a coincidence."

"Punishment, more like," Sam snorted. "No offense, but you're the worst thing that's ever happened to me. Had a bit of hope when I realized who you were, but I heard what you told the healer...no Fleet, no ship of your own. You've got nothing to offer, though I thank you for the *arkye*."

He toasted and drank. So did Elynor. Her racing thoughts had begun to slow for the first time in days, inviting fresh possibilities. Daring ones. "I can pay you. My father may be dead, but I'm still an heiress. I have coffers...name your price. But I *must* return to Erala."

"I watch your father's Fleet sail in and out of this harbor day by day, girl. Plead your charity off one of them. I don't sail."

Elynor changed tack at the hitch in his voice. "But you want to."

"Every Blessed wants what they're born for. Why do you think I do this?" Sam gestured with an unsteady sweep of his arm to the bottles. "Can't get drunk on the waves. Best get drunk on the milk instead."

Elynor had to admit, she saw the point of it. Every cup of *arkye* she tossed into the panged pit of her stomach helped silence the yearning to sail. But she had to convince him otherwise; she had to make him see this through her eyes.

Elynor tipped forward, folding her arms on the table's edge, her head spinning in a reckless whirlwind. "You aren't the only one who's lost much, Samwel Morlai. My father is dead and the Fleet rests in the hands of his killer. I'm here to thwart his plans, and then I'll return to Erala to thwart *him*. Believe me when I say I will let nothing stand in my way."

"Then why not sail yourself?"

Elynor's breath hitched. She wobbled back in her seat, brewing her most potent glare to fix him with. He met it with a crooked smile.

"Aye, that's what I thought. I saw the hints of it in your father's letter. Heard what your mother said to you, too. Not so different, are we, girl?" He topped off her glass and then his. "Both running from what we were made to be."

"I have never been anything but sacrosanct." Elynor's upper lip felt stiff, her mind humming and hissing. "It's how I've always lived. And how I'll die."

"Going to walk away from what you are, eh? Then how is it you intend to master the Fleet? One foot on land, one in the sea...can't have both. Quickest way to drown is not knowing your up from your down."

Elynor stared at him, simmering with anger and disdain even as her most brash plan of all leaped to the tip of her tongue. "You can have the Fleet."

Sam froze, the cup against his lips. "Beg your pardon?"

"The Azorian Fleet. It's yours if you take us home."

Her mind screamed at her to reconsider, to think of what she intended to do for herself now, with her inheritance, her legacy given up—but she banished it all beneath the drunken certainty that she would sort things out later. All that mattered now was winning Sam's aid.

He slowly lowered the cup again. "That is quite the generous offer. But it's not yours to give."

"It will be when Gavannon Al-Morral is dead," Elynor said. "And since I will be...refraining from the sea, it seems I will have no need of it."

Every word tore out of her like a blade unsheathed from her throat, cutting as it went. But she couldn't have both her humanity and the Fleet. And she was determined to remain Elynor Azorius of Bast, whatever the cost. Whatever that even meant anymore.

"You'll be in charge of your own charter again," she went on, forcing the temptations out on the long spool of a single breath. "The Caeruel at your feet. Free to go wherever you like, free to sail when and where you wish. You'll be responsible for the most powerful Fleet in any kingdom."

Her own dreams. Her own ambitions. She laid them all before him—for what use were they if she couldn't sail again?

Still. It felt like the coldest farewell to her father and to her old self. An agony like she'd never imagined clawed at her heart, trying to take the words back, but she refused.

Sam slowly sat forward, curling his hands together on the table, eyeing her shrewdly. "I'll want that in writing, girl."

"Whatever you wish," Elynor said. "But in exchange, you'll procure a vessel, sail us to Erala, and when our business is concluded, you and I will never speak again. And if you reveal my status to anyone in Erala…"

"I'm a sailor, not a pirate. Turning on my own kind's not in my blood." Sam rose, shockingly steady, as if the conversation had burned off the alcohol in his blood. Meanwhile the room tipped and swirled lazily around Elynor as she fought to track his movements. "Suppose you don't know much about contracts?"

Elynor barked with hoarse laughter, chafing the white scar on her thumb where she'd pressed her blood to Aeson Thalanor's paper, sealing her pact and hiring Sharek. "Just tell me where to sign."

***

An hour later, it was done. Elynor told Sam what to write and how to say it, ensuring there were no loopholes by which he could betray her. Then she signed and dated the contract, and once he'd done the same, Elynor took the open *arkye* bottle and stumbled toward the door. "I'll be back to check in on you."

"You do that."

"I don't trust you, Samwel Morlai," she added, though she had no reason not to.

He waved her off, tossing the other bottles into a barrel where they shattered and emptied. Elynor's hard-earned *tolvors* swelled the wood, and she choked on a muted jab of indignation. But she didn't have the clarity or strength to protest.

She wove down the street, bottle in hand, the bright eye of the moon blinking lazily down at her. Sam was right about one thing: she hardly knew up from down anymore. The palace was a long way away, and so was dawn. And so was Erala. And so was her father, her heritage, her dreams. The only things close tonight were shadows and doubt and grief.

Elynor stopped in the middle of the road and looked up at the cold stars. Tears rose on her lashes and snaked down her cheeks. "I'm sorry, Father. I had to do it. I can't be a Blessed."

A breath grazed her neck. "Elynor?"

She shrieked and spun, wielding the bottle like a club, aiming for a vaguely head-shaped lump in the darkness. Strong fingers caught her wrist, stalling her swing, and Elynor found herself squinting until Sharek's face distilled into focus from her wavering surroundings. "What are you doing, slinking up on me like that? I thought you were Rowan!"

"I followed you from the palace," Sharek said. "You left without telling anyone where you were going. I was concerned."

So he'd come all this way, and waited for hours while she haggled with Sam.

Waited. Just for her.

How many people in the world still cared enough to be concerned for her? To follow her and wait for her and escort her, because her safety meant something to them? Even if she was no longer sacrosanct, no longer *human*—

Of course that didn't matter to Sharek. It hadn't mattered when he was Blessed and she was his hirer, either. Somehow, he found means to forgive her, and to find things about her to believe in.

He was a good man, no matter what else he was. And she continued to hurt him by walking away from him every way she could. By humiliating him, and striking him, and doubting him.

Because she was *not* a good person.

Elynor didn't realize she'd said some of this aloud until she caught the faint flush on Sharek's cheekbones, and then he finally let go of her wrist and took her shoulders instead. "You are good, Elynor. A good woman. A good sailor. A good friend."

"I could be so much better."

"We could all be better. That's why the Empyreans give us long life: so that we have time to learn and grow."

"I hate your Empyreans."

Sharek's mouth twitched. "I know."

"But I don't hate you." They were so close, Elynor could smell mahogany and vetiver on his skin; he'd often smelled like that since the first time he'd bathed in Kaer Lleywel. Maybe he'd grown to enjoy the scent. And maybe she liked that she'd helped give him something to be fond of. "Whatever you are, Sharek, I think you're remarkable. I've never forgotten how you surprised and defeated my poor guard in nothing but a bathcloth that first night."

"Forgive me." Sharek's eyes glittered with dark humor. "Next time, I'll leave off the towel."

Elynor laughed and leaned her forehead into his chest. He stiffened at the contact, but then his hands slid from her shoulders to circle her back. And it was...lovely. Standing in the street, awash in moonlight, with his heart beating under her ear. "Thank you for following me."

"I would follow you to the depths and beyond, Elynor."

She believed him.

Elynor tilted her head back and watched the starlight glaze his hair and beard. He was tall—in fact, he seemed taller than usual tonight—but his mouth wasn't so far away. And with everything inside her still numb with what she'd done, and sizzling with the artificial courage only alcohol could bring, she found herself desperate to feel something real.

Elynor dropped the *arkye* bottle and slipped her shaking fingers into Sharek's hair. Slowly, she guided his face down toward hers.

Their noses brushed. She smelled the heat of his breath, felt it graze her lips, and frantic longing rose within her.

Then Sharek tensed. His fingers peeled back from her shirt, and he ducked his head away. "No. Not like this. Not when I can taste the *arkye* on your breath."

Abandonment crashed through Elynor, and something dark and ugly rose in her throat as she jerked backward. Her head spun, and she wobbled on her feet.

Sharek caught her shoulders again. She thought he said her name.

Then she vomited all over his boots.

Chapter Thirty-Seven

What Matters Most

There was no hope of making the trek back to the palace with Elynor as sick as she was, so Sharek brought her down to the coast.

She vomited many times as they went, into gutters and off docks, but she quieted when they came to the shore. The sand was a deep dust-brown, like Sharek's skin. Against its edge, Elynor was so pale she practically glowed. She sat with her feet draped in the water, and Sharek sat beside her, watching carefully for her to grow sick again. But she only stared with luminous eyes, made all the larger in the gaunt frame of her face, as the waves lapped against the harbor walls.

"Elynor," Sharek said, "you can't continue like this forever."

"I know." Her voice was calm, matter-of-fact. "But nothing makes sense anymore. I don't feel Blessed. I feel cursed. That name is a lie."

Sharek toed off his boots and sank his feet into the water, too. It was icy, but surprisingly refreshing. The heat hadn't quite puddled out of his core after he'd nearly kissed her—a moment sundered by good sense he nearly wished himself deprived of. "But what if the person you were before was the lie, and now you're becoming who you are meant to be?"

Elynor trembled, lowering her face to her bent knees. "I don't know how to become her without hating myself."

Sharek's heart ached with every beat. Not so long ago, he'd hated himself, too. Hated the killing Blessed he was. But when he looked at Elynor, he saw nothing that deserved hate.

He rested his hand on the back of her neck, and she moaned in relief. "You told me once that there was beauty in what I did," he said. "Beauty in my craft. There is beauty in yours, Elynor. When I saw you command that cog on the Caeruel, I saw strength in you like nothing I've ever witnessed before. I trusted you implicitly. When I said I'd follow you to the depths, I meant it. But I don't think you'd let me drown."

What was he even saying? It was a dull ramble to try and coax some joy back into her, some of the confidence she'd exuded when they'd sailed to Orleth. He wanted nothing so much as to breathe life back into Elynor Azorius.

Her shoulders rocked, and she burped dangerously, then settled with a groan. "You're a good man, Sharek Ransalor."

Moments later, she sagged sideways into his lap, fast asleep.

Sharek shed his cloak and draped it around Elynor's shoulders, and his Hunter's senses adapted immediately to the change in temperature; the cold slaked as his body warmed to silence it.

He should have been following Rowan tonight, not Elynor. He should have been trying to stop a war. But for now, he couldn't bring himself to think of anything but the water, and the stars, and Elynor's body curled against him.

And how he would give anything to help stop the war she fought against herself.

It was nearly dawn when Sharek finally slid into sleep, and then hardly any time seemed to have passed when he felt his arm being shoved, so violently it jerked the socket and sat him up with a groan. He wiped his eyes and looked at Elynor, who was scrambling back from him, her accusatory gaze snapping between him and the waves. "Why are we still here? Why did you not bring me back to the palace? You *know* how I feel about the water!"

Sharek held up his hands for peace. "You were too ill to be carried far. There was nowhere else to go but back alleys, and I preferred sleep over fighting off pickpockets and thieves all night."

Elynor opened her mouth, then shut it again and curled forward with a curse. "My head is *aching*."

"Sly will have some herbs for that." Sharek stood, offering his hand, and Elynor accepted it. She was unsteady, and paler than Sharek had ever seen her, but she stood stubbornly on her own two feet. When they clambered back onto the docks and went to the cobblestone street, she looked back, and Sharek did not think he imagined the longing in her eyes—or the resolve that firmed her mouth when she turned away from the water.

"Thank you, Sharek," she mumbled after they'd put a row of shops between them and the harbor. "For looking after me."

"It's what friends do." Though his experience with such things was tenuous, between Sylvester who wasn't always there, and Rowan who kicked him out of windows.

Elynor rubbed her arms as if against a chill, though she still wore his coat across her shoulders like a widow's shroud. "Yes, I suppose it is."

Sharek pocketed his hands as they passed a familiar keyhole-shaped door. "What were you doing with Sam yesterday, if I may ask?"

Some flash of emotion straightened Elynor's spine—pride, or an imitation of self-certainty even while her seams unraveled. "I was convincing him to ferry us back to Erala once we've thwarted Rowan."

His name in Elynor's mouth, full of hatred, raked uncomfortably down Sharek's spine. He'd long harbored that same resentment himself, but in recent days it had become more challenging to cling to. When he and Rowan were out hunting rats in the alleys or spearing fish in the shallows, taming Rowan's bloodlust by a Hunter's means, it felt different. It felt like belonging, something he so rarely had with Elynor and Sylvester when they were so entrapped in their own angles of this unfurling plot.

"Speaking of that gutless eel," Elynor said, "are you any closer to learning what he plans to do to start this war?"

Had he even searched for those answers lately? He told himself he was winning Rowan's trust, but it wasn't only that. He was reaping some personal gain from it as well. "Rowan won't give up his secrets lightly, particularly if he believes I'm searching for a means to thwart him."

"Well, keep looking. Killing him and killing Al-Morral go hand-in-hand."

"Then you ask me as my hirer."

They halted, tethered to the same thought, and the stream of foot travel broke around them as Elynor turned to face him. She banded his cloak tightly around her shoulders and stared at him with dark scores beneath her eyes. Sharek wondered if he looked half as sleepless. Half as weary. "Does it truly matter?"

Weeks ago, he might have said it didn't. But Sharek was beginning to realize he deserved more than her burdens to share as the man she'd hired to make swift end of her father's killer. He deserved her respect, and to stand on equal footing with her. He'd felt like they'd been there, that night above the falls when they were broken together. But she'd retreated so deeply into being Elynor Azorius, the sacrosanct heiress of the Fleet, that it was more like those first few days in Kaer Lleywel with her. Like all the common ground they'd crossed to meet one another in the middle had crumbled, and they were strangers again.

"It does," he said. "It does matter. Men don't deserve to live in cages, no matter how well-tended they may be. I will not return to a cage, Elynor. Not even to yours. I do this with you as your friend. But I can't be your hired hand anymore."

Her lips twisted in a humorless smile. "You sound like Rowan. His ideals. The ones he murdered my father for."

"And you're no better than Al-Morral if you would make a man believe he means more to you than he truly does, merely to keep him on your leash."

Elynor's eyes flew wide, and her lips parted in shock.

This time, Sharek anticipated the blow before it came. He caught her fist gently and did not take his eyes from hers. "*Do not* hit me to make your point. I'm not your target to beat on."

Elynor jerked back from him, tears lining her lashes. "Playing along with Rowan has made you cruel."

"No. It's made me sure of what I deserve. And this is not that."

And though it hurt in every inch of him, Sharek walked away from her, leaving her to follow him back to the palace.

Chapter Thirty-Eight

Solstice

For as long as Jamyson could remember, the Solstice had been his favorite day. He rarely woke with more of a spring in his stride. The kaer was always aflame with excitement and activity, servants scurrying to their tasks, the kitchens pumping out dishes and the nobles lacing the corridors with gossip and conversation. The regional accents of Ventia, Incandae, Teran, and Aqqor littered the air like foreign spice notes from one of Sylvie's favorite dishes, and everyone, no matter how politically inclined, looked forward to the King's speech and the banquet, the string quartet and dancing. It was the only time when all the bickering and land feuding between the lords and the disputes over the laws between the magistrates ground to a halt. For one night, they were all Eralanite. They all belonged.

It was for all those things—and for one other reason, far more personal—that Jamyson loved the Solstice.

But not this year.

This year, he crawled from the warm comfort of his bed to be greeted by a chilly, silent room and a stack of clothes left by the servant his Father had insisted tend to him, which Jamyson suspected was Al-Morral's idea of a spy. But the room was otherwise empty, the hearth burning dim. Frost laced the windows.

He was alone.

No Vestan sharpening blades and making wisecracks while Jamyson changed. No Elliott, Sylvie, Isaac, and Isla barreling through the door, already half-crazed with sugar, jumping up and down on his bed and only remembering at the last minute why this day was important to Jamyson in particular. And Esmae would be bound up in the kitchens all day; he'd never have a chance to see her.

Jamyson's heart was a pricked wineskin leaking misery into his empty chest. He finally belted on his ceremonial sword, bereft of Vestan's usual remarks about how he was threading the loops wrong, and let himself out into halls that did not teem with gossip for once. Instead a veil of whispers hung from the walls, thick and dismal as cobwebs in an unloved place; and everywhere he went, seeing to preparations and ensuring there were the proper number of Kingsgard at the barbican watching the bridge, and servants escorting the visiting dignitaries to their apartments, he was met with sunken stares and sudden silences that ached like old wounds.

The Winter Solstice was meant to be a time of joyous unity; but his father's mind sickness had pervaded the people, exposing them to His paranoia and panic. They knew by now of the royal siblings' fate and of the Queen's death, and the King's decrees, and had yet to realize they would be watching public hangings and signing a false treaty tonight. Jamyson felt nothing but the oppression of fear as he tended his duties, and no amount of forced grins or gaming wit dragged more than a reluctant smile from the guests.

By sunhigh, Jamyson's temples throbbed. The kaer overflowed with magistrates, lords, and ladies, and the dull murmur of nervous conversation only made the pain worse. He stole a moment indoors by one of the hallway hearths, warming his hands and feet at the fire. Snow had begun to sift down from lead-thick clouds, creating a picturesque landscape of the kaer.

It still felt wrong, beauty laced over broken bones. His siblings were dead. Vestan was dead. The Queen was dead. The King was losing His sanity, thread by thread. And Gavannon Al-Morral had positioned himself as one of the most influential figures in the kaer, opposing Jamyson's duties with his own booming presence.

He behaved as if the kaer was his; as if he was the King. And Jamyson would've decked him for it, for the fun and pleasure and the daring of it, if he hadn't known that instead of a hard reprimand and a night in the dungeons to cool his head, he'd pay with his life.

A boot scuffed the stone at the end of the hall, and Jamyson lurched back from the hearth, letting his hands drop from the mantel where he'd leaned. A rebuke was already on his tongue for whoever had caught him slacking from his duties, but it died when he recognized the figure standing at the mouth of the otherwise-empty corridor, looking both ways with palpable confusion.

For a moment, Jamyson did not move; he simply studied his father. Had the King always looked so gaunt? So disheveled? Perhaps the stress of the Solstice was expediting His deterioration; perhaps Jamyson ought to seek more of the King's time, not avoid Him. Instinct suggested they had little time left. Yet he stood rooted, watching the King wander aimlessly toward him, still studying the walls, and he couldn't bring himself to call out and feign cheer with the man who'd ordered His own children shot down from stone walls. Who'd hung both His wives.

The King was almost abreast of Jamyson and still didn't seem to notice him. He paused and turned back, arms akimbo at His waist, and Jamyson let out a silent, steadying breath. Then he stepped forward and touched the King's shoulder. "Father?"

The King swiveled slowly to peer at him, a waft of herbs on His breath that made Jamyson's stomach churn. Orson had clearly prescribed Him something, but by the stink of it, the King had taken far too much of whatever it was. Still, Jamyson didn't think that was the reason for the glazed, confused look in His eyes.

"Hello, yes," the King said. "I was just going for a walk, and I found…it's strange, I don't think I've ever visited this part of the kaer before."

Jamyson's heart sank. This was the only corridor from the King's tower to the audience chamber. His father must have walked it thousands of times.

"It's the drapes," Jamyson said lamely. "The servants changed them for the Solstice feast, and the color patterns on the walls make all these corridors look different. I've felt turned around all day, too."

The King's confusion softened into a relieved smile. "Of course. Naturally. Walk with Me to the audience chamber, will you, Jamyson?"

Jamyson turned the King in the proper direction. "Of course, Your Eminence."

If King Marcus sensed the tension that hemmed the air, He made no mention of it. His gaze fluttered from the arched ceiling to the windows on the right, looking out over the courtyard where dignitaries funneled inside to take their rooming assignments from the steward. "So many people. They'll spend half the night signing the treaty."

Jamyson saw the sliver of opening and pounced. "Then perhaps we shouldn't make them sign anything, Father. Forego the treaty and the hangings. It's been a long day, they're exhausted from traveling, and You're right...the feast will go on for an eternity if they're all signing."

The King's eyes swiveled to him, mired between looks of impatience and suspicion. "Jamyson, that treaty is for the good of us all. We've had too many enemies rise up around us of late. We cannot risk any others."

Jamyson wanted to roar in His face that the greatest enemy of all had risen up at His left hand, a sea-serpent named Gavannon Al-Morral, and He was blissfully unaware. He'd opened His eyes to lies and blinded Himself to truth.

But the King was ill, unable to grasp these things. And there was something sharp and insistent prodding Jamyson's chest from the inside, like a sword suspended over his heart, reminding him with every beat that if he pushed the King too far, he'd be the one publicly executed tonight.

So he forced yet another lying smile and dipped his head. "Come with me, Father. I'll have my new manservant bring a razor and mirror to the chamber. He gives the most excellent shave."

The King laid a hand on Jamyson's arm. It trembled slightly. "You are a good man, Jamyson. Don't think I've forgotten why today is so important to you."

Jamyson's heart lifted by the slightest detestable increment. It didn't matter why today was important, after he'd lost so much. But he couldn't silence the traitorous bit of his heart that inflated with the hope that the father he'd once loved just might not have left him entirely after all.

Whatever levity remained in the kaer was gone by sundown. It suffocated under the sheer number of cloaked bodies gathered on the inner mezzanines above the courtyard from the apartments and smaller ballrooms and meeting chambers, every one as silent as a corpse. They all watched with wide-eyed disbelief as the Kingsgard marched a dozen nobles to the gallows erected across from the King's viewing balcony.

Just as on the day the royal siblings were pronounced dead, Jamyson stood at the King's right hand, Al-Morral on his left, with a flawless view of the faces below. Jamyson wished the dusk would swallow the sheen of their tears and dull the fear in their eyes. He wished he'd managed to slip them a bit of whatever separated his father from His troubles now and again. He wished he could do *something* without damning himself to share their fate and ridding Al-Morral of his only opponent, and the King of His only foil.

And yet the terrible weight of responsibility on his shoulders was nothing compared to the burden of fear on the peoples' backs as they watched the nooses slip over the throats of these noblemen and women, distant relations with whom Jamyson had crossed paths and words over the years, and resented from time to time—but he'd never asked for this. He gripped his hands tightly behind his back and measured his breathing as the King began to speak.

"The men and women you see before you are charged guilty of consorting with the traitor Queen and her treacherous offspring to overtake the Holy Throne." King Marcus had rallied some strength to His voice, so now it cracked like a whip against the backs of His dignitaries. But His tone was monotonous and practiced, reciting every word with care. How many times had He and Al-Morral gone over this so the King would not falter in His speech and give way to doubt? "Let this be a lesson to all who see and hear of it: the King's wisdom will not be mocked. The sovereignty of the Throne will not abide challenge. And anyone who questions either will find the answers they seek at the end of a short rope."

The King made a cutting motion with his hand. Jamyson wanted to look away, but he forced himself not to. He kept his gaze on the gallows as the bottom went out. He let the gasps and sobs from the balconies soak into his ears, and reminded himself with every pulse of blood in his temples that he had to stop this. It was no longer serving Erala to keep the King's secret.

Somehow, he had to find a way to remove his father from power without handing another inch of it to Al-Morral. It was the only way to spare the kingdom's suffering.

The thought consumed him as the King announced the beginning of the feast and everyone straggled indoors, the gallows still creaking sadly below them. The King stepped inside first, and Al-Morral and Jamyson turned to follow Him, locking gazes as they swiveled.

"Delicate constitution, Sire?" the Fleetmaster asked.

"I think I could stomach another well-deserved death." Jamyson flashed an arm for Al-Morral to go first.

There was none of the usual chatter as the people filled up the kaer's largest ballroom. Terrified eyes followed Jamyson, Al-Morral, and the King to the head table, and the scrape of seats pulling out from the three-sided table was the only noise for a long while. Jamyson had seen more lively conferences after funerals; his gut twisted with pity for his people, rage on their behalf, and a determination that gave space for little else.

For the entirety of the meal, he ate little, and plotted instead. His mind traveled through a score of excuses to dethrone the King, each one less likely than the last. But it was a welcome relief from the pained, awkward silence of which his father seemed oblivious. For the first time in memory, Jamyson just wanted the Solstice feast to end so he could slide back into the comfort of his bed and dream of a better tomorrow.

Then the King dabbed His lips and pushed out His chair, reaching into His pocket for a scroll. His eyes traveled the room as He stood, and Jamyson's heart began to pound.

"Lords and ladies," the King read aloud from the scroll, "magistrates and madams. Here we're gathered from all corners of Erala, separate in our duties and dwellings but one in spirit and mind, to celebrate the end of another prosperous year and dream together of a glorious future."

The words of the Solstice speech clashed so corrosively with the atmosphere of the room that Jamyson wanted to sink into his seat and vanish. When he'd written those words, he'd never dreamed everything could go so horribly wrong for Erala. And even though the nobles didn't know he'd written this speech, he felt personally responsible for every disbelieving glance traded between them.

"Yet even as we look to that future, the present haunts us," the King went on. "How can we look ahead to a safe and bright tomorrow when today is fraught with danger and uncertainty?"

Jamyson pressed his elbows into his armrests and slowly swiveled his head toward his father.

Those were not his words. He had not written those things.

"Erala is not well," King Marcus said. "It is a sick kingdom poisoned by unbelief and heresy: prayers to the Empyreans among the common folk. Lies about the Throne's true power. Talk of fallibility in its Kings."

The silence was so absolute, Jamyson could only hear the crash of his own pulse. *Who wrote this? Whose speech is He reading?*

"That is why this Solstice is one of affirmation," the King read. "Of each of you affirming your loyalty to the Holy Throne. I call on you now to prove your devotion to Me and to My reign by signing your names to a treaty…"

Jamyson stopped hearing after that. His gaze sought Al-Morral behind his father's back, and he found the Fleetmaster beaming up at the King like a proper sycophant, hanging hinged on his every word. But that was not adulation in his eyes.

It was ambition.

"I will lay out the declaration of loyalty before Me," the King said, "and each of you will sign it. Anyone who does not put his name to paper will hang at sunrise. After you sign, you are free to drink and dance to your heart's content."

Not a whisper of sound as He gestured to Al-Morral, who produced the declaration and laid it on the table. The King sat, and for a moment, no one moved. Jamyson could feel the tension bracketing his father's body as He waited for someone to show Him loyalty.

The magistrate of Bast was the first to rise, and like a dark and dour wave, others began to follow. They trickled up toward the table, barely lifting their eyes as they signed and hurried away. The King gestured to the minstrels, and they struck up a tune far too cheery for this moment.

Jamyson was suffocating. He was in *agony* as he leaned toward the King. "What about the speech I wrote, Father?"

The King offered him a vacant stare, then a smile to mask His confusion. "It was an excellent speech, Jamyson. But I found Gavannon's to be more in line with our present struggles."

Of course He did.

Jamyson stood abruptly, and the King's eyes followed him, still gently bemused. "Where are you going?"

"To dance," Jamyson said stiffly.

But he didn't; while the servants cleared away the tables, forcing the nobles to stand in a great cluster that took up half the room, Jamyson couldn't bring himself to do anything but hover in the mouth of the side doorway leading out to the gardens and watch as they signed their lands and lives away to the Holy Throne. And he watched Al-Morral, the man who had ambitions on Jamyson's birthright.

First Elynor's. Now his.

Jamyson would kill him.

After some time, the hateful haze cleared and he realized Al-Morral was not paying any attention to the signing; his eyes were riveted across the room, watching one of the noblewomen. She was stunningly beautiful, honeyed hair spilling over the bare arch of freckled shoulders that peeked through her satin dress, her kohl-lined eyes taking in the proceedings with the greatest ease Jamyson had seen all evening.

Then Al-Morral rose, excused himself to the King, and hurried through the grand entrance to the outer hall. After a few moments, the woman pushed to the front of the line, scratched her name to the paper, and disappeared as well.

Jamyson leaned his shoulder to the doorframe and rubbed his mouth slowly, watching her go. In the flash of changing partners on the dance floor, she vanished.

Jamyson motioned one of the Kingsgard to him. "Who was that woman Al-Morral just left with?"

"That would be Abigale Cainwell, I believe, Sire," the man said.

"Of Guild Cainwell?"

The man nodded. "That's the one."

The Guild who supplied all his father's armor and most of His garments these days. Unsurprising that the Cainwells had sent their daughter to represent the family at the Solstice, but curious the way Al-Morral had stared at her.

Jamyson watched couples float past him in a familiar waltz, and with every strain of the music the matter of Al-Morral and Abigale slid further from his mind. Melancholy replaced suspicion, and despite the false smiles and the terror in every set of eyes he found himself dreaming of Solstices past. Of joy flowing as freely as the wine. Of his father laughing with the Queen at the head table while Elliott begged dances off pretty cousins and Sylvie gathered a crowd of boys and girls to discuss philosophy and politics while they devoured an entire cake by themselves.

He remembered twirling Isla in his arms and spinning Isaac on his shoulders, slamming back drinks with Vestan in the corner until they were both too deliriously happy to have a care in the world. He remembered begging Elynor to dance the requisite waltzes with him because he couldn't dance with the woman he really wanted, but his closest friend made an excellent partner and she always made a game of trying to pinch him while they twirled. And he remembered catching Esmae's eye across the room, making faces at the Queen's terrible jokes until they were both choking on forbidden laughter.

Swallowing the lump in his throat, Jamyson turned away from the dim, panic-addled room and strode out into the garden.

The snow had already laid down a thick blanket on the grass and hedges and the stone carvings that littered the inner yard, and more still fell. Strands of cut glass in every shade dangled between the dormant *Aljalam* imports throughout the garden, weaving a net of fantastic color through which the torchlight of the kaer's many levels fell. But Jamyson's heart still hung dark, the chasm in his middle yawning wider with every step.

He retreated to the edge of the music, to the end of all mimicry and pantomime, where he was alone beneath the stars and the firelight on a snow-furred terrace deep in the garden. He leaned against its railing and put his head down. Tears rolled from his cheeks and dabbed holes in the snow on the ledge.

"Jamyson?"

He didn't look up at the sound of Esmae's voice. He curled his gloves tighter around the railing as his legs shook. "It isn't the same without them."

Her hand grazed his back. "I know. I keep watching for them between the dancer's legs so they won't be stepped on. And then I remember..."

The snow misted around them, muffling the world in a thick, cold shawl.

"I feel like I've lost my shadow." Jamyson lifted his head to squint at the white-masked garden walls. "Like a piece of who I am is gone."

Esmae's fingers trailed lightly up and down his spine. "I'm so sorry, Jamy."

"It's not just them. It's Him. I've lost my father." He snorted wetly and wiped his nose on his sleeve. "He doesn't even remember what day it is. Not one mention this year."

"He doesn't. But I do."

Jamyson turned to face Esmae, and his breath caught. Here beneath these lights, here in the snow, she was more beautiful than ever—more than any satin-wrapped heiress. With smudges of chocolate on her cheeks and her red hair straggling loose from its handkerchief, she was a vision of perfection.

"I wish I could give you back your siblings and Vestan, but I'm afraid all I have is this." She pulled a small wooden case from the pocket of her slave's uniform and held it out to him. "Happy birthday, Jamyson."

His eyes wet again, Jamyson slid the top from the box and found a blade glinting back at him from the velvet interior: a black opal dagger, small enough to fit into the seam of his boot. "Where did you get this?"

Esmae shrugged. "I had Vestan purchase it for me. A kindly old woman paid me a few *duais* some months ago when I helped her carry her things at the market."

Gratitude lit the cold depths of Jamyson's heart like a forge as he took the dagger from the box and weighed it in his hand. It was small but wickedly sharp, its serrated edge grinning in the moonlight. He couldn't help but smile back at it before he tucked it safely into his boot and stuffed the box away in the waistband of his trousers.

"Thank you, Esmae." He took both her hands and squeezed them. "For everything you do. For everything you *are*."

She guided his arms around her back and slid hers around his neck. "You deserve to be remembered, especially today. Even if I'm the only one left in this kaer who can do it."

His tears dampening the sleeve of her uniform, Jamyson stroked his knuckles up the back of her arm. His hand wandered along the curve of her elbow, fingers separating hers from behind his neck so that they could entwine. He swayed them gently to the memory of music finding them between the hedges in this sanctuary of light and snow, with the spirits of his dead siblings and his closest friends, his stepmother and Old Anna twirling and those who'd hung today lurking around them in furrows their steps had created.

And then Jamyson and Esmae danced, a waltz for the lost and forgotten, a tribute to those who could never dance again.

Chapter Thirty-Nine

Princebreakers

Gavannon felt that glee might tug his heart from his mouth while he watched the nobles of Erala sign away their lands and loyalty to the Holy Throne—which would someday be his.

In that moment, he was certain he had never been happier, nor could he ever be happier.

And then he spotted Abigale through the crowd, decorated in light and smiling like a Queen, and his heart nearly stopped altogether before it burst forward in a wild, joyous gallop, and his mind raced for any excuse to be out of the King's presence for just a moment.

In the end, he chose the call of nature, not caring in the least if it seemed juvenile. Come morning, the King wouldn't even remember.

Gavannon waited out in the hall, pulse crashing with anticipation, and by the time Abigale joined him he could no longer contain his happiness. He swooped her up in his arms and spun her, his face nearly buried in her chest, and she laughed with her hands gripping his shoulders and her feet sailing behind her.

"I've missed you," he said into the dip of her bosom. "It's been too many days apart, my love."

"Gav, you absolute cad!" Abigale cackled. "Put me down this instant!" He settled her feet on the floor, and her mischievous eyes glinted as she framed his face with her hands. "Good. Now I can kiss you."

And she did, the dry aroma of wine on her breath, her fingers finding their way lazily through his hair. Gavannon leaned them back into a niche in the wall and let his hands wander along the lace ties of her dress, reveling in her curves until she drew back to peer into his eyes again.

"The speech was yours, wasn't it?" she said. "I heard your cleverness in every word."

"*Almost* every word," Gavannon said. "The beginning was the prince's. I had to concede it was a good place to start."

"Good enough." Abigale's eyes shadowed slightly. "But it's only a soft blow to his pride, Gav. Have you had any luck finding a way to remove him?"

"Not yet. The King is obscenely determined to trust him." Gavannon took her hand. "Walk with me, will you? And tell me what in the King's name you're doing here. I never expected to see you tonight."

Abigale shrugged as they started down the hall, fingers entwined. "I didn't expect to come. But then I started to think of the Guild, and how it'll be mine to command once Father is dead. He always brought me to these kinds of feasts as a decoration to be looked at, but now it's time I attended as the future head of Guild Cainwell. So I brought myself."

"I'm glad you did." He kissed her knuckles. "And you're right, your presence here shows your ambition and incentive. Have you made any new connections? Found a client or two?"

Abigale rolled her eyes. "Unfortunately not. All these nobles are shut up with fright."

"As well they should be. They see the same madness in the King as we do. But that's to our advantage…it will make them that much more likely to turn on Him when the time comes."

"But turning on Him is not enough," Abigale argued. "They must turn away from Him and to *you*, not to the Crown Prince."

Gavannon raked a hand back through his lard-slicked hair. "Convincing a sickly King to trust me with the world is one thing. Convincing all the people to accept a ruler who isn't descended from the Kings of Yore…that's another."

"They'll follow you once they're given enough reason to doubt the Venator lineage. All you have to do is cut out the legs from beneath the King and the prince in quick succession." Abigale squeezed his hand as they mounted a staircase to the inner balconies that looked down over the kaer's garden. "We're so close, Gav. Just a few more deft shoves, and this wall of lies and trickery will fall. Then we'll climb over it, straight to the Throne."

Gavannon froze.

Abigale, dragged to a halt by his hand in hers, twisted to peer up at him. "Gav?"

He laid a finger to her lips and nodded down into the garden.

There was a terrace in the heart of the snow-skirted foliage, separated from view of the Solstice ballroom by several hedges and rows of *Aljalam* trees—and the prince was down there, dancing with someone. They moved with the grace of nobility, clearly trained from a young age in the formal dances. But the woman's steps were arrested as if by an injury, and the prince moved seamlessly to compensate.

Gavannon tugged Abigale closer to the railing, squinting through the snow to see them. The prince twirled his partner and dipped her low, and she threw her head back in laughter. A handkerchief slipped from her brow, exposing locks of fiery hair.

"The Queen's slave." Hatred beat in Gavannon's temples like a drum.

"The one who caught you slipping the belladonna into her armoire?" Abigale hissed.

Gavannon nodded, his mouth dry with shock as Jamyson spun the woman upright again. Then he cupped the back of her neck and brought his mouth down to hers.

Abigale squeaked with shock, then muffled it with her hand. Gavannon gripped the railing as a cresting wave of triumph smashed through him, more thrilling than any chase on the high seas.

"This is it," he breathed as the pair in the garden started to dance again. "This is how we bring Jamyson to his knees."

Chapter Forty

The Villain

After her argument with Sharek in the mariner's district—which she thought about as little as possible—Elynor spent a great deal of her time alone, fighting to feel useful.

She had no chores to do or *arkye* to buy and she was too weary for the complex dance required to spin information from the *Khul* about her opinion of Erala. Some days she sat in their room watching the clouds trace the sky like whitecap on an endless ocean, and contemplated the gnawing ache in her middle—that terrible, fanged, hungry thing that had replaced her heart and was slowly eating away at the flesh around it, leaving her puddled with agony and spite.

She couldn't bring herself to smile at Sylvester's jokes or to apologize to Sharek or to bind herself to the cause they were all fighting for.

Perhaps this was what it truly was to be Blessed: to live numb and frightened, to be unmoored and at the mercy of winds that only blew against her.

But hadn't she also been Blessed when Sylvester had made her laugh? When her father had taught her to trust the sea? When she and Jamyson had shared secrets on balconies, when she'd gossiped and giggled with Abigale until their sides hurt, when Sharek had caught her in his arms after he'd slaughtered the Overseer and his guards in the mines to save her?

She had been Blessed then, and her life had been full of good things. Was it possible that it was not her nature, but her perception of her nature, that was the cause of her misery?

When those notions crept in, it felt as if King Marcus loomed in the corner of the room, hissing accusations of heresy and treason.

Finally, she couldn't endure it any longer. Waking alone yet again in their too-small chamber, Elynor cast off her blanket, stabbed her feet into her shoes, and all but ran from the palace.

Her feet carried her down to the harbor, but she told herself it was not the water she sought—it was Samwel Morlai. The man needed looking in on, after all. But even his very nature seemed to convict her; for she found him in his shop, not a bottle of *arkye* in sight, looking over maps and plans of something laid out in layers.

The moment she recognized its detailing, the words burst from Elynor's lips: "You can't man a schooner by yourself."

"Matter of fact, I can, girl." Sam's voice was rougher than she'd heard it last, but also clearer. "Rigged and built for two, but with a few touches and my own quick feet, I can bring it down to one."

Elynor studied the walls, the empty shelves, everything but the plans. Everywhere she looked was a reminder that Samwel Morlai, extraordinary drunk and bottom-feeding loach, was slowly swimming up to the surface, leaving her behind in the silt below the darkest fathoms of this treacherous sea. "I see you've stopped drinking."

"Aye." Sam didn't look up from the plans. "No need for the stuff. Sailing fills the body better than any spirits."

"I wouldn't know."

"Wouldn't, or won't let yourself?"

Elynor scowled. "Where will you get this schooner, anyway? I thought all your ships were repossessed by the *Khul* when her son died."

It was a cruel blow, but Elynor was desperate, punching at shadows to somehow be powerful. If all she could command was the conversation, she would captain it like a Fleetmaster.

But Sam didn't even look up when he said, "Stashed this one in a chink in the harbor wall when I saw the storm on the horizon. Couldn't bear to be parted with it."

Elynor folded her arms. "Sentiment?"

"Aye. Built it with my daughter."

Elynor's arms fell from their cross. "I didn't know you had children."

"Don't anymore." Sam rolled the plans. "Right, I'm off. If you came to lecture a drunk, I'll point you to the nearest tavern. If you came for company, best follow me."

Cheeks hot with embarrassment, Elynor readied the retort that she'd just come to check on him and now she'd be on her way. But the thought of their cavernous room at the palace loomed dismally before her, and what leaped from her tongue instead sounded almost like a challenge. "Lead the way."

She struggled to shut out the gentle lap of he water against the wharfs and shoreline as they wound through the mariner's district and climbed the stone clefts where the street ended. Sam had to check his stride to accommodate Elynor's sore leg, but he never complained; perhaps the excitement of seeing his schooner lent him endless patience. If only her own feelings were so simple to placate these days.

They finally reached the sand bars that ran abreast of the wall, and Elynor almost turned back yet again. But something stronger than boredom drove her hard on Sam's heels until he turned abruptly and climbed into a large seam broken into the wall. It was little less than a cave, water breathing into it and receding, and at the aft of the triangular divot a long, sleek shape crested and sank with the tide—the schooner, its masts nearly scraping the stone roof when it rose.

Elynor halted on the slick stones at the cave's edge, the sight of that depths-black hull and cherrywood deck bringing tears to her eyes. "What do you call her?"

"*Seabird*," Sam said. "My daughter named her."

The cruel irony wrenched a harsh laugh from Elynor. She waved off Sam's glance. "And this *Seabird* will bring us home, do you think?"

"She'll sail us anywhere I ask."

"Oh, wonderful. At least something around here will do as it's bidden." Elynor could coax no real vigor to her words, but Sam gave her that look she'd come to know in the wagon, swimming with unspoken things, as he swung aboard the schooner.

"Something on your mind, girl?"

Elynor used the distance as an excuse to sidle closer to the schooner. No sense shouting when conversation would do. "Too much on my mind."

"You know what would clear your mind would be a bit of sailing."

Elynor glared up at him. "I think I've made it clear how I feel about sailing anymore, Master Morlai."

"Aye. But we aren't talking about feelings. We're talking about who you are at the depths." He brandished a crooked finger in her direction. "Who taught you to fear that? Your father?"

"No! My father loved me for who I am. *What* I am."

"Ah. Your companions, then."

"Not them." Elynor had a blurry memory of Sharek telling her something about her craft—about how there was beauty in it—but the whole image felt like a dream.

"Your King."

Elynor flicked Sam a glance and found him watching her with understanding written on the planes of his face—and understanding edged too close to pity for her liking.

"Being Blessed is a curse," she rasped. "I would dare you to tell me otherwise after what you've endured."

"Don't blame my craft for that." Sam snapped the plans open on the schooner's deck. "Blame my poor choices. Blame the *Khul* for passing judgement. The craft is just a part of me. It doesn't decide my fate."

"But it does shape it."

"Aye. So does every choice I make. That doesn't make me cursed. Makes me no different from the sacrosanct. I'm only a villain in this story if I choose to be."

Elynor almost barked back at him to define what a villain was, then. What made them villainous?

But a quiet notion stopped her tongue.

It was villainous to use one's friends for one's own gain. To compel them against their will. To wield them as a weapon against greater foes, rather than trying to sort and solve things together. It was villainous to murder for gain…but not all death was of the body.

Elynor slowly sank to a crouch on her heels, and as she rested her hand on the black, opalescent water, she saw Sharek's face in her mind: the hurt, the betrayal that had framed his features when they'd argued in the street. After all this time, after all they'd endured together, she'd tried to wield him as a weapon once more; she'd yanked at the threads of his agency, tried to shape him again into a killing Blessed at her command to use against Rowan and Al-Morral, rather than trusting him to sort it out the best way for himself. All because he wouldn't do everything she wanted, the way she wanted it done, just like Al-Morral had killed Alden because he wouldn't do things his way.

If she came to see more profit in destroying Sharek's heart to meet her own ends than in working with him for a solution, she would never be any better than the man who'd ripped her father from her arms.

Ripples stirred the water as tears raced down Elynor's hot cheeks, dripping off the line of her jaw.

"Something wrong, girl?" Sam called down to her.

"I don't know how not to be the villain in my own story," she croaked. "How to stop treating the people around me like weapons against my enemies."

"Easier than you think." Sam's face appeared above the schooner's side, his eyes finding her in the gloom. "You let go of the idea you're in command of anything at all."

It truly did sound simple. But if she let go of those last few threads of duty and ownership that bound her to Sharek, he might drift away forever. And she would be utterly alone.

***

Elynor was glad of the long walk back from the harbor, up the honeycomb streets to the palace that evening; glad of the time to ponder why losing Sharek was so terrifying that she might fall on her own blade just to keep him with her. Was it because he was the only one who couldn't walk away from her by choice? Or was there something more?

Darkness swarmed the sky by the time she returned to the inner courtyard, and Elynor paused on the sleek, glinting tiles, tilting her head back to look up at the stars. Long ago, her father had taught her to navigate by those distant paths; yet here in Orleth, they didn't look quite the same. The ways charted into the sky were foreign in this place.

Her way forward was foreign. Her entire being was foreign.

Her hand hunted at the dip of her throat where Sharek's talisman had hung during her captivity. Were he in her position, he would have prayed—something she no longer resented him for. He prayed to his Empyreans, and he continued to rise from the fire each time fate dropped him into it. She prayed to nothing, worshiped the Throne and the King, and she'd become His sworn enemy. How could she blame Sharek for trusting in something better and brighter than himself?

"I need help," she whispered to the darkness within her where all her hope and belief in the way of things had once hung. "Relief. Deliverance. *Something*."

The words felt like screaming into an abyss. Utterly absurd.

"*Anything*?" Elynor's voice cracked. "If you're real, why would you listen to Sharek and not to me?"

The rustling of wind in the courtyard seemed to laugh at her. And why should the Empyreans, if they truly existed, give ear to an heiress who'd snubbed them and their Hunters and Blessed as heretics? They could laugh while she sank to the depths, and she wouldn't blame them. What sort of selfish woman only gave ear to power when she lost her own way? The whole world, it seemed, had turned its back on her. Why not the Empyreans as well?

She returned to their room chilled by more than just the night, and found Sharek outside, leaning against the door with folded arms. He didn't face the direction she'd come, but Elynor was certain he'd had every sense trained that way. A thin beam of gratitude sparked in her chest. "You didn't have to wait for me this time."

"Yes, I did."

No question or conviction in his voice. It was the first words they'd spoken to one another since their argument. Since she'd almost hit him. Since he'd walked away from her.

Elynor halted beside him. "I've spoken to Samwel. Plans are being made. We'll have our way home in the end."

"Good. I'm glad." Sharek turned toward her, leaning his shoulder and head now against the door. "And you?"

"What of me?"

His amber eyes lit into her, and with a stomach-flipping jolt as if she stood atop the mariner's honeycomb again, Elynor realized she couldn't remember the last time his gaze had held the dull look of an unloved ship's deck. He brightened even as she sank deeper into despair.

"I'd like to help you," Sharek said. "If I can."

A harsh laugh burst from Elynor's lips. "You know what we are, Sharek. What we must do. Even if this all goes exactly to plan, what then? Our paths are destined to diverge."

And then the laughter died from her lips at the next thought that slid into her mind, lodging at its forefront like a river's barricade, stopping all other sense behind it.

And all at once, she understood herself. Understood *everything*.

She couldn't afford to love one more thing that was going to walk away from her. Her heart would not stand to be broken another time. And that was the precipice she stood on. One more perilous notion, one more of those rare, devastating smiles, one more kind gesture or concerned look or moment when he understood her so absolutely, like her own face in the mirror...

Just one more, and she would fall utterly in love with Sharek Ransalor.

And then he would walk away, or he would face death again. One way or another, he'd be gone, and she would break in pieces. She could not need him, or Sylvester, or her mother. She could not need the sea, because that would be taken from her if the King or Aeson Thalanor ever learned what she truly was. The only way to not be left wanting with a broken heart was to never want anything at all...not even the Hunter standing before her, his inscrutable eyes traced with moonlight while he pondered the last thing she'd said.

She couldn't allow it to matter whether he walked away or not.

"I believe we're both destined for things, Elynor," Sharek said at last. "But whether we look after one another is not written into the paths the Empyreans laid for us to walk. It is a choice we make for ourselves."

Elynor swallowed the lump in her throat and forced the words that came in a choked whisper—the words that would protect what few pieces remained of her fragile heart: "Then *I* choose to walk away."

Sharek's eyes flickered, casting briefly away. But he only said, "As you wish, Milady."

And then he held open the door to their chamber and waited for her to walk inside.

Chapter Forty-One

A Familiar Cage

Elynor was drifting away from them, and Sharek was powerless to stop it. Sylvester encouraged him she would come around—women had their moods that seemed to come and go with the tides—but even as inexperienced as he was in the ways of women, Sharek knew this was not like that.

Elynor spent most of her time alone now, napping in their room, or she was down in the mariner's district with Samwel Morlai, keeping watch on his progress.

She was avoiding them, and it made his spirit ache.

"Ah, I know *that* look." Rowan's voice pulled him back to the Orlethian tavern they'd sequestered themselves in, trading the palace's fine gold-and-jade columns and perfumed incense for the familiar wooden walls and assertive reek of a common tavern. It rubbed harshly at Sharek's nose, as most scents did, but he could still smell the savory aroma of the spice district underneath it.

Empyreans. He'd never really noticed just how sharp his senses *were*.

"Sharek, if you're going to stare into the void and daydream, I'm going to go find a woman who will pay me a bit of attention."

Sharek rolled his eyes, coming back to the small table, to his cup of unfermented milk and Rowan's mischievous smirk with the bottle of *arkye* in his hand. "I forget sometimes that you begin to perish in increments if *someone* isn't paying attention to you."

"I think it's because I was the only son of my mother."

"So was I. Yet I prefer *not* to be noticed."

"Yes, but *that's* because you might actually have a fatal aversion to socializing." Rowan topped off his cup of *arkye* and took a long swig. "We've been in this tavern for an hour and you've spoken exactly six words until this moment. Even for you, that's an impressive record. Troubles with your heiress?"

Sharek's ears warmed. "She isn't mine."

"But you wish she was." Rowan wagged his brows, and Sharek merely shrugged.

He wouldn't tell Rowan the depth of his feelings—he'd told no one save the Empyreans—but he wouldn't lie, either. Lying would put Rowan on edge with him.

"You know it can never be." Rowan's voice was calm and factual, the same tone he'd often used to convey throat-slitting techniques or to remind Sharek that killing was not wrong, for the hundredth time. "She'll never be able to look at you and see you as anything but the power that runs in your veins. That's how the sacrosanct are."

Sharek's tongue knotted around itself. He'd wanted to believe that in the crossing to Orleth, in the days beyond that, things had changed. But with every step Elynor took away from them, Sharek felt more like her hired hand again. In the street when they'd argued, and on the walkway outside their room, it had seemed an ocean separated them. And now he wondered if what pushed between them was something Rowan could never comprehend.

Elynor had despised Sharek when she'd learned he was a Blessed carrying a Hunter's talisman against his chest and their prayers in his heart. How much more now that she knew he was a Hunter himself?

No wonder she would choose to walk away; no wonder she had looked at him so differently that night when he'd waited for her after her visit with Sam. He hadn't been able to pinpoint the emotion in her face—and he blamed his lackluster upbringing in the Sanctum for that—but now that Rowan's words dug into his heart, he realized what it must have been.

Disgust. She was disgusted by what he was, perhaps disgusted even by how her *arkye*-addled mind had suggested she kiss him that night they'd slept by the water.

A Blessed she could tolerate, but not this. She'd as good as told him when she'd mentioned what they were.

Sharek chugged the milk to cover the sudden dryness in his throat.

"You're right." He set his glass aside. "She would be better off if she went back to Erala and *I* stayed. As far from her as possible."

"Well," Rowan swirled his glass. "Perhaps not."

Cold dread chased the drink down Sharek's throat. "What do you mean?"

"I heard about Aeson's new rules," Rowan said. "After I disappeared, he went on a spree to train up Seekers. You know, those Blessed who would go to the homes of hirers who stole or forfeited another Blessed and take the due out of their sorry hides? Just a discouragement, I've never heard of it being followed through on. But if your Elynor ever decides to return to Erala without you in tow…"

Horrific notions seared through Sharek's mind: visions of Bracerath's Landing glazed with Elynor's blood as some Blessed servant of Aeson Thalanor demanded payment for Sharek's loss from her body. "She would never have agreed to such a contract. She knows better."

"If you really believe Aeson gives them a choice, you need a drink more than I do." Sharek didn't realize he'd jumped to his feet until Rowan flashed both hands and said, "Calm down, brother. It doesn't matter as long as you're both living here."

"Unless they send a Seeker *here*. If it doesn't find her at the residence she gave, what then?"

Rowan slowly lowered his hands, eyes wide. "It would track the scent of her blood."

"Could it come this far?"

"It might. If it had reason to. I've never crossed those things, they're one step shy of a dragnet. And you know how I feel about *those*."

Sharek shoved his chair in. "I have to go."

"Sharek!"

But he was already gone, tearing out into the night.

Sharek was breathless—and he wasn't certain if it was from panic or his damaged lungs—when he finally vaulted the steps to their chamber and slammed the door open. Elynor was alone, but not asleep, and she jumped at his entrance, jabbing her finger with the needle she'd been using to darn the ripped knees of her trousers. "*Sharek*! What in the King's name are you doing here?"

His eyes wildly sought every corner of the room, searching for danger that wasn't present. There was only Elynor, sitting under the window, staring at him with equal parts anger and morbid fascination.

The breath crashed out of him, and he rubbed his face with both hands. He was a fool. What had he expected—a Blessed already here, beating her on his behalf? "I thought..." he hesitated. "Nevermind. I'm sorry I frightened you."

Elynor's eyebrow climbed toward her hairline, and after a moment she slowly said, "Well, I need to get back to mending these. It's too cold to wear ripped clothes down to the harbor anymore."

Once again, Sharek hesitated. He couldn't imagine walking all the way back to the tavern and enduring Rowan's taunts at his panic-stricken flight. Nor did his cold, aching lungs encourage the notion. So he shut the door instead and slid to his seat against it, watching her. "Did you sign with your blood when you hired me?"

Elynor jabbed her fingertip again, then she met his eyes. The firelight by which she darned turned her eyes to deep pools, her gaunt face to a skeleton's frame. "Aeson wouldn't let me take a Blessed from the Sanctum if I didn't."

Sharek dragged a hand up and down the back of his neck. "Then, if something were to happen to me...or if I didn't return..."

The silence crashed down again, heavy and thick as an ocean tide. Elynor dropped her gaze and went back to darning. "It's your choice what happens with Aeson."

His eyes whipped to her, the implication spearing a deep disbelief in his chest. "You mean that you're setting me free?"

"I mean that isn't my place to do that or not. You're already free, Sharek. You were born free...a son of Ollanthyr. I have no right to tell you that you'll go anywhere. It's entirely up to you."

All his life, Sharek had feared to flee from the Sanctum; he'd feared Aeson's worst coming for *him*. Only in his most desperate times after Rowan's death had the notion of deserting and becoming a fugitive or worse been preferable to remaining in their cage.

But a Hunter could stay one step ahead of a Blessed. He didn't have to fear them anymore. And even if he looked over his shoulder the rest of his life, he would not give up this freedom for anything.

Except...

"If I do this," he said carefully, "if I stay away, they'll come for you."

"Let me worry about that." There was no fear in Elynor's voice…and no conviction.

"Elynor. I cannot do that."

"Yes, you can." She bit off the thread and glared at him. "Otherwise, what, Sharek? Would you return to the Sanctum and play at being a killing Blessed? How long before they find a dragnet like Rue and learn you're a Hunter? The only way you survive is by staying free. If I were you, I would seize that freedom."

Sharek frowned. "But you *are* free. As free as I am."

"No, I'm not." Elynor smiled a corpse's smile. "I may live my whole life never being found out, never belonging to Aeson Thalanor, but don't think for an instant that makes me *free*."

Sharek rested his head against the wall. "Sometimes it's easier to remain in a familiar cage than brave the truth of freedom."

"A familiar cage. You're referring to what I am?"

"Actually, I was referring to your status as the sacrosanct heiress."

Elynor snorted quietly. "You know nothing, Sharek."

But he did. He knew freedom was as terrifying as it was exhilarating, and that Elynor was afraid of the freedom to embrace what she was. Perhaps that was true of Rowan, as well; perhaps he'd left the Sanctum and bound himself to Al-Morral because the freedom to make his own way was more daunting than to trade a cruel master for a kind one.

But a leash was still a leash, and a noose was still a noose; and even as the tether slipped from around Sharek's neck, Elynor strained against hers.

And the danger in all of it was that she didn't even realize she wore it. Or that it was choking her.

Chapter Forty-Two

Promises to Keep

Despite his injuries, Vestan struggled to sit still as the healing came to his injured body.

Day by day, he was gladder of who had found them in the Valley. He did not fear these Hunters—he'd grown up hearing his father tell tales of their great feats in battle, defending Erala from its enemies both within and outside its borders—and he was glad to see the royal siblings warming to their companions and caretakers while he himself slowly mended.

They were shy at first, clinging to Vestan, who was familiar and safe. But over time, Sylvie hobbled to the cookfires, shyly asking them to teach her how to make this *multem* meal they ate each night; and Isaac and Isla gleefully wove dolls and wreaths out of the trimmings from the herbs the Hunters gathered. And Elliott, to no one's surprise, challenged everyone to duels. But the Blessed and Hunters were good for Elliott, too, in the blade and in balance to his temper.

They all shared the same anger, the same scorn toward King Marcus, but theirs was older, blunter. They'd learned to temper that fire so it wouldn't burn out of control. And as much as the Blessed swordsmen and swift, sharp-sensed Hunters taught Elliott of blocks and parries and footwork, they showed him just as much how to restrain his fury so it didn't fan so hot it consumed him entirely.

Vestan joined Elliott after another arduous training session one evening, limping over to sit next to the sweaty, scowling prince on a shelf of rock looking over the floor where Blessed and Hunters still dueled. He offered Elliott a waterskin, and the boy snatched it and drenched his hair before he drank.

"Your footwork is improving," Vestan remarked. "So is your arm. I see you can hold the block longer than you have before."

Elliott shrugged. "These people aren't like our swordmaster at the kaer. I never realized he was being soft on Sylvie and me until I fought Horase."

Vestan eyed the burly Hunter who was now putting Isaac and Isla carefully through their paces with sticks for swords. "They don't hold back at all, do they?"

"No. And I'm better for it. Stronger. And I can tell Horase *wants* us stronger."

"Does that frighten you?"

"No. It's what I want, too. I want to be strong enough to protect Sylvie and the twins, if it comes to that. I thought I was strong before, but now I know I can be better. And they're teaching me how." Elliott handed the waterskin back to Vestan and bent forward, resting his elbows on his knees and clasping his long fingers around his chin. "Everything we were taught about them was a lie."

Vestan drew in a shaky breath so his relief at those quiet words wouldn't leap out of him like song. "Jamyson would sometimes say the responsibility of the royal family is to tell the truth through clever lies."

Elliott snorted. "That's horsedung. Nothing Father did was truthful. He was wrong about *everything*." His gaze skimmed to Vestan. "Jamyson knew that, didn't he?"

"You should ask him, when you see one another again."

"You mean if Father hasn't thrown *him* off a rock wall."

"Yes. If that," Vestan grimaced.

Elliott watched him for a long moment; his eyes were shrewd, dark with the same intensity Vestan saw so often in Jamyson. It was the thing that was most alike about them, besides their coloring and their curls.

"You should go back to him," Elliott said at last. "Sylvie and I can manage the twins. And Horase and Ria will help. So if you need someone to release you, then since I'm the oldest, I'm releasing you, Vez. You need to go back to Jamyson."

Vestan arched his brows. "Did I need permission, Your Highness?"

Elliott stood and stretched, patting Vestan on the shoulder. "No, but maybe you thought you did."

Maybe he had indeed.

Gratitude half-strangled him as Elliott sauntered away to give advice to the twins. That steadiness of mind, and the way he could deliver an offering of aid without an ounce of cruelty or shaming...that was like Jamyson, too.

"They're good children." Ria's voice wafted from the shadows behind Vestan as she emerged from a cleft in the cavern wall, hands laden down with bandages and new splints for his sling. "May I?"

Vestan kept quiet as she worked. Down on the floor below, he watched a young Blessed horticulturist named Hessen help Sylvie walk across the pool's edge. He'd made her a crutch from a sapling with just enough flex to bob like a natural limb. Sylvie laughed breathlessly as she clung to his arm with one hand and maneuvered the crutch with the other, and Hessen tossed his chestnut curls from his eyes and said something that made the princess blush.

"Yes. They're very good children," Vestan murmured. "They shouldn't have to endure any of this."

"I know." Ria fitted the sling back over Vestan's head. "My son was about Elliott's age when he died. Life should begin in earnest for them now, not be cut short."

Vestan reflected on his own life, thrown into chaos when he'd been only a year older than Elliott and Sylvie. "Erala cares little for the wounds of its youth. There's an illness in it that's excused by rumors of infallibility and men who are less than human."

Ria shifted to sit side-by-side with him on the flat rock. "That's what we hope to change, you know. The fates of our people. Of children like these."

"How?"

Ria smiled crookedly. "I'm afraid I can't tell you that. Only those who have sworn the Hunterish blood oath of allegiance and secrecy are privy to that knowledge." She laid a hand to her chest, tapping her clavicle in a steady rhythm as if she played along to music only she could hear. "You could do it, you know. Swear the oath. Join us."

A sizzle of shock speared through Vestan at the casual offer. "You hardly know me."

"I know that you risked your life to save those children." Ria nodded to Isaac and Isla, wrestling now instead of hitting their sticks together, and Elliott chatting animatedly with a pair of Blessed swordmasters who teased him like a younger brother. "I've also heard the way that you speak of the Crown Prince—the loyalty and love you are capable of. And I won't lie...we could use a man of your strength."

Vestan's neck warmed, and he rubbed his unhurt hand through his hair. "I can't serve two masters." Then he said the words he'd been mulling every day while his strength returned, and that Elliott had finally unleashed in him: "I have to go back to Kaer Dorwenon."

Ria's eyes flashed wide and sharp with distress. "If you're caught, King Marcus will hang you as He hung the nobles at the Solstice."

Vestan grimaced. He'd heard that report from her spies—how the once-joyous winter feast had been a somber affair full of threats and treaty-signings. And if he knew Jamyson and Esmae, they were in the thick of it, at the very heart of the danger. Which was precisely why he had to go back.

"I won't be caught," he said. "I know all the secret routes. And I know Jamyson. He'll hide me."

"Will you tell him of his brothers and sisters? That they live?"

Vestan slowly shook his head. "Not with Gavannon Al-Morral spying at the walls. Jamyson will hate me for a while when he learns, but he'll be glad, too. I do this for them. And for all of you." He smiled at Ria. "You've been kind to me. I won't repay that kindness by sending the Kingsgard after you."

Ria dipped her head. "If you swear not to tell the prince they live, then we will keep the children with us until it's safe for them to return."

It would be a difficult promise to hold once he was face-to-face with Jamyson. But the only way to keep the royal siblings safe was to keep them dead in the eyes of their family until King Marcus was deposed.

He rose, and Ria rose with him, laying a hand on his arm. "Your loyalty is commendable, Vestan. And I understand why you go. But my conscience will not be clear unless I ask you once more to stay."

Vestan covered her hand with his. "I would like to stay," he said, and was struck by how much he meant it. "Perhaps when this is over, when Jamyson is King, he'll free me to go where I please, and I'll come back. But for now..."

"Duty calls." Ria's hand slid from his arm.

"I've been gone too long already. I missed the Prince's birthday...he's going to be furious enough as it is for that. Best if I go before he dies of neglect."

Ria laughed. "The carts returned just last night. I have a new band of spies heading to Dorwenon. You're welcome to travel with them."

Vestan dipped his head. "I would be honored."

Chapter Forty-Three

The Hunter's Dance

"I REALLY DON'T SEE why we have to do this," Elynor grumbled as Sylvester led her and Mide through the winding streets of the weapon's district. "Couldn't the *Daishi* have met us in the palace?"

"He is forbidden to return on pain of death." Mide's voice was cool as usual, but Sylvester caught a waver beneath it. "Even this risks much. I cannot ask him to risk more for my sake."

Sylvester chanced a glance back. The women walked side-by-side, and Elynor watched Mide from the corner of her eyes. The slant of her brows and the twist of her mouth might've been sympathy. Sylvester hoped it was; tonight, after all, was about moving forward in more than one sense.

"All right," Elynor relented at last. "What I don't understand is why you brought *me* along."

"Because you've spent plenty of time moping in that room, or moping down at the harbor." Sylvester folded his hands behind his head and stretched. "You remember that story I told you in Kirsagan's cart? Of Ardeth Lamruil?"

"The Blessed bard? What of him?"

"If you recall, his music lifted the lowest of spirits." Sylvester dropped back and elbowed between the women, slinging his arm around Elynor's shoulders. "Just for one night, wouldn't you like to hear music and dance and forget all the rest?"

"As if I could."

They didn't speak again until they walked beneath the amber rooftops of the musicians' district, and Sylvester's spirits begin to climb. He had spent enough time here since their arrival in Danje, spinning reels and putting his bard's talents to good use, that the weaving streets leading to the center of the district felt familiar. Homey. Something he had not felt in a very long time.

There was music everywhere in this place, and when the wind carried right it floated all the way to the palace. But tonight was a chilly one with snow sliding in from the west, the clouds hunkering so low the music crouched in the alleys. Lonely violin strains and soft piano melodies saturated the cold air as they made their way to the heart of the district. There was always a musical troupe playing here, and a bonfire every night. The flames heated the cobblestones and the people drank and danced their cares away. There was no talk of war here; the music staved off such fears.

A few appreciative hollers and cheers went up when Sylvester stepped into the open square. Elynor's brows rose. "You've certainly become legendary, haven't you?"

"I may have played a reel or two on the *shudraga*." The cheers grew thunderous when Sylvester slung the instrument from his back, and his grin grew with them. "While we're waiting for the *Daishi*, we might as well, hm?"

"Be my guest." Elynor dropped onto a bench at the edge of the square.

Sylvester had expected her to be difficult; he wasn't concerned. He turned to Mide. "Do you dance, *Khuless*?"

"It's been some time."

"Well, that may be about to change."

Sylvester sauntered over to the troupe. They greeted him with hoots and backslaps, making room for him on the stack of discarded citrus crates where they perched. Sylvester tuned the *shudraga* by touch and memory alone, keeping his eyes on Mide and Elynor. If nothing else, he was determined to make them smile while they waited for their next depressing conversation.

So he played.

Peace spilled through him the moment the music began. All his cares melted away, and joy sprang up in his heart as the people flowed to the voice of the instrument. They clapped and jigged, then grabbed partners and spun around the bonfire. The other musicians joined in, complimenting the *shudraga's* clean, silvery sound with drums and flutes and other Orlethian instruments Sylvester was still learning to name and play; the weaving of sounds was perfect and pure, almost ecstatic.

This was why he came here as many nights as he could. And why he'd brought Elynor and Mide while they waited.

The *Khuless* was the first to succumb. First her arms fell out of their tight cross. Then she began to nod to the beat. And then, when a man offered his arm, she took it and leaped into the ring of firelight, twirling and clapping with the rest of them.

Elynor was more stubborn. Her foot followed the beat, but her gaze was fixed on the flames. Sylvester could all but see the music breaking around her like a river around a stone.

She was strong, he'd give her that. But he'd prepared for this.

And just then, Sharek stepped into the square.

Sylvester hid a grin by dropping his head and letting his hair fall forward to shield his face, but he kept his eyes fixed on the pair as they met a few steps from the crates.

"Why are you here?" Elynor demanded.

Sharek shrugged. "Sylvester asked me to come hear him play."

They both looked at him, and Sylvester flashed an open-mouthed grin and raised his brows and chin in greeting. Elynor glared at him, stiffening as if to shout; but seeing Sharek had broken her defenses, and now the music washed over her, working its mysterious charm, easing her stance and bringing a slow smile to her face instead. After a long moment, she offered her hands to Sharek. "We might as well?"

He blinked. "I haven't danced in years. Not since Ollanthyr."

"Show me, then." Elynor dared him. "Show me a Hunterish dance."

Sharek's eyes blazed with a memory that sang through Sylvester's spirit in the same crescendo: the fires lit in their village, their mothers and fathers performing the ancient tribal dances of the Hunters from long ago. To Sylvester, it was akin to praying; it was the closest he could call the Empyreans to him and the only way he was certain they heard.

He changed the beat without a stumble, and for a moment the Orlethian musicians paused to listen. Then they picked up the patterns and played along.

Sharek spun Elynor toward the fire as the Hunterish jig began. They leaped and whirled, stomping and clapping, guided by the music like a third partner. Sweat poured down Sylvester's neck and back with the force of his playing, and he caught sight of Mide laughing, her hair finally escaping its stern knot; and of

Sharek, his face solemn in concentration but his eyes burning with their own fire as the steps of his people moved him to the beat. And Elynor was at his side, mirroring him perfectly.

Tears burned Sylvester's eyes as pure joy crested through him. If he could only have this, and nothing but this, forever—the music, the fire, the dancing, and his friends wrapped up in it—then he would be happy. Then he would stop looking back and mourning what had been taken from him and what he'd had to give away.

A sudden ripple of shadow moved among the people as they changed partners, and Sylvester saw the *Khuless* dancing next to a man in a hood and cloak. The moment he blinked and the fire shivered, the figure was gone. But something had changed, interrupting the pattern of the music; Mide sidled over to Elynor and gripped her arm. She too broke pattern, halting in place, and Sharek stopped beside her as Mide whispered in her ear.

And Sylvester knew.

He surrendered the music reluctantly and excused himself, encouraging the other musicians to keep playing. As he strung the *shudraga* in its sheath again, Elynor backed away, fingers slipping from Sharek's. Sylvester knew it wasn't just his imagination how his friend clung to her fingertips for a moment before he let go.

Sylvester bobbed his shoulders helplessly in Sharek's direction and earned himself a small smile and the shake of his head in reply.

Then Sylvester, Mide, and Elynor stole away from the fire and music for their clandestine meeting.

Chapter Forty-Four

Worth Every Risk

Elynor couldn't remember when she'd last felt so light. Her skin tingled with the memory of Sharek's hand, gentle on her waist as he'd guided her through the dances of his people; and though she'd only been a passible dancer in the prestigious circles of her youth, she could've gone on forever tonight. With him.

This was not walking away, and it was not reconciliation. But she didn't care; her feet were as buoyant as a skiff on the waves as she followed Sylvester and Mide away from the square, away from Sharek, to the next district—this one robed almost entirely in shadows with an odd feeling that chipped at her levity. "What is this place?"

"It was once a pleasure district." Mide's tone was stiff as ever; the lighthearted woman dancing with her people in the square might never have been, though the Orlethians likely would not soon forget her. "It attracted too much trouble, so the *Khul* disbanded it. But some cling to what wonders could once be found here."

Elynor's flesh crawled as they passed derelict stoops and small *gers* crammed between buildings. The smell of pipeweed and *arkye* issued strongly from a few doorways, rasping against her breathless throat. Mide ducked suddenly into one such structure with nail-studded boards recently ripped from its face, and inside, Elynor froze.

A man loomed just beyond the threshold, cowled and cloaked, and for a sharp, heart-dropping instant Elynor was certain it was Rowan, come to make a quick end of them.

But then the figure knocked back his hood, baring a shorn scalp aside from a long topknot, and an angular face with upswept Orlethian eyes.

"*Ezen.*" There was a smile in Mide's voice as she dropped to one knee, an arm across her chest.

"How many times must I remind you not to address me that way?" The man gripped Mide's shoulders and lifted her back onto her feet. "I am not your master. You are my *Khuless* and I am—I was—your warlord."

Mide snorted. "Very well. Shall I call you *koshin kun*?"

He flicked her forehead. "Not such an old man, Mide."

Their easy affection made Elynor's heart ache. How often had she and her father teased one another like that, setting all the sailors around them laughing as they bantered across the deck the way most men traded blows with swords?

She'd taken every word for granted, as if he'd always be there to laugh with her. As if anyone's presence was guaranteed for a lifetime.

Mide turned to face them, spanning her arm. "This is Sylvester and Elynor. We asked you here for your wisdom."

The *Daishi's* eyes tracked between them, somber with suspicion. Then he jerked his head. "Come with me."

They went deeper into the skeletal building, passing through crumbled doorways and empty rooms until they reached what might have once been a kitchen. It was bare, some of the walls knocked out to reveal support timbers like bones peeking through ruined skin. The *Daishi* lit a small fire in a stone pit at the center of the room, placed a pot of water over it, and filled it with leaves. Then he gestured them to sit.

Elynor was glad to; now that her sweat was drying on her skin, she was deeply chilled. She huddled by the fire, and Sylvester draped an arm around her, warming her with brisk rubbing. Mide sat off to one side of the fire, on her knees in the ceremonial Orlethian posture, which the *Daishi* mirrored across the flames. Elynor had the sense they'd conferred just like this, many times before.

"And tell me," the *Daishi* murmured as if there had been no break in their conversation, "what wisdom is so necessary that you called me back to this city?"

"The killing Blessed, Rowan," Mide said. "These two know him, from before he came to our shores."

Elynor quickly told the tale of Al-Morral and Rowan and their plot for war. The *Daishi* listened without a flicker of emotion, moving only now and then to stir and then pour the tea into cups. When Elynor had told him everything, he turned to Mide. "You have not brought him before your mother and questioned him with your gift?"

Mide dipped her head. "Mother listens to me less now than when you left, *Ezen*."

"I feared as much. Tamachi's death and this rumor of my betrayal have crushed her spirit, and he takes advantage of that wound." The *Daishi* sipped his tea, his expression remote. "But that is a sensible strategy. I would have advised against war with Erala at any cost...now he is her greatest advisor, and she may follow his word even to battle."

"What can we do?" Mide shifted forward. "Teach me to fight a war that has not yet begun."

"She may not accept your report." The *Daishi's* gaze tracked to Elynor and Sylvester. "But the word of another Blessed..."

"We aren't Blessed," Elynor lied quickly. "She wouldn't listen to us."

"But we know someone who is," Mide said. "Their companion, a man named Sharek."

"He's intimated himself already to Rowan, to uncover his treachery," Sylvester agreed to Mide's easy lie. "So far he's found nothing to convict him. But if *we* did..."

"We could present the findings to Sharek, and let him bring them before the *Khul*," Elynor said. "That's clever, Sly."

"But what evidence?" Frustration cracked Mide's voice. "Rowan has mapped his steps too precisely for us to accuse him."

"Have you searched the harbor?" the *Daishi* asked.

Elynor's skin reared with gooseflesh. "What of the harbor?"

"I saw him visiting that way now and again, before I lost my title," the *Daishi* said. "Now that I hear your story of his accomplice in Erala, I wonder if he receives word from him there."

Elynor and Sylvester swapped a look.

"The Fleet," Elynor said. "Al-Morral could be sending correspondences through the captains."

"If we could catch him with a note in hand..." Sylvester trailed off, biting the side of this thumb. "Mide, do you suppose the *Khul* would listen to Sharek if he hauled Rowan before her with a note from Al-Morral?"

"She might," Mide said. "But the evidence must be truly in his hand. She will not hear groundless accusations against anyone, and this *busar* least of all."

"We can take shifts watching the harbor," Elynor offered. "And Sly can ask Sharek to tell us if he hears of Rowan going to the docks." She felt Sylvester's curious glance when she didn't take that role herself; she ignored his look.

"I can perhaps take position in the mariner's quarter," the *Daishi* offered. "To watch for him when you cannot escape the palace."

"If you're seen, it will mean your death." Mide's voice cracked.

"And if his downfall will restore my honor and prove to the *Khul* that I did not betray her, it is worth every risk."

Gratitude swelled in Elynor's throat. So many lives had been threatened by Al-Morral's ambitions and Rowan's schemes. So many broken pieces, and she didn't know how to fit hers back together; but she could see the way forward, at least, to helping Orleth heal its heart. And perhaps through that she would prove to the *Khul* that no matter what lies Rowan spun, Erala's people were good, fair, and honest. All the good traits her father had instilled in her.

"All right," she said. "Let's catch our traitor in the act."

Chapter Forty-Five

Powers of Persuasion

A FINE FILIGREE OF dust flocked the walls of the kaer's library, proving just how little use it had seen since Sylvie's death, the Queen's imprisonment, and the King's madness. Joffrey, the elderly scribe who oversaw the southern turret, had been ill with a chest sickness for weeks, according to the gossip Esmae had overheard in the servant's quarters; and few people wanted to dwell on the history of Erala when the present was so disheartening.

Evers since the Solstice, Jamyson had been on high guard as if he was living behind enemy borders. The only place he could be himself, dropping the façade of the pleasant and carefree prince still trusting in his father's plan, was here in the library with Esmae.

She'd just come to join him again, a basket of fresh scones in arm, powdered sugar under her fingernails leaving a fine silvery trail as she slid into the bench seat of the broad, round table at the turret's center and scooted over to lean against him. "Anything?"

Jamyson pinched the bridge of his nose and arched back from the table, stretching the kinks from his spine. "Nothing so far about legal precedence to dethrone a King. Because of course there isn't…why would someone infallible need to be dethroned?"

"Not even for unjust hangings?"

"Nothing He does is unjust, because nothing He does can be without perfect merit." Jamyson slammed a hand down on the open book and swore. "If ever there was *proof* that the foundation of this kings-damned belief is flawed, here it is. A sick and addled man murders His wife and children, and the law *protects* Him."

Esmae frowned, tugging the book of Eralanite law out from under Jamyson's arm. "Jamyson, if you can't find *legal* recourse..."

"I'll have to challenge Him with the sword. I know."

Esmae's eyes slid to him sidelong. "You know what will happen."

"At best, I ascend to power as a kingslayer, the man who killed his father. The people will fear me and question my judgement from the moment I take the Throne." The words emerged colder and harsher than he'd intended, but it was the only way to keep his voice from shaking. "At worst, He overpowers me, and Al-Morral stands poised to take the Throne in my stead."

Esmae elbowed the basket of scones toward him. "You eat. I'll read for a bit."

Jamyson didn't protest. They'd been stealing every spare moment here, sacrificing sleep and risking the wrath of the entire kaer as they hunted for anything that would help them set the people of Erala free. And when he looked at these books of history and law and laid out his own failures and his father's side-by-side, the truth became ever more blindingly clear.

The sovereign infallibility and the Holy Throne were an absolute lie. The Kings of Yore had left a trail of deceit and mistakes and death strewn in their wake, and kept the people from ever daring to question with the greatest lie of all: that their wisdom was without tarnish.

It was a near-flawless trick, with only one small chink in its fabricant armor: in order to keep up the ruse, the King had to be sane enough to lie. And King Marcus no longer retained enough sanity to convince the people of His wisdom.

That was what worried Jamyson above all else. Because when it should have been Him his father leaned on to be the face of the kingship, to keep up the ruse, instead He huddled behind Gavannon Al-Morral. Ever since the Solstice, orders had come from the King directly through the Fleetmaster; and no one dared question the Friend of the King.

Urgency pricked Jamyson's back like a dagger poised to cut into it. He polished off a scone and bent over the book with Esmae, desperately hunting the pages for something that would save him from having to draw his sword against his own father.

"Jamyson." Esmae touched his face, drawing his frantic gaze away from the page. When he met her eyes, she bent forward to graze her lips against his. "It will be all right. We'll find some way to depose Him."

"That is a very interesting vow indeed."

Jamyson leaped back so sharply he almost tumbled to the floor, spinning on the bench with a pounding heart as Gavannon Al-Morral stepped from the seams between the bookshelves. Behind him, the black-clad Kingsgard dripped from the walls. And there, slowly rounding the end of another row, coming to face them—

Jamyson's stomach twisted in a vicious knot of dread. "Father."

The King's bloodshot gaze swiveled slowly from Jamyson to Esmae. "What is this?"

This wasn't happening. It couldn't be. After years and *years* of being so careful... "I was...researching. She brought me food."

Al-Morral arched a brow. "And fed it to you with her own mouth?"

Jamyson shot him a vicious glare and wished with all his heart he was Blessed with the power to incinerate men with one glance.

"I know you have had lapses in judgement when it comes to matters of the heart," the King murmured, "not the least of which was your desire to marry the woman who assassinated her own father and threatened Gavannon's life..."

Jamyson gaped at Him. "Marrying Elynor was *Your* idea, not—"

"*Silence!*" King Marcus roared, setting Jamyson back on his heels. "I have overlooked these lapses out of love for you. When Gavannon said he'd spotted you parading about the kaer with the slave from Oss Belliard, I thought him mad..."

Al-Morral. Of course he'd seen something, overheard something—and how long had he stalked Jamyson and Esmae, plotting to reveal them, maneuvering the King into position by feeding Him lies about Jamyson and Elynor, and now feeding Him the damning truth about Jamyson and Esmae?

Jamyson flexed his hands and imagined grabbing the Fleetmaster's head and twisting it off his shoulders with one cruel snap.

"But he is not mad," the King went on. "You have betrayed Me. Plotting with the magistrate's daughter to supplant Me."

Terror encircled Jamyson's throat. "Father, no. That isn't what this is about."

But here he was. With the books and with Esmae's powdered-sugar kiss still stamped on his lips, and his own words still hanging on the stagnant air.

King Marcus spread His hands. "You leave Me no choice, Jamyson."

"You're a fool." Esmae's voice was quiet and cold. It sounded nothing like her.

Silence swallowed the turret, swallowed the breath in Jamyson's lungs.

And then Esmae laughed, low and malicious, and it sent a chill digging down the planes of Jamyson's back. He swiveled his head slowly toward her as she glided forward, the whisper of her shackles like winsome chimes. She halted when the Kingsgard tensed and Al-Morral cast out a defensive arm before the King.

There was no hint of the slave who had walked the halls of Kaer Dorwenon for so many years. She was the magistrate's daughter once more, haughty and regal, and she managed to look *down* at King Marcus.

"You're an old and sickly fool," she repeated, and the King flinched. "I can see now why Your son was so easy to manipulate. It must be an inherent quality, that pliancy of mind."

Al-Morral's eyes narrowed. "What are you saying?"

"You really believe the Crown Prince would risk his inheritance with a slave?" Esmae scoffed. "It was *me*, You illiterate fool. He's been doing all of this at *my* behest."

"Esmae," Jamyson growled.

She didn't spare him even a glance. Her eyes were fixed on King Marcus, who gazed back at her unblinking. "From the moment You brought me into Your kaer to humiliate me, I've been carving the foundation from beneath Your feet. I seduced Your heir. I spied on Your wife. I turned Your children against You."

"Impossible," the King breathed.

Esmae laughed that guttural, horrific laugh again. "Are You *really* so gullible? You don't think I wanted to do it from the moment You took my father's life? And why did You do it, *Your Eminence*? It was for harboring Hunters, wasn't it?" Esmae took another step forward, and the King jerked back. "Did You never stop to wonder why he risked everything for them?"

Cold sweat broke out at Jamyson's hairline. The feeling deserted his fingertips and toes.

"It cannot be," the King said.

Esmae's smile was foreign, cruel, condescending. "I am a *Blessed*, You mad bastard. Blessed with the power of persuasion. And I turned Your whole family against You...even Your precious heir."

"You're lying," Al-Morral hissed.

Esmae shrugged. "Well, if You'd like to believe that, then hang the prince for treason. He's good for nothing to me if You suspect he's a traitor. But I dare

You to ask Yourself, Marcus...what if you're wrong, and You kill Your only heir because a Blessed *deceived* You?"

Jamyson's harsh breathing was the only sound that disturbed the musty air as his mind struggled to comprehend what was happening. The King's gaze darted from Esmae to Jamyson and back again, sweat gathering at His temples and sliding down His grizzled jowls. Al-Morral, wisely, kept silent.

Esmae took one more step toward the King, inclining her head. "The Queen told me Your secret. I persuaded her to. Shall I tell the prince?"

"No!" the King snarled. "No, I know that My son...My only heir would never betray me."

"Your Eminence," Al-Morral began.

King Marcus whipped away from Esmae. "Hang her and shut him in his rooms until she's dead. When she breathes her last, her power over him will break."

The word *dead* resonated in Jamyson's skull.

All at once, everything was not silent within him; it was roaring, bellowing, *wailing*.

He lunged, sweeping the legs of the first Kingsgard who grabbed Esmae, chopping the throat of the second, breaking the wrist of the third. "Esmae, *run!*"

But she didn't. Even as the Kingsgard turned on Jamyson, even as King Marcus shouted for them to subdue His son, Esmae held fast. She watched him with expressionless eyes, and when the men had secured his arms, she stepped forward and gripped his chin, forcing him to hold her gaze. "You've been a fun little plaything. I've even enjoyed a few of our trysts over the years. But I'm afraid I can't let *you* take the glory for destroying my father's killer. Goodbye, Jamyson."

She covered his mouth with hers, and against his lips he felt her words: *I love you.*

There was a dull clap of skin on skin as the King backhanded Esmae, breaking the contact between them, and the Kingsgard hauled her away from Jamyson.

"I should have beheaded you with your treacherous father," King Marcus snarled.

"Of course You should have." Esmae smiled, blood rising in the cracks of her teeth. "And a *wise* man would have. But You aren't that, are You, Marcus?"

"Get her out of my sight!"

Jamyson thrashed and hurled himself against the hands that bound him as the men dragged Esmae from the room, still smirking, still looking nothing like herself. But now there was a welt on her cheek and tears in her eyes, and he knew it wasn't from the pain of his father's blow.

"I love you!" Jamyson shouted after her as the door clattered shut. "I will *always* love you!"

"No, you won't, My boy," the King said. "Only until her power over you is broken." He nodded to the Kingsgard who remained. "Put him in his room."

<hr>

The march to his chamber, arms pinned and a guard's hand around his neck, was an absolute blur. Jamyson could think of nothing but escaping and freeing Esmae. The moment the guards cast him inside his room, he swung around and struck out; but a solid kick to the gut put him on his backside on the floor, and by the time he recovered his wind and scrambled up, they'd shut and barred the door from the outside. Jamyson hurled himself against the steely slab of wood twice, then rushed to check the others. But they were all latched.

"No," he panted, spinning toward the inner windows. "No, no..."

From his washroom, he had a narrow view of the inner courtyard. The gallows had never come down after the Solstice; they stood somber sentry, a promise of more hangings to come. And even now the executioner was mounting the steps.

Jamyson's heart lodged in his throat. This was a lie, a living nightmare—Esmae was not a Blessed, and she had not deceived him. He knew it better than he knew anything else in the kings-damned world.

She'd tricked his father. She'd sacrificed herself to keep him safe.

Jamyson wanted to fall to his knees before the King, to beg for mercy, for her imprisonment rather than her death so that he'd have a *sliver* of hope to sneak her out of the dungeons and set her free.

But the King would never listen. He'd grasped onto the hope that Jamyson had not betrayed Him, and He would never consent to believe otherwise. The die had been cast, the lot settled; Esmae had thwarted Al-Morral for now. But in turn...

She appeared at the edge of the courtyard on the fringe of his vision, dragged by six of the Kingsgard. They'd bound her hands as well as her feet now, the slave shackles winking in the sun as the men hauled her up the steps to the noose.

Jamyson hunted desperately for something to break the glass, snatched up a vase and broke it, but while it shattered, scraping his hands bloody, the window itself held—

—and Esmae's neck was in the noose now, and she was shaking her head at something, at the bag the executioner started to slide over her eyes—

—and Jamyson was roaring, grabbing his sword, pounding the pommel against the glass, but it was tempered by Blessed craftsmen, sturdier than natural glass so enemies could not break into the prince's chambers, and it did not give way—

—and through the glass, Esmae was looking at him.

Their gazes caught, and held, and Jamyson dropped the sword with a clatter and splayed his hands on the windowframe, shoving his brow to the cold glass. "No, no, no..."

Esmae shook her head, warning him to stand down.

Because he had to live. Because he had to keep fighting. Because if he didn't, then Al-Morral won and the kingdom would go to war.

Esmae couldn't prevent that. But Jamyson could.

It was not worth it. Not to him. Not to watch her die.

The executioner's hand was on the lever, and Esmae's lips moved slowly, framing the words again: *I love*—

And the world went out from under her feet.

Jamyson raged at the top of his voice, slamming his hands into the stones, screaming her name as she bucked and squirmed when the rope didn't snap her neck, when she started to strangle—

And then an arm looped around Jamyson's chest from behind, jerking him away from the window, an unnatural band of strength fighting against the whirlwind of his thrashing limbs, and a familiar voice rasped in his ear, "Don't look, Jamyson, don't look, I'm begging you..."

It was not possible—that voice, this moment, that any of this was happening.

But it *was* Vestan wrestling him down, and Jamyson squeezed his eyes shut, his jaw splitting in a soundless sob sucked inward that slowly built and built on every gasp until it rushed out of him as a pained, atavistic howl, a harsh and wobbling note of agony, of loss, of horror and hatred.

He slumped forward in Vestan's grip, sobbing Esmae's name until every last piece of him burst into ruin.

Chapter Forty-Six

Prayers for the Heiress

Moonlight spilled down from a cloudless sky, shedding generous dollops of silver light on the whitecap that roamed from the wall to the coast. The wind was firm and steady, lifting the waves and dropping them against the feet of the wharfs and the dark sand, the most soothing lullaby in existence. Elynor could've fallen asleep to it from her position in the attic of the *Daishi's* abandoned shack, where the boards pulled away from the shutterless window, offering a view of several wharfs—particularly the ones where Fleet vessels docked, the Eralanite standard run down for the night.

It was strange to be in the harbor but not with Sam. Elynor had considered inviting him, playing with the idea that he could restore some honor with the Orlethians by helping catch the greatest threat to their land in centuries; but he was where he needed to be, in that crevice of the wall, rigging *The Seabird* to sail. He'd offered a week, two at most, before she was ready. His time was better spent on that task, and anyway, the attic was a bit crowded as it was: Sylvester sitting at one wall, gently playing the *shudraga*, the *Daishi* resting his eyes in some sort of meditative posture at the other, and Mide taking the window.

Elynor surveyed them from the doorway, her hands weighed down with mugs of hot tea…an Eralanite brew, because the smell of Orlethian tea reminded her of Abigale's betrayal, and because the notes of citrus and rose petals harkened to home. She set one cup before Sylvester, who flashed her a nod and a smile without breaking the song; she set another before the *Daishi*, who didn't even stir; and then she joined Mide on the overturned fruit crate at the window, offering one cup and keeping the last for herself.

"Thank you," Mide said curtly.

"My pleasure."

They were silent for a time, as things often were in this attic; Elynor had been here several fruitless nights already the past two weeks, watching for Rowan and listening to the waves. She didn't know which was more satisfying, and that terrified her. She missed the water so much, it was like losing her father again every time she walked away.

"Anything?" she murmured to distract herself.

Mide shrugged. "The usual sailors and wharfmen coming and going. No one of consequence, though a new Eralanite ship ran into port this morning."

Elynor's spirits perked slightly. "What did it look like?"

"An enormous ship."

Elynor loosed a silent, aggrieved sigh. If she'd asked Sam, he could've told her its exact class, weight and length, the color of its siding and sails. And he would've shared her enthusiasm for every detail.

As if Mide could hear the strand of these thoughts, she slid a sideways glance to Elynor. "Sylvester tells me that when you come down the harbor, you are with Samwel Morlai."

Sylvester was a gossipy busybody. But there was no sense in lying; he had told her what the *Khuless* was capable of. "I do."

"Why?"

"He's crafting something for me."

Mide cocked her head, her eyes narrowing as she studied that vague truth. "He's dangerous."

"He killed your brother. I know."

Mide's sharp gaze lost focus, slashed apart by a grief that echoed in Elynor's chest. "He was so young. He needed to be protected. And Sam failed him. It was his mistakes that introduced the belief in my mother's heart that a Blessed could be deceived, could even fail at their craft. It is why she ha snot yet been convinced to go to war on their behalf, I think. And it's driven this great wall between us that I do not know how to tear down."

Her vulnerability stunned Elynor; but perhaps a woman used to living with truth, whether it was given freely or not, felt the responsibility to be just as honest with others. "I know...something of what that's like. My whole life has been built around the belief that our King is infallible. But then all of this happened, everything with Sharek and Al-Morral and Rowan, and now..." She scratched her temple. "Now if I believe Him to be right in all things, I must accept that people I love, even my family, deserve collars and tethers. That freedom should be denied to them from birth until death. And I must also accept that it's my place to marry His son and submit to His vision for my life, and give up everything I want."

Though, what did it matter if she married Jamyson now, since she had signed away the sea and the Fleet? Why not submit wholeheartedly to the King's demands, since she'd lost the desire of her heart?

Hadn't she?

"My mother doesn't care for what I want, either," Mide sighed. "I would rather become her warlord than a *Khul*...or worse, a daughter married off for alliance. She might have heeded me once in this. But ever since Tamachi's death, because there is no other heir, I embody the interests of Orleth. My own do not matter anymore."

Elynor swallowed, sinking forward, her elbows on her knees. "We deserve better than that."

Mide shrugged. "What can we do? Their word is law."

What *could* they do?

Rebel. Live in secret. Carry out their own dreams in clandestine ways. For a fleeting instant, she saw herself living on the coast, commanding the Fleet, commanding the Caeruel itself with her power; she saw an heiress become a Fleetmaster, hiding the truth of her nature for the sake of a peaceful life...but also embracing it, so that she could live to the fullest, unbound by anyone's shackles, even her own.

But could she accept the craft? The curse of the Blessed? All of it?

Even as her heart yearned, her spirit withdrew. "I don't know what we can do."

Mide's eyes slid to her again. "You can stop seeing Sam. He is wicked."

"I don't believe that. Infuriating, yes, and he doesn't know how to keep his opinions to himself. But I think that underneath all that, he suffers like you've suffered."

"His suffering will never be the same as mine." Mide's voice was cold and harsh as shipwrecking rocks.

"He mourns for Tamachi. And he mourns what he lost with you and your mother. I've seen it."

"Good. He deserves it for what he's done." But some of the conviction faded from Mide's voice.

"It was an accident," Elynor said. "Don't let your mother's callousness become yours. Don't hang blame where it isn't due. That's how people come to mistrust those who haven't wronged them." She raked her fingernails over her scalp. "It's how they justify putting innocent men and women in cages."

Mide opened her mouth, but Elynor gestured sharply for quiet.

Down in the street below, something moved amiss.

It was almost comedic, the figure in a dark cloak stealing away down the docks. He moved with hood raised, his definition blunted by the wool shroud, but even so his lithe grace was unmistakable: a familiar predator's stalk, like Sharek's movements, though Elynor knew now that in Sharek it was learned and in this man it was inherent.

"Rowan," she breathed, and Sylvester's playing stopped.

Mide slid forward to the edge of the crate. The *Daishi* took up his twin swords, strapped them to his back, and joined them. Sylvester came last, slow and slinking like a cat, and rested a hand on Elynor's shoulder.

Rowan swaggered with the confidence of a man protected by nobility, straight down the dock toward the newly-arrived Eralanite ship. Elynor bristled at the thought of Al-Morral in Kaer Dorwenon, doing the same with King Marcus, living his kings-damned life just as fearlessly.

A man met Rowan in the ship's shadow: Lars, one of the captains who'd sailed under Alden but preferred to drink with Al-Morral. Elynor would have to make note of which of these captains had betrayed her...but then, the Fleet would be Sam's. So she would have to warn him rather than managing it herself.

Elynor shrugged off the pang of sorrow that lanced through her.

Lars and Rowan exchanged unpleasantries, and something moved between them—a pale square Rowan unfolded and read by moonlight.

Elynor's breath caught in triumph.

Rowan nodded, folded the note, and tucked it away. Then he swiveled on heel and vanished among the buildings of the mariner's district.

Mide shot to her feet. "We must confront him. Now. While he has the evidence in his pocket that can condemn him to death."

"Patience," the *Daishi* warned. "He is killing Blessed and has proved himself ruthless. He will not give you these things lightly."

"Nor any of us," Sylvester said. "I'll speak to Sharek."

"Wait." Seized by compulsion, Elynor rose. "I'll do it."

And Sylvester, much to her relief, did not protest.

Sharek was not a difficult man to find tonight, which Elynor had predicted; if Rowan had excused himself for his clandestine journey down to the harbor, then Sharek had little else to do with his time.

He was sitting under the *Aljalam* tree in the inner courtyard, on one of the low benches between the hedges that surrounded it, his hands wrapped around his talisman. At the sight of him, Elynor's heart crumbled with shame and defeat. They'd danced that night in the square as they waited for the *Daishi*, but they'd never really reconciled from their argument; it was a cloud over their heads as dark and dense as the one that had haunted Bracerath's Landing their last few days there, and it settled between them again as she slid over the bench and sat at his side.

They were quiet for a time, listening to the wind stir the leaves.

"What are you doing?" Elynor asked.

"Praying."

"For what?"

"For guidance. For patience. For Erala." Sharek's eyes flicked to her. "Mostly for you."

Warmth radiated through Elynor's chest. She tried not to let it distract her. "I'm all right, Sharek."

"You aren't, but I know that you want to be. Which is why I pray." He swiveled on the bench to face her. "What do you need?"

She opened her mouth to tell him of Rowan, but what came first was, "I think that I need to apologize. I know I've been insufferable since Tariaga Falls. By the Throne, I can hardly stand *myself*." Humorless laughter chafed at her throat. "So I ask you to forgive me for my poor behavior. For how I am now. I try to be better, but...I struggle."

"As do we all. It's already forgiven."

"You've always been too quick to forgive me, I think."

He shrugged. "Because I see that in your heart, you wish to do good. And that counts for something, even when you struggle."

Elynor swiped her thumb along her eyelid. "Well. It's a long battle. And a difficult one."

"It is. But I believe you can win it. You are a natural-born sailor and a Fleetmaster in your blood...an heiress with a destiny to change Erala from coast to coast. And a Blessed who has always been that, at your highest and lowest. There is good in you, even if you can't fathom it."

His unwavering faith, steady as an ocean breeze, rocked her ship and sent everything spinning. It always had.

Which made this conversation particularly dangerous...because after speaking to Mide tonight, and after the days she'd feigned skulking around on Sam's heels to keep him in line, when truly he was her excuse to be near the waves, she was violently near to believing everything Sharek said; that she could somehow be Blessed, and still be good. Still be Elynor Azorius, heiress of the Azorian Fleet. That she could somehow not lose herself in this new title her mother had unleashed on her.

"Speaking of seeing things that others don't," she said, desperate to steer the conversation to safer waters, "I saw Rowan tonight. He was at the docks, receiving a letter from a Fleet captain named Lars. I suspect it to be his latest orders from Al-Morral."

The openness of Sharek's bearing shuttered into shadow again, and he slowly strung his talisman over his head again. "And you want me to confront him about it."

"It wouldn't be safe for anyone else to. He's a killing Blessed, Sharek. He killed my father."

Sharek opened his mouth, then shut it with a slight shake of his head. They were quiet again for a bit, the wind parting the leaves so Sharek's Empyreans could peer down on their conversation.

"I'll speak with him," he said at last.

"You will?" Surprise swept through Elynor's tone before she could marshal it under control.

Sharek's expression was unreadable. "You and I may have our disagreements, but I'm still here to prevent a war. And if that means confronting Rowan about his affairs, you know I will do it."

Of course she knew it. It wasn't his fault how her faith in everything had sunk into a spinning maelstrom. "Be careful. I know he's been friendly to you, but he's still dangerous, and I would not see you harmed."

Sharek's hand rested on her cheek for a moment, sending a warm, pleasant jolt through her body. "There is the Elynor I know. Tell her I said hello."

And then he rose, and walked away.

Chapter Forty-Seven

A Dance of Blades

Sharek had no name for the emotion that beat in his body when he finally confronted Rowan.

For days, he'd pondered how to do it, studying a thousand scenarios in private corners of the palace and praying a thousand prayers for guidance. And after all that time, he circled back again and again to the same desperate hope: he would be honest about what he knew, and then he would try to reason with Rowan along the tenuous bridge of friendship they'd rebuilt. And if the Empyreans were merciful, that would be enough.

He went to Rowan's room this time rather than summoning him to their usual tavern or to the alley where they hunted rats every other night. He'd didn't like to meet with Rowan on his own terrain, but it was better than risking a fight in Danje's sidestreets with a furious killing Blessed.

Rowan let him in without preamble, dressed in his ceremonial Orlethian garb. "Didn't expect to see you before the tavern tonight."

It was full daylight, the sun burrowing through the wooden shutters, but Sharek felt nothing but gloom and that dull, aching pound in his temples and chest. He surveyed the room for the glint of hidden weapons under the mattress, tucked into the armoire, lined up at the table where Rowan often sharpened them. He wore five knives of his own, and his senses were quicker and keener than Rowan's. That would have to be enough.

He faced him, keeping his back to the door. "I know you received correspondence from Erala this past week."

Rowan's eyes narrowed almost imperceptibly. "Who told you that?"

Sharek was familiar with this dance of bladed words. "No one. I followed you."

"I thought we agreed you'd stay out of my affairs."

"That's difficult to do when you've invited me into them on more than one occasion." *Dodge. Parry.* "What did the letter say, Rowan?"

Rowan shrugged—an upward thrust. "That it's time to strike."

Chills poured down Sharek's spine. *Backhand.* "Al-Morral."

"He's positioned Erala for war. Now it's time for Orleth." Rowan's eyes sharpened. *A heart blow.* "This is your last chance, Sharek. Fight beside me. Help me liberate our people."

"Last chance before what?" *Block. Evade.* "There are no windows this time, Rowan. And no poisoned blades."

Rowan slumped back against the wall and rubbed a weary hand over his eyes—a movement in the dance Sharek had never faced before. "After all this time, you still don't trust me. I'm not going to kill you, I've told you that. But if you choose out, I can't protect you from what's coming."

Sharek, too, broke the familiar dance, clapping Rowan by the shoulders and shaking him. "Rowan, enough. Let it *go*. Al-Morral is not the way to securing our people's future. He has his own ends. This is not about you! Leave his fold before he destroys you."

"I'm in no one's fold." Rowan shrugged him off. "I'm a freed Blessed. I make my own way."

"Then why are you milling around Danje waiting for letters that tell you when to strike? You're Al-Morral's weapon as much as you were ever Aeson's."

Rowan scoffed. "As if you're any better, prowling at Elynor's heels."

"I stay with her because I *choose* to stay. Because I'm *free* to choose, and out of a thousand choices before me, I choose her." The words left him lightheaded as they rushed out—because only in speaking them did he realize they were true.

Elynor was his choice. Whatever that meant, however it would shape his future with the Sanctum, with the Hunterish blood in his veins...he would not abandon her. He would follow her to the depths if he had to. To the Emperium. To whatever lay beyond. And he would ponder the ramifications of that when he wasn't staring down death itself in the eyes while trying to convince it not to be a killing thing.

"Al-Morral or the Sanctum is not a choice, Rowan, it's an ultimatum," he added softly. "And they've made you so desperate you don't even see you're still a slave."

Rowan's eyes were adamant, his jaw flickering with tension. "No one owns me. Al-Morral gave me my freedom."

"And I chose mine. No one had to hand it to me. Which of us do you think is truly free?"

Rowan broke his grip and slammed shoulders with him in passing, stalking from the room. Sharek rubbed his arm and watched the sunlight trace the frame of the shutters, his heart throbbing with anger. And with hurt. And with a hundred revelations all at once.

Betrayal. That was what he'd been wrestling with for days. He'd hoped Rowan would change for him, leave Al-Morral's schemes and truly grasp his own freedom when he saw the example in Sharek.

Because for the first time since Ollanthyr, Sharek Ransalor was truly free. And with that freedom, he would choose to stay.

It was terrifying. Thrilling. Exhilarating. And while it was still all those things, he would have to find a way to deal with Rowan once and for all.

Chapter Forty-Eight

The Meaning of Death

"Y ou're ridiculous, girl."

Elynor gritted her teeth. "I know *you* believe that."

She and Sam were walking back from the seam in the wall where once again they'd spent all morning and afternoon—Sam rigging and testing the lines, Elynor feigning indifference while she stole the unavoidable excuse to soak her feet in the water, serving as his second pair of hands.

Someone had to do it if they were ever going to sail back to Erala, and her father had taught her how to run the rigging. That wasn't her Blessed nature, it was knowledge she'd earned; so why not put it to use?

In moments of clarity, it frightened her just how easy it was to compromise. How much the lines between her inherent nature and her hard-won trade blurred, and how she danced with that boundary; and how little she regretted it afterward.

"It's clear you yearn for the Caeruel." Satisfaction and curiosity fighting currents in his tone, Sam peered past her down the shoreline. "What is it you gain by denying your nature?"

Elynor kicked a shell from her path. "A clear conscience, for one."

But it hadn't been that, ever since her conversation with Mide. And it certainly wasn't now, with her heart torn between the relief of a morning spent working *The Seabird* and the guilt that it felt good at all.

Sam sighed deep in his chest and hefted the burlap sack higher over his shoulder. Shelling was their excuse for their expeditions along the coast, collecting the brightest cones and sea glass to string into necklaces and other trinkets sold at his shop. "You know, girl, one of the things this wicked, wild place has taught me is that when it comes to sink or swim, we don't find out who we are. We *choose* who to be."

Elynor rolled her eyes. She'd decided long ago that she preferred drunk and caustic Sam to this sailor trying to feed her morsels of gruff wisdom. "And you think I've chosen wrong."

"No. Don't think you've reached the bottom yet."

Elynor could've screamed. She was already struggling to drag herself out of bed every morning; how much further down could she go? "Well, that's going to be glorious day. Any other wisdom you'd like to share?"

"Aye. You're about to step in gull dung."

Elynor skittered to one side, cursing. "Quit your laughing."

Sam chuckled. "Such a pain in my arse."

And he was a pain in hers, but Elynor didn't want to tell him that. She was still afraid to frighten him off. Like everything else in her life, her alliance with Samwel Morlai felt tenuous as a frayed roped.

"You don't have to offer me these little lessons, you know," she said when they reached his keyhole door. "You aren't my tutor."

Sam shrugged. "Can't help it. Your father would've hired me on to whip you into shape. Suppose I came prepared for it."

"Well, you can leave it off now. My father is dead."

"Aye, but you're not. You'd do well to remember that, girl."

And before Elynor could snap that she certainly hadn't hired him for remarks like *that*, Sam went inside and shut the door.

•••

Elynor Azorius was not dead.

But was she truly alive?

Sam's words haunted her every step up the honeycomb streets, through the glittering pockets of last light before dusk settled in. She didn't want to look closely enough at herself to know what it meant to be dead or alive, when she still breathed but the Elynor she'd known was gone, gobbled up by the great, dark ocean of everything she'd learned, of knowing what she was.

A Blessed sailor who couldn't swim the ripcurrents of revelation. She was pathetic indeed.

Spirit heavy, Elynor slipped into the room to find it, as usual, abandoned. When she didn't have Sam, she had this room.

She couldn't imagine having come to Danje when she still held the world in her hands. To be presented before a fair *Khul*, with her father at her side; to dine and laugh and dance among these people without the weight of saving their land spread across her shoulders.

But that vision, winsome and wonderful as it was...why did it feel empty?

Elynor wandered to her rumpled nest and began to smooth the sheets, giving her restless fingers something to do.

A dream of her father at her side in simpler times, without her nature or his fate pressed like a sword to the back of her neck, should not feel like it was missing anything at all. It should not seem empty without a laughing bard partaking of its splendors; or especially without a solemn-eyed Hunter whose radiant warmth filled every corner of the room, every dark cavern of Elynor's aching chest.

Her father would've liked Sharek. He would've tried to give him a job beyond the Sanctum. And he and Sylvester would've laughed for hours over the silliest things and the worst shanties.

Elynor didn't have him anymore, but she had them. And yet she was behaving as if they, too, had died.

Or as if she had.

Slowly, she sank down and picked up a pillow to beat into shape—and something slid out of the casing and onto the bed.

It was Orlethian stock, woven of the finest threads, almost too lovely for the simple note. The two taunting lines scrawled so carelessly on it:

Join me for dinner?
-Rowan

Those lovely, delicate threads crumbled in Elynor's fist as she strangled the note and hurled it to the floor.

So perhaps Sam was right. Perhaps she was a spiritless skeleton, a corpse inhabited by hatred. And if hating Al-Morral and Rowan was all that kept her alive, so be it. She was prepared to end this with her own two hands, if she must.

Snatching her cloak from the coat tree by the door and sliding Sharek's favorite knife from where he always kept it under his pillow, Elynor stole out into the growing dark.

Chapter Forty-Nine

Love, Deserved

ELYNOR HAD SPIED ON Sharek disappearing off at Rowan's side enough times to know where the treacherous eel made his bed. She strode in without knocking, even knowing he likely had a poison-tipped arrow trained on her heart.

But he didn't. There was a table in the center of the room, the other commodities pushed off to the walls to make room for it. Soft candlelight guttered, sending the shadows on the ceiling dancing. Two heaping portions of Orlethian fare almost entirely swallowed the genuine silver platters that held them, and sweet wine, not the sour notes of *arkye*, fletched the air. And Rowan stood by the table with the posture of a perfect gentleman, his hand on the seat that must've been meant for her.

The knife scraped inside Elynor's sleeve, begging for his throat. "What is this?"

"Lamb and rice. And some sort of pudding for dessert."

"You know damned well what I mean."

"Well, Sharek tells me you're making your home in Orleth now that Gavannon's secured the Fleet. Seeing as we may both be here a while, I thought we might as well clear the air. So, why don't you sit down?"

Her stomach was an ocean churned by numerous storms as she approached him, and he drew out the chair so she could sit. Tension banded every muscle until she all but trembled, watching him slink into his own seat across from her. The firelight paved his tattooed head as he drew himself closer to the table.

"I take it you don't pray," he said.

The casual words sparked some of Elynor's defiance, coaxing it up through the waves of terror that beat in her chest. "Let me be clear about this: there is *nothing* that will clear the air between us. You killed my father. And you nearly killed Sharek."

Rowan's eyes flickered with more than just the reflection of the fire. "I deeply regret that."

Elynor scoffed. "I'm certain you do."

Rowan picked up his cutlery. "Eat."

She stared at him. "You really believe I'm that foolish, after how you ended my father's life? You think I would eat or drink *anything* you offered me?"

Rowan set down his fork with a sigh. "What is the *point* of a dinner when no one else eats? You're as kings-damned bad as Sharek. *Here.*" He shoved out his seat, walked around the table, and shoveled bites of Elynor's meal into his mouth. "Convinced?"

She struggled to keep her expression impassive when the briny smell of his clothing filled her nostrils. "Hardly."

Rowan tossed up his hands, but returned to his seat. Elynor watched and waited for him to collapse from poisoning, but he didn't.

After several uncomfortable minutes of eating from his own plate, Rowan swallowed and spoke in a dull, dangerous rasp. "You know, the strange thing about a man blessed with killing is you can trust him better than anyone else."

"Is that so?"

"I could have shot you in the heart the moment you opened my door, I could've broken your neck. Stabbed you. Do you really think that puny knife in your sleeve will protect you from me, if I truly want you dead?"

Elynor gripped the table's edge to keep her hands from shaking. "Then what do you want from me?"

"To eat and talk, as I said." Rowan picked up his cutlery again. "It's your choice, but you're a fool if you believe I'd waste time poisoning you when I could just as easily throw this fork through your eye."

Elynor steeled her wits against the guile of his words. "You took the time to poison my father."

"Gavannon's idea. A fork through the eye is easy, but it isn't *subtle*. He wanted subtle, so it could pass for a sudden sickness."

That was what the magistrate had called it when Elynor brought Al-Morral forward on charges of murder: Alden Azorius had died of sudden and unpredictable illness. The fault of no one.

"You tied your own hands, do you realize that?" Elynor said. "You killed one of the only powerful men in Erala who might've listened to your people's plight. If you'd ever met with him, he would've listened to you. He would've even spoken to the King on your behalf."

She didn't know if that was entirely true. She never could know, now that her father was gone; but she had to believe that with a Blessed wife in hiding and a daughter kept ignorant of her craft, Alden Azorius would've moved the Emperium itself to break down those laws and set the Blessed free.

Rowan slowly stirred his soup. "That's probably true."

"And for *what*?" Elynor barreled on, her fury breaking the tight mooring that usually leashed it. "Is Al-Morral really the better catch?"

"It wasn't a matter of catching. Al-Morral offered. Alden didn't. I held no ill will toward your father. He was merely the latest in a long string of marks."

"He wasn't a *mark*, you rotting bastard's son! He was a good man, with a future and a family!"

"Not to Gavannon, he wasn't. He was a blockade to be blasted through."

Elynor rested her face in her hands, the anger bludgeoning her body until she ached as if she'd been thrown down and rolled by ripcurrents over reefs. "We never should've trusted that scab-picker."

Rowan snorted, and when Elynor looked up at him, he dabbed his mouth. "So Sharek tells me."

Elynor slowly sat back, resting her trembling hands in her lap. "He tells you much, doesn't he?"

"We're old friends, you know."

"Associates. Accomplices. Not *friends*."

Rowan studied her with upraised brows. "I wonder what that tone is about. You want him all for yourself? Or you can't stomach the thought that he could be friendly with the man who killed your father?"

Elynor shoved back from the table. "I didn't come here so you could lecture me about Sharek."

"Fair." Rowan held up both hands, baring his teeth in a sharp grin. "But I'll say this: he deserves better than to be strung along by an heiress who can't decide moment to moment what she wants."

She slammed her hands down on either side of her plate. "What in the King's name would you know about what I *want*?"

"I know because Gavannon's done everything in his power to take those things away from you. Sharek and I used to have a saying he learned from his mother: your greatest enemy is the one you make. And I suspect Gavannon has made quite the enemy out of you."

Elynor curled her lip. "He hasn't the first *notion*."

Rowan was quiet for a moment, the color paling slightly from his face. "And that's a pity. If you'd left well enough alone, he might've taken the Fleet and left it at that."

Elynor's skin prickled. "What do you mean?"

"I mean that the only reason you aren't dead right this moment is because I respect Sharek too much to make an enemy of my own," Rowan said. "But I'm afraid my contract with Gavannon is very specific. And you're going to help me fulfill it."

"As if I would ever."

"You already have."

And then Rowan choked. The last of the healthy ruddiness drained from his face. He slumped from his chair and slithered to the floor.

Elynor stood rooted in shock, staring at him as he started to twitch and jerk, as foam gathered in the corners of his mouth. His hand crawled toward her, a desperate plea in his eyes. She glanced at her own dish, confusion battling with her horror.

Her food *had* been poisoned?

But why had he eaten it?

Elynor stepped back toward the door, watching Rowan thrash and struggle, fighting to breathe. The cruel irony raised the hair on the back of her neck: he'd poisoned her father, and now he'd been poisoned. It was everything she'd wanted; she hadn't dirtied her hands, hadn't killed him herself. And she did not have to save him.

But what did that make her, if she sat by and watched him suffer as her father had suffered? Was it justice, or cruelty?

A flash in her mind, of Sharek's face when she'd asked him to confront Rowan; of the way he'd looked when he'd told her about him for the first time, that day in the Dru Farwell. The grief and loss in his face.

And suddenly her limbs unlocked, and she was at Rowan's side, yanking him up so he wouldn't choke on his own foam and pushing him against the table's leg to keep him upright.

"What...what are you doing?" Rowan wheezed.

"I don't know. Be quiet," she snapped. "I'm not doing this for you." Toward the door, she bellowed, "Help! We need help—someone, send for a healer!"

Rowan huffed wetly, his damp eyes struggling to meet hers. An odd tilt, almost a smile, yanked at his foam-flocked lips. "Perhaps...you do deserve him, after all."

And then his breathing stopped.

Elynor wrenched her hands back, falling onto her haunches and scooting away from him. Rowan slumped off to the side, his complexion waxy, his eyes fixed.

Dead.

The door sailed open behind Elynor with the stomping of many feet. She whirled upright, shaking and stammering as the *Khul's* guards swarmed into the room.

"We heard a commotion," one of them barked. "What—?"

He broke off with some odd Orlethian curse as he caught sight of Rowan; then he and another guard were at his side, crouching over his body, ministering to him.

"What happened?" Another of the guards demanded, whirling on Elynor.

"I don't know!" she choked. "The food was tainted..."

They looked between her and Rowan. One of the men picked up Rowan's platter. He sniffed it, and his face screwed up in disgust. "Poison."

Elynor gaped at him, her heart pounding, her legs weak. She was treading water above a fathomless abyss, the rogue waves poised to crash over her head.

Rowan hadn't poisoned her food.

Someone had poisoned *his*.

And then she realized the terrible implications of all of this, when one of the guards unthreaded the manacles from his belt and advanced on her.

Chapter Fifty

Eralanite Assassin

"This is nice, isn't it?" Sylvester sighed.

Sharek could only manage a halfhearted grunt in reply.

They were sprawled on the long rooftop that spanned the palace's outer walls, watching the evening stars peek out from behind the veil of clouds. A storm was rolling in, promising snow; Sharek could smell the harsh underbite of the wind's current, but it would be another day at least before it struck. For now, the rooftop was passably comfortable, warmed by the firepits in the rooms below; the cold Sharek felt tonight was only in his chest.

He'd intended to come up here alone, too weary to go out into the city and too restless to sleep. But he'd bumped into Sylvester leaving Mide's room, and with one look at his face, the bard had followed him up to the roof.

There, Sharek had told him everything that had transpired with Rowan the day before; and now he couldn't muster a word.

When he didn't speak, Sylvester folded his hands behind his head and shot him a glance. "Honestly, Sharek, did you expect any different from Rowan? You've been hunting him for a weakness all this time."

Sometimes it hadn't felt like it. Some nights he'd let his guard down and spoken of the Sanctum with the only person who understood the horrors he'd suffered there. Some nights had felt like he was hunting Rowan, and some had felt like he was begging him back from a precipice, praying to the Empyreans he'd somehow be heard.

"I don't know what I expected," he sighed. "Maybe I lived the lie so much I began to believe that all of us could have a life here."

Sylvester rolled onto his side. "You truly want that?"

"No. Not for myself. Erala is my home, and I was born to defend it. I couldn't be happy here, particularly if there was a war."

"I could be." Sylvester reached out, his touch as light as his voice, and trailed his fingertips over the long neck of his *shudraga*. "When I'm here, I'm not thinking of running to the next place. I'm not a bard or a healer or any other rocks-damned lie. I'm just...me."

Sharek swallowed. "Then perhaps you should stay, old friend."

Sylvester jerked his hand back from the *shudraga*. "And what, leave you to stop a war alone? I think not."

What did he need Rowan for, when Sylvester understood him so well? Almost every part of him, anyway.

"So," Sylvester said after a moment, "what *are* you going to do about Rowan?"

Sharek grimaced. "Bring him before the *Khul*, as I promised. With note in fist, if he hasn't burned it."

"And if he has? Do you suppose—"

A blur of distant sound masked his next words: pounding feet. The slam of a door. Shocked voices, growing louder.

Sharek sat up, raising a hand for silence, and Sylvester faltered. "What is it?"

And then Sharek heard the voice he'd been straining for, hoping against every instinct that he wouldn't hear it: Elynor.

Screaming.

He was on his feet and tearing down the slant of the roof before Sylvester could even shout his name.

The cool wind yanked at Sharek's clothes as he sprinted the length of the wall, past the *ger* in the center and over the inner courtyard. Across its span, interrupted by the shivering angles of the *Aljalam* tree, he glimpsed a host of Orlethian guards dragging Elynor from a room.

Rowan's room.

Sharek poured all his strength into running, cutting the two corners of the courtyard's end sharply and flying back along the roof toward them. Elynor was begging the guards to listen to her, resisting their hold, tugging against the shackles clamped around her wrists—

Shackles.

They'd put Elynor Azorius in *chains*.

The scars of old abrasions on his wrists sang a death-cry, and Sharek launched himself down from the rooftop, slamming into the guard who held Elynor and throwing him up against the railing, then knocking him senseless with a blow to the head. He turned on the second man and cut out his legs, chopped his throat, and dumped him into the courtyard. Then he brushed Elynor behind him, whirled to face her, and gripped her arms. "What—?"

Something struck his temple. The feeling went out of his limbs. Elynor screamed his name as his legs failed.

Sharek woke in a daze. In darkness. It was some moments before the dim outlines of things congealed into shapes, and by the distant glow of an oil lamp, he became aware his vision was arrested by black slats.

Prison bars.

He groaned, and something soft shifted under his head. Heat grazed his cheek and a steady, fast thumping brushed against his temple: Elynor's pulse. He hadn't even realized its cadence was familiar until he also registered her folded legs under his head and her fingers at his temple, stroking the hair from the throbbing gash where the guard had struck him.

"Where are we?" he rasped.

It wasn't Elynor who answered, but Sylvester, from somewhere in the darkness by Sharek's feet, his voice somehow both buoyant and hopeless in the way only he could ever be: "Did you know the palace had dungeons? Because I did not. Ah, the potent joys of discovery."

"You wouldn't be here with us if you hadn't jumped on that guard's back like a deranged monkey," Elynor said curtly—then added after a pause, "Thank you for that."

"My genuine pleasure."

Sharek slowly sat up. His head spun with discomfort, and he was certain he was concussed; but curiosity and dread prodded his limbs like knives, refusing him a moment more to lie inert. "Elynor, what were you doing in Rowan's room?"

"Having...dinner." Her voice was harsh, quiet, and full of disbelief, as if she couldn't fathom for herself that she'd dared do such a thing.

Sharek's heart raced. "Did he harm you?"

"No, he..." Elynor caught her breath. "Sharek, he's dead."

He stared at her, the firelight falling past his shoulder to caress the angles of her freckled face and paint the shock dulling her eyes.

Rowan is dead, I'm afraid. The memory of Aeson Thalanor's voice roared in his empty ears. *So now it's just you.*

"How?" Sharek breathed.

"I don't know. But I swear by the—by your Empyreans, it was not me. They think it was, that's why they put me in chains, but it wasn't."

"Why would they think that?" Sylvester demanded.

"Because I was with him when it happened." Elynor's voice shrank to a whisper. "And someone poisoned him. I recognized the effects...it was the same poison that killed my father."

Pity and rage tore at Sharek's heart. Over and over, venomous hands wound into Elynor's life, dragging the waters of her greatest fears until the silt gave up the cadavers of her past. Her father's passing. Abigale's treachery. Sharek's own near-death. And now Rowan himself, before her very eyes.

Poison, poison, poison.

Sylvester shifted his seat. "Could it have been Mide?"

"It's possible," Elynor admitted. "The *Daishi* might have supplied her with the herbs to do it, something he bought at the harbor."

"But why would Mide let you take the blame?" Sharek asked. "She seems like a fair woman, from what Sly's told us. She's worked hand-in-hand with you to do this the just way. Why now resort to murder?"

"Because you haven't accused him yet?" Elynor offered.

"No, he's right, Mide isn't the sort to go behind our backs," Sylvester said. "Besides, I was with her all evening discussing what to do about the *Daishi* once Rowan was gone."

"All right, fair. But who else is there?" Elynor demanded.

Sharek grazed his thumb over his talisman. "Al-Morral."

Their silence was so absolute, it made his ears throb.

"You think he's here?" Elynor hissed.

"No. But I think his hand is in it. Rowan told me that his time to strike had finally come…and now he's dead." The words ached strangely coming off his tongue.

To think he no longer had to fear Rowan's knife in his back…but then, when had he last?

"So, Rowan failed." Hope brightened Sylvester's voice.

"No," Sharek said softly. "Because as it happens, an Eralanite heiress has just murdered the *Khul's* left hand."

Elynor's fingers shot up to cover her mouth. Sylvester's head hit the wall, and he groaned.

"He's spent months feeding the *Khul* the lie that Erala is turning against Orleth," Sharek went on, the plan unfolding before his eyes as if Rowan lurked beside him, whispering it in his ear. "Elynor is a known ally of King Marcus. If she's blamed for Rowan's death, the *Khul* can easily conclude that she also killed Alden, all to frame Orleth…under the King's own orders."

"Implicating the King directly," Elynor whispered between her fingers. "Making Him the culprit."

Sylvester rubbed his eyes. "What better way to start a war?"

Sharek sank his shoulder against the wall. "He did it. He truly did it."

And Sharek himself had been right all along: one more person had indeed been sacrificed in the name of starting this war.

But he had never dreamed Rowan would turn that blade against himself.

Chapter Fifty-One

Ravenous Rage

Jamyson did not know how long he crouched under the veil of darkness, hiding his head in the shadows, until he couldn't sleep anymore. Until his body prodded him back to life.

He opened his eyes to a sight so familiar, he thought every horror he'd witnessed in recent memory must've been a dream.

For there was Vestan, sitting at the dining table like always, flipping a dagger to himself, red hair unbound over his broad shoulders and gaze lost in thought.

So he wasn't dead. And neither were the royal siblings. And neither was…

"Esmae," Jamyson croaked.

The dagger halted. Vestan sat forward slowly, not looking at him, and buried the tip of the blade in the table. "They took her body away some days ago. You've been asleep for a while."

Jamyson's eyes shuddered closed as the cold slap of reality struck him across the face.

This was real. This was his life now: this empty ache in his chest that could never be repaired, and his arms that could never again hold what was precious to him. Every moment of that hateful day, searing white-hot as a newly-forged blade, sliced into him again and again. Death by a thousand small wounds. "She did this for me. Lied to the King, sacrificed herself for me. So I could continue the fight."

"That sounds like our Esmae."

Jamyson rolled onto his back, slinging an arm across his eyes. Even knowing none of it had been a dream, he couldn't bring himself to be shocked that Vestan was somehow alive. He only felt a small jab of curiosity. "How are you even here, Vez?"

"Came in through the door."

"You know what I mean."

Vestan was quiet for a moment. "After the fall, I woke in the shallows of a branch of the river that runs along the valley floor. I must've fallen into that. That was how I survived, I think...that, and my strength."

Jamyson couldn't bring himself to ask after his siblings...Vestan would tell him if they'd survived. But he'd never expected to reap back any of his dead, and this alone was a gift. "I'm glad you're here."

Vestan's boots brushed the floor and came to a halt at the bedside. "Tell me what I can do."

"Turn back time. Revive the dead."

Vestan's weight depressed the mattress as he sank onto it. "For you, I would. But I'm not Blessed with such power."

Jamyson dropped his arm and peeled open his eyes. He stared at the canopy of his bed. "My father may have landed the killing blow, but Al-Morral was a part of this. It wasn't Esmae he wanted dead...it was me. And he used my father's sickness to drive a blade between us. If not for her, I'd be the one..."

He couldn't say it. Couldn't go back to that place, to the sight of her swinging on the rope.

"Then it's Al-Morral we must stop," Vestan said.

"Not just him." Jamyson planted his hands in the pillows behind himself and sat up. Every muscle ached as if with a terrible fever; his face was hot, and everything hurt. But he would press through it, because he must. His very survival depended on it.

The moment the thought settled in, some of the tension loosened, and the fog in his head abated. He pinched his temples with his thumb and middle finger.

"Not just Al-Morral," he repeated. "Things haven't been good, Vez. Hangings at the Solstice. Every lord and magistrate signing personal lands over to the Throne. It's gone far enough."

Vestan frowned. "What are you saying, Jamyson?"

He clapped a hand to his guard's shoulder and rose on unsteady legs, shuffling to the dining table where Vestan had left a hard loaf of bread and a plate of cheese. He picked at it, sorting through the problem. "You're going to follow Al-Morral again. There's something I need you to find out about him."

Vestan joined him at the table. "What is it?"

"There's a woman he crept off with at the Solstice...Abigale Cainwell. I want you to find out if she's in Dorwenon. Start at the Inn of Tryst. I saw him sneaking off there when I went to visit Cecile in the dungeon. If I have this right, she's important to Al-Morral, which makes her important to us. We need him removed by his choice or by ours, and I think she's the leverage that will make it possible."

Vestan nodded. "What will you be doing?"

Ravenous now that his palate had been stroked, Jamyson fell into his seat at the table and shoveled soft fruit from its pewter central tower into his mouth. "For now, I'll play the part of the faithful prince. The King believes I was under persuasion from Esmae, and I'm going to maintain that ruse right up to the foot of His Throne where I can finally do what needs to be done."

Vestan slowly leaned his hands on the table. "Jamyson?"

He swallowed, meeting Vestan's gaze, and the question there, without fear. He felt nothing but a simmering, sharp certainty that the only way to keep them alive was to do what was most dangerous.

"I'm going to kill the King."

Chapter Fifty-Two

The Seabird Set Free

The darkness of the prisons below the palace was slick and oily, breathing with the motions of its prisoners. Some wailed and sobbed; some cursed and raved. Thin glints of torchlight bled down the hall, grazing against Sharek's weapons, Elynor's compass, Sylvester's lonely *shudraga* all tossed into the corner where the guards had flung them that first night.

After two days, Elynor could hardly stand to look at them anymore.

To her left, Sylvester sat with his legs folded, quietly humming. He rarely was silent; silence belonged to Sharek. He sat with his face to the wall, clutching his talisman.

Elynor lifted her head from where she'd splayed out on her side, arm bent into a pillow, and studied his curved back and the creases of fear in his face where the torchlight touched his brown skin.

Sympathy joined the stranglehold despair held over her throat. She sat up, stiff and chilled from the cold stone, and pushed herself over to sit beside him. "Sharek."

His breath eased out, slow and tremulous. "The hovel beneath the Sanctum."

Of course this darkness, those cage slats, reminded him of his last prison. Heart thudding with pity, Elynor swiveled to mirror his posture, facing the wall. "A Hunter doesn't belong behind prison bars."

"Nor does an heiress of the sea."

A gentle spark of warmth bloomed in her chest, then cowered against the depths of the blackness hugging their cell. "What do you think will happen to us now?"

"I wish I knew."

Sharek stiffened suddenly, the moment the last word left his lips; and at the same moment several prisoners further up the dungeon's snaking path shifted from taunting words to cruel, provocative suggestions.

Elynor had spent enough time around swarthy seamen to recognize the hooting of vicious arousal reserved from brigands to women.

She and Sharek rose and turned together as *Khuless* Mide stepped into the open span beyond the corridor to their cell. She carried a torch aloft, and her upswept eyes ticked from Sharek to Elynor to Sylvester, lingering on the bard as he slowly came to his feet.

"I expected better from you," she growled. "More subtlety in the kill."

"I did not kill Rowan," Elynor retorted. "He killed himself to drive your mother toward war with Erala."

"This was all part of the plan I warned you about," Sylvester added. "Rowan took his own poison and implicated her for it."

Mide tipped her head, holding Elynor's gaze with cool ferocity; then she stabbed the torch into a bracket on the wall and came close enough to the bars that she could speak quietly. "I wish that did not seem sensible regardless of my power. But it does, especially with what's transpired since."

Sharek's eyes narrowed. "What do you mean?"

"The Blessed's body is gone. Stolen from the undertaker, we assumed."

Elynor gripped the wall behind her as weakness spilled through her knees.

It couldn't be. It *couldn't* be.

She'd seen his lifeless eyes. Felt the breath go out of him.

And yet...

"Stolen," Sylvester echoed sharply.

"No," Elynor whispered, the cold impossibility cracking her heart in two. "Not stolen. He had the guards provide a kings-damned *antidote*."

No wonder they had reached the room so swiftly, after so little commotion; no wonder they had ministered so feverishly over him, even when there'd been no breath in his body.

He knew poisons. And he knew *cures*.

A cure withheld from her father, but given to Rowan.

"He's going back to Erala," Sharek groaned. "Of course he is. Now he has veritable *proof* that Elynor tried to kill him with the same poison that killed Alden."

"And if Al-Morral has somehow convinced the King that Elynor was complicit in her father's death..." Sylvester muttered. "Oh, rocks, if He believes she's an Orlethian *spy*, that she did it on the *Khul's* behalf, and then attacked Rowan to keep her secret from being exposed..."

"Then King Marcus may think His only choice is to go to war with Orleth for meddling in Eralanite affairs," Sharek finished.

Mide's fingers wound around the iron bars so tightly, her joints popped. "Both sides have a sword at the other's neck for the same offense."

The trade agreements. The deaths. And in the middle of it, Elynor and Rowan.

"We should never have chased Rowan here," Elynor croaked. "We handed him the weapon he and Al-Morral needed to turn the *Khul* and the King against each other."

Sharek squeezed her shoulder. "I know Rowan. He had a hundred contingencies besides this one. We were only one possible course to starting this war."

"It hasn't begun yet," Mide said. "I know you speak truth about what you did and did not do. I will try to sway my mother to see that Rowan was no friend of Orleth. Perhaps now that his body has vanished without trace, she'll doubt him. The three of you—"

She tensed abruptly and turned away from them, facing up the corridor. Sharek stiffened as well, his hand sliding from Elynor's shoulder.

Something bumped along the floor, rolling to a halt at Mide's feet, hissing with steam.

Sharek grabbed Elynor and Sylvester and yanked them back from the cage slats. "Cover your faces!"

Mide drew her swords, then dropped them almost at once. Hacking and wheezing, she crumbled to her knees. Sylvester jerked forward, but Sharek held him back, his gaze fixed down the corridor toward three figures who came charging into the smoke. They wore thick handkerchiefs around their noses and mouths, but even so, Elynor would have recognized them anywhere.

The crashing surf of her pulse slowed to a whisper, hardly strong enough to fill a tidepool. "Mother."

Chapter Fifty-Three

The Legend of Ardeth Lamruil

Iracabeth struck a strange blue-green torch that burned off the smoke, though Mide still lay delirious when it cleared. Fury tightened Iracabeth's eyes as she reached the iron slats. "No one puts my daughter in a cage. *No one.*"

Despite the angry terms on which they'd parted, Elynor's heart soared. "How did you find us?"

"How do you think?" Samwel Morlai's gruff voice emerged from behind his own cowl as he moved to Iracabeth's side. "This blasted woman marched into my shop and demanded to know where you were—as if I was hiding you under my rutting table!"

"As if you'd have room for her down there," Iracabeth scoffed. "Honestly, your house is a sty."

"Better than a clay oven. Do you know you don't have to burn a fire every single hour of the day? I about sweated blood in your *ger*!"

"And how else was I to ensure you sobered up?"

Rue rolled her eyes, signed sharply at them—to which Iracabeth rolled her eyes in turn—then produced a set of keys and tiptoed past Mide, unlocking the cage. Sylvester brushed her arm in silent greeting before he knelt to touch the line of Mide's jaw. "She lives."

"Of course she does. We aren't murderers," Iracabeth said. "It's a simple sleeping drought. She and the guards will wake shortly."

Elynor slipped from the cell and stood before her mother, lost for words. She had intended never to see her again; how could she be both wary and relieved that her hopes were dashed? "*Why* are you here?"

Iracabeth raised a hand as if to touch her face, then let her arm fall. "I haven't been able to stop thinking about what you said to me...the asking price for this war. And you were right. The plight of the Blessed is crucial, but Alden's life was too high a cost to pay. And he would not have wanted Erala go to war in his name." Tears slipped from her eyes, disappearing below her cowl. "So, in his name, we don't break Erala. We heal it."

Sharek tilted his head. "We?"

Sam shrugged. "Seems our crew has grown by two."

Iracabeth's cheeks plumped with a smile. "It's time to set sail, Seabird. Back to Erala."

Fear, anticipation, wild relief all spilled through her. She did not know what to do with a single one of them.

Sharek jerked his gaze sharply to the corridor. "Guards."

All at once, Iracabeth was serious again, turning to follow his stare. "How many?"

"Two dozen. Maybe more."

Rue growled under her breath and signed to Iracabeth, who grimaced. "We've used up all the smoke."

"Sharek?" Elynor said.

"I can't fight two dozen alone without casualties. And I'm not certain Mide would take lightly to us killing her mother's guards."

Sam tossed Sharek, Elynor, and Sylvester their effects. "We'll do what we can."

Elynor pocketed her compass and followed him, but after a half-dozen steps she realized Sharek and Sylvester had not moved. Sylvester stared at the *shudraga*, and Sharek stared at him.

"Sharek, Sly, come on!" she urged.

Still, they didn't move.

"It's the only way," Sharek said as if in answer to some silent question.

Sylvester shook his head and jogged to catch up to Elynor, leaving Sharek to bring up the rear.

They followed the twisting corridor for some distance past other cells full of unconscious prisoners, not a waking guard in sight, though they hopped over countless sleeping ones. Following a gentle upward slope, they emerged into a round antechamber cluttered with tables where assumed criminals—and falsely accused ones—were logged before the guards dragged them into the prison.

There was only one door out. And no less than thirty guards between here and there.

Iracabeth thrust out an arm, sweeping Elynor and Rue back. Sam stepped before them, fists raised, his scowl like a storm. Elynor looked wildly at Sharek as the guards primed their rustic bows and took aim; but he was looking at Sylvester, and had not even touched his weapons.

"Sharek!" Elynor cried, fear hot in her throat.

"You have to do this!" Sharek grabbed Sylvester's shoulder and shook him. "Sly, I beg of you—"

The guards shouted at them to stand down. Sam stepped forward instead, jaw tight, goading them with curled fingers and aggressive strides to aim their arrows at only him; and all the while, Sylvester held the *shudraga* with shaking hands, his whole body trembling, his breaths heaving out in silent gasps.

A whisper of sound cut the silence as the first bowstring released.

"*Ardeth*!" Sharek bellowed.

And Sylvester cried, almost in tandem, "Get behind me, all of you!"

The first strum from his *shudraga* was like no sound Elynor had ever heard before. It was not music, it was a blade—a sharp wall of sound that crashed against the arrows, breaking them into slivers.

Elynor's hand flew over her mouth as the bard planted his feet, tucked his head, and strummed out another scythe of raw power that blasted the guards against the walls, knocking them unconscious in heaps.

The third stroke broke the prison door clean off its hinges.

No one moved. Elynor did not breathe.

"A Blessed musician," Sam growled.

At his words, confirming what Elynor had just witnessed with her own eyes and yet hardly dared to believe, she realized who Sylvester truly was.

Ardeth Lamruil. A figure of a story told in their prison cart...yet he was standing here. In the flesh.

Sharek took his shoulder and pressed his forehead against Sylvester's—Ardeth's—temple. "Thank you, old friend."

Sylvester's shoulders rolled with a silent breath as his secret released into the world. And Elynor, her heart crying out at his pain so like hers, wrapped her arm around his back and squeezed him gently.

Rue stepped before them, jerking both thumbs over her shoulders, and Elynor glowered at the dragnet. "You knew."

"I asked her not to tell you." Sylvester sniffed deeply and shrugged Sharek and Elynor off, lashing the *shudraga* to his back. "She's right. We must go, before Mide wakes up and sets all Danje's wrath against us."

Elynor was going to have a conversation with this bard. And soon. But for now, she followed him out into the light.

Chapter Fifty-Four

Sink or Swim

The slam of flying footfalls drummed in Elynor's temples, echoing the clash of warning bells that tolled throughout Danje. Black smoke peppered the air where archers mapped their small party's wild dash through the city streets, from the palace all the way through the mariner's district. People flocked the streets, staring in slack-jawed awe at the group of six that fled down the sloping avenues. The mosaic of colored light bounced along the rooftops, dappling their way as Sam took the lead, his feet familiar with every path.

They burst out on the docks at last, feet pounding the swollen wood, and Sharek stumbled with a curse, breaths wheezing in his scarred lungs.

Elynor dropped back beside him and yanked on the bulging muscles of his upper arm. "*Get. Up!*"

"I can't," he gasped, slowing even further.

Elynor met his eyes and silenced the plea there with a hiss. "Don't you dare ask me to do this again, Sharek Ransalor. I need you to get on your feet. Now!"

The dock shook as the first wave of guards reached the end, dashing toward them. Iracabeth and Rue doubled back with bows unleashed, shooting in tandem, and the guards scattered; Elynor yanked Sharek's arm around her shoulders and towed him to his feet, and they limped down to the end of the pier where *The Seabird* was moored.

A rogue wave of panic smashed over Elynor so hard she was nearly the one who halted this time. The thought of being on the waves again, frightening, and traitorous as it was...she'd never wanted anything so badly in her life.

Sylvester fell back beside them, and together they helped Sharek into the schooner where he collapsed on his knees, still struggling for air. Rue leaped in with him, gripping his hand and coaxing him into steadier, calmer breathing, while Sam prepped the sails and rigging and barked orders at Sylvester.

"Elynor, help me!" Iracabeth shouted, and Elynor lunged to the mooring bollards, helping her undo the knots, their movements so precisely attuned that Elynor saw her father's teaching in both their hands.

Iracabeth shot her a quick look and a grim smile that echoed the sentiment—and melted quickly as a great, guttural moan echoed through the harbor.

"Oh, Empyreans help us," she breathed.

"They're closing the harbor gate!" Sam roared. "Get into the schooner, both of you—*now*!"

Iracabeth all but tossed Elynor into the boat, diving after her as Sam and Sylvester cast off from the dock. Elynor floundered upright, gripping the edge of the schooner, her ears aching as the winches and pullies in the wall shifted in loud pops and screeches. Teams of figures, distant as midday shadows, manned the levers, heaving together at the gates set into the wall.

If they closed, Elynor and her friends would be trapped in the harbor with the *Khul's* guards—many of whom were running up their own sails, preparing to give chase.

They'd be fodder for the depths.

Sam and Sylvester struck like lightning tines along the schooner, letting out sails, manning the helm, working the rigging to lend them speed. Elynor's fingers flexed, feeling the lines sliding between them, the delicious burn of the ropes against her palms and forearms. Remembering how it had felt to be master of the water. Queen of the Caeruel. To make it her ally rather than her enemy.

Heat beat against her throat as they picked up speed and the gates continued to groan, flaking rust and barnacles while they trundled toward closed.

Sharek shouted suddenly, and his arm came around Elynor's back, forcing her down. A scattering of impacts along the side of the schooner raised the hair on her neck; arrows hailed down from clefts in the wall as archers took aim once more, their serrated tips tearing through the sails and burrowing deep in the schooner.

Elynor covered her head and Sharek rolled on top of her, shielding her with his body.

A vicious cry ripped at her ears, against her heart. Sylvester shouted Sam's name, and Elynor snapped her gaze up as Sam crumbled, an arrow jammed through the back of his shoulder.

Iracabeth crawled toward him, leaving a shaking Rue undefended. Sylvester dropped and jerked her into his arms, guarding her with his frame and holding the helm with one hand. And still the gate tolled inward, nearer and nearer to caging them.

The storm of arrows abated as the archers ran out their quivers. Sylvester shoved Rue toward Iracabeth and Sam and started to work the lines, but their speed flagged. As Sharek rolled away from her and scrambled to hold Sam down, Elynor sat up on her knees. She looked around at all of them, then darted her focus toward the gate, her heart plummeting at the distance.

This was what Sam had warned her about. This was sinking to the bottom.

It was Sam's blood on the schooner's belly and Sylvester helpless at the lines; it was Rue and Iracabeth stuffing their hands into Sam's chest and back to save him; it was Elynor's eyes finding Sharek's and knowing that any moment, he was going to die.

They both were.

And yet there was no fear in Sharek's face. There was something else, calm and focused, like the eye at the center of a maelstrom, like breaking through raging waters and cruel winds and finding peace.

Faith.

There was faith in how he looked at her.

Staring at him, the gate grinding inexorably on its wheels and the Orlethian vessels streaking closer, Elynor let go of everything.

She released the King's opinions. Her ingrained prejudices. Her own fear of what she was.

For one moment, in the calm of the storm, she looked at herself through Sharek's eyes.

She had brought them this far with scraps of training and the uncompromising will to stop a war and save Sharek's life. She had braved storms and rogue waves and pursuing vessels and kept them all alive, not in spite of her power as a Blessed, but only *because* of it.

They were alive today because of what she was. What she had always been. What she had fled from being.

And if she kept running now, they would descend to their watery graves in Orleth, and Al-Morral and Rowan would win. Because Sylvester couldn't sail this schooner alone, and Sam was senseless, groaning and thrashing as Iracabeth and Rue tended to him. They needed Sylvester's healing talents; and the schooner needed *her*.

There was no one else. But if she could lay hand to helm, they would *need* no one else.

With a jolt, Elynor's spirit struck the bottom.

Sink or swim.

Her fingers slid into her pocket, grazing her compass.

When the time comes, you will know the way to go. You have always known the way.

Her father's spirit hovered beside her, warmer than a sun-washed sea, begging to be let in. And rather than fleeing it this time, rather than resenting it, she let it in: the memory of his proud smile, his fathomless love, and everything he'd ever taught to her. It filled her like a cistern until she overflowed. It lifted her up from the bottom, touched her feet to silt and stone, showed her which way was up—a glorious light far above.

Sink.

Or swim.

Elynor lunged forward, shoving Sylvester out of the way. "Move! Help my mother with Sam!"

He staggered back as she took the lines, seeing her first step and then the next, a pattern of motions from here to the gate. Through it. Beyond.

She called Sharek to the helm and instructed him where to put his hands, her instincts and her father's voice booming out of her as she ran up the main sail and dropped the second to half-mast. At her command, Sharek spun the rudder, and they cut across the path of the nearest Orlethian ship, forcing the captain to drop his speed and turn to avoid collision. Elynor righted their course with a flex of the lines and tore for the gate.

"Sylvester. Sharek," she said, and their eyes snapped to her. She jerked her chin at the gate.

It would be so kings-damned close. But they could do it together.

Sylvester rose and snatched up the *shudraga*, sprinting to the bow, and Sharek called Rue to the wheel. He showed her how to hold it, picked up Iracabeth's discarded bow and quiver, and darted after Sylvester.

Elynor tied the lines and leaped over the sparse cargo Sam had brought aboard. They were picking up speed, drawing nearer to the gate—and nearer to the archers, primed once more and waiting for them to come in range.

"Please, please, please," Elynor chanted.

Sylvester stood on the bowsprit, his *shudraga* braced against his shoulder. Sharek stepped up on the railing, cocking one foot on the crossbeam and winding the other through the ropes that laced the wood. Then he drew, sighted, and released.

A volley of arrows flew askance as Sharek fired faster than Elynor could track, sending archers scattering on the walls, skewing their aim. Sylvester ducked his head and his fingers slammed down the *shudraga's* neck, sending currents of Blessed music screaming out from his instrument, a pulsing vibration on the air. The gates creaked to a halt, the deep scrape and howl of their joints sending lances of pain, hot and jagged, slicing into Elynor's temples. She nearly dropped to the deck, her hand to the mast the only thing that kept her feet beneath her.

The gate buckled and bowed out under the force of Sylvester's music. He played harder, quicker, punishing the neck of the instrument so hard his fingers bled, the current of sound barely holding the gap.

And then they were through, squeezing into a seam so slim it raked the sides of the schooner, showering wood splinters in the sea. *The Seabird* speared out into the Orlethian Channel, and the larger ship full of the *Khul's* men smashed its bow into the halves of the gate with a thunderous boom. The crew cursed in rage.

Pulse thundering, Elynor set her eyes to the horizon. The shadows of fear and resentment had retreated to her farthest corners, finding no purchase on her spirit now that she'd reached out to the sea in her moment of desperation, and it reached back—a cool embrace so familiar she nearly wept at its touch.

Erala's shores were far away, yet she felt she'd already come home.

Chapter Fifty-Five

Fate and Faith

After days of sailing the Caeruel, Elynor had relearned its dance like a familiar partner. Luck was on their side; the going had been smooth so far, the wind at their backs. It often was in the winter, Alden had taught her long ago; that was why their imports were better than their exports this time of year.

She missed him deeply, but he was with her now in the pieces that were slowly reawakening after so long a slumber.

Elynor looked across the schooner, taking stock of the crew: Sharek near the helm, enduring lessons from Sam while Iracabeth changed the dressing on his shoulder; Rue sorting out the rations, ensuring they had enough for six; Sylvester at the bow, sitting with his arms linked around his knees. It was the first time he'd sat still abovedecks; she hardly saw him out of the small cabin.

It was time.

Elynor tied off the lines and picked her way past Rue, offering the dragnet a small nod and lowering herself beside Sylvester. "So, then. Ardeth Lamruil."

He chuckled, scratching his neck. "It's a good story, isn't it?"

"Did you really play music for the King?"

He nodded. "For many seasons before He learned what I was. Then I fled Kaer Dorwenon to save my own skin. I changed my looks and my name, and Sylvester Munrow the bard was born. I took up healing as another layer of protection...cloaked myself in sacrosanctity."

"It *was* a good story," Elynor admitted. "I never even suspected. But why didn't you tell me?"

"I've had enough of being hated, and enough of running. I wanted you to think kindly of me, and I didn't suppose you would if you knew the truth...especially after Tariaga Falls."

Elynor winced. "Sly, if I had known..."

"You wouldn't have called us a curse, no, but it would've still been what you felt."

Elynor sighed and leaned her head back to look up at the stars. "But not toward you."

"Well, what's done is done." Sylvester shrugged. "It seems we were both fated to come into our own. Now my secret is out there, and you've embraced yours."

"I suppose. It's terrifying."

"Yes. Very much so, yes. But we helped our friends to freedom, didn't we? So maybe we aren't cursed after all."

Elynor desperately wanted to believe that her power was an answer to unspoken questions, not a problem to be solved. But only time would prove if that could be true, for she had not yet faced the King.

At the thought of Him, lightning pricked Elynor's fingertips. She jolted to her feet and offered a hand to Sylvester. "We have things to discuss with the others."

They joined them near the helm, where Sam had taken the wheel. His keen gaze followed Elynor's approach. "You walk with the waves under your step now, girl."

Elynor smiled at him. "No sense trying to flee from what I am anymore. I'd just topple into the water."

Sharek snorted, and Iracabeth laughed outright. But Sam watched her warily. "And our contract?"

The Fleet. She'd forgotten...it was rightfully his.

Her heart crashed against her ribs. "Let's have that conversation once the Fleet is actually mine to give away again."

Sam draped his arms through the wheel spokes. "You mean this Al-Morral bastard?"

Elynor nodded. "We'll have to get the measure of things when we reach Erala, but he must've made an in-road with the King. It's the only reason he would've spurred Rowan to act now."

"I shudder to think what Erala primed for war must look like," Sylvester said. "What's changed since we left?"

"We'll find out soon enough," Sharek said. "But we must go carefully, Elynor."

"I know. We ought to go to Kaer Dorwenon and meet with Prince Jamyson in secret. He's been at the beating heart of everything that's happened, he'll be able to tell us Al-Morral's standing with the King...and we can decide together what to do about it."

"Kaer Dorwenon it is, then," Sylvester said.

"For you lot, maybe," Sam said. "I agreed to ferry you back to Erala. Didn't sign a contract to be in the middle of a bloody war."

"Well, you're welcome to go slumming about in Bast," Iracabeth retorted. "But if we can't prevent this war, it will find you somewhere, Samwel Morlai. You might think of taking on a bit of discomfort now to avoid being inconvenienced in the future."

"And you cared for the *Khul's* family," Elynor said quickly. "You don't want to see them harmed. And they will be if Ergene goes to war. If not for us, then do it for them...to prevent another tragedy from falling on them."

After a moment, Sam scoffed. "All right, you swindling eels. But if this has me killed, I won't take it kindly."

"Fair," Elynor smiled. "If we make landfall near the southern coast, Bernian can drive us to Kaer Dorwenon."

"Do you trust him?" Iracabeth asked.

"I do. He and Gregor have been at my side since I first hired Sharek."

"Southern coast it is," Sam said.

"Let Elynor man the helm for now," Iracabeth ordered. "*You* need to rest."

"I'm fine, woman."

"Which of us is the healer, and which the stubborn arse?"

"Both, to the latter."

Iracabeth gave him a hard shove. "Go to your cabin. I'll wake you at shift change."

Sam grumbled, but he went, followed by Rue, who had taken generously to helping him in and out of his shirts to spare the stitches. Iracabeth leaned against the railing, watching them duck into the cabin.

"Will he be all right?" Elynor asked, filling the uncomfortable silence when Sylvester and Sharek also moved away.

"He will. We have plenty of herbs to stave off infection."

Elynor let out a slow breath. "I'm glad you were here to help him."

"I'm glad to be here at all."

Elynor peeked at her from the corners of her eyes. "Do you really mean that?"

Iracabeth blinked, frowning. "Of course I do. Elynor, I didn't leave for any reason but to keep our family safe. And now I'm returning because you need me."

Elynor pressed her lips together as a swell of fathomless feeling rocked through her. Being her father's prodigy had come as simply as breathing, because of what she was and how she'd been raised. She didn't know how to be her mother's daughter, to need someone who'd been so long away.

Sharek returned to the helm just then, and Elynor could've wept with relief. "It sounds like Rue is having some trouble making Sam take his sleeping drought."

Iracabeth rolled her eyes. "I'll go thrash him into shape, the fool."

Elynor bent against the wheel, easing the kinks from her back as her mother disappeared into the cabin. "Thank you, Sharek."

"I don't know what you mean." His expression artfully marshalled, he faced the horizon beside her and slid his hand slowly along the wheel, grazing the spokes.

Elynor smiled and shook her head.

Sharek's hand climbed over the spokes, one after the other, pausing when his arm was level with her shoulder. Elynor ducked so that he gripped the wheel on the far side of her, then linked her fingers with his free hand and brought it up to grip the wheel as well. With his arms enclosing her on either side, chasing off the chill of the winter-kissed sea, her shivers eased and heat puddled in her bones.

Off on the bow, Sylvester sat with his *shudraga*, playing a gentle song that fit the feeling that surged in Elynor's chest; it sounded like seafaring and wandering abroad, and coming home after so long away that one had lost and rediscovered who they were.

"Do you think it's a weakness to need someone in your life?" Elynor asked, thinking of her mother.

"If it is, then I am the weakest man in all the world."

She craned her head back to look up at him and found him already peering down at her, wearing that same look from the day they'd escaped Danje: faith.

But not just that anymore.

"I'm a liar." The words stormed from Elynor on a soft breath, and then she couldn't stop. "When I told you that I chose to walk away. I've tried, and I can't. I keep coming back. Because..." By the Throne, why was this so *difficult*? "Because I also need you."

Sharek's hands gripped both of hers around the spokes, that gentle squeeze both giving and asking permission. And Elynor gave into months of longing with a stretch upward, with the gentle arch of her back into his chest and her mouth finding his.

The kiss was a burst of majestic warmth and ecstasy that flooded through her at the softness of his lips and tongue—like diving from a cliff into unknown waters and finding them both foreign and familiar, warm and wild, dangerous and liberating. His fingers slipped from the wheel, his arms wrapped around her waist, and she let go of the spokes with one hand to grip the back of his head, keeping him with her as they learned the patterns of one another's breathing. Feeling. Opening themselves wide. *Belonging*. And needing, without shame, one another's touch. And their trust. And their love.

And their strength, to face the treacherous waters ahead.

Chapter Fifty-Six

Parting Ways

It seemed impossible that street scum from Bessidia could have the world at his feet, and everything he wanted. But Gavannon Al-Morral was a man who lived to defy expectations.

He'd risen above his stations from urchin to deckhand to First Mate to captain. He'd impressed the very head of the Azorian Fleet. He'd become partner, then Fleetmaster, and now Friend of the King. And with Prince Jamyson quivering like a kicked mongrel in the corners of the kaer, the Throne was so close Gavannon felt its sculpted armrests beneath his hands.

In the month since the slave girl's hanging, the kaer had all but become Gavannon's domain. The King's paranoia had grown enough that he'd begun to believe Orleth had wicked plans against Erala. He'd signed seven different sanctions on the trade routes in the past fortnight at Gavannon's advisement, and He spent less and less time making public appearances, welcoming news from His pages, or overseeing His kingdom. He'd entrusted all these things to Gavannon, and day by day Gavannon learned from tutors and advisers precisely how Erala was run.

If any of them had doubts about the Friend of the King taking on these duties rather than the Prince, they didn't voice them. The fraying rope of loyalty still tugged them between belief in the King's infallible choices—making Gavannon the obvious one—and their fear at what would happen should they raise concerns.

Gavannon always made certain to smile at them and be amiable; he needed their allegiance, not their loathing, when he took the Throne. And with the Prince's head delicately roped to the noose of his father's doubts, and the King Himself making scarce public appearances of late, the people were warming to constant, kind, and steady Gavannon.

Really, he only had one problem: that although the King doubted His Crown Prince, He still fought through the mania of mind sickness to somehow believe in him; not enough to circumvent all of Gavannon's advances on the Throne, but enough that He hadn't named Gavannon regent in Jamyson's stead.

Still. Gavannon Al-Morral was growing used to having everything he wanted, and he would not be thwarted by this grief-stricken Prince.

Resolution thumped his boots harder than normal on the steps of the Inn of Tryst leading up to Abigale's room, and he entered with every intention of plotting new ways to come between the Crown Prince and the King.

Instead he found Abigale sitting in the corner farthest from the door, head in her hands.

Terror shot through him, icy and precise to the heart. He crossed the room in three strides and tumbled down before her, taking her wrists and tugging desperately, trying to see her face. She jerked back from his touch with a soft cry, and then her frightened eyes focused with recognition, and relief cracked her tearstained features. She flung her arms around him and pressed against his warmth, trembling.

Gavannon scooped her into his arms and carried her to the bed, where he leaned against the headboard with her in his lap. He rocked her and stroked her back, torn between a fear that fought to understand hers and a slow, churning whisper of rage that something had happened, and he hadn't been here to stop it. "What is it? Abi, what's the matter? Are you harmed?"

"Not...not yet."

Gavannon tightened his arms around her. "What happened?"

Abigale sucked in several unsteady breaths, then planted her hands on his chest and pushed herself upright, her raw gaze holding his. "I was at the market today, buying the week's food, and...I think someone was following me."

Gavannon tried to quiet his breathing, to stifle the killing rage that rose up at those simple words. "It might have been a messenger. Or an admirer."

"No, I've had plenty of both. I felt ill intention. Whoever was watching wanted to do me harm."

Gavannon rebelled against the visceral urge to draw his sword and hunt this person down. "Did they follow you to the Inn?"

"No, I retraced my steps and changed my patterns. I kept to the open-air market where it was crowded, and when I was certain I wasn't being watched anymore, I ran. But..." she gulped shallowly, her fingers threading his collar.

Gavannon slid his knuckle beneath her chin, tilting her head up until their eyes met. "But?"

"But the feeling was in this room. And my notes are gone, Gav."

The blood fled his head so swiftly he was left dizzy and hollow, a husk, a rattling coffin for his unbeating heart, his unbreathing lungs.

"I thought...I thought you took it with you everywhere, every time you left this room."

"I usually do! But I've forgotten it now and again, and today was one of those days where I didn't remember until I'd left, and I thought it would be such a quick foray to the market that it wouldn't *matter*."

But it did matter. Because her schemes to supplant the King through His wife, His children, the Crown Prince...it was all there. All the damning evidence that could hang them.

Gavannon ached to stand and pace, but he didn't want her to think he was furious with her. "Was anything else taken?"

"Some of my mother's finest jewelry, and my red day gown, the one you love. Why?"

"It may have been nothing more than a petty robbery...someone who sniffed out your wealth and decided to attack in your absence. The malevolent presence you felt might well have been the thief's accomplice ensuring you hadn't yet returned to the Inn."

He warmed to the idea even as he spoke it, a kernel of relief igniting in his chest, but Abigale sawed her lip in her teeth and shook her head. "Even so, what's to stop them taking the journal to the King?"

She was right. There was no guaranteeing a lowly thief wouldn't bring such damaging evidence to the King for status. As a boy, Gavannon would've done the precise same. And if such treason came before the King, He would task Gavannon with hunting down the one to whom it belonged. Or worse, He would offer the hunt to the Prince to prove himself.

Either way, Abigale would be the next to hang.

Gavannon slid his arms from around her, and Abigale sat on her knees, facing him. In her eyes, Gavannon saw the terrible reflection of what had to be done.

"You must go." The words were the last breath of a dying man passing his lips. "Go back to your family's estate in Bast. Play as if you never left except for the Solstice. Your father's men will vouch for you as they've always done. You'll be safe there."

Fear sliced through her gaze, and he thought at first it was at the notion of being under her father's roof again; but then she framed his face with her hands. "But what about *you*, Gav? If the King learns of this and remembers seeing us together at the Solstice..."

"He's too far gone for that. A few more well-aimed blows, and the Throne will be ours. But for now, Abi, you must run."

Abigale wrapped her arms around his shoulders and laid her mouth to his, a desperate kiss full of regret and longing, tasting of farewell. "I'm so sorry," she whispered against his lips. "I'm sorry, Gav."

"I will never blame you for this," he said. "We all make mistakes, we all forget at times. My only concern right now is that you're kept from the gallows. Come, I'll help you pack your things."

"No, there's no need. If I'm accosted by Kingsgard along the way, I don't want to be found with any of the items the thieves might've noticed in my room. I'll just go with the clothes on my back. I must make my own way, for both our sakes."

Emotion sat heavy in Gavannon's throat. "At least let me go along to hail you a carriage."

"It's too dangerous for us to be seen together now. You know that." Abigale's smile freed tears as she laid a hand over his chest. "Here is where we say goodbye. I'm sorry, Gav...this is all my fault."

Gavannon gripped the sides of her neck and kissed her once more, pouring every inch of passion and promise into the few short moments they had left. And still it was not enough...it would never be enough. He would only be satisfied when they were together again.

And as he stood at the window of her abandoned room, watching her hooded head disappear into the throng of marketers at the heart of Dorwenon, he realized he'd been foolish and tempting fate to ever think he could have absolutely everything he wanted.

Chapter Fifty-Seven

A Feeling of Home

Erala had never felt less like home.

After a flurry of embraces with Gregor and Bernian, a tearful reunion between them and Iracabeth, and a rushed explanation of all that had transpired and where they must go now, Elynor and her friends climbed aboard Bernian's carriage and flew at breakneck speed from the southern coasts toward Kaer Dorwenon. Along the way, Gregor told them of the disastrous Solstice, the deaths among the royal family, and Al-Morral's appointment as the Friend of the King. Rumors had begun to spread of sanctions against Orleth for trade offenses and suspicions of meddling. Fear sickened the heart of Erala.

Elynor listened to all this in silence, hiding her tears for the loss of Jamyson's siblings and the state of her home by staring out the carriage window at the endless shadows of a dark winter's night screaming by in a sinister continuum; all the while, Sharek gripped her hand on the seat between them so tightly it ached.

She welcomed that anchor and the warm comfort of his presence, as steady and quiet as when they'd first left the Sanctum together. So much had changed, and yet so little had. Once again, it was her and Sharek against Al-Morral.

They arrived at Dorwenon after several days, taking shelter in the skeleton of an abandoned inn while Bernian and Gregor made a quick escape with the carriage. Elynor crafted an unsigned note to Jamyson, praying he would recognize her script, and asked Rue to deliver it to the kaer. Then they waited, crouched in the must and mire of the neglected building, listening to pigeons croon in the rafters. Elynor alternated between pacing and sitting while claws of restless energy raked her body. Always, Sharek watched her.

"Will you tell me what you're thinking?" he murmured at last.

Elynor sank onto an old sawhorse in the corner beside him and cradled her head in her hands. "That Al-Morral is winning this. That perhaps he's already won."

"He hasn't."

"But he easily could. Sharek, I would never have conceived that the King could put His own wife and children to death, no matter what the perceived offense." Grief choked her. "What's Al-Morral done to Him?"

Sharek stroked her back. "We'll learn soon enough."

Elynor glanced up at him and found him gazing out through the window, toward the kaer. "What are *you* thinking about?"

"I'm thinking...I'm not certain." He was quiet again for a moment. "Have you ever smelled something that reminded you of home?"

"By the Throne, yes. Especially after my father died, I'd sometimes smell musk and brine and think if I turned around, he'd be there."

Sharek's hand went still on her back. "I smell...something. I can't place it, but it reminds me of Ollanthyr."

Just when she was prepared to ask him what it was precisely he smelled, the battered door creaked open. Elynor lunged to her feet as Vestan entered, blade drawn. Sam also rose from where Iracabeth had been bandaging his shoulder, drawing his own sword.

"It's all right!" Elynor hissed. "I know him."

Vestan's eyes lit on her, bright with relief. "Elynor."

A muscled shape barged in on his heels, and in the dim cuts of moonlight through the untended wood Elynor recognized Jamyson—somewhat. This gaunter, more haggard version with his dark curls grown out nearly to shoulder-length and bound at the back of his head hardly fit her memory of the prince who'd tossed his boots up on her table at Kaer Lleywel and comforted her at the loss of her father. But he was still undeniably Jamyson, brown-skinned, bright-eyed, royally garbed...and before she could even say his name, his arms were around her, sweeping her up against him.

"I knew you weren't dead." Relief and affection utterly shattered his usually-arrogant tone. "Thank the Holy Throne you're all right, El."

Tears stabbed Elynor's eyes at his raw voice—and at the nickname he hadn't dared call her since they were children. "Gregor told me everything. Jamyson, I'm so sorry...about your siblings, about Esmae."

His breath shook and his arms tightened around her. Then he stepped back and looked her over with a critical eye. "There's something different about you."

"It's been quite the journey." Though she loved Jamyson dearly, she wasn't quite prepared to tell him the truth of her heritage.

"Clearly, it's been *something*. You have quite a few new friends." Jamyson's eyes darted to all the faces that lurked in the dark. Rue, who had been staring at him in slack-jawed awe, hastily averted her gaze. Jamyson's focus lingered on her a moment before he peered at Sylvester. "Have we met?"

"I'm sure I've never had the pleasure," the bard replied blandly.

"I'll go fetch us some food and wine from a tavern," Iracabeth said. "I think we all have plenty of tales to tell."

She grabbed Rue's arm and dragged her from the inn—perhaps to lecture her on the dangers of staring with such ardent fervor at a Crown Prince—and Jamyson frowned after them. Then he said, "That woman looks suspiciously like—"

"Yes, she's my mother," Elynor said, and shock spread across Jamyson's face. "As I said, it's been *quite* the journey."

Chapter Fifty-Eight

Tales of Two Kingdoms

An hour later, they were gathered in the thin, shivering beams of moonlight with food and drink to go around. Elynor picked at her portion, her appetite suffocated under the sheer magnitude of the tale Jamyson had just finished telling. It was so much worse than Bernian or Gregor had known.

"Mind sickness is a terrible thief," Iracabeth murmured after a heavy pause. "Among the cruelest I've seen."

"Is there nothing you can do for Him?" Elynor asked.

"Not when the paranoia has progressed this far. He's beyond even my reach."

"It's worse than paranoia." Bitterness laced Jamyson's tone. "He trusts no one but Al-Morral. I already knew that was dangerous, but now…I should kill Him, and damn the consequences."

"No, you shouldn't," Sylvester argued. "Erala will need a good King to pick up the pieces after your father's gone. And if Elynor is right about anything, that King is you. Your position matters."

"Assuming the kingdom can survive Al-Morral and the King it already has."

"He's not infallible, is He?" Elynor asked, though it seemed so obvious now. "He's never been."

Jamyson shook his head. "I realized it when He hung my mother, but I never knew how to tell you. Or anyone else, for that matter."

The revelation didn't rock Elynor as badly as she'd expected it would; perhaps because she'd slowly begun to realize it ever since the King had first demanded that she come to Kaer Dorwenon against her will, give up the Fleet despite her deepest desires, and marry his son against *both* their wishes.

It ached. But it was somehow the most sensible truth she had learned in recent months.

"Have you had any success finding a means to oust Al-Morral?" Sharek asked.

"Legally, no," Vestan grunted. "And the King will hear no charge against him."

"Then run him off," Sam offered.

"We're working on that." Jamyson reached into the inner pocket of his doublet and tossed Elynor a small notebook. "There was a woman staying in Dorwenon he seemed to have association with. Vez broke into her room at the Inn of Tryst and found this."

Elynor's fingers already knew the supple leather, the tooling of wildflowers along its face. "This is Abigale Cainwell's."

Jamyson sat forward sharply. "You know her?"

"Better than I'd like. I gave this to her when we graduated from our lessons." Elynor flipped the book open, but the familiar script was difficult to read...washed in the dimness of the roo, and ciphered. She nudged Sharek, and he scooted closer, planting one hand on the packed dirt floor behind Elynor as he leaned over to read with his Hunterish sight.

"I remember little Abigale," Iracabeth said. "She's in league with Al-Morral?"

"More than that," Vestan said. "We think he's in love with her."

Elynor looked up at Jamyson. "Then she may be the key to cracking this armor he's built around himself."

Sharek cocked his head. "I've seen a cipher like this before...this is a bandit code."

"Where would Abigale have learned such a thing?" Iracabeth demanded.

"She could have charmed it from anyone in a tavern between here and Bast," Elynor scoffed.

"She may well have learned it in Rimbourg, even," Sharek added. "But these are schemes against the royal family. Strategies. Poisons. Have you brought this to the King?"

Jamyson shook his head. "Al-Morral is in our way. And if he intercepts this notebook, we'll lose all the evidence. I've been saving the last of the King's good will toward me for when it counts."

Elynor's guts writhed at that reckless tone in his voice. Jamyson always flirted with danger like a beautiful woman, tempting and toying but never consummating with a kiss. But the way he spoke now, and the dangerous glint in his eyes...he was plotting something truly mad.

"The same day we secured these notes, Abigale disappeared from Dorwenon," Vestan added. "We don't know where she's gone."

"And without her, we lose our leverage against Al-Morral," Jamyson finished grimly.

Elynor stared at the notebook as a dark notion danced in her mind. "I know where she's gone. And more importantly, I know how to apply the leverage we need once she's there."

Jamyson slung his arms around his bent knees, inclining toward her. "I'm all ears."

Elynor shut the notebook, stroking the soft leather. "Abigale is safest hiding behind her father's guards at their homestead in Bast. She told me once she'd charmed all the boys there so thoroughly they'd fall on a sword for her."

"So how do we reach her there?" Sam demanded.

"*We* don't." Elynor swiveled toward Sharek. "The Sanctum does."

His eyes widened, comprehension breaking in them like a bloody sunrise over dark waves.

"I'm not sure I follow," Jamyson said.

"Sharek is a killing Blessed," Elynor lied, turning back to the prince. "I hired him to assassinate Al-Morral...but I didn't want the King to ever find out, so I gave my mother's family name as alias, and I gave them Abigale's homestead as surety I'd bring Sharek back."

"If Aeson Thalanor believes I've been released, he'll send a Blessed to find Elynor," Sharek murmured. "And the first place that Blessed will go is Abigale's home."

"I've heard what the Sanctum's Seekers are capable of," Jamyson said. "They'll beat this woman to within an inch of her life if they suspect she's the one who lost their Blessed."

"Yes. And then my mother will save her," Elynor said. "If, and only if, Al-Morral agrees to confess his crimes."

"That would certainly draw Al-Morral away from the King." Vestan and Jamyson exchanged a long glance fraught with unspoken things.

"It's a good plan," Jamyson admitted. "But you're talking about sending a Blessed after someone who used to be your friend, Elynor. You're certain about this?"

Elynor tossed the notebook onto the floor with a dull clap, silencing the hiccup of guilt in her throat. "She conspired to kill everyone you love, Jamyson. People that *I* love. She wanted to play a game of murder...this is the price of that game."

Vestan nudged the prince's shoulder. "She's right, Sire. And with the word we received from Bast, we can't afford to delay."

A chill spidered up Elynor's arms. "What word?"

Jamyson grimaced. "The Orlethian *Khuless* has brought a royal envoy to our shores, demanding audience with the King. There's some rather serious charges involved...something about escaped spies."

Sam swore, and Sylvester passed a shaking hand over his eyes. Sharek pushed himself to his feet. "I leave for the Sanctum tonight."

Shock rooted Elynor to her seat as she watched him go; and then, in the shadow of his absence, the stares of the others spurred her to move.

Pushing upright, she hurried out into the bitter chill of the night, catching up with him partway down the winding path toward the heart of Dorwenon. "Sharek, wait! Are you certain about this? We've hardly devised this scheme."

He slowed to match her stride. "Time is short. Al-Morral and Rowan must be stopped, and if this is the part I play, then so be it."

"Time was short when we left Kaer Lleywel. And you know what became of that."

He glanced down at her, his gaze softening. "This is not like that."

"Easy words. But you're still going."

They halted as one. Sharek faced her, the hard planes of his face gentled by moonlight. "You should travel with Iracabeth to Bast. If the Seeker chooses to hunt by the scent of your blood as well as by the location you left Aeson, you must be close by the Cainwells."

Elynor folded her arms tightly. "Then I'll see you afterward."

Sharek laid his hands on her shoulders. "I will come back to you. I swear it."

Elynor didn't know why she was so afraid he wouldn't; but the panic was heavy as lead in her chest, a stone sunk deep in the sea at her center. She gripped his biceps and stretched up to kiss him, the sweet taste of wine and meat on his breath, fighting to hold onto him this way. "Be careful, Sharek."

A flicker of a smile traced his mouth. "For your sake, Milady."

Then he was gone.

Chapter Fifty-Nine

The Prince and the Heiress

Long after Sharek departed Dorwenon, Elynor still sat on the roof of the ramshackle inn, watching the distant horizon and wondering if every flicker of motion in the veil of night was him, riding away from her on some stolen mount. Her heart strained with poignant notes of farewell to every glimpse in the dark that might've signaled his disappearance to fulfill this duty.

Not even his duty. His choice. And he had chosen to help them by going back to that nest of his own horrors.

A faint scuffling below signaled she was no longer alone, and Jamyson climbed onto the roof and flopped against the smokestack beside her. Arms crossed, he stared at the kaer, faintly framed with moonlight. Shadows scoured its flanks; the same shadows haunted Jamyson's eyes.

Elynor dragged her gaze to follow his. "It hardly seems like the same turrets and towers we conquered as children, does it?"

Jamyson snorted. "It hardly feels like *home*."

Grief carved out a portion of Elynor's heart. "I'm so sorry about Esmae. She was a good woman...a good friend, in what few ways we were able to know one another."

A small, nagging bit of her heart reminded her that she would have known Esmae better had she not seen her enslavement as just, somehow, in the King's own judgement. Another loss endured because she'd placed her faith in false sovereignty—a fast friendship that would never be.

For it seemed, given Jamyson's tale, that Esmae had been among the best of them all...a clever, compassionate woman, fearless and faithful to the truth, even to her end. And yet Elynor had only known her fleetingly as a magistrate's daughter, and then as the woman Jamyson had loved...though she had never truly fathomed *why*, when his own father had deemed her unworthy.

Now Elynor knew. And now she ached for all the things that could never be, for any of them now.

"I wish I'd gotten to know her better," she added softly.

"I wish you'd had the chance." Jamyson wound a hand around his neck, rubbing it slowly, his eyes stained silver beneath the moonlight. "I wish we'd all had plenty of chances for things we'll never get."

"That's true. And I'm also sorry I was gone when you needed me most." Elynor squeezed his shoulder. "And I'm sorry I'll be going again."

"I'm not. It's what Erala needs. We do this for the kingdom." He scratched beneath the tight knot of his hair. "I'll do my part. You'll do yours. And let's hope your Blessed does his."

"He will. Sharek is a man of his word."

Jamyson stretched forward. "A killing Blessed. Really?"

"Don't tell me you disapprove, when Vestan is down there shaking this whole place with his snores. You choose your friends the same way I choose mine."

Jamyson shrugged, peering past her at the kaer again. "We've been wrong about what the Throne is. What the King is. I think it's safe to consider everything we know about the Blessed is wrong, too."

Elynor's heart swelled. "Then, when you're King...I suppose things will be different?"

A quiet scoff. "I don't know. If this pulls through, the kingdom will owe a portion of its freedom to at least one Blessed. That can't be overlooked. But with the people already shaken by what's happened with the King...it will take time to change the laws. And longer to change their hearts."

"As long as you aren't tossing children into the Sanctum."

Jamyson arched a brow. "Since when did you become such an advocate for the Blessed?"

"I saw what they were like in Danje. Some were cruel, no doubt. But if we imprison the many for the cruelty of the few, then all the sacrosanct ought to be in chains in the name of Al-Morral and the King."

Jamyson rubbed his jaw. "You're suggesting a case-by-case basis, then. Blessed roaming free, and only those who misuse their craft being punished."

Elynor's pulse fluttered in her wrists. "I am."

"I'll consider it." He folded his arms on his knees and cocked his cheek to them, studying her. "There really is something different about you, Elynor. You're not the same woman I last saw in Kaer Lleywel."

"And you aren't the same brash prince who came to comfort me about my father."

"Well, it's been a long few months, thanks to Al-Morral and this Rowan. And the King."

The belligerence and determination returned to his tone. Elynor sat back, studying the glass-sharp cuts of grief on his angular cheekbones, the adamant of his dark eyes.

"Jamy," she said slowly, "swear to me that you'll only do what you and Vez agreed to…your part in stopping Al-Morral. Swear that you won't do anything rash."

A familiar smile flickered across his mouth, so quickly Elynor wasn't certain it had ever truly been there. "Nothing rash."

Elynor didn't press the matter. But deep in her heart, she wondered if the measure of rashness from a prince who'd always walked the edge of danger truly counted for anything.

Chapter Sixty

Oaths Fulfilled

The Sanctum of the Blessed was said to be a sanctuary, but to Sharek Ransalor it had never looked more like a whitewashed prison. Through the eyes of a free man, the jutting towers and thrice-barred latticework on the windows screamed of captivity, imprisonment, a cage—a discordant rhythm against the trill of winter birds in the forest that fletched the grounds.

Sharek's lungs throbbed as he slunk through the painfully-familiar halls, making his way toward Aeson Thalanor's private chambers. He'd ridden most of the way on horseback, but crossed the last few miles on foot for stealth.

Wrestling down the guards at the doors had been simple now that he knew to rely on his Hunterish senses rather than fighting against what he'd long believed to be the instinct of a killing Blessed. They'd been little match for him, and he banded that knowledge around himself like armor as he stole from sparse shadow to sparse shadow and finally slipped into Aeson's study. Its broad windows looked out over the lawns to the southeast, toward the Fai Alora, and Sharek's heart clenched at the familiar dance of the treetops in the stroke of the wind. He'd never been able to concentrate when he was in this room; Rowan had always covered for his distraction, smoothly taking the contract and informing Sharek of the details later.

It was always the trees, the memory of Ollanthyr. Just like that smell back in Dorwenon.

He shook his head, snapping back to attention. He could dream of home later. For now, he had a mission of his own.

Sharek slid down in the shadows of the tall bookcases and draped his cloak tightly over himself, relishing the moment to catch his breath; those miles were the longest he'd run since Danje, and his lungs seared like fire. He prayed to the Empyreans that Hunterish healing would one day restore his old stamina. For now, their answer to his prayer was in the long minutes he waited, in silence and early-morning shadows, before Aeson Thalanor entered the study.

He'd hardly changed since Sharek had seen him last: tall, gaunt, and long-limbed, his beard brushing his clavicles as he sauntered to his desk and lit the candle tree on its corner. Sharek fought not to tense at the man's every movement.

Besides his scarred lungs, Sharek had much else to heal.

He clung to the shadows as Thalanor laid out the day's duties, humming quietly to himself in utter oblivion to the Hunter lurking in the seam of the bookcases, watching and waiting like a predator carefully studying his prey.

When Thalanor reached for his quill, Sharek lunged.

He drove his fist into Thalanor's throat first, crippling the voice that would've brought the Hunterish commands down on his head. When the old man choked and shoved his chair back, it struck Sharek's chest. He wrapped his hand in Thalanor's long, thinning hair and wrenched his head up, laying a knife to his neck. "The only reason I do not spill your throat this moment is because without you, the Sanctum falls, and the Blessed with it."

A soft, wet syllable fell again and again from Thalanor's gritted teeth as he tried to form the name of his attacker—a name he'd gleefully denied was Sharek's to have.

Sharek towed him flush to the seatback and rested his mouth at Thalanor's ear. "This is the last you will ever see of me. I'm a freed Blessed now. And I came here to warn you that if you send anyone after me, I will kill them. And I will keep killing, again and again, until the cost of the Blessed who hunt me becomes greater than the profit I reaped for the Sanctum."

Disbelief and triumph surged through his veins, hearing himself utter those long-coveted words.

How many nights had he laid sleepless in his hovel, dreaming of this moment? How many times had he stared at Thalanor and envisioned his blade at that craggy throat? And at last, it was happening.

"May my face haunt your dreams until your well-deserved death," he snarled, "for that is the only place you will see me after today. Goodbye, Aeson Thalanor."

Sharek slammed the man's forehead against the desk, skirted around it, and rushed to the door.

The moment he swung it open, an iron weight drove into his face, flinging him to his seat.

Sharek spat blood as his gums tore and his broken nose opened in a fount. Dazed, reeling, he scrambled backward on his hands, his face throbbing, gaining some distance from a pair of Blessed who stepped into the study—tall, broad, banded with muscle. There was no warmth or emotion of any sort in their eyes as they took up stance between Sharek and the door.

They must have found the unconscious guards near the Sanctum's entryway and come to defend their master.

So be it.

Sharek scrambled to his feet, drew his deadliest sword, and lunged, driving it against the first man's neck.

It broke against his skin like it was made of stone and the blade of glass. Pain pierced through Sharek's sword hand at the impact. He dropped the broken hilt and tore backward, staring at the men, horror cleaving through his aching head.

Armored Blessed—the perfect foil for one blessed with killing. He had only ever heard tales of them from his father. Where in the Emperium had Thalanor dug them up?

They advanced on him, and other Blessed streamed into the study behind them—men and women Sharek knew. Fighters, strongmen, those blessed with speed and with dealing out pain.

Sharek bolted to the windows and did not give himself a moment to think of Rimbourg, of a knife in his side, of Rowan. He hurled himself at the glass with all his might—

And rebounded. The glass was tempered.

Sharek's shoulder ached, but not as cruelly as his pounding heart as he spun back to face the Blessed who advanced on him.

Though he was not a killing Blessed, he was not above killing *them*.

Sharek drew his knives and lunged.

Around the broad desk and the unconscious heap of Aeson Thalanor, Sharek dueled the Blessed. He threw himself onto the might of his senses, feeling the way impending blows warped the air, listening for the shift in pulse and breathing whenever another fighter prepared to lunge.

There were a dozen of them, and one of Sharek. And it would have been an even fight.

But his *lungs*.

In minutes, they were burning like flame. He gasped through his bloodied nose and mouth, sweat pouring down his back and chest heaving as his body fought to push air through the scarring that crippled him.

A kick to the sternum from a fighting Blessed put Sharek on his knees. This time he only regained his feet by grabbing the desk and thrusting himself away until his back struck the tempered window. His wild gaze flashed over his remaining opponents—half a dozen, and then the two armored Blessed at the door, waiting silently. They would not have to fight him; they would merely have to stand in his way.

Sharek's eyes heated with dread.

He never should've come here alone. He'd overestimated his own talents. Forgotten the limits of his ravaged lungs. Foolishly believed the Sanctum could not hold a Hunter.

But it had always managed to hold *him*.

He'd made an oath. Sworn he'd never go back. Made a vow to himself that it was death before the Sanctum for him.

The knife was in his hand, the blade arcing toward the racing pulse at his throat—

Her face flashed in his mind. Smiling. Sunkissed. Full of trust and hope and something too powerful to name.

Elynor.

He'd made another promise, too.

Sharek's hand stilled.

I will come back to you. I swear it

His eyes brimming with eat, Sharek let go of the knife. Let it clatter at his feet.

And then Aeson Thalanor's men were upon him.

Chapter Sixty-One

Wildfire Fears

Purpose, ambition, and Kaer Dorwenon all seemed so much emptier without Abigale.

Gavannon floated through the days from duty to duty, wondering at every face he passed if this was the thief who'd stolen Abigale's book and driven her away from him. In the moments between one appointment and the next, he questioned everyone he could—Kingsgard assigned to Dorwenon, people at the markets, those who worked at the Inn of Tryst.

None could aid him. None had laid eyes on the thief.

He was no nearer to assuring Abigale's safety.

The ache to protect her was a constant distraction. And that, he assumed, was the only reason the Crown Prince managed to corner him before his lessons on Eralanite law one day.

"Fancy seeing you here."

Jamyson's casual drawl halted Al-Morral with a grimace at the end of the hall. The prince stood between Gavannon and his rooms, shoulder propped to the wall, a smirk floating on the edges of his mouth. His eyes were bright, his hair groomed back into a knot behind his head. He looked more alive than he had ever since the slave girl had hung—as if something had poured new purpose into his veins.

Gavannon clenched his jaw and swept forward. "Yes, fancy seeing me outside my own rooms. Forgive me, Your Highness...I have pressing matters to attend."

"No, of course," Jamyson shrugged. "The Friend of the King, always busy. Between the kaer and Dorwenon."

Gavannon froze in midstep.

Silence gobbled up the space between him and the Prince with that knowing smirk still framing his lips.

"What do you know of my business in Dorwenon?" Gavannon growled.

Jamyson shrugged upright, a waft of menace traveling before him. "You should have kept her close by, Al-Morral. Where you could protect her."

Dread punched a hollow hole in his gut.

The arrogant little son of a bastard knew about Abigale.

"What have you *done*? Gavannon snarled.

"Nothing. What's coming has nothing to do with me, except that I'm turning a blind eye to it," Jamyson said. "And thoroughly enjoying the notion that soon you'll have to make the same choice you gave me: between the kingdom I'm set to rule, or the woman I love."

Gavannon's molars ached. "If you harm her..."

"Oh, don't flatter yourself. I'm not chasing down your blushing consort," Jamyson scoffed. "I'm staying right here in Kaer Dorwenon. Where *I* belong."

Bristling, Gavannon stepped nearer to him. "I will bring the King's wrath down on your head!"

"You do that." Jamyson didn't fall back an inch, arms folded, casual as anything. "And while you're busy talking Him over to your side, Abigale dies."

The last two words fell like an executioner's axe, chopping the last threads of Gavannon's resolve.

There was no pity or mercy in the Prince's eyes.

Gavannon had pushed him too far.

For endless seconds, neither of them spoke. Or moved. Then Jamyson dipped his head. "Enjoy the dilemma you presented *me* with. And always remember I gave you a better chance than you ever gave me. Gave *Esmae*."

Then he turned and sauntered up to the bend in the hall. Gavannon stared after him, choking for air as panic ripped his chest with razor talons. His fingers ached to draw his blade and ram it through the Prince's back, but then he would never have what he wanted. What he *needed*.

At the end of the hall, Jamyson glanced back. "Elynor Azorius and her killing Blessed send their regards."

Her name slammed into him, all the implications tumbling out from the blow, and Gavannon turned from his rooms and fled.

"Gavannon!" The King's greeting was, as always, full of relief and glee, as if all His problems were solved the moment Gavannon marched into His rooms.

Except he didn't march this time; he broke inward, gasping for breath, and bent with his hands on his knees while he struggled to catch his breath. "Your Eminence! There is an urgent matter I must attend to in Bast."

The King frowned, struggling up from His desk across the solar. He moved more slowly than ever these days, as if He no longer trusted His feet beneath Him; or perhaps it was because He ate so little, fearing the kitchen staff was trying to poison Him. Gavannon had barely kept Him from executing the lot of them just a fortnight past.

With him gone, they'd have no protection. But he couldn't be swayed.

"What troubles you, Gavannon?" the King demanded. "Tell Me, and I'll make it right. Whatever I must do."

Gavannon stared at Him, and for half a moment, He pondered. He could stay and turn the King against His son, right now, twisting this dagger until it went all the way through to Jamyson's heart.

But if he waited, he would never reach Abigale in time.

"Elynor Azorius has returned from death," Gavannon said. "She and her killing Blessed have set their intentions against the woman I love."

Just speaking the words, the truth he'd realized at the Prince's parting, drove a blade of terror into his heart. Rowan had told him about that killing Blessed, and Abigale had encountered him in Rimbourg. He had her scent. And with Elynor holding his leash…

The King staggered back against the desk. "She's come for Me."

Fury ripped through Gavannon. "Not for you! For Abigale!" The King blinked, shock breaking in His face, and Gavannon swallowed a curse. He hated when his rage made him sound like his father. "They will not harm You, Your Holiness. But they will absolutely harm her. I beg Your release so I may go to her before it's too late."

King Marcus gazed at him for many heartbeats, and a strange, maniacal determination hardened His glassy gaze. "I will do far more than that." He snatched His cloak from the back of His seat. "I have thought much about this in recent weeks, Gavannon, ever since that treacherous slave girl hung. What you bring Me today only confirms what I have most feared."

Oh, Gavannon did not enjoy the sound of those words spilling from the King's lips. "And what is that, Your Holiness?"

"That the Blessed are a blight on our kingdom. My ancestors dealt gently with them in the days of Yore, but are their talents worth their trouble? They have infiltrated My kaer and turned My loyal family against me. They are no tamer and no better suited for our halls than the Hunters who whelped them."

Disbelief nearly closed Gavannon's throat altogether. "Your Eminence?"

The King halted beside him and gripped his shoulder gently. "Go to your love, Gavannon. I will assemble the Kingsgard in your absence, and we will deal a blow to the Blessed from which they will never recover. The Kingsgard will tear down the Sanctum and destroy the Blessed. Rid us of their trickery once and for all. I do this for you, Gavannon. And for Me. So that no one else will ever suffer as My family has."

And with more strength to His stride than Gavannon had seen in weeks, the King departed.

Gavannon stood rooted in solitude, clenching and releasing his fists, suffocated as waves of panic crashed down from all different directions.

The King's fear was a wildfire raging out of control. But what could Gavannon do? If he stayed, he would lose Abigale.

He tore from the solar.

The kaer thrummed with activity by the time Gavannon reached its lower levels. Already the outer courtyard teemed with black-clad Kingsgard preparing to ride, and more joined them by the second. Gavannon kept behind the stone archways that ringed the courtyard and hurried toward the stables; he could not afford to be seen or accosted by anyone, not even King Marcus Himself.

And then a shadow detached from a nook in the wall ahead of him: a familiar figure, broad and hooded, with a glint of iron-and-woad tattoos peeking from beneath the hair growing into tight curls against his head. "There you are, Gavannon. You're a hard man to track these days."

Gavannon's heart dropped from his chest.

This couldn't be happening. Everything couldn't be going so horribly wrong all at once.

"Out of my way, Rowan!" he barked, shoving around the Blessed without breaking stride.

"Why do you look like you just sucked on a sour *Aljalam*?" Rowan strode after him. "Gavannon!"

"My enemies have found Abigale. Elynor and her killing Blessed—"

"Sharek?" His name launched from Rowan with far more intimate knowing than Gavannon had ever heard. "What would Sharek want with Abigale?"

They barged together into the stables; Gavannon rushed to the first stall and wrenched open the half-door. "I'll explain everything after I find her."

Rowan slammed the door shut. Gavannon twisted around, pulse thundering, as Rowan's greater height crowded him against the wood. "You'll explain *now*. Why is the Kingsgard is assembling? To protect *her*?"

Gavannon stared at him, the words no longer willing to come.

Slowly, Rowan dropped his hand from the door and stepped back. "They're going to attack the Sanctum. Because you told them of Sharek's involvement."

"I didn't want this," Gavannon hissed. "It's the King's paranoia, He believes every Blessed must be destroyed."

"Then stop Him, damn you!"

"I can't! He won't listen anymore...He's beyond my control." Gavannon put the stall door between himself and Rowan and mounted up, so he was slightly above arm's reach. "I can plead with Him, or save her. And I must save her, Rowan."

Rowan's lip curled. "After everything I did for you—the lives I took, the trusts I broke—this is how you repay me. By betraying Sharek to the King, and killing my kind."

"I don't have time to argue with you. I'll go to Abi, you go to the Sanctum. Save as many as you can."

"Oh, I will," Rowan growled. "And when I'm finished there, Gavannon, I'll come for *you*."

Death's slick fingers reached out from that quiet vow, clamping around Gavannon's neck. But he couldn't pause to put Rowan in his place—not when Abigale was in danger.

He kicked his horse into a wild gallop from the kaer.

Chapter Sixty-Two

Defending Elynor

Darker and more tomb-like than ever, Bracerath's Landing was as foreign as the halls of the *Khul's* palace now. Elynor tried not to dwell on how utterly empty it all seemed, and *why* it struck her that way; not only because her father was gone, but because these steps leading down to the pool belonged to picnics and conversations with a Hunter who was not here.

It was difficult to find anything she could safely think about when she was also fighting to ignore the drip of blood from her fist into the small glass vial in Sam's hand.

He'd already cleaned her blood from his blade and sheathed it again, and Elynor was glad not to have to look at the sinister wink of dying sunlight along the sleek edge that had scored her arm. It was a shallow cut, and Iracabeth would tend it as soon as the task was done.

Still, Elynor didn't want to stare.

She focused on Sylvester instead; he was pacing up above the steps, while Rue sprawled near the pool's edge, stirring her bare foot through the cool water. Elynor had done the same thing many times while she was deep in thought, always drawn to the water.

She didn't realize her hand had dipped until Sam propped it up with his. "All right there, girl?"

"A bit shaky," Elynor admitted. "Nothing I can't manage."

"We're almost done here."

Elynor eyed the vials skeptically. "You really believe this will work?"

"It ought to." Sylvester's words emerged brittle through clenched teeth. "We know that once the Seeker realizes Abigale is not you, it will seek your blood. The best way to distract it long enough to capture it is if we spread your blood all across the Port."

"I hope you can run quickly," Elynor said to Rue. The dragnet raised a brow and nodded.

Sam capped one vial and tossed it to Rue. "Still say we should kill the thing, not capture it."

"We need it to hunt Rowan," Elynor argued, as she had many times on the carriage ride from Dorwenon to Bast. "He's a slippery eel. Let his own kind handle him."

Sam's brows peaked. "The longer you hold onto that grudge, the worse it's going to be for you."

Before Elynor could frame a retort, the antechamber door swept open and Iracabeth entered, carrying a bag of food in one hand and her medicine satchel in the other. A frown drew her resemblance to Elynor in the most poignant sweeps yet. "The Seeker has entered the Port. He's making his way to the Cainwell estate as we speak."

"Time to go." Sam corked the second vial and tossed it to Sylvester, then filled another with a squeeze of the wound on Elynor's arm and pitched it to Rue. "I'll keep watch on that estate. Soon as the Seeker is finished there, we take the vials and separate. We'll bring it back in chains, or not at all."

"Be careful," Elynor said. Sylvester shot her a quick smile, then sprinted out. Rue nodded and was swift on his heels.

"*You* be careful," Sam said to Iracabeth as he passed her in the doorway. "If the thing comes here, shoot it. We'll find another way to corner Varodan."

Iracabeth nodded and squeezed his shoulder, then came down the steps to sit beside Elynor. "Arm."

Elynor couldn't aptly express her gratitude that her mother was staying here with her while the others managed the Seeker; so she sat quietly instead, biting back every hiss of pain while Iracabeth cleaned, powdered, and bandaged the knife wound.

With that seen to, Iracabeth produced a basket of cinnamon-sugar rolls from the bag. "I hope they're still your favorite."

Cheeks warm, Elynor accepted the offering. "You remembered."

"I remember every little detail about you from back then, Seabird. I memorized those things to keep you close."

Throat tight, Elynor stared at her roll. "Abigale and I were friends back then, but I don't feel badly for doing this tonight. You recall the good of me, but the good has no hold on my choices now. What does that say of me?"

"That you may have a small issue with unforgiveness," Iracabeth said. "Abigale is reaping some of the consequences of her treachery. But if you dwell on your hatred for too long, Elynor, it will infect you. You'll become little different from her. That's what happened to the Kings of Yore...how they came to justify killing the tribal leaders and setting the Hunters on the run. It's how the Venator bloodline came to be so twisted and full of hate."

"Except for Jamyson."

Iracabeth frowned thoughtfully. "Yes. Except for him."

She rose and began to pace, making slow laps around the top step, and Elynor watched her go. Her mother's face was full of storming thoughts, and after a time Elynor could no longer bear the silence—or that look. "Are you all right?"

Iracabeth tapped her fingers slowly over her lips and shook her head. "This place..." Her voice was husky, dry, and she dipped her gaze to the floor. "I never thought I would see it again."

"Did you miss it?"

"The Landing, no. But the people in it." Iracabeth wandered to the window and glanced outside. "Does the seaside cottage still stand?"

Elynor nodded. "I always wondered why Father didn't tear it down when you left. But now I know he always hoped you'd come home."

"Alden was a great man," Iracabeth murmured. "The kindest and maddest I'd ever met. His dreams for the Fleet, for how to build those ships..."

"I know." Elynor snorted with quiet laughter. "The shipbuilders wanted to flee whenever he came bursting into their workshops. Who knew what wild ideas Alden Azorius would dream up next?"

"Visionary," Iracabeth said. "Dreamer. And the most loving man I ever knew. When I told him I was Blessed, do you know what he said to me?" She choked out a damp laugh, swiping hastily beneath her eyes. "He said that *he* was the one who was blessed. Blessed to have married me."

Elynor rubbed her face with both hands. "I wish he would have told me. When I think of how I hated Sharek when we first met—how I hated *myself*—"

"I know," Iracabeth said. "Alden was great, but he was not without his faults. I wanted him to teach you to love the Blessed the way he loved me, but he was frightened it would draw the King's attention. You've been outspoken and opinionated from the time you could first form words, Elynor. Alden feared you would say the wrong thing to the wrong person and land yourself in the Sanctum." She sat next to Elynor again, taking her hand. "So he decided to lead you by example and hope you would form your own opinions by what he modeled."

Elynor wondered if perhaps, in some way, he'd succeeded after all. She'd had her reproach for the Blessed, and for Hunters; but she'd chiseled away at them bit by bit, ever since she'd met Sharek. And now she was exactly like her father, blessed in many ways. Alarming ways. Frightening and breathtaking ones.

"I miss him." It was the first time Elynor had spoken the words aloud since his death—the first time she'd let herself truly feel how deep the wounds went, through her core and beyond. "Does it ever stop—the missing? The longing?"

Iracabeth wrapped an arm around Elynor's shoulders and pulled her close. "No, Seabird. You never stop missing them. But that's how we keep them alive."

Elynor did not realize she had fallen asleep until she was suddenly awake again, startled by the murmur of voices nearby.

She was lying at the top of the steps, her head pillowed on her mother's cloak, and she could see through her lashes that Sam had stumbled in through the doorway and knelt in the stains of blood that Sharek had left behind the night he'd come back from Rimbourg.

And Sam was adding to it with his own blood seeping from a shallow cut across his chest.

Elynor inhaled sharply and started to rise, but footsteps rushed across the tiles. And just like that night when Sharek had staggered in, bleeding and crumbling, there was an Azorian woman tending to the wounded again: Iracabeth, crouching before Sam, already applying pressure to his injury and asking in harsh whispers what had happened.

"It's done." A thin vein of triumph sizzled in Sam's voice. "It was a kings-damned *fight*, but we chained the thing in the end. The bard and your dragnet are hauling it down to some empty cottage at the base of the cliffs. They'll keep watch until it's time to leave."

"Thank you," Iracabeth murmured, "for helping us keep Elynor safe. I know she isn't yours, but you treat her like she is. I'm glad for that."

Sam sank back on his elbows to give Iracabeth a better vantage over his wound. "She's a good woman. Like her mother."

"And you're a dangerous flatterer, Samwel Morlai."

His chuckle was jagged with pain but full of warmth. "I'm not the only one who had reputation in Orleth. I'd've rather had yours than mine. Healer, savior of the Blessed—"

"Friend to the *Khul's* family?" Iracabeth murmured. "And a damned good father when it mattered most, from what I'm told."

Sam was quiet for a moment. "Thank you for that."

Iracabeth hummed in her throat. "I wish I had still lived in Danje when that chest sickness came through. I could have saved your daughter."

Elynor frowned. Sam had never told her how his family died, but he'd told her mother?

"Aye. Well," Sam inhaled sharply with pain. "If she'd have been anything like Elynor when she was grown, it would've been the death of us both anyway."

Iracabeth laughed. "Don't tell me you don't love this. The excitement, the adventure...and what it means to the kingdoms."

"I suspect that's something else we have in common."

The warmth of his tone brought a dim memory of a firelit room and whispers in her doorway.

Of what it felt like to be a whole family.

Elynor settled back, binding the cloak nearer to her face, inhaling her mother's scent from between the folds. And then, secure in the knowledge that Sam, Sylvester, and Rue had survived the Seeker, she drifted back into slumber.

Chapter Sixty-Three

Savior in the Shadows

He had been in darkness for many days. Deeper than an Orlethian prison. Darker than his most vicious nightmares.

They'd beaten him and flung him back into his old hovel and locked the door behind him; and no matter how many nights he dreamed of Thalanor's torch lighting up the dark, bringing with it the vision of an heiress in a dress too fine for this place, with fury in her fists and vengeance in her eyes, he only woke in the pitch blackness and the silence and the utter aloneness, again and again.

Every time he woke, the nightmare was what he lived.

He had no name and no face and no future outside these walls. Only a bruised and aching back, traitorous lungs, and a groove of stinging flesh on his neck where he'd chosen this sham of an existence over the Emperium.

He tried to gather memories of what mattered most, to comfort and keep him company, but they shattered and skittered away from him, bleeding into the shadows. And he was alone again.

Alone. For Empyreans knew how long.

And then he woke from dreams of the sea breeze and salty kisses, emerged from sunlight into darkness, and felt something shift in the world. The shadows were no longer absolute; light bobbed against the wall in front of his face where he'd curled up on the stone bed with his back to the prison bars.

Thalanor's torch, after all. Soon they would drag him from his stone bed and force him to his knees in the sparring rooms. They'd smash his bones with crops until he begged for death, and then they'd send him to bring that death to others. They'd dispatch another Blessed to keep him from running or turning the knife against himself again. The world would think him dead, and he'd become a shadow seen only in the nightmares of the marks the Sanctum sent him to destroy.

He was never getting out of this.

He gripped his talisman and tried to whisper prayers, but the darkness swallowed them whole.

The light stopped. Fingers tightened on rusted metal, sending a shower of flakes to the floor. Another sound, deep and vibrant, wobbled and fought to crawl across the space toward him. The vibrations caressed his wounded back, sending deep shivers through his body. But he would not give them the pleasure of answering their summons like a whipped mongrel.

The sound came again, and again, rattling, banging, and then a sharp voice cut through the addled thickness in his ears.

"*Sharek?*"

He knew that voice. That loathsome, hated voice.

Sharek Ransalor dug his hands into his bed and flipped with a groan, turning his gaze toward the door of his cell.

Rowan clung to the bars with white-knuckled fists, torch secured in the bracket on the wall. His eyes were wide, his jaw slack. "What are *you* doing here?"

Stone dust shook loose above them. Sharek frowned at the ceiling. "What is that?"

"A siege. The Kingsgard are here to wipe out the Blessed. I came to help whoever I could, but I didn't expect...how did Aeson get his hands on you?"

Old anger shivered through his bones. "Does it matter? Aeson or the *Khul*...one prison traded for another."

Rowan stared at him for a long moment. Then he drew a special knife from behind his back—the twin to Sharek's own favorite dagger—and hacked at the lock.

Confusion prodded Sharek's muddled head. He swung his legs off the bed. "What are you doing?"

"What does it look like? I'm getting you out of here." Rowan whooped in cold triumph as the lock gave, then swung the door wide. "Hurry. We don't have much time. Don't want the Kingsgard to corner us down here." Sharek slid from the bed and staggered, and Rowan caught him with a hand to his chest. "You're heavy. Is that from your worthless morality or your inflated sense of honor?"

"Let go of me, I can walk." Sharek shoved himself out of Rowan's hands. His shoulder hit the wall, and he hung there, panting. "Why are you doing this? After Danje—"

"Because I didn't want *you* in that Orlethian prison! You put yourself there, not me." Rowan took a step toward him. "Apart from other Blessed who don't know my name and would fear me if they did, you're the only person in this Empyreans-forsaken perdition of a kingdom that I give a damn about. I wouldn't leave you in this place of *all* places…not this time. And never again, brother."

Sharek knew that vicious note in his voice from all the times he'd argued for the freedom of the Blessed. All Blessed. And what had Elynor told Sharek once? That those blessed with killing were also capable of saving.

Rowan could've left him to be crushed by the bowing, breaking ceiling, but he'd opened the door for Sharek instead. A door to freedom he'd feared might never swing wide again.

For now, Sharek could trust this unlikely answer to his prayers. He stuck out a hand. "Give me a weapon."

Rowan freed a falchion from his hip and tossed it to him.

Sharek turned it backhand and rushed Rowan, tossing him against the wall and pressing the edge to his throat. They gazed at one another over the cold, impartial curve of steel.

"If you betray me or Elynor ever again," Sharek growled, "if you make a deception of your death to deceive me *once* more, I'll end you."

"Noted." Rowan brushed the weapon aside, and Sharek let it fall. "Though I doubt that's much of a threat from you right now. Can you fight in your condition?"

"I'm more adaptable than you might think." With every moment spent on his feet, his senses were sharpening. Purpose pounded in his blood again, a Hunter's need to do that for which he'd been created. "Let's save our people."

Together, they charged from the hovel beneath the Sanctum for the last time.

In the upper halls, there was nothing but fire and dark armor, blood and screams. Sharek had never heard so much screaming in all his life. The Kingsgard were killing their way through the Sanctum, cutting down every Blessed they crossed paths with. Young girls and boys, old men and women, and those of healthy mid-age were all heaped indiscriminately at the bases of sweeping staircases and piled before doorways where they'd tried to flee. Sharek's ears rang with their pleas for mercy and the cold reply of steel hacking the smoky air as he and Rowan battled through the ranks of the Kingsgard side-by-side, carving paths for the Blessed to escape.

Sharek's Hunterish nature did not change the years of training he and Rowan had together. They still moved like twin swords wielded in Sabrathan's hands, cutting into the Kingsgard fold and spinning out of reach. But even with his shirt tied around his mouth and nose to guard his lungs as best he could, Sharek tasted ash and grit on the air.

They were losing time.

A Kingsgard blade tripped past his defenses, and Rowan's falchion met it an inch from Sharek's chest, knocking it aside. Sharek whirled under Rowan's arm and impaled a guard who'd crept up from behind, his dagger flashing at Rowan's back. They did not need to speak or glance at one another to know where the other was; Sharek's sense of Rowan's place in the world was sharp as a blade, and Rowan knew his patterns.

Together they stripped open a barricaded door to the basement and released the Blessed from the kitchens. They dragged children from under the blazing rubble and bundled them out the doors. Then they turned back to duel again. It was sheer insanity that there was no one else Sharek wanted at his back in this battle; Rowan might as well have been Empyreans-sent.

"Keep moving, will you?" Rowan shouted, and Sharek realized he'd halted for a heartbeat to stare at him as the utter lunacy of the moment truly occurred to him. "Check the upper levels!"

Sharek nodded and bounded up the staircase, nearly tripping over a heap of fine robes at the top. He caught himself on the railing of the mezzanine and looked back.

Aeson Thalanor had made it only to the top of the steps before a Kingsgard dagger, wrapped in the colors of the royal family, had found its home in his throat.

Sharek bared his teeth in a satisfied scowl and began to hunt again.

His senses pierced the smoke, leading him to rooms where the Kingsgard had blocked the Blessed inside to burn. He freed them, one door after another, until the wall of heat ripping through the wood-paneled rooms became unbearable and there was no sound beneath the crackle of flames and the clash of Kingsgard with Blessed below.

Sharek charged back down the stairs, his lungs aching. He couldn't endure the inferno much longer.

"Sharek!" Rowan hauled an herbalist Blessed from her cowering sanctuary behind a fern pot and flung her to Sharek, who ushered her to the Sanctum's front doors, pushing her outside and taking a moment to gasp in the clean air. Across the lawn, the Blessed they'd freed were bounding away into the wilds like deer freed from a paddock. As the herbalist choked her thanks and streaked away after them, Sharek's heart soared.

The King would not have what He wished today. This would not be the end of the Blessed—it would be the beginning for all those who survived.

Survived...because of him. And because of Rowan.

Sharek whirled back into the Sanctum just in time to see Aeson Thalanor's armored Blessed charge into the support pillars of the nearest balcony, bringing it crashing down on the Kingsgard.

And with it came the roof.

Sharek dove inside, snatching a pair of Blessed bakers out of harm's way and slinging them out the door. He leaped free of the raining clots of the stone that buried the Kingsgard, the armored Blessed—

And with an agonized cry, Rowan went down as well, dragging a small boy into the shelter of his arms while the rock plummeted around them.

A surge of panic ripped Rowan's name out of Sharek, and he dodged from cover, heedless of his own safety. Smaller stones nicked his arms and back as he covered his head, crossing the parlor and sliding on his knees beside the heap where Rowan had fallen.

Sharek tore away the flagrant debris, his hands blistering, his palms gashed open on jagged heaps of stone. But still he dug, and kept digging until he unearthed Rowan's soot-powdered curls, then his shoulders.

The boy lay beneath Rowan's brawn, his temple dented, blood pooling under his head.

Tears silvered Sharek's vision as he jammed his heels into the stone and hooked his hands under Rowan's arms, dragging him inch by inch from beneath the debris. Then he slapped out the fire that still ate at Rowan's limbs and gripped the sides of his neck, feeling for a pulse.

It was there. Thready and weak, but it was there.

Sharek ducked under Rowan's limp arm and tugged him up, weaving through the graveyard of ruined marble colonnades and smoke-scarred porcelain walls. The façade Aeson Thalanor and his predecessors had maintained over this torturous prison was gone now, its broken bones showing it for what it was. And the surviving Kingsgard still swarmed it, searching for anyone else to stick their blades into. They couldn't feel what Sharek felt, or hear what he heard. Or didn't hear.

There were no sounds of life or flickers of movement but for the fire. Any Blessed still huddling in the Sanctum when the roof caved in were dead…everyone but him and Rowan.

Sharek let the guards pluck over the boneyard they'd created of innocents unable to flee. He hobbled away from the wreckage of his prison, dragging Rowan's blistered, wheezing, fire-scarred body with him, deep into the Fai Alora. Moving south toward the only true sanctuary they would find.

Chapter Sixty-Four

The Villains We've Made

A SLIM SKIRT OF snow hugged the Aqqorian coast far below as Gavannon sprinted through the most prolific district in Bast. His heart clawed into his throat as he slipped and skidded along the ice-polished street tiles, the fine homes he'd once admired from afar as a poor deckhand first come to Bast flashing past him without concern now.

None of the riches mattered. None of the elegance. All he cared about was reaching Abigale.

He'd abandoned his horse in a jammed avenue where carriages fought through the snow, and now he ran with all his might, the cold biting his lungs, venomous dread pounding the base of his throat as he reached the edge of the Cainwell estate and took in the sight before him.

The gate was dented, the latch no longer fit to its catching. Inside the grounds, blood stained the fine stone fountains, the opalescent gravel indented in the shape of fallen bodies. There were far fewer guards lurking about the estate's perimeter than had ever accosted him the few times he'd crept onto the grounds to see Abigale before her parents had fallen ill; and of those who remained, none of them accosted him at all as he lunged up the prominent steps beyond the snowy drive and burst through the front doors.

Someone cried out over the shriek of a knife being drawn. Gavannon drew his own sword and blocked it, and over the blade he held the gaze of the Cainwells' household steward, Vincet.

The man fell back in recognition and relief. "Lord Al-Morral! Thank the King it's you."

Gavannon sheathed his blade. "What happened here?"

The person who'd screamed—the head of the maids, Luetha, whom Gavannon had met a handful of times—folded over on a settee against the wall and buried her face in her hands. "Attack."

"By *whom*?"

"A Blessed," Vincet growled. "Killed our guards and attacked Milady Abigale."

Gavannon's knees wobbled, and he clung to the doorframe. "*No...*"

"He was incensed, he was *mad*," Luetha wailed, devoid of all the composure with which he'd seen her command the estate to cleanliness in visits past. "He told her this was her debt from Aeson Thalanor. She told him she doesn't know any Aeson Thalanor, but he wouldn't *listen—*"

Confusion wrecked itself against the shores of Gavannon's understanding.

It had not been Elynor's killing Blessed, then. But what had transpired here?

It didn't matter. The finer points were nothing. The creature would meet the same end regardless when he got his hands around its neck. "Is it still here?"

"Left, suddenly," Vincet said. "That was yesterday."

"Where is she?" Gavannon rasped.

"In her room." Vincet swallowed sharply. "Her father passed not long ago. She's all that's left of the family, and I fear..."

Gavannon didn't want to hear his own terror echoed by the steward. He barged past him and made straight for Abigale's chamber.

He'd never been allowed inside it from this way—he'd always climbed the rose trellis in the garden, and then the wisteria tree to her window, like a lovestruck boy—but a current of concerned, harrowed faces led to her door.

His hand shaking, Gavannon walked uncontested into her room.

Abigale was laid out on the bed like a porcelain statute, her skin too pale in the moonlight, her hair arrayed on the pillow in golden threads.

She was beautiful.

She was broken.

Her eyes were sunken in bowls of bruising, her temple stained with blood, her lips chapped with rust-red flakes. Bandages turned the smooth angles of her body bulky, the contours of a frame he'd loved so well made unfamiliar by this brutality. Everywhere he looked, there was evidence of wounds, of this heinous crime done against her.

She did not wake when he knelt at the bedside and clasped her cold hand, breathing against her knuckles, "Abi. Abigale, I'm here."

No stirring. Not even a squeeze of her hand around his.

Panic soaked his throat.

He was losing her. And if he lost her, he would lose everything.

Gavannon slipped an arm around her waist, careful not to touch a single bandage. Then he wrapped his fingers tightly around hers, laid his head against her side, and wept.

He did not know how long he cried before the sleep he'd sacrificed in favor of reaching her as swiftly as possible finally stole over him. It was a deep and dreamless slumber, and when he woke again, the room was veiled in pitch-darkness.

Yet Gavannon knew he was not alone.

Prickling awareness shot through him, lifting him up straight from the bed, his hand to his sword as a pair of figures moved from the shadows gathered up beside the armoire and from behind the thick satin drapes. They were spirits reflecting each other, one older, one younger.

The older, Gavannon did not know. But the sight of the younger sent hatred and disbelief spearing through him.

Elynor's face was expressionless as she held his gaze. "Hello, Gavannon."

A sea of lost love and betrayal surged between them. Gavannon's neck prickled, and he glanced toward the closed doors. Would the maids and attendants come running if he raised his voice?

"Don't bother with them," the other woman said. "A sleeping drought has taken them. There's no one to interrupt this conversation."

Gavannon dragged his gaze slowly back to them. "Come to kill me, Elynor?"

Her jaw flickered. "Much as I'd like to, no. That wouldn't solve the larger issue at stake."

She was so calm, so cold, and her eyes didn't even stray to Abigale—her girlhood friend. Sweat budded on Gavannon's top lip, and he flicked a glance at Abigale. "Why kill her? She was not the one you had contention with."

"You of all people should understand collateral, Al-Morral. You made it of me easily enough when you killed my father."

"Elynor," the woman murmured.

Elynor paused for a beat. "It isn't too late for Abigale—my mother can heal her."

Gavannon's attention darted to Iracabeth Azorius, practically a legend Alden had told over pits of fire with too much wine in his blood. She looked as if she could snap him in half. As if she *wanted* to.

He swallowed. "Heal her—for what cost?"

"You return to Kaer Dorwenon with us and confess before the King, His Orlethian guests, and all of Erala that you and Rowan precipitated this conflict between the kingdoms."

"You will tell them it was you who had Alden murdered, and why," Iracabeth added.

"And that Rowan falsely accused the *Daishi* of Orleth of treason," Elynor said. "And falsely accused *me* of killing *him*."

Gavannon's fingers formed and fell out of fists, slowly and painfully. With every word they spoke, another vapor of his dreams blew away like smoke from a fire that had blazed far beyond his control. "Even if I confess to everything, the conflict has gone too far already. They will never believe me."

Elynor smiled, a cruel, dark flicker of a grin. "I think that you'll find the Orlethian ambassador is *very* astute when it comes to dividing lies from truth."

"The time for talking is over. Choose, Gavannon." Iracabeth's voice was uncompromising. "Your ambition, or this woman's life."

Gavannon wrenched his gaze away from them to Abigale. She was so still, breathing so shallowly. She had perhaps hours left, if this woman did not help her.

The King was becoming too difficult to manage. Rowan had vowed to kill him. And he had made a dangerous enemy now of the Prince. But he could wipe them all out with a few deftly-aimed strokes, assume the Throne, hang Jamyson, and send the full might of the Kingsgard against Rowan. Then he could kill Elynor, Iracabeth, and every friend they had. He would have his security, his provision, his *power*.

But what good was any of it if he didn't have *her*?

Gavannon dragged a hand down his face and rested it over his mouth as the way became clear, from here to a troubled horizon. "I'll do it. All of it. The confession. The chains. If you save her."

Elynor's gaze flicked past him. "Sam."

A third figure emerged from the shadows of the doorway, a brawny sailor with bloodshot eyes. He swept Gavannon's feet with a kick and yanked his arms behind his back, then clapped a pair of dented irons cuffs around his wrists.

"You just stay there, mate." The man patted him on the shoulder, a promise of pain radiating from his fingertips.

Iracabeth sat at the bedside and smoothed Abigale's hair from her brow. The motion was so tender, it knocked the breath out of Gavannon. Hope surged in his chest.

"I'm going to find Sylvester and Rue," Elynor said curtly. "Remember, don't let her suffer, but don't heal her completely until we have his confession secured."

"You heartless wench," Gavannon hurled at her back. "She was your friend. What made you like this?"

Elynor paused with her hand on the door, glancing back at him. "You did."

And then the enemy Gavannon had created stepped from Abigale's room without a backward glance, leaving him in the ruins of his own downfall.

Chapter Sixty-Five

Kingkillers

It was time.

The Sanctum had been the last straw. When Jamyson thought of people like Vestan, good and loyal, being butchered in their prison—when he thought of the promise he'd made Elynor to do better by the Blessed, and how he'd never had the chance to keep it—the anger in his blood boiled into a steaming bath of pure rage.

Jamyson had put this off long enough. Argued with Vestan. Argued with *himself*. Wondered if this was the right path to take...and if he could ever be forgiven for it.

But the span of opportunity was rapidly shrinking; Al-Morral would return soon, with or without Abigale Cainwell, and when he did, it would be all-out warfare for the King's mind. And in that struggle, it was the people who would suffer most. Innocent people, like Jamyson's siblings, like the Queen. Like Esmae.

Jamyson had to do this now. Before it was too late.

So he slipped out while Vestan was still asleep, hidden behind the changing screen in the corner, bringing only his blades, wits, and the clarity of the hard choices and difficult duties demanded of a prince.

His father was in His private solar, as usual; Jamyson quietly sent away the guards, and they left, the same fear in their faces as in every face in Kaer Dorwenon these days.

It was Jamyson's responsibility to heal that fear. He would do it the only way he knew how.

He entered the solar and shut the door behind him. Then he put down the bar across it.

The King looked up from His desk, papers arrayed before Him, untouched. His eyes were hooded, a mask of contempt that had been foreign to Jamyson only a season ago. But now it was the look he'd come to associate with the King. "I had wondered when you might come."

Jamyson rested his hand lightly on his sword. "I know about the mind sickness."

"Of course you do."

Jamyson swallowed a stab of pain at that condescending tone. "That's why I don't want to hold You accountable for the havoc You've wreaked on this kaer and on the people of Erala. But what You've done to the Sanctum...this ends it. You can't keep doing these things."

"I am the Infallible Sovereign," the King said with a spike of arrogance. "Whatever I do is already just. This was justice against the Blessed."

"It was paranoia. And it was murder."

"The Blessed are tools. Weapons. You cannot *murder* a weapon."

"And what of Your wife and children?" Jamyson's tone hitched, but he forged ahead. "Do You deny *that* was murder?"

"I do not deny it was necessity. They, like you, were persuaded by a Blessed."

Jamyson's teeth ground painfully together. "Do You not see how Your fear has cost You *everything*?"

"Not everything." The King slowly rose. "I am not the reason Gavannon left the kaer. That was your doing, was it not?"

Ice pricked Jamyson's skin. "I don't know what you mean."

"Liar." The King's tone was clearer than Jamyson had heard it in months. "You think I haven't seen how ambitious You've become? You drove Gavannon out of this kaer so you could secure your inheritance of the Throne. You're the reason he's gone."

It was almost laughable how He could be so right and so very wrong at once. "The Throne *is* my inheritance. And if You truly desire what's best for the people, You'll step down before any more harm is done."

The King barked a scathing laugh. "And let the traitorous son of a Hunter-lover, a puppet of the Blessed, take the Throne? I think not."

Jamyson's pulse beat in his throat. The King had all but declared him unfit; if Elynor's plan did not succeed, and Gavannon returned of his own volition to Kaer Dorwenon, the Throne would pass to him in regency.

Jamyson couldn't let it happen. Damn his own heart.

He unsheathed his blade. "What I do now, I do for the people You once professed to love. I'm sorry."

He catapulted toward the desk. The King shouted for the guards even as He plunged a hand into His robes and drew His own sword from His hip. Steel beat against steel, throwing sparks, and Jamyson jerked back. The King kicked the desk against his stomach, knocking the wind from him, and brought His own weapon down in a two-handed stroke. Jamyson flung himself out of reach at the last moment so the King's sword bit deep into the desk; then he shoved it aside, taking his father's blade with it, and lunged to make the killing blow.

But the King still retained a trace of the nimble fighter He'd once been. He dodged, picked up one of His books, and hurled it into Jamyson's face. The corner stabbed him above the brow, unleashing a blinding wave of pain that blurred his vision, and when he shook his gaze clear the King had freed His sword and charged once more.

The current and future sovereign dueled for their lives, and if Jamyson was caught in the act, he would hang for it. Heir apparent or not.

The only way he would survive this was if he left this room the only man alive.

The thought filled him with fresh vigor, and he drove in against the King. With every flash of steel, he saw his brothers and sisters; he saw Queen Cecile; he saw Esmae, her lips forming words of love as the King's command ripped the world from under her feet. Jamyson's teeth gnashed and tears streaked his cheeks as he battled the man who'd taught him to hunt and fight and lead, who'd showed him how to walk tall through the kaer with his head high. The man who'd killed Jamyson's mother and stripped away everything he loved.

The man he'd cared for and hated for so many years.

A heartbroken shout stormed through Jamyson's lips, and he ducked beneath his father's next slash and swiveled, yanking his new dagger from his boot. He drove upward toward the King's sternum, but His fingers wrapped Jamyson's wrist, and with a kick to the hinge of Jamyson's elbow, He drove the knife into Jamyson's shoulder.

Jamyson's cry blended with the smashing of the solar door—the bar broken in half like a twig, the hinges shrieking as the entire thing bent inward. And then Vestan was there, crashing into the King and hurling Him away from Jamyson.

He yanked the knife from Jamyson's shoulder and twisted with him to face the King as He peeled Himself up from the desk, a feral smile turning His face to a stranger's. "And this is why you defy Me. I kill one of your Blessed pets and you bring back another."

"Not all that's gone is lost forever," Vestan growled. "But You might be the exception."

"You dare speak to me that way, Blessed?"

"I dare do more than that, You feckless bastard." Vestan squared his stance. "This is for the royal siblings."

He and Jamyson lunged together.

The King was ready for them this time. He yanked an offhanded dagger from the sheath behind His back and hurled it straight toward Jamyson's chest. Jamyson lunged aside, breaking off his assault, and Vestan flung himself at the King; the old man wielded His sword backhanded, cracking the pommel against Vestan's brow. When Vestan staggered, the King knocked his legs from under him and hurled him against the table's edge so hard he dropped to the floor. Then He raised Jamyson's dagger and drove the tip down into Vestan's exposed back.

Jamyson cried out in fury and tackled the King to the floor. They rolled, fighting for dominance, and it stunned Jamyson just how much power remained in the King's body, as if He'd stored up what little reserves He had for this moment—this inevitable struggle between father and son. Jamyson thrashed and hit at everything solid, denting his father's ribs and slamming blows into His soft middle, but paranoia seemed to dim His every notion of pain.

All that was left in Him was the desire to kill Jamyson.

And then something smashed into Jamyson's head—the same pommel that had stunned Vestan—and black stars floated across his vision. Before he could recover his wits, the King kicked the sword from his grasp. Then His fingers circled Jamyson's throat. "Heretical traitor! Do you think you can wrest the Throne from Me? I *am* the Throne. I am infallible, I am sovereign above all else, and if Erala must *burn* before it falls to its knees before Me again, then so be it!"

Dimly, Jamyson saw Vestan trying to crawl toward him, the blade still stuck in his back. With trembling fingers, he drew it from the sheath of his skin, then arched and buckled in agony.

The King's grip tightened, crushing, breaking something deep in Jamyson's chest. "Go to your treacherous mother and your lover in death. And know that Erala is better without you than it ever was with you. That you were a worthless son!"

Something sizzled in Jamyson's veins as his gaze found Vestan again, his guard slowly uncurling again, raising the opal knife Esmae had gifted to Jamyson. A fire he'd grown used to feeling ever since his scrape with the belladonna poisoning slithered through his blood paths again. But this time it was not merely a stroke of energy; it was something brighter, something white-hot that built on itself as the King's fingers pinched tighter around his throat, and Jamyson stopped breathing—

With a mighty cry, Vestan flung the knife. It jammed into the King's side, loosening His grip. And then the energy burst out of Jamyson, a furious surge of power, and he swung one last desperate blow at the King's chest.

The impact hurled his father off him like a battering ram, straight upward into the ceiling, so hard His body cratered among the tiles and hung there, limp as a doll. Jamyson gaped up at Him as breath shuddered back into his lungs. Gaped at the impossible sight of what he'd done.

And then the King folded gracelessly from the tiles and smashed into the floor. Blood pooled around His body, and His eyes gazed sightlessly at the wall.

He was dead. Jamyson had killed Him...by flinging Him into the *roof* with the weakest punch of his life.

Vestan's hands fastened in Jamyson's shirt, hauling him up. Jamyson stared at his father's corpse, gasping for breath, fighting to comprehend what he'd done. "*What was that?*"

Vestan's gaze branded him with shock. And comprehension. "It was strength when you needed it most. Like when you drank the belladonna and couldn't keep it down, even without the antidote. Rocks...that's it. That's always *been* it, that thing about you I couldn't make sense of..."

"That's *what*?" Jamyson roared. "Vez, you aren't talking sense!"

"Jamyson, you're Blessed," Vestan croaked. "Blessed with survival."

Jamyson swung his gaze to his bodyguard. Took in the certainty and reverence in his eyes.

And felt his own world plummet out from beneath him, just as it had with Esmae. A death-blow.

"No. That isn't *possible*."

"How else do you explain this?" Vestan flung an arm toward the King. "How do you explain how you walk away from every scrape and disaster hardly scathed, with or without armor? How you pick yourself up after everything? And how reckless you are—you dance with death because your Blessed nature wants to be unleashed. It goads you to take risks so it can help you survive them."

Jamyson grabbed Vestan's collar in turn and shook him. "Will you stop talking! I am not *Blessed*!"

"Jamyson. Why do you think your mother freed those Hunters when you were a boy, even knowing it would mean her death?"

Jamyson stared at him, the feeling draining from his face.

It made too much sense. *Perfect* sense, even. His mother, a Hunter, laying down her life to free her own kind. A *Hunter* sitting on the Queen's throne. And when Hunters bred with humans, the offspring...

Jamyson scrambled back from the King, horror ripping through him so hard and swift, he couldn't breathe. "No. No, no, no..."

Footsteps pounded in the hall—the Kingsgard, no doubt alerted by the impact of the King's body with the ceiling. Vestan stumbled upright, blood soaking above his hip, and yanked Jamyson to his feet. "Take the passage behind your father's bookcase. Get to your rooms. I'll tell them I did this, that you tried to stop me and I stabbed you in the shoulder. It looks like the work of a strong Blessed, anyway. They'll believe me."

"They'll kill you."

"You won't let them."

Jamyson's gaze flashed to the King's broken body...no. Not the King. In death, he was only Marcus Venator. Jamyson was the King now.

The strength rushed from his limbs. He staggered, and Vestan hurled him toward the bookcase. "Run!"

And with the weight of Vestan's sacrifice crashing over him, Jamyson Venator, Blessed, *cursed* forever, fled for his life.

Chapter Sixty-Six
Great Deceptions

ELYNOR HAD NEVER ENDURED a carriage ride so uncomfortable as the return to Kaer Dorwenon from Bast—not even when she'd first taken Sharek from the Sanctum. She sat on one seat, pressed between Sylvester and Rue, while Sam held the chain linked to Al-Morral's shackles and Iracabeth held the Seeker's. That Blessed was always watching Elynor, its gaze intent and hungry. Elynor tried to ignore it, and the way Al-Morral glared at her, too.

It was a relief to finally reach Kaer Dorwenon, but the sense of levity did not last long; for no sooner had Elynor led her entourage onto the bridge toward the barbican than she realized all the flags on the towers were flapping at half-mast and the torches burned even in the daylight from the sconces on the walls.

The Flame of Remembrance. She hadn't seen it lit since Jamyson's mother died.

Elynor's stomach dropped. She abandoned the others and fled indoors, up staircases and around corners, her bandaged arm throbbing, her fingertips scraped by the stone in her haste. She shouldered past a pair of guards at the Throne room doors and burst inside, steeling her heart for the sight of a prince's coffin laid in the middle of the hall and people gathered to pay their respects.

Instead she came face-to-face with *Khuless* Mide, rising from a stiff bow before the Throne, flanked by her armed and helmed Orlethian guards; and of

Jamyson Venator sitting on that Throne, looking haggard as if he hadn't slept in days.

Elynor froze, shock anchoring her feet to the stone floor.

The silence deafened for endless moments.

"As I was saying," Jamyson's tone was dry when he spoke at last, "I haven't seen Elynor Azorius in months. Except I suppose I've seen her now." His pleading gaze flashed to her. "Good to see you after all this time, Lady Azorius."

Under Mide's quelling glare, Elynor jolted back to focus and curtsied. "Your Eminence. *Khuless* Mide."

"I've been sent to retrieve you," Mide growled, "and your companions, and to return you to Danje in chains."

"That won't be happening," Jamyson said. "Lady Azorius is under my protection."

"And is that worth starting a war?"

"There's no need for war," Elynor said. "I've brought proof of the duplicitous actions from those who intended to pit the kingdoms against one another for profit."

Mide's sternness held, but brightness licked her eyes. "Have you?"

Elynor sidestepped as Sam entered, dragging Al-Morral beside him. Sylvester and Rue entered next, and Mide's eyes cut to the bard, lingering until Iracabeth led a pair of Kingsgard inside with the Seeker bound between them. "What is this?"

"A confession." Al-Morral's tone strained with reluctance; but with Abigale still in desperate need of Iracabeth's continued care, he would not renege on his promise. Elynor was confident in that, if in nothing else.

Mide approached him, and the Orlethian contingent moved with her like the tilt of a dark bird's wing, their hands on their weapons. "What sort of confession?"

Resignation aged Al-Morral by no less than a decade. "Alden Azorius's death was a ploy by myself and my associate, Rowan Varodan. Rowan poisoned him and then traveled to Orleth to plant blame among your people, to incite Erala against Orleth."

"*How?*"

"At first, the *Daishi* was to be found with the same poison on his person. But then Elynor Azorius chartered passage to Orleth, and we thought she made the better culprit. Orleth would believe King Marcus sent her to plant the evidence.

Rowan plotted to stage his own death, to make it seem like she'd come to silence him."

"And where is Rowan now?"

"Alive. I saw him here in the kaer just before I traveled to Bast."

Elynor's pulse quickened at the thought of Rowan, loose in the wilds of Erala again.

"And what of my father?" Jamyson demanded. "What was your scheme with Him?"

Al-Morral shot Jamyson a glare. "At first, it was only to make Him believe Orleth murdered Alden through his daughter, to provoke Him to war. But then I had my ambitions, and…one thing led to another."

The spirits of Jamyson's dead family haunted his face as he slowly rose and descended from the Throne, halting shoulder-to-shoulder with Mide. "Tell us *why*."

Al-Morral shrugged faintly. "Profiteering. I own the Fleet. I have connections to guilds throughout Erala. If we were at war with Orleth—"

Mide struck him across the face, whipping his head to the side. "You gutless, heartless flake of *busar*. Good men were executed for your deception."

"And women. And children." Jamyson punched Al-Morral's head back the other way.

"You ought to be executed." Mide wrapped her hand around Al-Morral's throat and pushed his head back until his eyes locked with hers.

"Agreed." Jamyson laid a hand on her wrist. "Unfortunately, the law protects him. Everything he did was under the King's approval. I can't hang him without just cause, and I can't begin my reign by executing one more person who *appears* innocent."

Mide's fingers flexed. "What are you suggesting, then?"

Jamyson jerked his head. "Confer with me, *Khuless*?"

Elynor sidled within earshot when they retreated. Uncouth, perhaps, but she didn't care; she wanted to know what would become of her father's murderers if they wouldn't be dead by sunrise.

"I'll deal with Al-Morral," Jamyson muttered to the *Khuless*. "It's Erala he betrayed, so Erala will try him and put him away in a prison so deep and dark, he'll spend the rest of his miserable days stewing in regret. Would this Rowan make a fair prize for Orleth?"

"Better than." A feral smile yanked at Mide's mouth. "I'll make certain he suffers before he dies."

Jamyson hooked his thumbs in his ornate belt and gestured with a full-body slope toward Al-Morral. "I think a signed confession ought to put a stop to what that one started. Would your mother agree?"

"I believe she would. And we will make certain that Rowan confirms it. A wise choice, Prince Jamyson."

The two swiveled as one, and Jamyson shot Elynor a raised-brow look when he noticed how close she stood to the dais. She offered a bland stare in return.

"The *Khuless* and I have conferred," he announced to the room at large. "Gavannon Al-Morral will sign a written confession of all these crimes you've born witness to. That confession will travel back with *Khuless* Mide and the Blessed called Rowan to Orleth, where he'll stand accused of his crimes against their kingdom."

"And Al-Morral?" Iracabeth asked.

"Gavannon Al-Morral will repeat his confession before a conference of magistrates and then rot in a prison of my choosing for the assassination of Alden Azorius."

Elynor's heart broke open, a wash of relief flooding her body so fiercely her knees shook. Al-Morral might not be dead, but he would be stopped. And that was all that mattered.

Rue signed rapidly to Iracabeth, and she nodded, turning to Jamyson. "To make this effective, Rowan must be found. Might I suggest the services of this Seeker?"

Jamyson studied him with narrowed eyes. "You there. Blessed. You know Rowan Varodan?"

"I do." The Seeker had an eerie voice, chillingly light, like a cold winter breeze stirring snow. "I have smelled his blood."

"And you value your life, I take it."

"Yes."

"Then on pain of death, you're to hunt him and bring him back to Kaer Dorwenon alive, at which time you'll receive a full pardon from the Throne and your freedom. On the assumption you'll leave Elynor Azorius in peace."

The Seeker's gaze flicked to her. "I have no quarrel with the woman. If Aeson Thalanor does not order me, her contract is forfeit."

"Then consider it forfeit. You serve the Throne now." Jamyson nodded to Sam. "Release him."

The Seeker flexed his wrists as Sam slowly unthreaded the chains around them. He drew in a deep breath, jaw twitching, a hound scenting the breeze. Then he turned on heel and loped from the room.

Jamyson cleared his throat, folding his arms and tapping his elbows. "Speaking of leaving Elynor Azorius alone…"

"She did not kill Rowan, clearly," Mide said. "Though it is the *Khul's* discretion to lift the bounty on prisoners, I am certain she will reconsider the object of her rage when she realizes Rowan is a cheat and a liar."

"I'm glad we understand one another." Jamyson offered his hand. "It's been an honor preventing war with you, *Khuless* Mide."

"And with you, Prince Jamyson." Amusement softened the edges of her tone, and she shook his hand. Then they strode toward the Throne room doors, flanked by their guards. Mide slowed abreast of Sam, her gaze cutting sharply across him. "If you ever set foot in Orleth again, it will be your head."

Sam averted his gaze. "Understood."

The *Khuless* lingered, studying his downcast posture. "Be free."

As Sam's eyes shot up to her again, tears lining his lashes, Mide strode from the room.

Chapter Sixty-Seven

The Art of Healing

A THREAD OF GENTLE music still rang through the heart of Ollanthyr, but Sharek could hardly hear it anymore. It was lost within the silence itself, swallowed in the vastness of the Fai Alora and the pause that hung over the world, holding its breath at the ruined wooden wall of the village, the modest homes decayed into gravemarkers, the heaps of bones lying at doorframes and along the road where families had left them to rot when they'd fled all those years ago.

Ollanthyr had become a haunting place for the spirits of memories. They haunted Sharek as he paced the confines of his childhood home.

They had been here for days. Sharek's lungs had finally eased from their ache, and his wounds from the battle were beginning to mend, but the Sanctum still burned in his dreams. In his nightmares, he was shut up in the hovel while it collapsed around him; he never escaped, and death finally found him precisely where he'd first welcomed it with open arms.

He didn't welcome death anymore. But it still followed him here.

Sharek traced his fingertips over the filthy tabletop, the wood swollen with many seasons of rain, battered by the elements. He brushed away the fluff of mouse nests and ran his thumb over notches buried in the wood, and remembered.

A glorious day of golden warmth and green light filtered through the bedheaded spring growth of the Fai Alora. Nymeria was out gathering herbs, and

Sharek and Castian sat at the table: Castian skinning hares, and Sharek watching, tracing the tabletop with his own blade—a smaller imitation of Castian's, just as Sharek was a smaller imitation of his father in every way.

"Why do you always hunt more than we can eat?" Sharek asked.

"Have you seen how much hare your mother can put away in a meal?" Castian arched a brow, and Sharek laughed. His father joined in as he returned to skinning. "No, I do this to feed the poorer villages out there. Not all have Blessed who can help them survive the harsh climes, much less Hunters."

"That's an awful big responsibility." Sharek had just learned that word. Everything was a responsibility, from making his bed to using the privy pot.

Castian smiled. "Yes, but Erala is ours to protect. Its people are ours to look after. It's why we were made."

"Then why do we hide?"

"Because the Kings don't want our help, but we protect Them all the same. Just as we protect the people, though they fear us."

Sharek considered that as he traced his knife tip over the tabletop. "They hunt us, don't they? Kill us if they find us."

"Yes."

"Then why do we protect them? I don't understand."

Castian laid aside his deboning knife and held his son's gaze with solemn courage. "Because it isn't about them. It's who *we* are. Do you understand, Sharek?"

"*Sharek.*"

He drew his hand back from the mildewed tabletop, turning toward the corner. For the first time since they'd stumbled into this broken place, Rowan's eyes were open, fixed on the cratered ceiling. He rasped Sharek's name again.

Sharek returned to him, sitting cross-legged at Rowan's head. He helped him sit up and drink from a dented bowl full of melted snow. Rowan screwed up his face in disgust, but didn't complain. "Where are we?" he groaned when Sharek laid him out again.

"Ollanthyr," Sharek said. "My family's home."

Rowan rolled his head to the side, taking in the patchwork of broken furniture, the caved-in ceiling, the limp door on its rusted hinges. "No wonder you're so miserable all the time."

"It wasn't always like this."

"I know. Fausto Hagan."

Rowan had dragged that story out of him not long after he'd come to the Sanctum. A tearful, hate-seething mess of a boy, and Rowan had made him spill that story like blood while Sharek punched his palms until his own knuckles turned black with bruising.

He couldn't remember what it had been like to be so young. Or to trust so easily.

Rowan struggled to prop himself up on his elbows, then groaned and gripped his side. "*Rocks*. What happened to me?"

"The roof caved in on you."

Rowan's brows shot up—the only movement that didn't seem to cause him discomfort, so Sharek braced himself to be subjected to that look many times. "And you dragged me out?"

Sharek shrugged and hauled a broken stone pot from the corner. The *multem* inside was still faintly warm from the previous night's meal, and he offered Rowan the crooked ladle. "Don't worry, I washed all these things before I used them."

"Thank the Empyreans. Wouldn't want to snort up the dust of your dead ancestors." Rowan's arrogant retort was deadened somewhat by the way his hand shook in the simple motion of feeding himself. "Why here?"

"I couldn't think of anywhere else we'd be safe."

It was more than that, though Sharek would never tell Rowan; after being locked away below the Sanctum, certain he'd squandered his only grasp for freedom, there'd only been two places he'd wanted to run: straight to Elynor, or back to the spirits of his parents. And he wouldn't bring Rowan near Elynor again.

Rowan handed the ladle back and reclined against the musty heap of blankets Sharek had fashioned into a bed for him. "And you've been pining at my bedside all this time."

"I've kept busy."

Rowan's eyes drifted across the room and back to him. "The Sanctum?"

"Destroyed." The word echoed hollowly. Though the structure of stone and mortar had been torn down, the essence of what the Sanctum was would live in the hearts of every captive until they learned to heal from the suffering they'd endured there. A person or a place could only hurt a man for so long, but a wound left unhealed could torment him for the rest of his life.

In Rowan's eyes, he saw his same hollowness reflected. As much as they'd talked of tearing the Sanctum down with their bare hands while they lay in its dark holes, as often as they'd stormed up ideas of what they'd do if they were ever free, there had been tethers that bound them to that place. Aeson Thalanor was the only constant figure in their lives after their interment; the Sanctum had been the only semblance of home they'd known for so many years.

But now, for Sharek, home held the shape of foggy kaer grounds at dawn and wind-bathed waves and the scent of juniper and rosewood. Brown eyes and dark hair and skin pale as beach sand.

He had a moor. An anchor. But Rowan did not. His face was rearranging itself now into the usual mask of playful antagonism even as his body tightened and lifted slightly with a spasm of pain from his broken ribs and contused innards. "It must terrify you, knowing I'm alive and now there's no Sanctum walls or Aeson Thalanor to restrain me."

"In fact, I'm relieved."

Rowan's crooked laughter caught, and his whole body eased out of its rigor. "Why are you doing this? Why pull me from the fire at all? I don't deserve your charity."

"No, you don't. But it's not about what you deserve. It's about the sort of man I am. I won't leave you to die after you saved my life."

Rowan scowled. "So where does that leave us?"

Sharek shrugged. "Wherever we decide to go. That's what freedom is...it's the choice. It's the chance to set the course of your own destiny."

"Well, our choices are few. There's no place for us in this world, and less for me. I'm not as tame as you. I have to kill. It's my nature."

"You don't have to kill men. I could teach you to hunt, the way my father taught me. Deer and things. There's never a lack of need for game, particularly in the poorer villages."

"And to what end? You'll never trust me again."

"I might. If you prove yourself worthy of that trust."

Rowan scoffed. "Seems a dull existence. Killing stags and winning your approval."

"Naturally. Because you have so much else better to do." Rowan glared at him with red-rimmed eyes, and Sharek inclined, linking his arms around his bent knees. "Rowan. The Sanctum is in rubble. The Blessed are free to make their own way. You have no reason left to hate or to hunt."

"I could kill what remains of the Venator bloodline, for what happened at the Sanctum." But Rowan's tone was halfhearted.

Sharek shook his head. "Jamyson Venator did not do this. And if we punish the innocent for the crimes of their ancestors, we're no better than the King who did it to us."

Rowan curled his lip. "Then what do you suggest we do?"

"Let go of what we were. Release the spirits that once bound us. Grow. Heal."

"I don't know how to do anything like that."

"I'll show you," Sharek said. "Trust me, brother."

Rowan's gaze flickered as Sharek released the word from within himself—a word he'd trapped under lock and key, buried deeper than any Sanctum hovel, the moment Aeson Thalanor had callously passed along the news of Rowan's death that first time. "I don't know what's worse. That you truly believe the nonsense you're spewing, or that your arse-shaped face makes me want to believe it, too."

Sharek snorted. "You'll learn to. Now lie back. You need to rest."

"Overprotective nursemaid is not a good look on you."

"Death would look worse."

Rowan scoffed under his breath. But he laid back down.

Chapter Sixty-Eight

Edits and Interventions

Elynor hadn't bathed properly since the palace in Danje...nor did she allow herself the luxury upon her return to the kaer until she was certain Al-Morral was interred beyond any notion of escape in the dungeons, under a guard of fifteen men including Mide's own. Only then did she submit to what she had longed for in every bucket of lukewarm water she had subjected herself to in the crossing of the Caeruel and beyond.

And true and proper *bath*, with soaps and shampoos and water that stayed warm as long as she liked.

It took hours to scrub all the filth from her body, and by the time she emerged from the wooden tub she was pruned like a raisin and dizzy from the steam. She planted herself facedown on the bed in the chambers Jamyson had assigned to her and breathed out a long, delirious sigh. She was so kings-damned happy to be free.

But Sharek's absence still gnawed at her, vicious and constant, and wouldn't let her fully embrace that this horrific ordeal was over.

There was a knock at the door, and Elynor rolled upright, banding her robe around her waist and smoothing her tangled hair. "Enter."

Jamyson slipped inside. "Hope I'm not interrupting anything."

"Only a silent victory dance."

"I'd join you if I wasn't so exhausted." He stripped off his swordbelt, tossed it onto the dining table, and flopped down beside her. "The *Khuless* and her people will remain with us until the Seeker finds Rowan, so we'll have to be on our best entertaining behavior for the time being."

He rubbed his shoulder as he spoke, and Elynor frowned. "What happened?"

"Battle wound."

Elynor's heart raced from more than the heat now. "Jamyson?"

He stared at the wall. "I...Vestan killed my father."

Shock blew out the breath from Elynor's chest. "But *why*?"

"He was attacking me. Vez had no choice. It was my life or the King's." He bent his head into his hands. "It was me or Him."

Elynor laid a hand on his back. "I'm sorry."

"I'm not." Jamyson's tone was leaden, the words breathed out like heresy toward the floor. "And that's what frightens me. The only thing I regret is that my first act after my coronation will be to hang the man who saved my life."

Elynor yanked her hand back. "You're going to *hang* Vestan?"

"He assassinated the King. If I don't exact justice, I'll lose the Throne."

"But the King was a madman!"

"He was. And the people will never believe that." Jamyson sat back, his troubled eyes fixed on her. "A Blessed killed the Infallible Sovereign. That's how it will be remembered."

"Jamyson, we've lost enough friends."

"I *know*," he growled, running a hand through his hair. "But I can't let my first edict be that a man who murders a King can walk free."

Elynor scratched her temples, frowning at the floor, then lifting her head to stare at the wall. "It isn't an edict you need. It's an intervention."

Jamyson's eyes narrowed. "All right. What is *that* look for?"

She turned her gaze fully to him. "I think you need to speak to my mother."

Chapter Sixty-Nine

Finally Free

Now that Rowan was awake, his restless energy fumed through the house, making it seem too small for them both; so Sharek spent a good deal of his time in the Fai Alora, stalking and trapping game, imagining his father's spirit was with him, silently approving his choices. Half the game he brought back alive to the house, and as Rowan's strength returned, he made clean kills of them. Each time, his vigorous energy quieted some, and those nights they cooked meat in the old hearth, filling the home with the smell of burning dust and flagrant cobwebs, and talked about things: the Sanctum, their past missions, Aeson Thalanor. There was no talk of the future, and Sharek didn't press for it yet. Rowan wasn't ready to envision such things; his gaze was still trapped backward, looking at the spirits that hounded his heels.

"It's strange how much a war doesn't matter now that the Sanctum is gone," Rowan remarked one morning. They sat at the table, plucking pheasants, heaping up more meat than they could ever hope to eat before it spoiled. In his mind Sharek mapped the old trails that connected Hunter villages throughout Teran, wondering if Rowan was ready yet for so long a trek.

Now he paused, glancing up. "Do you regret what you did to start that war? Any of it?"

Rowan shrugged. "I was taught never to regret the kill. Guilt's an unkind companion, you know that."

"It's what the Sanctum taught us. That never kept me from feeling guilty."

"Because you're too soft." Rowan plopped another pheasant on the heap and bent forward, curling an arm around his middle to grip his ribs. "I'm told Alden Azorius was an advocate of the Blessed, in his own way. That he never hired them."

"That's true."

Rowan's gaze emptied as he stared at the tabletop. "Him, I regret."

Sharek set down his own pheasant, searching for something to say to those words he'd never expected to hear.

And in the silence, he caught the brush of a footstep outside.

Sharek rocked to his feet at once, scooping up his deboning knife. Rowan's gaze flicked between him and the door, his senses a hairsbreadth too dull to alert him to the danger. Sharek motioned him down and turned to face the door.

But he did not have to go looking for the trouble; it came straight to them this time.

There was an eerie stillness in how Aeson Thalanor's Seeker filled up the doorway, only his long, bound hair stirred by the breeze, and Sharek's heart dropped to his knees. This was undoubtedly the Seeker who'd gone after Abigale.

He curled his hand over the knife. "Who sent you?"

"Jamyson Venator. By the word of Gavannon Al-Morral."

Rowan stood too, slower, unsteady. He stepped forward and raised an arm, barring the way to Sharek. "Which one of us have you come for?"

The Seeker's gaze sharpened with primal focus. "You. I'm to return you to Kaer Dorwenon alive, to face justice for your crimes."

Sharek's gut coiled in a tight, ugly knot.

Elynor's plot had succeeded. He knew exactly what sort of justice was coming.

He barged forward, and Rowan shoved him back, still glaring at the Seeker. "If I go quietly, you leave this one alone. Agreed?"

"I care nothing for him unless he stands in my way."

"Then you're about to care very *much*." Sharek laid a hand to the falchion Rowan had given him in the Sanctum.

Rowan stabbed his elbow into Sharek's middle. "Don't even think about it."

"Rowan—"

"This is Al-Morral's doing. Protecting his traitorous throat from my hands." Rowan's laughter was pitiless. "You were right. I never should've trusted that son of a bastard. He was always going to betray me if it was in his best interest."

The words were resigned. They were giving up.

"No." Sharek couldn't watch someone else he cared about be dragged from this house, never to be seen again.

Still guarding his ribs, Rowan stepped forward. "I'm ready."

Sharek snagged him by the pit of his arm, towing him to a halt. "If you go with that creature, at best, you'll be dead inside a month. At worst, you'll be an Orlethian prisoner. You'll never be free again."

"And if I don't go, we'll be fugitives forever and you'll never be reunited with your precious heiress. You said freedom is the choice. So I choose not to turn the kingdoms against you by letting you fall on a sword for me." Rowan yanked his arm loose, gripped Sharek's neck, and pressed their brows together. "Consider this my penance for what I did to you in Rimbourg. In Danje. And for leaving you to rot when Al-Morral offered me freedom."

Sharek's eyes burned. He squeezed them shut.

"I'm done. It's finished," Rowan said. "Our people are free."

He released Sharek and stepped back toward the Seeker, spreading one arm slightly, still holding his ribs with the other.

"*All* of us are now, Sharek."

And then he let the Seeker lay hold of him and lead him away.

Sharek kept his feet until they were gone. Then he folded down to his knees, whispering prayers to Sabrathan for Rowan's quick death as clouds rolled across the sky above Ollanthyr, stealing the sun.

Chapter Seventy

The Execution

For days, talk around Kaer Dorwenon was of nothing but the visit of *Khuless* Mide. Then it was about Jamyson's coronation, passing without fanfare because he didn't feel like celebrating or feasting, and he knew the stunned and frightened people didn't either. Then it was all about Vestan, presumed dead, who'd risen from the depths to kill the former King.

Jamyson's crown was light, but the Throne was an abyss. He was glad to leave it even for a public execution.

Khuless Mide stood with him on his left, the position of a foreign dignitary. To his right was Elynor, and he was glad to have her there, regardless of the sort of message that sent. Her steady presence and her confident faith in their plan helped him keep his feet as he looked down at the crowd gathered in the kaer's inner courtyard, where the Kingsgard escorted Vestan, bound and gagged, to the gallows.

Gallows that would be deconstructed at long last after today. And perhaps Jamyson would find the strength to dance around them in relief while he burned them to cinders…but for now, every muscle weighed like stone.

He had longed to steal a moment with his bodyguard in the dungeons to thank him for his sacrifice, for interceding at all. But Jamyson's every move was being watched now, and the people would take no kindlier to his sympathy for Vestan than they would to his release. So Jamyson's only communication with his friend had been a scrap of paper slipped by Rue, who used her muteness like a cloak that made her utterly invisible.

And as Vestan stepped onto the gallows and his eyes found Jamyson on the King's viewing balcony, Jamyson hoped the steadiness of his guard's gaze meant that Vestan had received the message in full.

Jamyson had not bothered to prepare a speech. He would not paint a veneer over this day, nor would he begin his reign by lying to the people about how he felt toward King Marcus or Vestan. He would not use the pretty and expected lies to corrupt his bodyguard's reputation any more than it already would be.

The hairs on the nape of Jamyson's neck rose in a sudden, shivering sweep, and he fought not to look to the left, forcing himself to meet the executioner's eyes as the noose slipped over Vestan's head.

Forcing himself to nod.

The dip of the wood, the plunge of Vestan's body nearly sent Jamyson to his knees. For a flash, he saw Esmae, thrashing and struggling as the life choked out of her, and his heart cracked once more.

And from the mezzanine across the courtyard, a bowstring twanged.

The arrow whistled out, straight and true, and sang through the cords of the noose. With a fraying hiss, they snapped.

Vestan's boots clapped the courtyard cobblestones, and he was up and running before he'd even caught his breath. The people leaped away, crying out in terror; Jamyson pretended to be stunned for one instant before he called the guards.

And that was all Vestan needed to lose himself in the throng. By the time the guards winnowed between the innocents with their weapons, Vestan was already gone. And Jamyson knew he would never be found.

He was glad. Relieved, even. The plan had worked.

But he'd never felt so alone in his life, as his closest friend—the only one who knew the true nature of him—took his leave of Kaer Dorwenon for the last time.

Chapter Seventy-One

Jamyson, Restored

Restless energy conferred into Jamyson through the very bones of the kaer, full of whispers about Vestan's escape and the fruitless hunt for him. He couldn't bring himself to take the seat when he returned to the Throne room, the iron, finial-tipped chair his father had so often lounged in, so certain of His own wisdom, convinced of His infallibility. Jamyson circled around it instead, running his hands over its grooves and divots, hating every inch of the thing. Just as he'd feared from the first moment he'd sat in it, no powerful surge of awe-inspiring knowledge had come over him. No enlightenment or fierce revelation had paved his steps into a better future. He wouldn't have even been able to save Vestan without Elynor's help and her mother's swift shot.

He was still just Jamyson Venator, a frightened man with the weight of a kingdom on his shoulders and no clear path forward to protecting it.

No, not just a man. A *Blessed*.

His knees buckled, and he leaned a moment against the detestable Throne. In so many ways, it was the only thing keeping his feet beneath him.

To his relief, the Throne room door opened just then, sparing any more thought to his own nature, and *Khuless* Mide joined him, flanked by a pair of guards. She'd stopped bringing the entire entourage with her everywhere she went, which he hoped meant the tensions were abating. He did not want to inherit his father's near-war along with all the other sins He'd left Jamyson to sweep up.

"I had no idea Eralanite executions were so exciting." As usual, the *Khuless* kept a steady tone, but there was a hint of mirth in her eyes.

"They usually aren't." Jamyson kept his voice just as bland.

Mide's lips pursed and she cocked her head. "You know, it's very strange. We have tales in Orleth of an archer with such precise aim. A woman who haunts the Amasandji province."

Jamyson's pulse quickened. "That's an interesting coincidence."

"I thought so, too."

The pause lengthened into awkwardness, and Jamyson hunted for something to break it. But it was Mide who finally shrugged. "Well, archery is a craft practiced by many, myself included. Anyway, I came to tell you that my people and I are departing for the coast. The Seeker has delivered Rowan Varodan to the edge of Dorwenon. It's time we brought him back to Orleth to face justice."

Jamyson dipped his head, surprised by the faint tinge of regret that accompanied the motion. "It's been my pleasure to entertain your company these last few weeks, *Khuless*."

"It's been my pleasure to be so entertained." Mide's eyes danced. "Your ways here are very interesting indeed. Quiet coronations and lively executions, and a King who was not ashamed of his Blessed bodyguard though the man murdered his father. I suspect we will be seeing much more of one another now that you are King."

Jamyson extended his hand. "I would be honored by that."

"Yes, you would." Mide clasped his hand warmly; and then she was gone, taking the last of the distractions with her.

So there was nothing for Jamyson to do but slump in his Throne and try to think through the whirlwind of everything that had happened in recent weeks and what still needed to be done.

He had a eulogy to write for the King and the interment to conclude. He'd need to replace the advisers his father had hung and offer incentives for the stricken nobles not to pack up their things and flee to other cities—beginning with dissolving the treaty that had consigned their lands and livelihoods to the Throne itself. And he needed to have words with a certain magistrate in Bast about a pair of wills that were still, absurdly, under review.

He had to put the kingdom back together. And he had to do it alone.

There was a gentle swish of movement at the Throne room door, and Jamyson muttered, "Enter."

"I have."

He glanced up, stiffening at the unfamiliar figure leaning against the doorway. The folds of clothing draped against her curves marked her undeniably a woman—one strung with weapons, and hooded and cloaked.

Jamyson shoved himself to his feet and reached for his sword. "Who are you?"

She raised a hand. "Peace, King Jamyson. I don't come as an enemy. I bring good tidings."

"I find that difficult to believe. You have the look of an assassin."

The woman tipped back her cowl with both hands. Her warm brown skin and sharp eyes were unfamiliar, and yet Jamyson felt a faint stab of recognition when her somber gaze held his. "There. Now we are equals, you and I."

Jamyson kept his hand to his sword. "How did you convince my guards to give you entrance?"

"They're currently dealing with a matter at the barbican. Don't worry," the woman added as Jamyson jerked forward a step, "it's all good news. I come on behalf of Vestan."

Jamyson hesitated. "Vestan."

"We met when he was wounded in the Valley. My name is Ria." She paused for a moment, then added softly, "I come also on behalf of someone we both loved very much. Esmae."

Jamyson let out a soft huff as her name socked the breath from him. "How...how did you know her?"

"My people still live because of her. She and her family sacrificed their lives and freedom for ours."

Tension rippled through Jamyson, but it was still not enough to pull his sword from its sheath. "You're one of the Hunters she protected in Oss Belliard."

"I am."

Yet she did not attack him—the last living Venator. Jamyson narrowed his eyes. "Why are you here?"

"Because Vestan spoke highly of your love for Esmae," Ria said. "And because I know that she loved you. Even in Oss Belliard, she spoke of Jamyson Venator in glowing terms. And now you are King, and I am curious what sort of King you will become."

Slowly, Jamyson peeled his fingers from his blade. "The law says I ought to kill you where you stand."

"But you can change the law. As our King, you can change everything."

That was true. A Blessed on the Throne could do a great deal of harm; he could also do a great deal of good.

He'd made promises to Esmae he could never keep, swearing oaths and freedom and fairness that were beyond his grasp. But standing at the mouth of the Throne room was a woman like him...someone Esmae had sacrificed something to save. They were indeed equals, linked by the courageous gifts from a brave and proud magistrate's daughter. And Jamyson owed it to Esmae with every breath in his body that he would choose his next words carefully.

"Esmae told me that Hunters were strengthened to defend the kingdom," he said slowly. "Gifted to protect it from enemies the sacrosanct Kings couldn't see."

"That is what our stories tell us, too."

Jamyson swallowed and searched for a corner of his spirit that felt guilt or raised an apology to his dead father.

He found none.

"Erala is going to need all the defense it can muster in the dark times ahead," he said. "It's shaken by the actions of its last King. So if protection is what you offer...if Esmae trusted you, then so do I." And in the spirit of the Queen who would never be, Jamyson took his hand from his sword. "You do right by her. Or we will have war."

Ria held his gaze for a long moment, eyes glinting with sorrow. "Our spies did everything they could, but King Marcus moved too swiftly even for us. I am sorry we did not reach her in time."

Jamyson's breath struck the very bottom of his lungs, and he looked sharply away. "So am I."

After a long moment of silence, Ria added, "Vestan and I will carry this mantel for you. He rides with us now. And in time, perhaps we can tell the people that the Throne and the Hunters have found peace. It begins with us, Your Majesty."

There was no deceit in her words. And there had been no deceit in Esmae when she'd spoken fondly of these people who'd taught her the knowledge she'd used to crack Al-Morral's schemes wide open. To help Jamyson save his kingdom.

He knew what it was to be sacrosanct, and now to be Blessed. And he was beginning to learn what it was to have been wrong about everything.

"Tell Vestan…" His voice broke, and he cleared his throat. "Tell Vez he reports to me. In secret."

"It will be done." Ria stepped back, towing up her hood. "I hope you enjoy the coronation gift we've brought you. Long live the King."

Then she turned and vanished like smoke into the hall.

Jamyson sat down, trembling, and held his head in his hands. This day could not be any stranger, nor his beliefs any more challenged. And he did not want to know what gift this Huntress had left for him.

He sat in silence for some time, stunned that he'd encountered a Hunter and lived to tell it. More than that—he'd seen his grief for Esmae reflected in her eyes. And he'd believed it.

He shook with that grief, with disbelief, and with the realization that Erala was going to continue to change whether he wanted it to or not. And *he* would keep changing, also against his own wishes. And somehow, while all of it was happening, he'd have to keep the kingdom from crumbling.

The Throne room door creaked, and he sighed. "What *now*?"

"That's really not a Kingly thing to say, idiot."

That voice—high and strident, and full of familiar humor—

Jamyson's gaze snapped to the doorway.

Standing there, rumpled and filthy and with his hair badly in need of a trim, wearing peasant clothes and a crooked grin and spreading his hands on the doorframes to hold them wide, was Elliott.

Elliott.

Jamyson wrenched to his feet, leaving his stomach and heart and his sane head along with every other broken piece of him stuck to the Throne. Before his wide eyes, the doorway crowded with Sylvie's lean form, and Isla with flowers woven into her hair, and Isaac wearing a necklace of cannibal fish teeth.

Their names pulsed through his head, pulsed in time to a single word: *Alive. Alive. Alive.*

Jamyson shouted and leaped from the dais, and Isla and Isaac slipped under Elliot's arms and dashed forward to meet him. Jamyson snatched them up and spun them, their laughter shredding the cold walls that had slammed down around his heart after Esmae's death, and then he let them go to catch Sylvie as she limped forward and crumbled against him, and to hold Elliott's head against his chest when his brother collided with his side, crying like he hadn't since he'd turned ten and decided he was now a man.

And Jamyson was crying, too, breaking down to his knees, clutching them against him, and Isla leaped onto his back and wrapped her arms around his neck, whispering a litany of "love yous" in his ear. Isaac squirmed into his lap and buried himself in Jamyson's stomach, and Sylvie framed Jamyson's wet cheeks with her hands and pulled his head to her shoulder, and told him it was all right, that they were here and they'd never let him send them away again. Elliott harshly and vehemently echoed that vow.

Jamyson kissed their cheeks and sent up a prayer to anyone who was listening; a prayer of thanks for this last gift, something Vestan and the Huntress Ria had sent him from beyond the yawning chasm that separated their worlds. This hidden treasure kept safe from the King's treachery to the very end.

It was the most priceless thing Jamyson had ever known.

It was life. It was purpose.

And it was the gift of no longer being alone.

Chapter Seventy-Two

Forgiveness

IT WAS OVER. AL-MORRAL was in chains. Abigale would join him once she'd recovered, and Rowan was muzzled and bound and being led away by Mide's contingent.

And still Elynor fought not to be afraid.

She ought to be glad. Especially that the royal siblings were alive, another miraculous resurrection no one in the kaer could understand. Their shrieking presence, running down the bridge to the kaer and then to the Throne room, had been the talk of the halls all evening, imposing over the fearful murmurs of the archer who'd shot Vestan free.

Elynor ought to be grateful for that, too. She ought to be rejoicing. But she couldn't, because it had been weeks since the Sanctum fell, and now the Seeker had brought Rowan back in chains. But Sharek had still not returned.

Elynor stood on a west-facing turret of Kaer Dorwenon, watching Mide's people ride away. She'd had a stilted farewell with the *Khuless*, and in the end Mide had thanked her for the wisdom she'd shared in the mariner's house as they'd drunk tea together. Elynor supposed that was the closest thing to common ground they'd find, at least for now, and she didn't care about the rest of it. She was consumed with scouting the horizon for another rider.

The door to the turret opened wide, flooding lanternlight on the star-kissed tower as Sylvester sauntered out to join her. He set the lantern down, leaned back on the stone, and unlashed his *shudraga*, playing a few gentle notes that coaxed peace over her. Elynor shot him a grateful smile, which he returned—but it hung oddly on his lips.

"Missing Mide already?" Elynor teased.

"She is...an imposing woman," Sylvester said.

"Careful, Sly. You might sound like a man who's becoming interested in love."

"If I were, it would not be with a woman who carries so much title. And besides, there's only room for one love-struck fool on this tower tonight." Sylvester sheathed his *shudraga* and turned to lean on the wall beside her. "Still looking for him?"

Elynor rubbed her arms against the winter chill and faced the horizon again. "I thought once my father's death was avenged, I'd finally feel like myself again. But it just feels...empty."

"Because your father is still gone? Or because you found something else that made you feel like yourself in the meantime?"

Heat prodded her cheeks. "Did you come up here only to tease me?" Nevermind that she'd started it.

Sylvester flicked invisible lint from his collar. "As a matter of fact, I came to say we should go and get him back."

She blinked. "Do you know where he is?"

"No. But I have an idea of who does." And he gestured down at the bridge.

Elynor and Sylvester caught up to Mide's contingent at the edge of Dorwenon. Though the warriors turned at Elynor's shout, spears raised, the *Khuless* forced them to a halt with one word. Her narrow, curious eyes lit on Sylvester first, then followed Elynor as she barged through the ranks straight to Rowan and snatched him by the collar. She yanked the gag from his mouth and drew him close to eye level. "Do you know where he is?"

His eyes were dull—with exhaustion, with pain, with drug, Elynor didn't know or care. She held his gaze anyway as it sought hers, glazed with confusion. Then he nodded.

She jerked him closer. "*Where?*"

"Home."

Sylvester drew in a short breath. "Ollanthyr."

Rowan's eyes sharpened slightly, boring into hers. He wetted his dry lips. "He needs you." His voice cracked. "Look after him. Do better by him than I did."

Elynor let go of him and stepped back, holding his hooded stare.

Those dull eyes. Those bent shoulders. She had seen them before: Sharek, in the hovel below the Sanctum, before he had climbed out to the sun. A creature willing to kill and fight its way to freedom at almost any cost.

But Sharek had drawn his line. He'd drawn it at respecting his family's legacy, at protecting his kingdom as he'd been born to do. And Rowan...Rowan had found his line in the sand at the same place as hers.

At the feet of Sharek Ransalor.

All at once, the veneer of hatred around Elynor's heart shattered. The anger and reproach she'd held onto for so many months slipped through her fingertips, and she let go. And with its parting, something ugly and rancid poured out of her, filling her eyes with tears.

It was the poison she hadn't realized she'd ingested, consuming her ever since her father had died. Ever since she'd first begun to hate Al-Morral and Abigale and Rowan, all fighting for something just as strongly as she had fought for her inheritance.

They'd wounded her, scarred her for what they wanted, and she would never love or trust any of them. But now it was a new day. A new life, with a new King on the Throne. And Elynor didn't want to carry the poison with her anymore.

"I forgive you," she said.

Not for him—not because he deserved it.

But for herself. And for Sharek.

And as Rowan's eyes widened, shock and clarity piercing them in earnest, and something else—something that wanted to name itself gratitude, perhaps—Elynor turned and ran back down the bridge with Sylvester on her heels to the sanctuary of the kaer's courtyard. They went straight to the stables, to different stalls, and Elynor reached for the tack hanging from the wall.

"How far to Ollanthyr?" she demanded.

"A few days of hard riding, and that's if we don't encounter rain or snow...which I suspect we will," Sylvester replied. "But I don't believe he's dead or injured. Rowan wouldn't have come quietly if he were."

"We'll find him," she muttered to herself as she readied the horse's bridle. There was truly no other future to consider.

"Elynor."

Heart racing, she froze.

She'd summoned that voice. Brought it to her by sheer might of will.

A hand skimmed her shoulder, the touch as fleeting as always. Elynor spun on heel, and Sharek stepped back, raising blister-scarred palms; there were cuts on his face, half-healed, and sadness and tiredness stamped his eyes in the shadows of the stable.

"You're hurt," she murmured.

He shrugged.

The stall door popped open, and Sylvester slipped inside, wide-eyed. "I don't believe it. When did you get here?"

"Just now. I found a horse. I followed the Seeker and Rowan back."

Sylvester shook his head. "Still full of surprises, old friend."

"Rowan said that you were in Ollanthyr," Elynor said, her mind still struggling to comprehend that he was not there, after all; that he was *here*, where she had wanted him for so long now. Weeks, even.

"I was. *We* were." Sharek's expression shifted into something so downcast, it cut a jagged dagger's slice down her heart. "He gave himself up so the Seeker would leave me be."

Elynor's chest ached at the pain in his voice, for the loss he felt that she couldn't understand; for the bits of himself he'd given up, for Rowan, for Sylvester, for the Sanctum...and for her. And for what was left behind that bled beneath his surface.

She took Sharek's face in her hands and traced his new wounds with her thumbs, smoothing the hair from his brow. "Are you all right?"

"No."

Sylvester slid a hand over his shoulder. "Why didn't you come back to Kaer Dorwenon once the Seeker was on the hunt for Elynor? We were worried ill about you."

Sharek's dull eyes found Elynor's face again. "I was...in the Sanctum. Beneath it. Thalanor's men captured me."

Sylvester cursed, and Elynor's heart clenched so hard she sucked in her breath. "*Sharek.*"

"I thought I would never be free." His voice shook. "I thought I would never see your faces again." Sylvester's eyes shot to Elynor's, and she knew even before Sharek spoke the words. "Rowan freed me. And I still let them take him."

His voice broke, and he broke down as well, falling to his knees in the straw. Elynor and Sylvester crouched with him, and Sylvester put an arm around each of them, and Elynor wrapped both of her arms around Sharek. He leaned into her and cried into the side of her neck, and Elynor's heart wept with him for everything in the world that was changing, and would continue to change in ways they could not control.

But she also cried with relief that both Sylvester and Sharek were here, all of them with their arms around each other. She cried for the forgiveness she'd given to Rowan, and for Sharek's pain on his behalf, and for all the ways they'd set themselves free. And she wept with gladness that after all these weeks of fear, Sharek had kept his promise.

He'd finally come home.

Chapter Seventy-Three

The Inner Circle

Soft snoring filled Jamyson's room as his siblings drowsed in his bed, tangled in a dogpile while he sat at the dining table, his broken heart close to bursting at every remaining seam. He had still lost Esmae, and Vestan was beyond his reach now; but he had them, and with that he could see a way forward into the dark future.

It was Sylvie and Elliott who'd given him the notion; after the younger two had gone to bed, they'd joined him at the dining table like a war council, and he'd explained what happened with their father and Al-Morral, and why he hadn't been able to stop to it. And how sorry he was for that.

"It wasn't your fault." Sylvie had squeezed his hand tightly. "You weren't just fighting against Father, which would've been impossible enough."

"Right." Nodding, Elliott had rocked back his chair. "You were fighting the idea of Him."

Jamyson had looked at his brother and sister differently after those words, finding in them the wisdom imparted by a brush with death—and by learning to live among the people their kingdom had taught them to hate. They'd found friends where they'd expected to see enemies, and it had matured them. Changed them. "So how do we fight an idea?"

Sylvie had been the first to speak. "You know, before the Kings of Yore declared themselves infallible—"

"Which we all know is a lie," Elliot had growled.

"Don't interrupt me. Rude. Anyway, Jamy, there were real councilors to a King back then. A trusted Inner Circle who advised Him and helped Him look after the people."

Elliott had leaned himself forward, catching on. "You should have one of those. Friends you can trust. People who can help you clean up the mess Father made."

And all night, Jamyson had been thinking about that. Now he was so restless he felt he might crack apart at any moment. So he hopped to his feet and slipped from the room, locking the door behind him. Just in case.

The halls were mostly deserted; though Jamyson had lifted the curfew Al-Morral and the King had instated in the last weeks before His death, most nobles seemed to favor the early retreat still. Perhaps they'd just grown used to retiring at sunset; or perhaps that didn't want to face the memory of King Marcus that still haunted these halls.

Jamyson walked unaccosted for some time, deep in thought, panging with anguish for Vestan and Esmae and the insight they would've shed on the notion of an Inner Circle. It wasn't until he emerged onto the King's viewing balcony that he encountered another living spirit.

Iracabeth Azorius perched on the edge of the balcony, alone for the first time he'd seen. He cleared his throat. "Care for company, Lady Azorius?"

Iracabeth whipped her head around and laughed. "I haven't been called that in so long. Yes, Your Majesty. Please, sit."

Jamyson rubbed the back of his neck as he joined her at the balcony's edge. "And I haven't been called *that* long enough to be used to it. Call me Jamyson, please."

"All right, Jamyson." Iracabeth's smile reminded him of carefree days of mischief in the kaer halls, and of his own mother's half-forgotten face.

They sat in companionable silence for a time, watching candles wink out in apartment windows around them like stars fading into dawn.

"It's quite a storm of chaos out there," Iracabeth said after a time. "Apparently there were some bandits spotted in Dorwenon who the Kingsgard have never seen before. One of them looked suspiciously like a former bodyguard of the royal family, but, well—who can prove it?"

Ria and Vestan were watching over the city. And there was some comfort in knowing his bodyguard was still close by, if out of reach—watching over *him*.

"Thank you for what you did for Vez. Elynor wasn't overstating your talents. That was quite the shot you made at the gallows that day."

"It isn't the first noose I've shot through. It has long been my duty to protect innocent Blessed."

Jamyson rubbed his face. "Vestan is grateful, I'm sure."

"I'm not only referring to him."

Fear arrowed through Jamyson, bright and sharp, and he jerked his head up to meet Iracabeth's solemn gaze. His tongue felt swollen suddenly, his head a swarm of nerves. "I don't know what you're implying, but I'd consider your next words very carefully."

"No need to take your father's tone with me," Iracabeth said. "I know you're Blessed, Jamyson. Rue is a dragnet. She sensed it the moment she met you."

Jamyson's pulse thrummed in his temples. "So. It's really true, what I am."

"Does anyone else know?"

"Only Vestan. And you and Rue, apparently."

"I suppose we ought to keep it that way." Iracabeth's earnest gaze reminded Jamyson even more fiercely of his own mother, who'd given him his laughter and wildness and his sense of justice. And now, he knew, his Blessed craft. "When Elynor first came to Orleth, I thought the only way this kingdom would ever have peace was through war. But now that I see you again, Jamyson—so grown, and wise in ways no King before you has ever been—I realize how wrong I was. I had forgotten what the future already held for Erala."

"How do you mean?"

"I mean that, Blessed or not, war or not, this kingdom was destined to have a noble and fair ruler when Marcus died," Iracabeth said. "Your mother was the dearest friend I ever had. I didn't know for certain that she was a Hunter, but I suspected. She always spoke of unity between Hunters and Blessed and the sacrosanct over sovereign infallibility. And she was honor-bound to raise you to be a good man who believed those things, too."

"I hardly remember her." The words pained him to say. "But that does sound like her."

"She loved you fiercely," Iracabeth said. "And she feared for you. But I don't think she would fear now. You have all the power to see the plights of every side. To shape a new future for Erala."

"Where do I even begin, when the nobles either fear or hate the Throne now?"

Iracabeth thinned her lips thoughtfully. "You start with those who know the truth. Those you trust with *yourself*. They're the ones you can trust the kingdom to."

She was right. As complicated as it all was, this was also the easiest, most sensible decision he would ever make.

And Jamyson realized exactly what he had to do.

Chapter Seventy-Four

A Table of Friends

Elynor had never seen such a motely bunch gathered in a King's chamber for supper. She'd assumed the invitation slipped under her door was only for herself to dine with Jamyson, but she'd arrived to find Rue already there, lounging at the dining table and helping herself to an *Aljalam* fruit, and Sharek, who'd scurried over to Elynor the moment she arrived with the air of a man rescued from a den of wolves. "Do you know what this is about?"

Elynor shrugged. "I thought it was just a supper between friends."

Sylvester had appeared next, looking as mystified as the rest of them, but at least with a bit of playing on the *shudraga* he'd tempered all their nerves; and then Jamyson finally arrived himself, with Elliott and Sylvie in tow, the First Princess laden down with cakes and followed by a stream of servants carrying more food.

And so here they were, bellies full, and somehow as the wine flowed they'd begun to tell stories. Sylvester dominated that conversation at first, putting Elliott and Sylvie into side-splitting laughter over tales of Ventian gambling houses and wild escapes through mountain heights. Then Elynor told them about sailing across the Caeruel that first time, pursued by Al-Morral's men, the Orlethian Channel welcoming them as the rogue wave raced toward their cog.

"Were you frightened of it all?" Sylvie asked.

"Yes," Elynor said, her eyes on Sharek. "But not as much as I was frightened of what I might lose."

The silence that followed, with his eyes on hers, belonged only to them.

Rue tapped Sylvester's back and signed something, slow and careful, and the bard watched with arched brows and a puckered lip. Then he translated, "What I'd like to hear is a story of how the royal siblings survived the perilous wilds."

Elliott folded his arms and Sylvie dashed a fleeting glance at Jamyson. He shrugged.

"It was...Hunters," Elliott admitted. "Them and the Blessed found us. They kept us safe while Vestan went back for Jamyson."

Silence descended over the table so rapidly it raised the hairs on Elynor's arms. Jamyson watched their faces with a cool, contemplative refrain. Then Sharek sat forward, lips parted in shock, hands trailing back through his hair. "What were they like?" His tone was warm, unrushed, but his eyes danced in the candlelight.

Sylvie cast another nervous glance at Jamyson, who bent his elbows to the table and rested his clasped hands against his cheek. "Tell them, if you want. We're all friends here."

"It was...nice," she said shyly. "I didn't like it at first, not having kitchens or books. Or, you know—servants."

"You complained *so much*," Elliott snarked, and Sylvie hit him.

"Not as much as you did! You didn't even want to get *dressed* without someone helping you!"

The First Prince turned a mortified shade of red. "That's not—I wasn't being *serious*—"

"You were saying, Sylvie?" Jamyson's smile was patient, but laughter bubbled in his tone.

"That it was nice?" Her voice lilted, turning the words to a question. "The food was nice, and I liked learning new ways to cook for myself. And...the people were good. Fair, and honest. And very, very kind." A rosy blush filled her cheeks, and Elynor fought down a smile.

"All of that," Sylvester said, "even though they were Hunters?"

Sylvie's eyes rounded with fright, but then her jaw set and she threw back fiercely, "Just because they're Hunters doesn't make them terrible people. My Father was sacrosanct, and He put my mother to death."

"And He tried to do the same to us," Elliott added just as sharply. "The Hunters saved us from Him. So if anyone wants to attack Ria's people, they'll have to go through Sylvie and me to do it."

Sharek blinked, his expression inscrutable. Rue sat up tall, eyeing the royal siblings with newfound interest. Sylvester grinned like a fool. And warmth surged from Elynor's chest and spread through her body in the headiest tide.

This was the start of a new future at the very bones of Erala, with its youngest nobles who would one day shape it.

Jamyson shifted in his seat. "As my sister has just so adorably demonstrated, Erala should be a kingdom of free thought, where differing opinions are not outlawed as heresy. Where people are unafraid to speak their minds among friends." His gaze traveled around the table, frank and sincere, full of the maturity of grief and the wisdom of carrying a new weight on his shoulders. "It begins with us. Some of you I know very well...better than I'd like." He winked at Elynor and smiled at Elliott and Sylvie, who pulled faces of mock offense. "Some of you, I know less. But you come highly recommended by those I do trust."

Elynor tipped her head as comprehension slowly began to dawn.

Jamyson folded his hands on the table and looked at Sharek. "You're a killing Blessed, is that right?"

Sharek hesitated for a moment, then nodded.

"And you," he said to Rue, "a dragnet?"

She nodded rapidly, her eyes round and anxious.

Jamyson gestured to Sylvester. "And you're a healer, correct?"

"So they say."

"Good. It's a starting point, anyway." Jamyson spanned an arm to them. "I want the six of you as the foundation of the Royal Inner Circle. Rue, you'll vet everyone who comes to the kaer. If they're Blessed, I'll want to know what their skills are. Use that natural stealth of yours to keep up with the whispers floating around here, so we're prepared for anything. And Sharek, you'll keep the worst from happening with anyone who slips past Rue's guard." He pointed to Sylvester. "I need a healer around I can trust...someone who isn't afraid to tell me if I'm going mad. That disqualifies the current court physician, and you happen to come highly recommended by two women I trust implicitly. Care for the job?"

Sylvester's eyes widened. "You know I'm also a bard, do you not?"

"If you're referring to that ridiculous law my father made because of that Blessed who used to play in our halls, it's already undone. I couldn't care less if you play music, so long as you do it on your own time."

A sheen of tears coated Sylvester's eyes, and he laid a hand to his chest. "It would be my genuine honor, Your Majesty."

"And you." Jamyson's eyes flicked to Elynor, full of teasing.

She held up both hands. "You know my opinion on living in Kaer Dorwenon, Jamyson."

"I'm not asking you to be my wife. Something tells me I would have the fight of my life if I tried." He aimed an amused smile at Sharek, who turned an unnamable shade of red. "I want you to oversee the Azorian Fleet and report to me on its dealings. And I want regular reports on Orleth. *Khuless* Mide may have come to respect us during her stay here, but I'm not so certain about her mother. We'll need to keep a close watch on the horizon, and there's no one's eyes I trust more."

Stunned, Elynor looked at her companions. Sylvester had already given his affirmation; Elliott and Sylvie were in no question; and now Rue was signing rapidly at the King.

Jamyson studied the dragnet for a moment, his expression vacant with confusion. "You're going to have to teach me that language of yours if this is going to work." She signed something else, smirking. "*What*? What are you saying to me?"

"I believe she said *Obviously, silly King*," Sylvester translated.

Sylvie replicated her hand motions. "*This* means *silly King*?"

Rue nodded. Jamyson arched a brow. "Oh, you two will get along splendidly."

Elliott and Sylvie burst into laughter, and as they scooted closer to Rue, Elynor met Jamyson's eyes. With heart in throat, she nodded.

The Fleet might be Sam's to own, but if it was hers to guard, with one eye on the horizon toward Orleth, she would still have a place in it. A piece of her father's legacy, to safeguard and invest her heart in. And she and Jamyson would never have to concern themselves with the notion of marriage when something just as powerful bound them: trust. Belief. Alliance based on friendship, not forged through a reluctant matrimony.

Jamyson looked at Sharek, who pushed back his seat. "I need a moment to think."

Jamyson frowned, but nodded. And when Sharek hurried from the room, Elynor excused herself and followed him out.

They retreated to one of the upper balconies, looking out across the city of Dorwenon as it slumbered in darkness. For a time, neither of them spoke, simply leaned their arms on the railing and drank in the world around them: the chilly breeze and tufts of clouds soaked in moonlight. The floor of the Valley a dizzying distance below. The Emperium wide-open above.

"Will you tell me what you're thinking?" Elynor asked.

Sharek heaved a heavy breath. "That it's an honor. And a great responsibility."

"It is," Elynor sighed. "Jamyson is ambitious. And reckless...he's always been that. I'm not certain he's thought this through to the end. But I know he wants what's best for Erala, and he believes an Inner Circle of Blessed is part of that."

"But he doesn't know how many Blessed are truly part of it. Or those who aren't."

They glanced at one another, the gulf of their own secrets dark beneath their feet.

"You know, with Jamyson on the Throne, and Elliott next in line...perhaps things will be different now," Elynor murmured. "Perhaps, in my lifetime, I'll be willing to step forward and say that I'm Blessed."

"But not yet?"

She shook her head. "I'm still learning what it means to be Blessed myself. I can't allow anyone else to define it for me...for good or ill. That's my journey to take."

"I'm glad you won't take it alone."

Elynor slid her hand into his. "So am I."

Sharek glanced down at their entwined fingers, chuckling. "I was referring to Sam, actually."

"Well. Him, too. I'm beginning to feel as if my father sent him to me, somehow. A gift to guide me in the next leagues of my voyage—the place where I learn what it is to be Blessed. And to make peace with that."

Sharek was quiet for a bit, his thumb stroking her knuckles as he gazed into the distance. "My father," he finally said, "used to bring me to the Valley of Embra from time to time. It was a grueling journey by foot, but we'd come to the lower mountains and watch the sun set behind Kaer Dorwenon. He'd tell me that life is but a dawn and a sunset, as brilliant as we make them. But what matters truly are all the moments between."

Elynor squeezed his hand. "Moments like this?"

Sharek's eyes turned to her, full of warmth. "Exactly like this."

He bent his head as if to kiss her; but with their lips an inch apart, he froze, drawing in a deep breath through his nostrils. Scenting. Questing.

She pulled back slightly. "Sharek?"

"That damned smell again," he growled, jerking back from her and looking west toward the craggy cliffs where Dorwenon perched. "How do I *know* it?"

Elynor frowned. "The one form the night we arrived here? That reminded you of Ollanthyr?"

His gaze swung back to her, eyes wide, jaws parting in a soundless hiccup of shock. Then he dropped her hand. "I must go."

"Sharek?"

Elynor reached for him, but he'd already turned, tearing away down the balcony.

Chapter Seventy-Five

The Hunter's Choice

Sharek crashed through the undergrowth beyond Dorwenon, his heart slamming into his throat like a smithy's hammer. His scarred lungs begged to rest, but he ignored the tingles of icy pain pricking through them. The shimmering outlines of the trees, gently kissed in waning moonlight, ripped past as he tore into the forest, following a memory of scent, a wild hope that went beyond all reason.

He hadn't recognized that smell when it first touched him, hadn't realized *how* he knew it until he'd heard the words from Elynor's mouth. And all at once, it made sense, even though he'd given up ever smelling it again, tucking that portion of himself so far away and so deep he'd all but locked it in a cage.

But now it was here, growing stronger, until he crashed out into an open meadow where the path leveled out, and he saw her: a woman, hooded and cloaked, facing away up the path.

Panting, his voice ragged from the run, Sharek forced out the word.

"Mother?"

The woman stiffened. Then she turned slowly to face him, and the sight of her face struck him like a blow to the chest, stopping his heart. She was every inch as fierce and wild and beautiful as he remembered, every inch the quiet warrior he'd always known. But for the first time, knowing what he knew of himself, and of *her*, he saw her for what she truly was.

The graceful lines of the Hunter. The attunement of her senses in the way she tilted her head and angled her body toward the quietest stirrings in the undergrowth. And how her eyes flashed golden in the light, the way Elynor told Sharek his sometimes did, when he was catching sight of something no human eye could see.

She was just like him.

"Oh, Sharek," Nymeria whispered.

He stumbled forward and crushed her against his chest. She was so much smaller than him now—hardly taller than Elynor—and he was almost afraid he would break her. But the embrace she returned was just as fierce, even setting off a dull ache in his ribs from the struggle in the Sanctum.

He winced, drawing away, and Nymeria gripped his forearms. "You're injured?"

"Nothing I cannot recover from. In time." He forced an unsteady smile, confusion battering its edges. "How is this possible? How are you *here*?"

"I have lived near Kaer Dorwenon for many seasons, watching the royal family. Watching the King and the Crown Prince."

"But *why*?"

"To help those we could. To protect Erala." Nymeria's lips thinned with sorrow. "Your father and I lurked in the shadows far too long, thinking concealment would keep us alive. If we'd been wiser, we would've tried to change things for our people, rather than hiding from our enemies. So, when you did not come back, Sharek...when I had exhausted every avenue to find you, when I thought Fausto Hagan had killed you, I struck off to start changing hearts and minds."

"How?"

"I began with lords and magistrates, offering them the gifts of our people: our strength, our senses, our knowledge of healing. I led them to trust by example. And then, Oss Belliard. Where everything changed."

That name pricked Sharek's memory. "The magistrate...Basithia, and his family. You led the Hunters they helped set free?"

"Sharek, I *am* a Hunter." With the smallest smile, his mother confirmed what Iracabeth and Rue had first laid before him in the *ger* all those weeks ago. "To the people I lead, I am called Ria."

Sharek's heart clenched. "Father's name for you."

Nymeria's breath trembled inward. "I couldn't let it die with him."

Sharek paced around her, dragging his hands through his hair. "Mother, all this time, you knew...you *know* what I am."

"Yes," Nymeria said. "I feared Hagan killed you for it. It wasn't until we were scouting the kaer one night several weeks ago that I caught scent of you. I couldn't believe it was true...you were there and gone so quickly. But then you came back. And I've waited for you to find me."

So that he would not feel impressed upon, or hunted—just like all the countless times he'd stomped off into the Fai Alora alone after arguments or discipline, and she had trailed him at a distance, ensuring his safety without foisting her uninvited presence upon him.

Gratitude for her tenderness, unchanged after so many years, welled a fresh ache in his throat. "I knew you were here, as well. I've sensed you ever since I returned, but I didn't know what I smelled." He'd felt like a man chased by rogue spirits, as if visiting Ollanthyr had infected him with a different sort of poison. He had never dared entertain the thought that what he'd *felt* was his mother's presence. That she'd found him after all this time.

"I feared you kept your distance because you did not want to see me," Nymeria admitted, every word taut with anguish. "I never found you, despite the talents you now know I have...that you and I shared. I never set you free. Now I hear from my spies around the kaer that you lived as a killing Blessed, that Aeson Thalanor kept you all those years...I could understand if you never wanted to lay eyes on me again."

"The Sanctum was not your fault." Sharek came back to her, laying a hand on her cheek, catching a tear as it rolled down her weathered brown skin. "I was in a terrible place, but the Empyreans made something good of it. Something better than I could've ever hoped for."

Nymeria rested her fingers over the talisman tucked above his heart. "You kept this. You still pray to them?"

"I have *always* kept them, and you, with me."

Joyous laughter broke through Nymeria's lips, and she pulled his head down to kiss his hair. When she stepped back, she looked exactly how Sharek had made himself remember her: reckless and happy, and mischievously plotting something. "Sharek, come with me tonight. To our people. There are many of us...Hunters I've found over the years, and free Blessed as well. We do as the Empyreans command, as Sabrathan always wished: we protect Erala. And in the dark times ahead, we could use your arm."

Shock set Sharek back again. "I don't...I'm not fit for such a life."

Yet even as he said it, he heard his father's voice slipping through the trees, the strong arms of his memory wrapping his wife and son in a warm embrace, a breeze that felt like spring: *The Kings don't want our help, but we protect Them all the same. Just as we protect the people, though they fear us. Because it isn't about them. It's who we are.*

Nymeria smiled, her eyes glistening with tears as if she too could hear Castian's voice gliding among the leafless limbs that rattled above.

This was Sharek's purpose, the thing he'd been born for. The ambition of all his people. And it was being offered to him by none other than his own flesh and bone.

A band of Hunters and Blessed, joining together to guard and protect the kingdom. And him, a part of it, right hand to his mother. He'd never dared to dream so far or so lofty. His heart practically sang at the notion.

But if he accepted this offer—if he went with her—

Elynor.

Sharek swallowed. "Do you need an answer immediately?"

Nymeria shook her head. "But by week's end, I will. I have others who depend on me now, and I must meet them at the mouth of the Valley of Embra to ensure Gavannon Al-Morral is delivered to the magistrates and then interred. I cannot wait forever, *mal ga'el.*"

That was only fair. But a piece of Sharek wished his mother had never found him; for even as he hugged her, breathing in her woodsy scent, the smell of the home he'd all but forgotten…even as he left her there, draped in silken strands of moonlight, he knew what impossible choices he faced.

And his heart began to crack in two.

Chapter Seventy-Six

Winds of Joy

E LYNOR RETURNED TO HER rooms after nearly an hour on the balcony, nervousness churning in her gut, her ears trained for the sounds of Sharek's return while she bathed the day from her skin. Her mind was an equal whirlwind, humming with Jamyson's offer of overseeing the Fleet and all the potential that lay within.

For the first time since they'd sailed home, her future was not void of the sea; even her power purred with joy, satisfied by the offering.

When she finally emerged from the bath, it was only because she'd pruned; and she'd barely slipped into her nightgown when a knock came at the door.

Sharek. Heart thundering, she glanced at the hopeless snarl of her wet locks in the mirror, then forsook them. "Come in!"

But it was not Sharek who entered; it was Iracabeth, dressed in wool for winter travel, setting a sack of provisions down at the door.

Elynor's heart sank. "Leaving for Bast?"

Iracabeth nodded. "I'll oversee the rest of Abigale's treatment, then hand her off to the local authorities."

A twinge of true concern slithered in Elynor's chest. "Do you think she'll be all right?"

"Scarred and destined for a harsher future by far than if she'd remained true to herself...but yes, she will live," Iracabeth said. "I'll stay however long I must to ensure she does."

"Good," Elynor said, and meant it. She would never love Abigale like a sister again; but with the hate released from her heart, she'd begun to hope she'd survive. "And...afterward?"

"Afterward..." Iracabeth's lips twisted in a way Elynor knew hers did, too, when she was nervous or deep in thought. "I thought I'd come to Bracerath's Landing and stay with you. If you'll have me."

Elynor searched her mother's gaze for a hint of flightiness, hardly daring to believe. "You'll truly stay this time? You swear it?"

"I swear it." Iracabeth smiled. "We have many years to make up for, Elynor...and plenty of healing to do."

"Of course." Happiness nearly strangled those two words. "Yes, you can stay with me, Mother."

"Then I'd best be on my way. The sooner this is done, the sooner I'll see you again."

"Well, before you go," Elynor said quickly when Iracabeth reached for her satchel, "would you mind...it's a bit knotted in the back." She gestured to her hair. "I was going to ask Sylvie to help, but I suspect she's in bed by now."

Iracabeth's eyes softened, even silvered a bit. "I'd be glad to, Seabird."

They went to the dressing table in amicable silence, sharing the same sort of peaceful moment that so many mothers and daughters did. Happiness ached in the base of Elynor's throat while her mother pared away the knots in her unkempt hair...something she'd dreamed of her doing for so many years.

"How was your dinner with the King?" Iracabeth asked after a time, meeting her gaze with a touch of mischief in the mirror.

"Intriguing. Unexpected." Elynor hesitated, toying with several jeweled hair pieces arrayed on the table. "He offered for me to oversee the Fleet and report on it to him."

Iracabeth smiled broadly. "I think that's wise. Besides your father, no one's ever known the Azorian Fleet better than you...he told me as much in his letters."

Pride warmed her goosefleshed body. "He did?"

"Many, many times."

Elynor bit her lip, but still a grin slipped free. "How do you think Sam will feel about it?"

"Oh, he doesn't seem the sort to mind being put in his place by a clever woman...he was close with the *Khul's* family, after all." Iracabeth winked, setting aside the brush and gathering Elynor's hair to braid. "Besides, one talented sailor to another, it's plain as day he respects you. I think you can achieve much together."

"That's true. And I don't want to be unfair to him...I promised him the Fleet, and I intend to be a woman of my word." She passed the brush from hand to hand, consumed in thought for a moment. "I know Father tried to be fair, but his partnership with Al-Morral was unbalanced, and I think that's where the struggle for power really began. I won't make an enemy of Sam by denying him his due."

"That, darling, is wisdom," Iracabeth tied off the braid and settled beside her on the seat. "Learning from the mistakes of your predecessors so that you don't repeat them."

Elynor propped her elbows on her knees, scratching her temples. "None of this was as simple as I thought when I hired Sharek. Father wasn't always the perfect, fair Fleetmaster. Al-Morral loved and feared to lose things. Rowan cared for Sharek. And I was so cruel to everyone when I learned what I was."

"And that is *life*." Iracabeth rested a hand on her curved back. "Messy and complicated and infuriating. But what a privilege to live it. And to live it *together*."

Elynor leaned into that touch. At long last, she leaned into her mother.

"I'm glad to live the rest of it with you," she confessed quietly.

"And I with you." Iracabeth pressed a kiss to Elynor's brow. "I love you, Seabird. I'll see you soon."

Then she rose and strode from the room, taking up her satchel as she went. And this time, Elynor did not fear she would be gone forever.

She tried to stay awake until Sharek's return, with books and tidying the room, and finally writing a note to Sam; but eventually the wine and exhaustion of the long day caught up to her, and she drifted off in the windowseat, watching for him to arrive.

She woke to the feeling of a blanket being draped around her shoulders, and snorted sharply, sitting up from the glass. Blearily, she squinted up at Sharek, his face half-haloed in daylight. "There you are," she mumbled, her mouth cottony with slumber. "Where did you go?"

He stared down at her, and his pained look yanked the breath from her lungs. She drew her knees up to her chest and sat tall. "*Sharek*."

He slowly sank down on the windowseat, facing her. "It was...my mother was in Dorwenon."

Disbelief spiked through Elynor's chest. "*Nymeria*? She's here?"

"She has been for some time, leading a band of Hunters and Blessed who give aid to the provinces."

Caution settled along her bones at the refrain of his tone; there was not the joy she had expected from such a reunion, only a depthless sorrow in his gaze. "And what did she say?"

"She wants me to help her lead these people."

Relief shook laughter from Elynor's chest. "Of course she does! You're more than capable, and it would be an honor to your father's legacy. That's wonderful, Sharek."

"It is." His fingers played restlessly with his talisman.

Elynor frowned. "Why do you look so upset? Is this because of Jamyson's offer? He may still let you be a part of his Inner Circle, even if you're traveling."

Sharek blew out a long breath. "I'm upset because you're returning to Bast, and if I do this, then I will be everywhere across Erala. And I don't know when I'll see you again."

Elynor stared at him, her mind grasping the words but her heart refusing to pick them apart, to fully comprehend them.

And then, all at once, reality settled in.

"Oh," she murmured. "*Oh*."

No other words came.

With all the changes that had transpired—Al-Morral gone, her father avenged, Sylvester and Rue staying on in Kaer Dorwenon, Jamyson the new King and the Fleet under her supervision but headed by Sam—Elynor had begun to craft a vision for a new future. And with every iteration, whether her mother came with her or left, whether she had a place within the Fleet or not, even if Rue stayed with her mother and they had to learn how to share the title of daughter, Elynor saw herself facing these changes with Sharek at her side. He'd become an integral part of her dreams for her life without her ever realizing it.

And now he was playing himself into a different song, because he was not hers to say that he must stay or go.

Elynor did not own Sharek. She did not own any Blessed. And how selfish would she be if she begged a man to live apart from his purpose and his people, only to keep her own heart from falling to pieces?

In silence, Elynor felt out her own anguish. She let her heart ache. And she found that as painful as it was, saying goodbye to Sharek was better than having not known him at all.

It was the same with her father. His death would always sting, like a badly-mended bone or a bruise that begged to be pressed on every now and again. But she would not trade all their glorious years of sailing and learning and growing together, or their many picnics and fits of laughter and nights spent dreaming under the stars, for a heart that felt nothing. Just as she would not trade away her mother for the pain of healing through what was broken.

And she would not have traded the pain of loving Sharek Ransalor for all the numbness the world could offer. Even if he would leave her again.

Heat limned Elynor's lashes, and she brushed it hastily away. "I want you to choose what will make you happiest, Sharek. Even if it takes you away from me."

Sharek's head jerked back. "You do?"

"I know what it is to be separated from your purpose. And it might be different for Hunters than for Blessed, but it's still an ache I don't wish on you. You told me yourself how you longed to do right by this kingdom, not by killing, but by defending it. And I think the Empyreans are showing you how…by protecting its people. I think you should fulfill that destiny."

Stranger than that the words fell from her lips so easily was that she believed them. Utterly and absolutely believed them. If his Empyreans were real, then she knew they loved him, too, and that they dreamed the brightest future for him even if it meant he was parted from her.

And in that way, Elynor finally found common ground with them.

Sharek was quiet for a long time, looking out through the window, wrestling with the choice. Presently, a tear snaked down his cheek; Elynor reached for his hand and squeezed it with all her might.

"How blessed am I," she added softly, "to have something it hurts so *much* to lose."

Slowly, Sharek turned his face toward her, gaze touched with anguish and that precious uncertainty. "It would not be forever. A few seasons, to learn what it truly is to be a Hunter. And whenever I'm within a day's run from Bast, or anywhere I catch your scent, I will come to you, Elynor Azorius. Always."

Elynor's breath caught, huddling in her chest. "To the depths and beyond?"

Cupping the back of her neck, he leaned his brow against hers. "Even beyond death. I will find you there."

And that vow at last gave her the strength to do what had seemed impossible when he was poisoned, when her world was crumbling, when she'd felt like a villain who did not deserve him.

Elynor could finally let him go...knowing this time, without a tinge of doubt, that he would return to her in time.

"When do you depart?" The question emerged wet with the tears bobbing in her throat.

"Soon. But I have another vow to keep first, if you'd accompany me."

Bristling with curiosity, Elynor decided she had time for one more adventure.

Chapter Seventy-Seven

The Storm and the Sunrise

Elynor had never traveled so much of Erala by horseback. There was something exultant in the breeze, promising an early spring as it tangled its rogue fingers in her hair; something magnificent in beholding the breadth of it, down through the Valley of Embra and across the glorious Teranite meadows budding with the first wildflowers of the new season.

And there was something wonderful in having this time alone with Sharek.

The world was carrying on without them; somewhere his mother was waiting for him to join their people, and in Bast, Sam would soon arrive and await her return to learn the Fleet's inner workings. Her mother would be in Bracerath's Landing before long, readying it to be a home for them. Jamyson would expect reports forthwith.

But for now, this was enough: these long days of riding, and late nights where she built fires and Sharek hunted, and they talked about everything: her father and his mother; Al-Morral and Abigale. Rowan. The Sanctum, and what Sharek had suffered there both times he was captured.

With every passing day, more poison left the wounds inside her, and Sharek sat taller in the saddle, some of the anguish passing from his eyes. They both slept deeper at night, Elynor tucked into the curve of Sharek's body, memorizing the patterns of his breathing. Memorizing what *together* felt like, so that when they were apart, she could bring him back to her in the dark.

Finally, they made camp in the trees one night rather than in the meadows, and it was still dark when Sharek roused Elynor again.

"Entirely too early," she grumbled, prying her tacky eyelids apart. "What are you *doing*, Sharek? You still haven't even told me where it is we're going, or why we're going there."

"I'm keeping my word." He offered his hand. "Come, it's finally time. Let me show you something."

Muttering and cursing, Elynor followed him into the trees.

The cool morning air woke her slowly, and in the predawn dimness she relied on Sharek's Hunterish senses to guide them through pockets of forest that all looked the same. The world was barely beginning to grow pink when she spotted something too dense and dark to be a tree or even an old stone crouched among the foliage ahead.

She slowed. "Where are we?"

"The Fai Alora." Sharek glanced over his shoulder. "As promised."

Elynor halted altogether now, staring at him.

How long ago had he made that vow, and yet still she recalled the moment he'd spoken it? The shade of his skin, the glassiness of his eyes with fever and poison raging through him...and how he'd promised to bring her here. To show her the greatest sunrise in all Erala.

Sharek stopped as well, watching her without speaking. Elynor shook her head. "After all these months..."

He shrugged. "I keep my word. Now let me show you where I come from."

Elynor took his hand and let him lead her through the memories of his home.

Ollanthyr was a simple place, gutted by long-ago fire, but Elynor could see that it had once been beautiful: its gardens well-tended, its homes much-loved, its paths gathering the footprint memories of children running at play. She could almost hear the spirit whispers of Ardeth Lamruil's first songs weaving into the murmur of wind through the leaves; she could almost imagine Sharek Ransalor's laughter as his father swooped him up on his shoulders.

And she could almost envision herself in Sharek's world even then. That somehow, the Hunters would have heard of the injustices done to the Azorius family, and they would have sent someone to make it right...a strapping warrior with his mother's talisman around his throat; a quiet, introspective, noble Hunter who would have swept into her life like a storm raging across the Caeruel. And he would have changed everything. He was always destined to change things.

Elynor's eyes welled with tears that for once were not full of sadness.

Thank you. The prayer rolled through her mind like a sob. *Thank you for watching over him all these years. For bringing us to one another.*

Elynor didn't realize how tightly she'd gripped Sharek's hand until he squeezed back. "Is all well?"

"Everything is perfect," Elynor said. "Will this forest sing for us?"

"Soon. My mother always taught me that there was a song in the world, you know. That it was my duty and privilege to learn my place in it."

"I remember how you told me that, in Bracerath's Landing," Elynor said. "Have you found it now?"

"I think we both have."

And that was true. They had found their part to play: him the subtle drum like a trusted heartbeat, and her the chaos of cymbals, a crashing surf. Yet their melodies blended perfectly. He had been the notes missing from her life, the void in her music, the harmony unsung until the day she'd walked into the Sanctum and they'd begun to set one another free. And she could no longer hear that song without him.

Together, they were something more than music. Their lives were a symphony beyond all words.

They passed beyond Ollanthyr's farthest edge and went on a bit further. Then Sharek stopped, peered around, and nodded. "This is good."

Elynor leaned into his side. "Thank you for bringing me here. For always keeping your word, even if you must defy death to do it."

"Always for you, Elynor." Sharek turned his face to her, his smile full of childlike glee, amber eyes dancing. "It's time."

So it was, and Elynor had to force her gaze away from him to take in the Fai Alora. For just then the sunrise broke through the trees, gilding the leaves in streaks of gold, encasing the whole world in an emerald shell that cupped Elynor and Sharek in its gleaming heart. Their bodies danced with the colors of spring, the season of new life, and the age of a world reborn.

Erala would never be the same after all that had happened; and *they* would never be the same. Elynor did not know what her future held when they reached the coast, but she knew that whatever awaited, Sharek would be a part of it—forever with her, a brand on her blood and bones and heart. And that was enough.

In a last breath of silence that spoke of everything, both old and new, they joined hands and watched the sun rise over the Fai Alora.

And all around them, the world broke into song.

Epilogue

The gleaming halls of Kaer Dorwenon burned so brightly with the splendor of daylight, Elynor Azorius squinted against a roaring headache.

Though that, she supposed, might have also been owed to the unholy hour at which she'd risen, riding barebacked and at breakneck speed from the last inn beyond Dorwenon proper to reach the kaer halls. She'd sung the dawn up from its hiding place within the Valley of Embra, the same way she'd greeted its golden cresting over the waves of the Ocean Caeruel countless times in the last year.

It never failed to make her heart sing its own refrain—and on this day more than most.

Yes, this was a special occasion, a joyous one...grand enough that she'd conceded to travel far from Bast, to leave the waves in the care of Samwel Morlai and Iracabeth Azorius and whatever Empyreans-damned tension floated between them these days. Something she gave herself no time whatsoever to dwell on, that had her knocking at doors several times before she dared step through them in Bracerath's Landing...even in the newly polished east wing.

What a year it had been.

And now, here she was, striding through halls where the King's household bowed and his numerous advisers offered her nods and *helloes*; many of these faces she had known since childhood, but never wearing such levity. Crags and clefts she'd thought permanently carved into countenances worn down by the former King were shallower now, some nearly erased by grins as bright as the halls they traversed, going this way and that—to meals and meetings and all sorts of places where their voices were heard. Where their cares were considered by the King's Inner Circle, or by King Jamyson Venator himself.

Their greetings ebbed and flowed with an easy camaraderie that blazed in her chest—for what they were to their cities and towns and villages all across the kingdom, so she was for its burgeoning naval fleet. An overseer, an ambassador of *Morlai & Azorius*...the charter which dealt directly in trade and peacekeeping with their neighbors across the Ocean Caeruel.

It was truly a new dawn in Erala—a dawn which went on and on, so bright and full of hope that Elynor could hardly greet it full-faced.

Damn this headpain.

But as she crossed the inner courtyard where once there had been gallows, now there was only brilliance; and there were mere steps between her tired feet and the place where she would enter the Inner Circle's private meeting chamber, and greet those her heart ached with missing almost as much as it missed the waves she had left behind to report here.

Sylvester and Rue, who had been tasked with the health and secrets of the kaer...and by the look of those under their watch, were doing quite well.

Sylvie and Elliott, who made frequent forays under the Venator banner, establishing good will with those their father had slighted—both Blessed and human.

And as for the Hunters long in hiding, and the gifted people—*her* people, sold off to bidders, in all the places that lurked in the shadow of what the Sanctum of the Blessed had once been—there were others to give report. Others who made it their purpose to set the Blessed free, to raise the Hunters back from the grave, to tell them the news of the throne and its new regime.

No longer a Holy Throne. But one sat upon by the sort of King who put his ancestors to shame.

It turned out a king as fallible as his subjects, and humble about his shortcomings, was one much easier to love. And they did love him, from ocean ports to the depths of the provinces. Elynor could hardly wait to tell him of all the goodwill the last year had wrought...how it healed her heart into something that almost remembered its levity from before her own father's death.

The sturdy sole of Elynor's leather seafaring boots grazed the lowest step of the staircase that swept up from the inner courtyard to the doorway of the private meeting chamber above—and even that quiet chafe was nearly loud enough to mask the rumble of an intonation from the shadow below the stairs.

"Milady."

Her foot halted.

Her heart halted.

How many times had she dreamed of that voice as she'd sailed this last year—had she clung to its vestigial rumble on the cusp of waking, before it was stolen away by shanties and shouts and the breaking of the sea against the ship's prow?

How many times had she gone back to it in her memory, clutching syllables like lovelorn letters to her chest, holding the brand of his mouth against hers by the touch of her fingers to her trembling lips?

Had memory and dream ever once speared such heat to her middle as this? Frozen her as utterly as this, so that she was still as prey in a hunter's eyes when his broad, leonine shape slipped from below the stairwell?

He looked...well.

So much better than when she'd seen him last, when he'd been gaunt still from poisoning and breakneck travel, and the shadows of his brief but ruthless return to Aeson Thalanor's clutches and the loss of Rowan had haunted his eyes.

Those eyes were bright now, and his hair trimmed above his shoulders, his beard groomed and his frame fuller—even more muscular, somehow, than before, in a lean and healthy way that spoke without words that he had been doing what he loved best. He had been out in the wilds, attuning his senses, falling in step with his mother—and with Vestan and the others—in defense of Erala; he had been among his people, learning the ways of his father.

He had been healing in a fashion he might never have if he had stayed with her.

She slipped her foot back from the step, all at once struck with a barreling wave of vulnerability that made her acutely conscious of how she must seem so different to him, too; no longer in the dress of an heiress, but the vests and linen of a sailor, her skin tanned deeply by the sun's kiss, new freckles sprayed across her forearms and the bridge of her nose.

She crinkled that nose as he stepped toward her, so that it might excuse the hitch of her breath...the way her stomach pitched and rolled like a ship in a storm as she drew in the smell of mahogany and vetiver from his skin.

"Well met, Milady." Sharek's voice was so quiet, and that murmur so deep, she practically felt it in the soles of her feet. "You look happy."

And if anyone in any kingdom in any realm would know how hard-fought and hard-won that happiness was...it was him.

Him. Sharek...who was such a piece of that happiness. Who she had kept with her by letters awaiting her in Bracerath's Landing each time she returned to port. Who she had yearned for so painfully, she had sacrificed sleep and comfort on the journey here from Bast, just to see him this much sooner.

And all at once, that happiness took wing as joy—a playful sort of unbridled relief that had her deciding to tease him.

"Now, you, sir...you can't possibly be Sharek Ransalor." Wrinkling her nose even further, she shook her head. "You're far too cleanly...Sharek doesn't bathe. Despises baths, to wit! And he doesn't look a thing like you. His hair is a long and tangled mess, and his beard...a sanctuary for mites. I'm fairly sure he's allergic to the razor."

He cocked his head. "Elynor?"

"And he certainly wouldn't stride up to, much less carry on a conversation with, a woman he hasn't seen or spoken to but for letters here and there in a whole year." She stepped around him, feigning a dramatic search of the courtyard—and fought to ignore the sizzles of primal energy that pinioned over her skin as he moved with her, his eyes never leaving her face. A hint of gold flashed at their edges, a lick of desire that almost strangled her next words before they even emerged—that made them feel an utter lie. "He's dreadfully awkward and painfully shy, unless he's giving out wisdom, at which point he can talk himself breathless. Such a contradiction."

His eyes narrowed. "*Elynor.*"

"Or," she added, entirely breathless now, "he won't speak in full sentences unless there's something he very much wants."

He stepped into her path, the broad lines of him unfairly complimented by his sleeveless leather vest, his well-trimmed trousers tucked into fur-lined boots—and by the talisman that lay over his beating heart. "Tell me more about his man, then. Perhaps I can help you find him."

"What else bears remarking on?" Elynor leaned her head back, holding his gaze even as it made her feel as weightless as an unmoored ship. "His face? Gentle and wild. His eyes flash gold when his senses are piqued. And his lips...his lips could make the saltiest sailor go weak at the knees."

He slid his hand around the back of her neck. "And his tongue?"

She stopped breathing entirely. "Absolutely devastating."

For the first time in a year—since they had said farewell in these very halls—Sharek Ransalor brought his mouth down to hers, destroying and remaking her all at once. The ache of missing and longing caught fire with relief all at once, and Elynor looped her arms around his shoulders, drawing herself near to him so that, after far too many months of wishing and wanting, there was no more space left between them.

When they broke apart to breathe, there was laughter in his eyes. It echoed in her heart.

"Oh, Sharek. It *is* you! What a surprise," Elynor exclaimed.

Sharek nuzzled his nose against hers and nipped her earlobe. "I see you found your sense of humor floating out there on the Caeruel."

Elynor smacked his chest. "And I'm truly stunned to realize you have one at all."

"I have that, and more." He took her hand from his chest and pressed a kiss to her knuckles. "Because at last, I have you again."

Heat burned her eyes as if she'd squinted too long against the sparkling of sunlight on the waves. "I have missed you more than I thought possible."

The gold in his eyes flared as he tilted his head to one side. "And I you, Elynor. More than I have words to say."

He kissed her again, and this time it was slow, and savoring—an apology, a reunion, a promise that made her spirit soar.

So she held tightly to Sharek's hand, and when the kiss ended far too soon for her liking, she drew him up the steps; and by the time they struck the landing above, she was telling him all about the Fleet. And when she paused to rest her tingling tongue, he spoke with a gilded gleam in his gaze of all he and his mother and the other Hunters and Blessed had done to free their kin and stoke faith in Jamyson's reign.

And for the first time in a year, Elynor Azorius's heart was at peace.

With Sharek's hand in hers, fingers fitted easily together as if they had always been there and would never let go again, she found she truly wanted and lacked for absolutely nothing at all.

And she would not think today of going away again; she would not think of waves or wilds or what kept them away from each other. They were here, and would be here for the foreseeable future—until Jamyson was satisfied with all of their reports, and until they had time to strategize and sort out any complications that reports from across the kingdom might bring.

In that time together, with nothing more between them than doors and corridors and so much wanting and missing now undone...the future might become whatever they wished.

And in that future, for the first time since her father's death, Elynor found no fear.

For within that future, with Sharek once more at her side...anything might be possible.

Acknowledgements

First and foremost, as always and ever, to my Father God.

For giving me new stories to write and new lessons to learn and teach, even when I think I've come to the end of all that I am. For the patience You have with me when I fumble my way through the dark. For the wisdom You granted as I was trying to figure out where to stick the landing on this series. Through all the back and forth, I knew I was never alone—and that empowered me to do what needed to be done. Thank You, thank You, thank You. Each time I reach that place and finally let go, I find You waiting for me. When I leave the shores and brave the treacherous seas of doubt, I find I know the way...because You are the way. Help me to keep walking on water, my eyes fixed on You.

To my family, all of whom showed me limitless patience while I muddled my way through the middle of this trilogy. Whenever I doubted and strayed, you were all there to encourage, uplift, and inspire me in your own unique ways. I love you for that, and for so many countless other reasons. And especially to my mom, an unwitting vessel and mouthpiece of God's inspiration. For the simple, misspoken name, "Sharek", that had me running to write down the image of a man in a prison hovel, Blessed with the power of killing despite his soft heart. You spent my whole childhood helping me chase inspiration in the weirdest of ways and the wildest of places; thanks for still doing that now that I'm an adult.

To JD, for the long, sweet nap-and-snuggle sessions as an infant where I worked with baby in one arm and free hand on the keyboard. I will forever cherish those whirlwind days when all I could do was edit these books while curled up on the couch with you. To JD, who continues to remind me to look up from my books and take heed of the world around me, to use my time wisely and not burn it up with the need to produce, produce, produce; who helps me strike a balance my life sorely lacked when it comes to measuring the beauty of writing with the beauty of the world outside the tales I tell. May I always love you and support your dreams like Alden did for Elynor...but with much less vengeance and poison and stabbing in our story. ;) For me, *THE CURSE OF THE BLESSED* as it is today will always belong to the two of us. Teamwork, kid. <3

To Annelisa, who took me on a tour through the prettiest parts of Epcot where I wrote the first chapter of this book. I can never read the opening without thinking of early mornings tucked away in pristine corners of Canada, or the smells and sights of a French bistro and the taste of strawberry crepe. Thank you for being my guide, my sounding board, my friend...and for helping me finally find Elynor's name!

To Danny, for encouraging me all the way through drafting during what was arguably one of the toughest times of both our lives. For finding a new favorite coffee shop for us to love, and letting me linger in the pauses this story demanded even when they took my mind far away. I needed the escape, and you made it happen. I will forever be grateful for that.

To Lina, who long ago took a chance on a relative newbie on Instagram as her critique partner. Who bonded with me over our eerie likemindedness on stories about sailor girls with dead fathers, depths-bent on revenge. For showing me new intricacies and beauty in writing I had not yet explored...for being my critique partner, telling me I could do this, helping me finish a book I sometimes doubted I had the strength to write, and letting me disappear into reading *Daughter of the Deep* when I needed to escape my own world. I know for a fact I would not be the writer, the author, or the woman I am today had you not reached out a hand of friendship to me and invited me aboard your vessel. Forever and ever thankful for you.

To Cassidy and Miranda, who came along into my shy life and turned it upside down as I wrote this book. To Cassidy for fearlessly bombing my Twitter and telling me "*Yes, have them cuddle on the raft,*" and to Miranda for first writing—and then letting me print off—her gorgeous poetry that helped me find my way through learning who Elynor was. The first sparks of friendship were born in the belly of writing this book, and I will never forget that wonderful time.

And to you, reader—for taking the time to read this duology. You are holding in your hands a story that challenged and grew me in unique ways as it forced me to navigate difficult subjects, from power imbalances to a fleshed-out antagonist's point-of-view. So much new territory came about in the journey to write this book...and I'm grateful you embarked on it with me!

About the Author

Renee Dugan is an Indiana-based author who grew up reading fantasy books, chasing stray cats, and writing stories full of dashing heroes and evil masterminds. Now with over a decade of professional editing, administrative work, and writing every spare second under her belt, she has authored dozens of books. Living with her husband, son, and not-so-stray cats in the magical Midwest, she continues to explore new worlds and spends her time in this one encouraging and helping other writers on their journey to fulfilling their dreams.

Also by R. Dugan

You can find other R. Dugan books, including...

The Chaos Circus (Young Adult Portal Fantasy)
The Curse of the Blessed (Adult Fantasy Trilogy)
Tales Of Wonder And Woe (New Adult Epic Fantasy Series)

at online retailers Amazon, Barnes & Noble, and more,
and at reneeduganwriting.com/shop

Find Renee Dugan online at: Reneeduganwriting.com
And on social media: @reneeduganwriting

www.ingramcontent.com/pod-product-compliance
Lightning Source LLC
Chambersburg PA
CBHW031410010625
27464CB00003B/120